BY ACCIDENT
OF BIRTH

BY ACCIDENT OF BIRTH

THE QUINN SAGA

THOMAS E. SIMMONS

OPEN ROAD
INTEGRATED MEDIA
NEW YORK

Copyright © 2015 by Thomas E. Simmons

ISBN: 978-1-5040-7928-0

This edition published in 2022 by Open Road Integrated Media, Inc.
180 Maiden Lane
New York, NY 10038
www.openroadmedia.com

To my wife Katherine, the original woman

PROLOGUE

Mississippi, 1915

The rasping ring was as irritating as it was startling. Bethany Quinn put down the book she was reading, *The Ambassadors* by Henry James. She walked into the central hall and looked down at the recently installed device. It rang at her like a barking dog. She grasped the unfamiliar receiver from its cradle and pressed it to her ear while eyeing the candlestick mouth piece as if it were the head of a black snake. The questioning voice from the other end sounded weak and tinny.

Bethany picked up the candlestick phone and spoke into the mouth piece. "This is she, only it's Miss Quinn, not Mrs."

"Pardon my mistake, Miss Quinn, but are you the owner of the Quinn estates in Cuba?" The voice was unmistakably British.

"Would you please speak louder and tell me who you are and what this is about?"

"Yes ma'am. I am Major Mallory Renfroe of his majesty's special service calling from the British consulate's office in New Orleans."

"What on earth for?"

"Miss Quinn, it seems you own certain items in storage in Cuba which my government would be most interested in purchasing."

"If this is a joke from one of Jonathan's old friends I wish you would tell me."

"I assure you this call is not a joke. I beg your patience, Miss Quinn. It has taken me no small amount of time and effort to find the rumored items of interest, and even longer to locate you. I only today discovered you have a telephone connected through the Vicksburg switchboard. I was prepared to leave New Orleans tomorrow to find you in person."

"Major, just what are you talking about?"

"I'm speaking of ten thousand such items manufactured by Mauser. They are in a warehouse in Santiago in crates mislabeled, deliberately I assume, *machinery parts* and consigned to Quinn-Alacon Sugar Mill. According to warehouse records, they have been stored there since 1903. My information is that you are the owner of Quinn-Alacon Sugar Mill."

Bethany' heart missed a beat. She couldn't catch her breath and had to sit down on the bench seat built into the new ebony telephone stand.

"Miss Quinn," the tinny voice continued. "As you know, England is at war. My government would be most interested in taking those items off your hands, all hush hush of course. We wouldn't want the Germans or Turks to discover them."

Bethany was silent a moment. "You must be mistaken, Major. I own the Quinn-Alacon Sugar Mill in Cuba, but I don't know a thing about any such crates in Santiago."

"Perhaps not, Miss Quinn, but the items are there. I've confirmed that fact, discretely of course. Do you understand what I mean by items of interest? I hesitate to use a more descriptive term. I will mail a detailed description of the items and how you may contact me. Time is of the essence in this matter, Miss Quinn."

She closed her eyes and whispered to a ghost. *My God, Jonathan, will it never end?*

"Miss Quinn? Are you still there, Miss Quinn?"

"I'm here, Major. It's just that you have taken me unawares. You will have to give me a little time to . . . to see if what you say is true, I mean about me being the owner of the items you mentioned. If I am, I will be more than happy to be rid of them. And Major, don't you worry about the Germans and Turks. We Quinns never sold to despots." Bethany hung the ear piece back into its cradle.

For Beverly Bethany Quinn the call was a klaxon from hell. It had taken years to subdue the personal demons that had ridden her to the edge of madness. Now one phone call had unlocked their cages, freed them to roil up from the catacombs of her memory. She knew them well, knew they would once more curse her sleep and fill her waking hours with irreconcilable conflict.

She sat on the bench by the phone in the hallway for a long while, a kaleidoscope of images flying across her mind's eye. The only sound in the house came from a tall, Herschede case clock standing in the shadows. As she listened to the authoritative tick at each swing of its pendulum, Bethany had the peculiar sensation that the great sidereal movement by which time is reckoned had reversed and was inexorably dragging her into the past.

"Miss Bethany . . . Miss Bethany! You alright? You look like you done seen a ghost."

Bethany looked up to see a worried expression on her housekeeper's face. "Maybe I have, Lizzy. Would you get me a tall glass of ice and put a little bourbon in it? Might as well bring the bottle. I'll be on the veranda."

"Miss Bethany! It ain't even five o'clock yet."

Bethany ignored the remark, stood and walked down the hall, out the screen door and sat in a wicker chair set with cushions covered in flower-patterned chintz. It was a lovely, late-March spring day. Azaleas, camellias, day lilies, peonies, even some Louisiana iris were in bloom. The dogwoods were on the cusp of snowy splendor. Bethany didn't notice. She was lost in thoughts of Cuba, arms and war.

Directly, Lizzy backed through the screen door holding a silver tray laden with a glass of ice, a bottle of bourbon and a linen napkin. She turned and set the tray on the table beside the wicker chair, rolled her eyes at Bethany, and left without a word.

Ice tinkled as Bethany lifted the glass to her lips and took a taste of chilled bourbon. *I knew I should not have had that telephone put in out here at Shamrock. Cost me a fortune.*

She took a second sip and lifted her eyes to the panorama of flower beds, lush greenery and great oaks draped in feathery Spanish moss.

Major Renfroe, you just spilled death all over my lovely spring. We Quinns have seen enough violent death haven't we Jonathan? You know those fools in Europe have started another war? That damn British agent has crossed an ocean to give me a part to play in the killin'. How much death will spit from ten thousand Mauser rifles? Damnit Jonathan, you should have told me about the rifles. That's how the Cubans paid us the last of their debt isn't it? Those are rifles the Spaniards surrendered. You mentioned the Cubans had cleared what they owed, but I never saw anything on the books except where you crossed out the debt. When Cuba was freed you said we were through and we were, but you didn't tell me about the rifles. Were you just sick of it all, just stuck them away and forgot about them? Well damnit, Jonathan, somebody didn't forget.

Bethany sat in moody silence sipping bourbon. A beauty all her life, she thought herself a freak, an accident of birth, the daughter of war . . . fortune's whore. There was a secret part of her that those who loved her were never able to fathom. Jonathan was the only one who knew why and he never told.

Of all things on Earth, war must sadden God the most. He gives us the freedom to think and the will to act, and maybe guardian angels to try to save us from ourselves. When they fail, when Earth rings with the sound of war, the horror of it, do great invisible clouds of His death angels descend over battlefields to collect forgiven souls from the pieces, sometimes less than pieces? Remember Jonathan, remember when I went crazy blaming myself for the death of all those American boys? I asked you how God could find them when there was nothing left. You told me God would gather them from the dust. I do so hope that's true.

She drained the glass, picked up the bottle and poured another measure over what was left of the ice.

Here it is a beautiful day and I sit brooding over death. Why not? Death was my father wasn't he? I was not conceived of love, or joy, or passion or even lust . . . just war, pain, and death.

Carrying the bottle in one hand and the glass in the other, she walked into the house and stood in the long hallway with the ticking clock.

Well, Jonathan, you've put me in the arms business again. What price will I pay this time? It won't be madness or drug-induced lethargy. I've been there. So how does one do penance for putting weapons of death in the hands of strangers? Is it time that dulls our memory of the sins, the guilt? I would think one should have to recall all the details of one's life in order to determine proper penance. God will require that before judgment won't He?

Bethany walked into the parlor, sat at a mahogany, roll-top desk, set the bottle and glass on the green felt-covered desktop, and unlocked the bottom drawer of the right side pedestal. It contained a nickel-plated, over-under double-barreled derringer with ivory grips, an unusual pendant on a gold chain and a dusty, paper-wrapped parcel. She lifted the parcel, laid it on the desktop and stared at it for a while. Written on the heavy brown wrapping paper were the words, *For Ansel Quinn. To be delivered upon my death,* and her signature, *B. B. Quinn.*

After another sip, she untied the string and carefully unfolded the paper exposing two journals. One had her name inked on its cloth cover. She had not touched it in over 17 years. The other was leather bound with the name *Annielise* embossed in gold on its cover. The leather was cracked with age. Small bits of the embossed gold lettering of her mother's name had flaked away. Kept from her as a child, it had been given to her at age 17 on the day her uncle Jonathan had taken her from the only home she had ever known. The revelations she found in its pages were so shocking and painful she had never opened it again. Holding it now, she experienced the almost palpable presence of her mother and family whose faces she could not remember.

Mama, I know Nannie helped you with this, and Doctor Ted, bless his heart, had to finish it. He did it knowing it would be all I ever knew of you and Nannie and Great Grandfather and what happened that terrible day up by the old place here at Shamrock. What of your stories and mine have I locked away? The parts too painful to remember? The parts time mercifully shoved into the shadows? The part about me no one would believe? Can I believe it even now?

A phone call from a man I don't know has dredged up my own shadows, Mama. I have a trip to make, a task to perform, a last salute to a past I doubt you would have approved for your baby girl. I promise you it will be the last of its kind. Perhaps, after almost half a century, it's time for all of you to tell me again your stories and mine. Maybe that will be penance enough, but I doubt it.

Bethany unlatched the tarnished brass clasp, opened the diary to the first page and began a hard journey.

BY ACCIDENT OF BIRTH

War is the father of all

—Fragment 53, Hippolytus Ref. IX, 9, 4

BOOK ONE

THE QUINNS, 1863

CHAPTER 1

The harder life got inside the ring of fire, the more tenaciously the besieged attempted to preserve some semblance of civilized society. Although the bombardment proceeded uninterrupted day and night, week after week, the shelling was shifted randomly from one section of the town to another. When the barrage lifted from a neighborhood, its citizens, grown accustomed to hell, defiantly ventured out of their basements, damaged houses or hastily dug caves to socialize as if nothing taking place around them was out of the ordinary. Random shells crossing high overhead occasioned little comment. Women were seen walking down ruined streets holding parasols to protect their skin from the sun, ignoring the odds against a stray shell finding them. Witnessing such activity, a rational observer could argue that the sane had become insane.

Animals, the few that had escaped the cook pot, didn't adapt as well. Ruled by instinct, they lacked the human ability to pretend, to hope, to trade sanity for insanity when reality became unbearable. Dogs took to whimpering when their tortured ears sensed a shell flying overhead. If one exploded nearby they would commence an awful howling.

As mournful as such sounds were, the most lugubrious of sounds didn't come from the plaintive cry of an animal. Sporadically, as the sharp crack of an exploding shell died away, there would come the tormented wail of a human witness to the sudden maiming or death of a loved one or neighbor. On one such occasion, a woman and the little boy she was leading from their backyard privy toward the safety of a cellar was engulfed in a deafening flash of fire and smoke. Seconds later, as the smoke thinned, stunned neighbors saw the woman, shocked silent, standing like a blackened, disfigured Greek stature. She was missing the forearm that had held the hand of the little boy, a little boy who had vanished into smoky, pink mist.

Such harrowing sights and sounds were imprinted in the memories and repeated in the nightmares of those citizens of Vicksburg yet untouched, waiting their turn.

The Quinns, caught in the town under siege, were living absent the comforts of Shamrock Plantation. Nor could they enjoy their once lovely Vicksburg townhouse that had so gaily served as the center of society when the planters moved to town between planting and harvesting. That had been a time for parties, courting, marriages, gay excursions up-river to Memphis or down-river to New Orleans . . . but no more. For the Quinns and their neighbors, life was now a raw, miserable quest for survival.

Sixteen years prior while serving with Lee's Mississippi Rifles during the Mexican War, Daniel Hillary Quinn had gained a healthy respect for artillery. When the Quinn town house began to suffer damage from shot and shell, Daniel insisted that his daughter-in-law, granddaughter and house servant move to the safety of a cave quickly dug into a wooded hillside some distance behind their home.

It was dark, damp, musty-smelling and tomb-like. There were two sections. The largest was timber braced and crowded with four cots, a table and oil lamp. A small grotto cut into the cave wall served as storage for food and water. The only touch of luxury was an oriental rug brought up from the house to cover the dirt floor. Out front, a canvas tarpaulin supported on posts stayed with ropes served as porch and kitchen complete with wood burning cook stove, chairs and a kitchen table, all carried up from the house. This *veranda* provided the cave dwellers a shady place to dine and to gather when the daily shelling shifted from their sector to some other. The air outside was rarely untainted with drifting smoke and the acrid odor of spent gunpowder, but it was better than the dank staleness of the cave.

May 27, 1863 began as ordinary a day as could be expected in a town under siege. Shortly after dawn, the Quinns gathered under their awning for breakfast. Nannie Keturah Quinn handed Daniel a fine china plate, linen napkin and sterling silver fork, items as out of place in a cook-tent as she was. Even in a plain cotton dress and soiled apron, Nannie was as beautiful and graceful as always. She had been the center of the Quinn family since the day she married Timothy Ansel Quinn, the only son of the widower Quinn.

Daniel held out his plate to Arabella Dupuis who spooned a ration of salt bacon and a single hoecake onto it muttering the admonition, "I ain't listenin' to no more complaints about de cookin'. This here town be runnin' short of near about ever'thing and I does the best I can wit what we got."

At forty, Arabella took no foolishness from anyone including her master. Over the years her official role at Shamrock had progressed from house servant to nanny to chaperon of Daniel Quinn's granddaughter, Annielise. To hear the senior Quinn tell it, her role had progressed from slave to Tzarina. She had taken care of Massa Quinn's granddaughter, now sixteen, since the day the child was born, slept in the nursery when Annielise was a baby, and now slept close by her in the cave. It was Arabella's duty to chaperone Annielise Quinn everywhere she went, especially in a town full of soldiers.

Annielise was a blonde, blue-eyed Southern belle blossoming into womanhood. Although she was raised in a privileged household, she was neither a spoiled nor demanding young lady as were so many daughters of Southern gentry at the time. On the other hand, she was independent, spirited and as stubborn as her grandfather Quinn. She never issued a complaint about the increasing hardships, nor cowered to the danger inherent in a town under siege. That meant aggravation for Arabella who found herself following the determined young woman running errands and visiting friends during lulls in the shelling. Always struggling a step or two behind, Arabella complained continuously.

"It ain't fittin' for no young lady to run around out here like you doing. Ain't no need for it neither."

"Arabella, I am not gonna let those Yankees make me afraid to leave that hole we live in."

"Well, I *is* afraid. You goin' to get us kilt, that's what. I seen some high foolishness in my time," Arabella stated, "but runnin' round in de middle of dis here war is crazy and you knows it. White folks is crazy. You look round dis here town and tell me dey ain't." Arabella was very nearly correct. After weeks of living in a city subjected daily to a rain of fury previously unknown by civilians, the population had little choice but to fight stubbornly for survival. Like the Quinns, some moved into dirt caves dug into the yellow clay hillsides of the town and surrounding areas. Some continued to live in their houses, either in foolish defiance of a hated enemy, or because of a terror-driven inability to leave the familiar.

Each day the citizens of Vicksburg had to make do with less. A few undamaged wells and rain water stored in home cisterns provided the only water besides that collected in muddy shell holes and ditches. As pantries and root cellars were emptied and backyard gardens stripped bare, town folks and soldiers alike were forced to eat mules, horses, dogs, cats, cow peas, cane sprouts, songbirds, and sometimes worse. Rats, skinned and dressed, sold in the marketplace at the outrageous price of a dollar apiece.

On that day, 27th of May, while the Quinns were having breakfast, an 18-year-old soldier named Zeke Pittman sat in the dirt in a section of trench line overlooking the wide, muddy Mississippi. Cleaned up, young Zeke was strikingly handsome. He had his father's strong jaw, his Irish mother's bright eyes and had inherited high cheek bones and shiny black hair from his grandmother who was full-blooded Choctaw. In his present condition, not even his mother would recognize him, much less a stranger think him handsome. Zeke's face was streaked with dirt, his cheek blackened by the residue of gunpowder. His coal-black hair was dull, dirty, shaggy-long and uncombed. He was caked in mud, infested with lice, hadn't washed or changed his threadbare, sun-bleached uniform in weeks. He was thirty pounds underweight, had deep circles under his eyes, and like those around him, his body odor was overwhelming.

The only thing about Zeke that seemed undaunted was his natural good nature. He could kill, had killed, but he would rather joke around than fight. In spite of the pestiferous times, he often brought laughter to his battle-hardened fellow soldiers and they loved him for it. On this morning, Zeke sat lacing his unit's tattered battle flag to a new staff freshly cut and debarked from a skinny pine sapling. The old staff had been shot in two.

"Them damn Yankees burn up a hunnerd dollars worth of lead a day on my flag. They can't shoot for nothin'."

"How come you fixing a new pole then?" asked Jeremiah Dunn, 17-year-old, freckled-faced, redheaded kid. He was sitting barefoot in the trench watching Zeke.

"Hell, Dunn, that was luck. They couldn't do it again if the Devil was to fart in their ears."

The two had been on the line together for weeks. Crouching in the open trench they were chilled by rain, burned by the sun and subjected daily to sniper and artillery fire. They spent nights repairing the damage their breastworks suffered by day. They lived in filth, complained, told jokes, talked of girls, thought of home, tried to hide their fear and dreamed of food. Like the men around them, they slept when they could and went hungry on rations reduced by half.

Below them, the bluffs were erratically eroded into craggy fingers that reached down to the river below. The silt that sluiced down them with every rain enriched the accumulated earthen flats and wild vegetation. It was a riverbank adequate to afford concealment for enemy sharpshooters daring enough to cross the river at night and entrench themselves at the foot of Natural Fortress Vicksburg.

Later in the day, Zeke was napping when a soldier down the line named Clem Barfield nudged the man next to him. "Would you looky thar. Here come a Yankee Boat!" Barfield yelled to the others, "Look yonder boys! They gonna try to run the river."

News quickly spread through town of a Yankee ironclad coming down river! Citizens gathered on the lawns, balconies and rooftops of Vicksburg in anticipation of the battle to come. Several young ladies, Annielise Quinn among them, were visiting at the stately, Corinthian-columned Tillman townhouse on Washington Street. From the rear second-floor gallery they had a grand view of the river.

The townspeople watched in silent awe as the dark monster hove into full view. Tongues of flame and smoke billowed from *USS Cincinnati*'s gun ports as she opened thunderous fire. The solid shot and explosive shells from her huge guns gouged enormous chunks out of Confederate works on the bluff.

The Rebel batteries above answered with devastatingly accurate fire. Great plumes of water like the steps of giants walked across the river to fetch *Cincinnati's* range. Her mast, pennant and flag were quickly shot away. While her armored sides repelled Confederate shot, the repeated heavy hammer blows against the iron cladding splintered the thick supporting timbers behind into ragged chunks of wood that tore into her sailors with lethal force. In turn, *Cincinnati's* terrible guns took tally tearing apart the flesh and bones of defenders on the bluffs above.

In the midst of the furious exchange, a single Rebel shell fired by the Fort Hill battery found a weakness at *Cincinnati's* stern and opened her to the river. Tons of turbid water swirled into her iron-laden hull. Spewing great clouds of smoke and steam, the mortally wounded vessel swung sharply toward the far shore. Laboring vainly for the shallows of the west bank, she settled slowly into the river like a hog into mud. Her surviving crew, those with rapid access to hatches, those who were not scalded to death by steam or maimed by splintered wood, those who could swim, entered the eddying river current and struggled for shore. Some drowned, some died swimming amid the fountains raised from shot fired from the bluffs. The Rebel shelling continued until only *Cincinnati's* blue-striped, black funnels remained above water to mark her grave.

Annielise and her friends, watching from the second-floor gallery of the Tillman home, witnessed the spectacle and joined in cheering the victory. The great chorus from Vicksburg rolled off the bluffs and rippled across the water to lap faintly onto the western bank where lay the exhausted Union survivors of another failed attempt to open the river.

For the surrounded, besieged, starving citizens of Vicksburg, the sinking of *Cincinnati* was a moment for exultation, a singular triumph, a last hurrah.

"Look at them Yankee rats swim fer it," shouted Jeremiah Dunn. Zeke Pittman raised the pole from the trench and waved his flag. Soldiers around him whooped and hollered. "Wave it, Zeke, boy! Give 'em the flag!"

Zeke climbed up out of the trench onto the breastworks. Bracing himself with a wide stance, he waved his flag back and forth for all to see. Rousing cheers came from up and down the Confederate line echoed by the civilian spectators in town.

Sharpshooters hidden below along the flats at river's near-edge weren't nearly so amused. Caught in the excitement of the moment, his ears filled with the cheers of the crowd, Zeke didn't see his sergeant, bent low, running down the trench, didn't hear him cry out, "For God's sake, Zeke, get down!"

Fire! A terrible, clawing fire erupted between Zeke's widespread legs. The boy let go of the flag and reached to hold his manhood but found only blood and pain. Screaming, Zeke stood staring down at his bloody hands. Before Jeremiah Dunn could scramble up from the trench to pull his friend down, a second ball slammed into Zeke's pain-twisted face, blowing the back of his head and brains all over Jeremiah. Zeke's body clumped heavily beside his crumpled flag.

With the town's one hospital overflowing, several aid stations had been set up in tents. At one of them located two hundred yards behind a section of trench line facing the river, Doctor Theodor Perkins was on duty when casualties from the *Cincinnati* engagement began to arrive. They were laid out under the hot sun—some on stretchers, some on blankets, many on the bare ground. Some moaned, some screamed, some whimpered, "Is it bad?" Most were silent, their eyes shut tight, afraid to look at their own wounds or those of their comrades. Body odor competed with that of blood, torn entrails, urine and excrement.

Doctor Perkins stepped carefully among the wounded giving reassuring words to each man while quietly indicating to his orderly which among the more seriously injured he thought had a chance to live. They would be tagged for surgery. All Ted Perkins could do for the others, the ones with gaping abdomen or head wounds, was to try and ease their agony for as long as Death took to call. It was a heavy, almost unbearable burden. Irreplaceable supplies of chloroform, morphine, and laudanum were dwindling. He had to reserve what was left of them for those who stood a chance of recovery. There would soon be little but whiskey available for a patient's pain, and in too many cases, for the anguish and fatigue of the doctors. The one product the South could manufacture in sufficient quantities was whiskey.

For now, the pitiful sounds of men pleading for him to save their shattered limbs could be stilled by chloroform, the stillness followed by the nicking sound of the bone saw. When the supply of anesthesia was gone, the sound of the bone saw would be lost in the screams of fully conscious men held down while arm, hand, leg or foot was sliced and sawed away—the limb thrown aside, the unwashed, blood-slick table cleared for the next man . . . and the next.

Unlike so many doctors of the period who had obtained their medical knowledge from the common but vastly inadequate system of a year or two apprenticeship, Doctor Theodore Perkins had graduated from the Nashville School of Medicine where he studied surgery under Doctor Paul F. Eve, and later under Doctor Joseph Newman. Doctor Newman had served in the war with Mexico and made it a point to introduce his students to his firsthand knowledge of the horrific wounds that result from armed conflict. After graduation, Dr. Perkins had set up practice in his home-town of Vicksburg never expecting to treat such wounds.

When the topic of secession first began to dominate conversation in the parlors, poker games and meeting halls of Vicksburg, Perkins had taken a stance against it. After war was declared, he refused to join the Confederate Medical Corps. Instead, war came to him. His civilian practice became second to the terrible demands of treating Confederate wounded.

Ted Perkins was trim and fit at war's beginning, but the long days and nights now spent attending both Confederate and civilian sick and wounded were taking a toll. The once robust doctor had the haggard look of the overworked, underfed and sleep deprived.

Pausing to take out his handkerchief and wipe away the sweat from his brow, Perkins sensed movement in the periphery of his vision and turned to see Daniel Quinn staggering breathlessly toward him. Ted had always looked up to Daniel almost as a big brother. Without hesitation he told his assistant surgeon to take charge and fetched his medical bag. Perkins saw the worst kind of fear in Daniel's eyes.

"All right, Dan, let's go. I can only leave for a few minutes."

"How did you know?"

"I know an old bastard like you couldn't run like that if his own life depended on it. It has to be Nannie or Annielise. Tell me what's happened, and slow down before you kill us both."

"It's Annielise. Arabella was hysterical by the time she found me. I got her calmed down enough to tell me Annielise has been shot. Don't know how bad. They were out on the gallery at the Tillman place watching the battle, for God's sake. Nannie left for the Tillman's while I came to find you. We got to hurry, Ted."

"I'm trying, damnit. She's *my* godchild, remember?" Perkins, short of breath, muttered, "Damn a town that ate all its horses."

Arabella stood wringing her hands and crying at the front gate of the Tillman house. When she saw the two men puffing up the street, she whispered, "Thank you, Jesus!"

Neither man had enough wind to speak. Doctor Perkins moved on up the brick walk, urged every step of the way by Arabella. Daniel held to the iron gate and fought to catch his breath.

A crowd of chattering young women fell silent and moved aside as Arabella dragged the doctor past them down the wide central hall and up the graceful, curving stairway toward the second-floor bedroom where Annielise had been carried from the gallery.

Pale and wide-eyed, the child lay on a tester bed, both hands pressing a folded, blood-stained towel to her wound. Nannie held a damp cloth to Annielise's forehead.

"Hello, precious. We're going to take care of you."

"Uncle Ted. I'm scared."

After one look at Annielise's bleeding wound, he wasted no time bellowing orders.

"Arabella, go down to the kitchen and have 'em tear a bed sheet into bandages, boil the strips and dry 'em in the oven quick as they can." Arabella hadn't made it to the door before she received more orders. "Tell Mrs. Tillman I said to send those young ladies home and ask if she has any whiskey. If she does, ask her to wash down the dining room table with it."

Ted Perkins was one of a handful of doctors who had begun to suspect the use of soap or alcohol to clean instruments and wounds before and between surgeries might lessen the prevalent onslaught of infection. Most surgeons didn't bother to wash their hands, instruments or operating tables between patients. They simply wiped their hands on dirty aprons and used the same blood tainted bowl of water to rinse instrument and sponge in preparation for the next patient. 25 to 50 percent of surgery patients died of infection.

Ted looked back toward the bedroom door to see Daniel laboring for breath.

"Dan, you're gonna have to help me carry her down to the dining table. I can't operate on this feather bed. Nannie, help me git her clothes off." He turned back to his patient. "Annielise darling, moving you is gonna hurt but we have to do it."

The 16-year-old, pale with pain, tried to cover her fear with bravado. "Save that Yankee bullet for me, Uncle Ted. I just might wear it around my neck as a souvenir." She screamed as they lifted her off the blood-stained bed.

Annielise was gently placed on the Chippendale table. It smelled strongly of bourbon. Mrs. Tillman and a house servant were on their knees spreading old quilts over the Oriental rug beneath it. She whispered to her servant so that Annielise wouldn't hear, "I don't want blood on this carpet! Lord knows if we can ever afford another one."

The doctor cleared the room except for Nannie and Daniel.

"Arabella, you slide those pocket-doors shut and don't let anyone disturb the surgery."

"Naw sir!" Arabella said, "Ain't nobody gittin' through these doors till you makes that child better." As she pulled closed the ten-foot high, mahogany doors she added, "Til's you do, you ain't gittin' out neither."

Ted Perkins took a pint tin from his bag. It held the most precious substance throughout the Confederacy, chloroform. He poured a measure of the volatile liquid over a thickly-folded, flannel cloth. "I want you to breathe as deeply as you can, Annielise. This is going to make you feel a little funny, but don't fight it." He pressed the cloth over her nose and mouth. Annielise fought the sharp fumes like a tiger. It took all three adults to hold her down.

When she was quiet, Ted told Nannie, "Don't take your eyes off her and tell me if she has any trouble breathing." Ted wanted Nannie busy so she wouldn't watch what he had to do. "Dan, you stand on the other side. Don't look if you can help it, but you'll have to hold her still if she starts to squirm. I have a little brandy if you need it"

"Just do what you got to do Ted," Quinn replied.

Ted Perkins set to work with the skill of a surgeon who had treated over a thousand bullet and shrapnel wounds in the last three months. The location of the wound frightened him. Deep abdomen wounds were almost always fatal.

"It's not as deep as I thought," he said as his probe quickly found the bullet. "It must have been about spent. I have to open the wound, see how much damage has occurred. We can't leave any internal bleeding."

Daniel turned away when Ted picked up the scalpel. He was out of practice, but he prayed.

So did Dr. Perkins. He now knew the wound alone wouldn't kill her, but infection might. Ted spoke as he worked, more out of habit in training apprentice surgeons than in explanation to Daniel and Nannie. "The bullet has made a ragged entry wound in the lower left abdominal parietes several inches below and to the left of the umbilicus."

With forceps he carefully lifted the bullet from its resting place, held it up for inspection. It appeared more deformed than he would have imagined from the relatively small amount of damage it had inflicted in the soft tissue of his Godchild. "This young lady will have her bullet."

Looking around for a receptacle, he dropped the bloody chunk of lead onto a sterling silver bonbon dish on the Sheraton sideboard and turned back to his surgery.

"The bullet has damaged her left ovary and barely penetrated the womb. It's serious, but she has a good chance of full recovery." He cleaned the wound and began to stitch up the damaged tissue.

"Arabella," Ted Perkins called. The door slid open and the short, plump black woman hurried in past the doctor to look at her child. Satisfied, she shifted her attention to Perkins.

"Arabella, go ask Mrs. Tillman if she can set up a cot down here in the hall. I think it best if we don't move Annielise for a few days. I certainly don't want her carried upstairs." Then he whispered so the others wouldn't hear, "Why in heaven's name did you let Annielise out on that balcony?"

"Let her!" Arabella bellowed, and then in a loud whisper, "How I asposed to stop her? She stubborn as her grandfather. It's all I can do to keep up wit' her. Half de town out watchin' dat battle, Doctor Ted. You knows I rather dat bullet hit me stead a dat child."

"It's alright, Arabella. Go see about that cot, and fetch me those bandage strips. They ought to be ready."

Theodore Perkins left the Tillman house and walked toward the aid station. He ignored the damaged homes, shops and rubble scattered streets, but an agitated mockingbird fussing about in a shell-shattered oak drew his attention. It was the only songbird he had seen in weeks. Songbirds that had not been driven off by the fury of siege had mostly wound up in soup pots.

"You better fly out of here fo' someone knocks you out of that tree with a rock." The mockingbird cocked its head at Perkins, trilled a few notes in answer, then flew off toward the river as if it understood the warning. Ted watched the bird climb over the treetops into the cloud patched sky and disappear in the distance. *Wish I could do that.* He wearily continued toward the aid station.

As he walked, his thoughts turned to what waited him at the charnel house, for that is what he feared his surgery now resembled. Every day, all day and into the night the wounded, maimed and sick moaned with pain, fever, infection, malnutrition and fear. Worst of all was the unmistakable vacant stare of a patient resigned to death.

It's hard to save someone who has lost hope, Lord. Ted wasn't much of a church-goer, but since the war he had fallen into the peculiar habit of talking to God direct-ly. *I do the best I know how but it's never enough is it, Lord?* Ted's thought turned to the army graves detail that arrived at day's end to collect the dead and the piles of limbs, and how he tried to avoid watching their morbid work. *It's the same for the other side isn't it Lord? This war visits hell to all in its terrible path. Is this war your doing, Lord? We're all fools and sinners down here. Have you brought this war down on a nation to cleanse its soul for the sin of slavery?*

Ted's conversation with God was interrupted when Union artillery resumed shell-ing the town center. *Damn 'em Lord! Damn us if you must, but damn them too for the terror they rain down on women and children in this town.*

Perkins reached the aid station to join his assistants in attending the day's wound-ed. By early evening he was so tired he could hardly lift his arms, his fingers trembled. In the dim light of dusk he addressed the last of the day's casualties, a sergeant with a dirty, blood-soaked rag wrapped around a nasty flesh wound to his left arm just above the elbow.

"What's your name, Sergeant?"

"Tunnard, Sir."

"Well, Tunnard, whatever it was took a little hide and muscle but missed the bone. This arm probably won't gain back its full strength, but you'll likely heal up all right provided you can keep this wound cleaner than the rest of you. Sit down in the chair here." By lamplight Ted used tweezers to pick bits of cloth uniform and unidentifiable detritus from the wound, rubbish that had been carried into the sergeant's arm when the shard of shrapnel tore through it.

The sergeant said nothing during the procedure—just clenched his jaw. Ted applied a salve of elemental sulfur to the open wound, then picked up a needle. Its tip was a flat, curved, double-edged blade, grown a little dull from use, with a round shank ending in an eye at the top. He held it up to the light and threaded a length of silk suture.

"This is gonna smart a bit," he told Tunnard, and began to stitch the ragged wound closed. "I'm going to bandage this up to keep the wound clean. You know a little soap and water wouldn't hurt the rest of you, sergeant."

The sergeant grimaced but didn't complain as the doctor worked to close the wound. Instead he struggled to continue the conversation. "I can hardly stand myself,

Doc, but we barely git enough water to drink. Them Yanks don't exactly invite us down to the river to bathe."

"That's alright, son," Ted replied as he pulled the needle through for another stitch. "It's a wonder any of you fellows up there can move at all without getting your ass shot off." Ted tied the last stitch and began to wrap the arm with a roll of homemade bandage. "God knows, I've treated enough of you."

"Can't say I've showed my ass to the enemy, Doc, but I'd rather get hit there than what happened today. I had a kid git his balls shot off."

"His balls shot off! I haven't treated any such wound as that."

"I don't reckon so on account a second bullet kilt him. Fool kid was standing up on the works waving a flag after we sank that ironclad. I tried my best to git him down. He was a good looking kid. Claimed to be part Choctaw. Died all full of victory and hurt, I reckon."

"Well, Sergeant, you're gonna hurt a while with this arm. Say your name is Tunnard?"

"Yes sir. My home's just down river at Warrenton, what's left of it."

The doctor finished bandaging the arm and fixed it in a sling tied around the sergeant's neck. "Tunnard, I can put you on the wounded list and get you off the line."

"That's tempting, Doc, but I can't do it. I got to look after my men."

"Well, be careful with that arm, son. You don't want to start it bleeding again. Come back every couple of days to let me look at it and get that bandage changed. Living in a trench is a good way to lose that arm to gangrene."

"I'll do that Doc. Thank you."

The sergeant walked toward the bluffs and disappeared into the darkness.

By the next morning, Annielise was drifting in and out of fever-induced delirium. With the town center under shelling every morning and afternoon, Daniel insisted she be moved to the safety of the cave. Ted sent two stretcher bearers to carry her to the cave and checked on her himself that evening. He didn't say so, but he feared the worst. "I've done all I can," he told Daniel. "The rest is up to God."

On the forth morning, Annielise's face no longer glistened with sweat. Nannie gently felt her daughter's forehead. It was cool, the fever had broken. Nannie bowed her head and said a prayer of thanksgiving.

Near noon, Annielise opened her eyes and announced to the ever present Arabella that she was hungry for some biscuits. As scarce as flour was, she got a biscuit.

A week later, Ted Perkins brought Annielise a present. He had commissioned the sole jeweler in town to make it. The man had been thrilled. The doctor's strange request was the only commission the jeweler had received since the siege began. He couldn't eat his merchandise and had begun to barter it for food as the price of a barrel of flour had risen to $500.

With a sly smile, Ted Perkins handed Annielise a blue velvet box. Nannie, Daniel and Arabella looked on as Annielise opened it. Inside was a deformed Minié ball wrapped in a gold teardrop setting threaded onto a delicate chain.

Annielise kissed Ted on the cheek. "That's for saving my life and this Yankee bullet." She fastened the gold chain around her neck.

"That's the tackiest thing I've ever seen," Nannie said. "I never wanted to see that awful thing again."

Arabella, hands on hips, mumbled imprecations about "trashy folks."

"It's a badge of courage and my granddaughter can wear it if she wants to," Daniel declared.

"It's a badge of foolishness, 'dat's what it is," Arabella said. "I'm leaving," Ted declared. "They'll be looking for me at the hospital."

"That's right! All the menfolk is leaving so this child and her mama can get some rest. Miss Nannie is done woe' out. Dere ain't no shelling going on round dis here part of town so you-uns git. Do yo' smokin' and talkin' out yonder."

Quinn and Perkins emerged from the cave into bright sunlight. "First it was my wife, God rest her soul, then my daughter-in-law, and now damn if it's not a slave ordering me around. Come on to what's left of my house, Ted. See if we can find an unbroken bottle of bourbon and maybe a cigar or two."

Annielise made the civilian casualty list in the Vicksburg newspaper, *The Daily Citizen, J. M. Swords, proprietor.* It was printed on the back of wallpaper for lack of newsprint.

Last week the following ladies of our city were wounded: Mrs. Major T. E. Reed, Mrs. C. W. Peters, Mrs. W. S. Hazzard, Mrs. W. H. Clements, Miss Lucy Rawlings, Miss Annielise Quinn, and Miss Eileen Canovan. The wounds were all from fragments of shells except for Miss Rawlings and Miss Quinn who were struck with Minié balls.

A month later, June 27, 1863, the 41st day of siege, Annielise celebrated her seventeenth birthday. Her wound had healed. She fussed about "the ugly red scar on my tummy," but had recovered sufficient strength to walk. During an afternoon lull in the shelling, the Quinns held a little party for her in the shade under the canvas tarpaulin. Annielise wore a white linen dress for the occasion. Nannie combed her strawberry blond hair and tied it back with a red ribbon. The sparkle was back in her deep blue eyes.

Grandfather Quinn brought out a bottle of French wine salvaged from his cellar. Nannie produced a small jar of homemade fig preserves, enough for everyone to have a dollop on the half dozen biscuits Arabella had managed to make from flour, one egg, water—milk was unavailable—and a little bacon fat.

Ted gave Annielise a thick, leather bound diary with a brass lock. He had the jeweler emboss her name in gold on its cover. "You should record these times." he said. "Such an important literary task should keep you out of further mischief."

"That's a wonderful idea, Uncle Ted. I'll write everything down: the history of the Quinns and Shamrock, the war here in Vicksburg, our brave boys, and the stories I've heard about you and Grandfather. Y'all were bad boys."

"Your grandfather was years older. He led me astray."

"I led you astray?"

"That's right, but I'll forgive you, Daniel, if you show me where you're hiding that French wine."

A few nights later the most massive bombardment the town had yet suffered was laid down upon Vicksburg. Shells fired from gunboats and mortar barges rained down on the Confederate bluffs facing the river while Rebel trench works forming the landside defenses were pounded by a seven-mile semi-circle of Union artillery. Fired high into the darkness, thousands upon thousands of shells trailing sparks from powder-train fuses and burning wadding arced over the city. Initially mimicking a falling star, the flight of each shell ended in a thunderous flash and concussion thick with the whizzing whine of razor-sharp shards of red-hot iron. It was as near to hell on earth as anyone in Vicksburg that night would ever experience.

At first, the whomp and crack of shell bursts commenced safely distant from the Quinn cave, but slowly the terrifying sounds crept ever closer. Dirt began to dust down from the timber-braced ceiling. The flame of the oil lamp fluttered wildly, casting eerie shadows on the walls. The very ground began to shake. Not a desperate word was spoken. Transfixed by fear, the cave dwellers screamed silently until, like a passing tempest, the barrage rolled over them into the distance. Numb, stunned, ears ringing, hearts pounding, mouths gritty, lungs full of dust, those in the Quinn cave lay awake for hours until fitful sleep granted miserable relief to stressed minds and dirt-sprinkled bodies.

Just after dawn the next day, July fourth, 1863, Nannie awoke inexplicably frightened. There was something eerily unnerving about the morning. Several minutes passed before she realized what made it so. For the first time in 47 days and nights the guns were silent.

Annielise and Arabella were sleeping. Daniel Quinn's cot was empty. Walking from the cave into sunlight, Nannie found the dead calm uncanny. Spread before her was a landscape of scattered shell holes and splintered trees. All that was left of a great oak nearby was a smoldering trunk shorn of all limbs. Wisps of smoke drifted low to the ground like riptides on an ocean. The sky was hazy, laden with dust, the air heavy with the acrid smell of spent gunpowder. One corner of the tarpaulin at the cave's entrance hung limply. Sunbeams streamed through the shrapnel-torn canvas patterning the shaded ground beneath with flecks of sunlight. The raucous caw of a crow flying overhead shattered the unfamiliar serenity. Nannie thought, *The scavengers are wasting no time arriving.*

"Nannie!"

She looked up to see Daniel hurrying toward her from the direction of town.

"Get everyone up! We're going back to what's left of the house. Vicksburg is surrendered. Grant will be in town by ten o'clock. I don't know what's going to happen but I want you and Annielise off the street. Y'all go on right now! I'll git some help to bring everything down soon as I can."

While Arabella stayed at the cave to pack, Nannie and Annielise walked a worn path across a weed-choked field to the street that led into town. They were both dressed in the latest fashion . . . long cotton dresses grown thin and faded from wash-pot boiling and hard scrubbing.

The two women passed small groups of ragged, filthy men with downcast faces. Almost none wore a complete uniform. Many had no shoes. Some had tear streaks down their dirt-caked cheeks.

From one such group, a young soldier stepped into the street in front of the Quinns and took off his cap. "Miz Quinn, Miss Annielise," he said, "I'm Seth Whitfield. I know your boy, Jonathan, Miz Quinn."

The soldier took a grimy, bullet-holed battle flag from inside his shirt. "They say them Yanks most probably gonna search all us when they git here." He held out the flag. "My brother, he died carrying this flag. I don't want no Yankee touching it. I'd be obliged if y'all would take it, Ma'am."

Near tears, Nannie nodded and took the flag without a word, wrapping it in her silk shawl. The two thin, blond women walked on down the littered streets passing damaged homes, some burned out, none untouched. From the verandas of several of the houses, gaunt women and old men silently watched them pass. Some nodded. Along the way, many of the once stately oaks that had provided shady canopies over the street stood splintered, bereft of limbs and leaves, mute testimony to the fury of siege.

Directly, the ladies approached their once beautiful Greek revival townhouse. Many of its windows were shattered, its columns and walls pocked from shrapnel. There were two holes in the roof. To reach their home, mother and daughter had to skirt a long, slow-moving line of troops, each man in turn laying his weapon on a growing pile of arms in the street in front of the Quinn house. Annielise climbed the front steps and entered the house. Nannie stopped at the front walk. She had noticed a small boy dressed in dirty, ragged clothes standing in line with the soldiers. *That child can't be more than twelve.* She couldn't take her eyes away. When his turn came, he looked up at a sergeant standing by the stack. The man nodded. The boy unstrapped his drum, laid it gently at the foot of the pile, put his drumsticks beside it, then hid his face against the grizzled soldier and clung to him sobbing. Nannie ran up the steps, closed the door behind her, and for the first time since the siege began, wept uncontrollably.

Near noon, the Quinn women watched from behind torn parlor curtains through a broken window as the first of the enemy troops marched down their street. Some took charge of the Confederate prisoners and marched them away while others began collecting the surrendered weapons and loading them into a wagon. From the direction of the shell-scarred courthouse the women could hear a Union Army band playing gay, triumphant tunes. Down on the river, Admiral Porter's gunboats and supply packets steamed up and down, endlessly blowing their whistles.

All day the long blue lines marched into Vicksburg. Each side was awed by the other; the men in gray, that the Blues were so many, those in blue, that the Grays were so few. The victors did not make sport of their Confederate prisoners. The Grays of Vicksburg had not fallen under direct assault of arms and the Blues knew it. Rations were shared, respect given.

What the newly-arrived Union troops saw were ragged, dirty, sick and starving human beings, soldier and civilian alike. Until the well-fed soldiers of the United States of the North entered Vicksburg, those living there had no standard but each other by which to compare their condition. Deprivation had descended upon them a day at a time for 47 long days. Food trickled out, water was scarce. Flesh and muscle shrank away, soiled clothes and uniforms deteriorated, hair went unkempt, bodies un-bathed. Scurvy, malaria, and dysentery had begun to take a toll. It all came so slowly. One might notice a neighbor looking bedraggled, but in one's own mind, one was holding up all right. Each clung to their former self-image and dared look only in the mirror of their memory.

The senior Quinn arrived at the house with Arabella and several borrowed servants carrying pots, china, silverware, bedding, clothes and other items of use from the cave. Using a borrowed hand cart, Daniel and the servants returned to the cave to fetch the rug, cots, table, lamp and finally the stove.

Daniel, too worn out for further chores, sat on the back steps. His daughter-in-law came out on the back veranda and sat beside him.

"Daddy Quinn," Nannie asked, "what happens now?"

"Nannie darling, I been sittin' here thinkin' about that. The first thing we do is see if we can get some help to clean up this place, get the holes in the roof and walls patched and find something to cover the broken windows. It won't be pretty, but it'll be a sight better than a cave. We should have stayed at Shamrock. I never should have brought you here. I thought you and Annielise would be safer in town. I don't know what occupation will mean—martial law I reckon. As soon as we can, Nannie, we'll return to Shamrock and begin again, you and Annielise and, God willing, Ansel and Jonathan and me.

Three days following the surrender of Vicksburg, Nannie heard a knock at the front door. She looked through the cracked, beveled-glass side light to see Thomas Boatner, her husband's lifelong friend from Natchez, standing on the porch. He wore a soiled, threadbare gray uniform of a Confederate major. He had been best man at her wedding. Thrilled to see him, she threw open the door.

"Tom Boatner, you come in this house and let me hug your neck."

Nannie remembered him as carefree and handsome with laughing eyes. The Tom Boatner she saw standing before her was thin and hollow-cheeked. He looked at her with the saddest expression she had ever seen on a man's face.

A shiver ran up Nannie's spine. *Oh God! Which one will it be?* Taking off his sweat-stained, wide-brimmed hat, Boatner held out an envelope. "This came in a bag of our mail captured by Sherman's men." Nannie couldn't move her hand to take it. "It's been a long time arriving, Nannie K. Grant's headquarters people opened all our official letters before they let us have them. When this one came across my desk, I thought it best if I delivered it myself." Unable to make eye contact, he placed the letter in her hand.

Motioning Tom inside, Nannie sat down on a dusty, horsehair-upholstered divan. Her hands trembling, she pressed the soiled, wrinkled paper flat on her skirt and stared down at a broken wax seal bearing the imprint, CSA. She turned it over and saw the address. *Mrs. T. Ansel Quinn, General Delivery, Vicksburg Station.* Nannie carefully unfolded the plain sheet of tablet paper.

Dear Mrs. Quinn,

It is my sad and terrible duty to inform you that your husband, Colonel T. Ansel Quinn, was mortally wounded while leading his troops in fierce battle near Oxford, Mississippi on the 15th day of May 1863. He was loved by his men, respected by his peers, and by his devotion and courage honored his family, his country, and this command. With deepest sympathy I remain,

Very respectfully, Your obedient servant,

N. B. Forrest, Gen. CSA

Cheerful sunlight streamed into the room in cruel contrast to the dark cloud Nannie felt creeping over her heart, shrouding it in unbearable sorrow. Tom Boatner, watching her beautiful face twist into helpless agony, sat down beside her and gently folded her into his arms. Unable to find words, he offered silent comfort. Nannie buried her head in his shoulder.

Finally, Nannie raised her head, wiped the tears from her eyes with the backs of her hands, and looked up at Tom. "Thank you for bringing it yourself, Tom. I know how hard this must be for you." Major Boatner nodded and stood up. He held her hand a moment. "We have word the Yankees are gonna distribute some food. I'll bring you what I can." He stepped back, turned, and walked slowly out the front door, quietly closing it behind him. Nannie Keturah Quinn sat alone in the dead silence of a once happy house. *Oh! Ansel. I love you so. I need you so.*

When Daniel came home, he found Nannie in the front hallway sitting pale and drawn at the foot of the stairs. Teary-eyed, she looked up at him and held out the wrinkled paper. "Daddy Quinn, I need you with me when I tell Annielise. I just don't have the strength to do it alone."

Daniel Quinn read the note, absently handed it back to Nannie. "Nannie, I . . ." he paused and started again. "I just need a moment or two. Forgive me." He stood there, his face gray, quick shallow breaths leaking pain through clenched teeth. Finally, holding tightly to the banister with one hand, the other gently touching Nannie's bowed head, he started slowly up the stairs.

Struggling to walk under the paralyzing weight of sorrow, Nannie followed him. *My husband is dead. My Ansel is gone.* The terrible finality those words conveyed ripped into her very soul. As she fought for strength to console her weeping daughter a new fear clawed at her heart. *My son! Dear God, where is Jonathan?*

CHAPTER 2

Jonathan Hillary Quinn had his mother's blue eyes, rosy cheeks and reddish blond hair, his father's strong chin and trim build, and the headstrong ways of his Grandfather Quinn. It was the latter trait that landed him, at age sixteen, at Marion Military Institute in Alabama, one of several Southern military schools known for their ability to impose discipline as well as scholastic excellence upon the young hot bloods of wealthy planters. At the time, his parents had a more furtive reason for sending their son to Marion. There was wide talk of secession. They hoped sending their son away to school would keep him out of war . . . if it came.

War was declared during Jonathan's second year at Marion. Like the other young men at the school, he was caught up in the naive enthusiasm of the uninitiated, but his expressed interest was distinctly different from that of his classmates. They talked of saddles and sabers. His room was decorated with model ships.

"What you want'a be sailing for, Quinn? All the fightin' gonna be on land. Hell, we don't even have a navy," his friends chided him.

"We can't win without one," he answered. It was a prophetic statement, but his friends at Marion considered the discussion purely academic. Jonathan didn't. He saddled his horse and left.

Strong willed, but no fool, young J. Hillary Quinn had a plan. Before dawn, he headed for Montgomery, sixty three miles away. There he hoped to enlist the aid of his great uncle, Judge William Quinn. Confederate States President Davis had appointed him an advisor on maritime affairs.

The judge, the main source of Jonathan's interest in ships and the sea, found himself listening to the last male heir in the family argue in favor of enlistment in the fledgling Confederate navy.

"Uncle Bill, Daddy has raised a company of infantry, you are an advisor to President Davis, everybody we know is gonna join up sooner or later. I won't be the only man in the family not to do so."

"It is precisely because you are the only son in the family that you should stay out of this war."

"You ran off to sea when you were my age."

Judge Quinn had run away at age seventeen to spend his early manhood at sea before returning home to read law.

"There was no war then, Jonathan. The sea alone is dangerous enough. You mix in war, it becomes deadly."

"It was pretty deadly at Manassas I hear, and that's a long way from the sea."

Judge Quinn began to pace back and forth. He was hard put to rebut the boy. He had taught him to sail at his fishing camp on Bon Secour Bay, south of Mobile.

"Jonathan, what you are setting out to do will be hard, dangerous, and lonely. You'll have to stand on your own merits before the officers and men of your ship. Once you sail, there'll be no turning back. God knows how long you'll be gone. Your family will worry, and I'll carry the burden of having helped place you in harm's way. We love you boy, damn your stubborn ways."

Jonathan didn't say a word. The judge paused to look at him eye to eye, saw determination in the boy's expression, shook his head in resignation and resumed pacing. *I reckon I know when I've lost a case. Better to help than to let the boy go off on his own.*

"All right, Jonathan, here is my offer. There's an important new ship being built. Her officers will be hand-picked. I'll send a telegram recommending you to Stephen Mallory, Secretary of our Navy. He's a friend of mine. If you are accepted as a midshipman aboard the new ship, so be it. If you're not accepted, I want your word that you'll return to school and stay there."

"You have it, Sir."

By week's end, the Judge received answers to the two telegrams he had sent, one to Richmond, the other to Mobile. He sat the boy down in his study.

"Jonathan, Mallory has gotten you a berth on a new ship that won't be completed for a while yet. In the meantime, this is how it will be. I've asked a favor from an old sea dog in Mobile, a certain Bosun Jones. I'm placing you in his rough but able hands until your ship is ready. You'll clean fish, mend sails, tar skiff bottoms and do, without complaining, whatever else you're asked to do to earn your room and board. My advice is never argue with Bosun Jones. Do what he says when he asks and say, yes sir, and damn little else. If he takes a liking to you, and you pay attention, you just might learn enough to keep yourself alive aboard a ship of the line."

"And if he doesn't like me, Uncle?"

"Then God help you, boy. He'll probably drown you himself before the Yankees have the chance. Now, you think about that tonight and give me an answer in the morning. I'll hear no more from you this evening. Maybe a night's sleep will change your mind."

The old judge watched seventeen year old J. H. Quinn board the morning train for Mobile. Back in his office he composed a letter to Jonathan's parents, one to Marion and another to his brother. For days he agonized over his part in sending the boy to sea instead of back to school.

He shouldn't have. The next year the cadet corps at Marion marched to Selma one bright, sunny day. Almost every boy died there defending God, country, and a large store of Confederate munitions.

Mobile was a lovely town shaded by grand oaks feathered in Spanish moss, its busy waterfront commerce softened by their grace. Young Quinn was met at the train station by a barrel-chested, gray-bearded, raw-voiced, dirty-bellied elder who smelled of tar, sweat, and whiskey.

"You be Master Quinn, I presume."

"I'm Jonathan Hillary Quinn, Sir."

"Are you now? Well, I'm Deuteronomy Jones, and you will address me as Bosun Jones, and do what I say do or be carted back to your school or fed to the fish as you please. Now tote your bag on down to Water Street. You'll find a catboat moored at the foot of Dauphin. I'll meet you there directly."

Deuteronomy turned on his heel and marched away in a gait peculiar to men who have spent more time on the deck of a rolling ship than on land. Jonathan was left standing on the platform without a clue as to which direction lay Dauphin Street or the river. His training had begun.

South down Mobile Bay at the mouth of Dog River, Bosun Jones had a dock, two large, open-sided warehouses and a cabin that served as both sleeping quarters and office. In addition there were a couple of small sheds where rope, tar, marine hardware, paint and the like were stored. Jonathan was assigned quarters in the one nearest the dock. It afforded him barely enough room to string a hammock.

Most days he spent cleaning fish, caulking skiffs, splicing rope or mending sails, all skills he learned under the watchful eye and instructions of Bosun Jones delivered in rather colorful language. If he didn't learn anything else at Dog River, he certainly would learn the art of proper cussin'.

There came a day when a sleek blockade runner named *Virgin* anchored off Dog River. Bosun Jones explained, "Look at her and pay mind to what I tell you boy. That one's a beauty. She's fore and aft rigged, shallow-draft, swift of sail, equipped with an auxiliary steam engine, but light on guns to save weight. Her mainstays of safety in a dangerous business are speed, stealth, the indiscriminate use of flags of several nations and the skill of her captain, a tough old Scots-Irishman named Molony. She rendezvouses with English and French ships at Cuba, the Bahamas and other Caribbean islands to exchange cotton for cargos of military contraband and luxury items for her dash here to Mobile Bay.

"Whenever she anchors off Dog River, you gonna see a freed black called Gator show up here with a crew of slaves he hires out to man a whaleboat to tow lighters between *Virgin* and the dock there until her cargo is safely stowed in my warehouses. I expect you to go with Gator and bend your back with him and the rest of 'em."

Jonathan found the work back breaking hard. He learned the cargo was divided between arms, munitions and medicines for the war effort, and scarce items like lace, finished cotton cloth, china, rum, wine, perfume, spices, Cuban cigars, and sugar to sweeten profits. The outbound cargo was baled cotton destined for foreign textile mills.

Jonathan was surprised to learn that Deuteronomy Jones owned *Virgin*.

"If you own a ship, why aren't you addressed as Captain Jones, Sir?"

"You got to figure things every way you can, boy. There's more warships out beyond the mouth of the Bay there than most people ever seen on one ocean. If this here port was to fall, what Yankee would believe that a beached, worn-out, poor old bosun could be a blockade-running ship owner? I don't aim to be hanged or put in no Northern prison for aiding the Rebels, or for that matter, in no Southern prison for war profiteering. Don't ever get yourself in a corner with no way out, boy."

In the evenings after supper, Jonathan attended school of a sort at Bosun Jones' cabin where his hard taskmaster pounded seafaring knowledge into his brain. "By God, you got a heap of learning to do, boy, and not much time to overhaul it all."

Jonathan filled notebooks with the endless knowledge of seamanship that poured from Bosun Jones like saltwater from an open seacock. He had to memorize the name and location of every mast, spar, sail, shroud, brace, sheet and line of a sailing ship, and the proper commands to trim sails, bring a ship about or jib or 'wear' one whether square or fore-and-aft rigged. He had to study steam engines and paddle wheels, side wheels and propellers. Added to his burden were studies of weather and navigation. His brain ached from study as much as his body from hard physical work.

"You better pay attention, Master Quinn. This ain't idle knowledge, boy. You gonna learn that soon enough. You've learned how to navigate a ship at sea. That's one thing. Navigating your way into a blockaded port is another barrel of fish, all of 'em sharks."

And so it went until, on a stormy, moonless night, Bosun Jones stood on shore in the rain watching *Virgin*, showing no lights, disappear into the darkness. Standing on *Virgin's* wet, storm-swept deck, Jonathan breathed in the salt air, filling his nostrils with the heavy aroma of tar, hemp, cypress, oak and pine, and not least, the intoxicating scent of romantic adventure that exists in the minds of boys stretching for manhood.

In the early spring of 1862, *Virgin* returned once again to Mobile where Bosun Jones boarded her to see how his student was faring. When she departed, to Jonathan's surprise, Deuteronomy remained aboard. In Santiago, Cuba they rendezvoused with a British merchantman from Liverpool. While their cargos were transferred, Jonathan's trunk along with a sealed pouch marked C.S.A. were put aboard the English ship. The pouch would be delivered to James Dunwoody Bulloch, the Confederate agent in charge of acquiring ships in England. Among the official papers was a letter of introduction for Midshipman Jonathan Hillary Quinn, assigned to "that vessel presently referred to as hull number 290."

Deuteronomy handed Jonathan a leather money belt. "Here's money enough to buy proper uniforms with a little left over for essentials." Jonathan started to protest, but Deuteronomy cut him off, "This ain't no gift. You earned this money." Then, for the first time, he put his arms around Jonathan in a fatherly hug. "Remember all I taught you, boy, and you'll come through all right. Now git along with you, and do me proud, boy. I've got to make sail for home."

Jonathan stood at attention with a big smile. "Yes, Sir, Bosun Jones, Sir."

"You'll do, Master Quinn, you'll do," Deuteronomy said with a smile on his rugged, sun-wrinkled, sea-weathered face.

Unarmed, and in spite of protests filed by the United States, Laird Brothers Hull Number 290, christened *Henrica*, sailed from England flying the Union Jack. Aboard her were 23 Confederate officers, among them, Midshipman Jonathan Hillary Quinn.

The mixed foreign crew consisted of 120 men who, according to the ship's Captain, Rafael Semmes, *"had been picked up promiscuously about the streets of Liverpool, and were a reckless, improvident, hard-drinking lot."*

In an isolated bay off the island of Terceira in the Azores, *Henrica* rendezvoused with the supply ship, *Agrippina*, and spent two days transferring aboard her cargo of cannon, powder, shot, coal, and food stores.

On the twenty fourth of August 1862, the Union Jack was struck and the Confederate naval ensign raised. The Southern officers, in the words of Captain Semmes, *". . . were astonished when the unenthusiastic Englishmen, the stolid Dutchmen, the mercurial Frenchmen, the grave Spaniard, and even the lone, serious Malayan, to the man joined in a soul-stirring refrain of 'Dixie'."* The officers sang in loyalty to a cause, the foreign crew to a voyage for which they would be paid in gold. The name *Henrica* was painted over and replaced with a name the world would recognize as that of the most successful naval raider in history, *Alabama*. Young Jonathan Quinn would cross her decks into hell.

CHAPTER 3

Daniel Quinn assembled the women in the parlor. Eyes cast down at the floor, brow furrowed, he spoke in a subdued tone a preacher might have used at a funeral. "The Yankee provost marshal put out another proclamation today."

Daniel paused in thought.

They already been turned loose at Shamrock, I reckon, all of 'em, nearly a hundred thousand dollars invested and not a penny for the lot. Now I got to do it here by damn Yankee orders under threat of arrest in my own town, in my own house in front of my family. Hail the conquering heroes the Yankee sons of bitches.

The room was silent. He realized the three women gathered before him were waiting for him to speak. He struggled to find words.

"The proclamation orders all slaves in surrendered Vicksburg freed. Arabella, you are free to go as you please. I don't know what in your heart you hold toward us Quinns. I thank you for the loyalty you have shown Miss Nannie, Miss Annielise and this family." He paused and finally lifted his eyes up to Arabella. "God knows where all the freed people will go or what they'll do. The Yankee army will feed 'em for a spell, I reckon." He lowered his eyes back to the floor. "You're welcome to stay if you want, Arabella, but a little food and a leaky roof over your head is about all I have left to trade for your services."

The Quinn women, standing behind Arabella, didn't say a word. Daniel focused on a spot where shrapnel had torn the Oriental rug and gouged the heart-pine floor beneath.

Head held high, Arabella broke the silence. "Ain't nothing right 'bout slavery," the black woman said. "Never was. Don't know what's gonna happen to black folks now, but it be better 'en what's gone befo'e."

Standing in front of Daniel Quinn, her brow wrinkled, her mouth set with pressed lips Arabella paused. Daniel looked up expecting her to walk out of the house.

After a long, agonizing moment the freed slave continued. "You is a good man, Massa Quinn, and yo' family is the only family I gots. I reckon I loves Miss Nannie and dis here child I hep'ed raise. I ain't ashamed fo' saying it. I ain't got no place to go. I be staying on."

Both Quinn women hugged Arabella Dupuis. She shrugged them off, "I ain't got no time to put up with no foolishness. I got work to do." A freed woman, she started up the stairs so her proud, happy tears wouldn't show.

It was Daniel Quinn who walked out of the house. Hands shoved into empty pockets, he set out walking along town streets mottled with sunlight scattered through the remaining limbs and leaves of war-scarred oaks. *I've just been humbled in front of my family by the decision of a black woman to stay with us, and God help me, I was afraid she was gonna leave.*

Daniel Quinn had serious reasons to be depressed. Prior to the fall of Vicksburg, Washington had sent out a draconian order that made it the duty of Union occupation forces to: "*. . . seize and apply to the support of the United States Army, the property of any and all of the following: Any officer in the army or navy of the Confederacy; Any president, vice president, member of congress, judicial or cabinet officer under the Confederate government; Any governor, member of the legislature or convention, or any judge of a state in secession; Any officer of the Confederacy who had formerly held an office under the United States; Any person in a Confederate state who had given aid, assistance, or comfort to those in arms against the United States.*

As that covered nearly every adult white person in the state of Mississippi, and certainly every citizen of Vicksburg, their private property could be and was occupied, destroyed or taken at will by the occupation forces. As it turned out, much of what was seized did not *apply to the support of the United States Army* as the order directed. Many field grade Union officers set their duty aside to engage in cotton trafficking using army quartermaster supply wagons to confiscate from warehouses that which belonged to the destitute survivors of Vicksburg and transfer it to river packets or rail cars for transportation to market. The practice became such an embarrassment to the Army that a major Northern newspaper asked in print whether "*any Mississippi citizen had ever received so much as one penny for their cotton?*"

The more Daniel mulled over the prospects of his family the more depressed he became. *My cotton stolen, my investment in slaves gone, my land burdened with debt and taxes. Every damn bank I know of has failed. There's not a cent of credit to be had. What the hell am I gonna do?*

Prior to the war Daniel Quinn had been a man of means. He owned some 3,000 acres of land, most of which had been under cultivation. In 1861 he had more than 500 bales of cotton in storage at Vicksburg. When war was declared, two hundred bales were pledged as security against a loan. One hundred bales were pledged toward backing Confederate "cotton" money, Confederate treasury notes backed by 1861 cotton bales stored in warehouses. He gave fifty bales for the defense of the city. They were physically incorporated into Confederate earthworks.

Daniel had learned that cotton prices on the international market had never been higher. Shortages brought on by war had raised the price to the unheard of level of almost two hundred dollars a bale. Even in a defeated South, he figured the sale of his remaining cotton would bring enough to begin anew at Shamrock. He now knew he had been wrong. His reserve of cotton was gone, "stolen by the damn Yankees."

As Daniel walked and pondered his hopeless situation, his frustration was not salved by the sight of long lines of Confederate prisoners waiting for parole passes. *Damn it to hell! Will they ever get to us civilians?*

Daniel was desperate to get to Shamrock. When he applied for parole for himself and his family, he was told that as an elected official and former slave owner, he would have to wait his turn. Paroling prisoners came first.

Under the terms of surrender, General Grant agreed to parole his prisoners at Vicksburg provided they took an oath not to bear arms against the Union. Mounted troops were allowed to keep their horses (those few that hadn't been eaten or killed by shelling), and officers were allowed to keep their sidearms. Grant's decision to parole prisoners was not a humane act. It was a military necessity. If he was to swiftly follow up on his victory, he could not afford the time, men, and supplies it would take to imprison some thirty thousand surrendered Confederates, as many as a third of them sick or wounded. Grant placed Vicksburg under martial law, put Major General McPherson in charge and moved out.

The task of governing the city and paroling prisoners was put in the hands of the military provost. Unlike those who had fought to take the city, the occupation troops brought up fresh from the rear held little respect for the courage of the defeated, soldier or civilian.

After all the cotton was gone, Vicksburg's occupation authorities returned to proper military details, one of which was to order the reverent W. W. Lord, minister of the shell-damaged Episcopal church, to reinstate that portion of the *Book of Common Prayer* dealing with a prayer for the president of the United States. (In the South, the passage had been changed to a prayer for the president of the Confederacy.) As a result, church attendance became very light, composed mostly of Yankee officers and enlisted men.

When an old and much-respected Episcopal bishop was allowed through the lines to visit Vicksburg, rumor spread that he would simply omit the prayer for the Yankee president. As a result, the congregation of occupying Union officers and men was swelled by the old congregation of Southern citizenry. However, the good bishop, having been threatened beforehand with military arrest, read *"We pray for the President of the United States and all others in authority,"* when he came to it in the *Book of Common Prayer*. He had hardly finished the passage when a young lady stood up and walked out of the church. She was quickly followed by several other young ladies. Inspired by their courage and defiance, the entire Southern congregation followed suit leaving the church to the soldiers in blue.

A few hours later, copies of a remarkable order were posted around the city: It read: *Headquarters 17th Army Corps, Vicksburg Mississippi. The following named persons having acted disrespectful toward the President and government of the United States, and having insulted the officers, soldiers, and loyal citizens of the United States who had assembled in the Episcopal church . . . by abruptly leaving the church at that point in the services where the minister prays for the welfare of the President and all others in authority, are hereby banished, and will leave the Federal lines within forty-eight hours, under penalty of imprisonment.—By order of Major General McPherson.*

A second order was quickly issued giving the following instructions: *The parties ordered to proceed outside the Federal lines will report at the depot tomorrow at 10 o'clock. They will be permitted to take their private baggage. A conveyance will be in readiness at Big Black Bridge with a flag of truce to take them to the Confederate lines, or so far as the flag may be permitted to proceed.—By order of Major General McPherson, James Wilson, Lieut. Col., Provost Marshal*

"Miss Annielise Quinn" was the first on the list of six young ladies named in the order. Livid with anger, a white-knuckled Daniel H. Quinn stormed down the street leaving in his wake the futile pleading of Nannie Keturah and the wailing of Arabella. Two young soldiers guarding the steps of the provost marshal's headquarters, a confiscated townhouse on Crawford Street near the corner of Cherry, made only half-hearted moves to bar him from entering the building. He was an old coot, they figured, but he was one mad, mean-looking old coot.

If the rage in a man's eyes could kill, the officer on duty reckoned the cold, steel-gray eyes of the man standing before him would have wiped out the entire headquarters.

"I will not insult your vile ignorance by beginning with the word 'gentlemen', for no sons of mongrel bitches such as you and your general could possibly understand the meaning of a word used to describe a civil man, much less one deserving the title 'officer'."

"Just who the hell do you think you're addressing, old man?" the major snapped, and stood up behind his desk.

"A coward and cotton thief who makes war on women and children and orders young girls out of their city. I'm addressing a wad of scum who is unfit to wear the uniform of an officer in even the poorest excuse of a backwater, bureaucratic, paper pushing command; a usurper of a uniform who isn't worthy so much as to empty the slop jars of the men who did the fightin' before he arrived. Those fightin' men conducted themselves as soldiers. You and your general come as leaches to prey upon the civilian survivors of siege and vent your retribution upon young girls, one of whom is my granddaughter, goddamn your soul to Hell! You withdraw that order or by God I'll kill the first man who comes to get her."

The last sentence was stated with such icy calm that there was not the slightest doubt by anyone in the room that he meant it.

"Sergeant! This man, by threat, has assaulted an officer and the Army. Take him away and lock him up! Now!"

In spite of his age and arthritis, to put Quinn in irons and haul him from the room required the strenuous efforts of the sergeant, two of his men and the officer's drawn pistol. As a token of his esteem, the elder Quinn left behind one private with a blackened eye and a Sergeant with a bloodied nose.

Nannie was frantic when Daniel didn't come home that evening. Warned that no woman was safe on the streets after dark, she went early the next morning to the Provost office only to be informed by the officer of the day, a lieutenant, that the senior Quinn had assaulted an officer and soldiers of the U.S. Army and been summarily sentenced to a year's imprisonment.

"May I see him please?" Nannie asked, and was shocked by the officer's answer.

"Mr. Quinn is considered a dangerous criminal. As a result, he was placed in irons and is, at this moment, enroute down river for transshipment to imprisonment at Fort Jefferson."

"But he's an honorable and elderly man. He was trying to prevent your general from sending my daughter, his granddaughter, alone out of the city to God knows where. It's cruel and unjust."

"Please understand, ma'am, for his actions, he could have been shot."

"Where is this Fort Jefferson? Can I visit him?"

"I'm afraid not, ma'am. Fort Jefferson is on the island of Dry Tortugas located seventy miles off the coast of Florida. It's used to incarcerate dangerous military and civilian criminals."

Nannie walked out of the provost headquarters full of a crippling uncertainty as to what to do. *Oh! Lord help us. Ansel is dead, my daughter is to be banished to we know not where, and now Grandfather Daniel is being taken from us. I don't even know if my son is alive. Dear God, what more can this horrible war take from me?*

Nannie returned home to find a guard posted at the house to ensure that Annielise reported later that morning as ordered. She gathered her daughter and Arabella to tell them that Daniel had been sent away to prison.

"I don't know what to do," Nannie confessed. She looked into the faces of the two stunned women.

Arabella was the first to speak. "I knows what you do, Miss Nannie. You fetch Massa Quinn's gun and shoot de first Yankee what tries to take our baby."

"It's all right, Mama," Annielise said. "I'm glad to get out of here. I'll be just fine once we reach friendly lines. From there I'll get to Shamrock. I'll be safe there."

Nannie knew better. A seventeen-year-old girl alone, especially a pretty one, wouldn't be safe among the lines of any army, blue or gray, and she certainly wouldn't be given an escort all the way to Shamrock.

She determined her daughter would not be sent into exile alone. *They may put Daniel Quinn in prison, but they won't put a mother in prison, not out in front of the whole town.*

They didn't, but only because of a freed slave. When Nannie, Annielise and Arabella arrived at the depot, each carrying a small trunk, they found a large crowd of citizens already gathered. The army had anticipated trouble and assigned twenty soldiers and a squad of cavalry to maintain order. Two wagons were waiting, one with bench seats and an opened-sided, canvas sun canopy for the ladies. A second open wagon was for their baggage. Each had a large white flag attached to a long staff lashed beside the driver's seat.

At the appointed hour a sergeant called out the names of the young women on the list. Some tearful, some defiant, the young women stepped from the crowd as their names were called and walked to the wagons. Nannie tried to walk with her daughter, but was stopped by a soldier. "Just the young ladies on the list, Ma'am."

Arabella walked straight past the soldier restraining Nannie and through the blue line of soldiers separating the crowd from the wagons. A trooper tried to stop her. She jerked away and caught up with Annielise.

"Just a minute there! You can't go, woman."

"I been taking care of dis here child since she was born. She been wounded from yo' bullets, and I is going with her."

"You're free now. You don't have to take orders from anybody. Don't you understand?"

"Is dat so?" Arabella put both hands on her hips, a signal of impending perturbation even Daniel Hillary Quinn had learned to recognize and respect.

A captain from the office of the Provost stepped up and answered for the soldier, "Of course that's true. You don't belong to this girl's family any longer. You don't have to serve them."

"You saying I is free to come and go as I please?"

"That's right," he answered.

"Then I'm pleased to go with this here child. You done put her Granddaddy in jail, kilt her daddy, shot her and now yo' wants to send her away and leave her mama over dere wit' nobody. You set her mama up in dat wagon with her daughter and put them three little trunks yonder in de other one. Dere means to be trouble if'en you don't."

The captain weighed his options. The crowd was a smoldering tinder box. He abhorred the thought of using troops with bayonets against mostly women and old men. *Damn that fool general and his order.*

"Sergeant! Let the mother and that free and loyal citizen through and be quick about it."

Nannie and Arabella were helped up into the front wagon beside Annielise. Their baggage was tossed into the second wagon. The other young ladies were already in place when Nannie and Arabella were allowed into the wagon. As a result, their mothers commenced demanding to be allowed to go too.

"Lieutenant!" the captain yelled, "Get those wagons rolling! Now!"

The hostile crowd, shouting encouragement to the young ladies while murmuring curses to the soldiers, were parted at the point of bayonets to allow the wagons, escorted by the lieutenant and twelve mounted cavalrymen, to move out toward Jackson forty miles to the east. They left behind a near riotous crowd excoriating the Yankees with curses and handfuls of dirt and gravel scooped up from the roadway. The Captain and his men, dusted and spit upon by a mob of Southern ladies, quick marched from the scene in less than good order.

Sitting on the rough board seats, the women were jostled and jolted as the wagon navigated the long neglected, deeply rutted, potholed road. There was not the hint of a breeze. The canvas top did little to protect the occupants from the sultry heat as the sun climbed into the hazy August morning. Determined to maintain their dignity, the women rode in stoic silence.

* * *

At a road junction several miles outside of Vicksburg, the Union detachment came upon a Confederate soldier in a tattered uniform astride a skinny horse standing in the middle of the road. A pair of pistols in worn leather pommel holsters hung from the saddle. The young lieutenant halted the procession and walked his horse forward. As he approached the horseman, he recognized the uniform of a Confederate Major. The Rebel officer saluted. The lieutenant did not return the courtesy. The ladies could see the two men talking, but were too far away to hear what was said.

"Lieutenant," the major began. "I was paroled this morning. I'm going down river to my home in Natchez, but I've waited here for your caravan. I know one of your charges, the girl that was wounded. Now, I see her mother and a servant are also with you. The family's home place is south toward Natchez. I hope you will allow me to take the burden of responsibility for them off your shoulders. I give you my word as a gentleman to escort them safely to their home."

"My orders are to escort these women to the Confederate lines, or as close thereto as possible. They'll have to ride with the rest of my charges."

"Not if, for the ladies in question, this is as close thereto as possible."

"But this is not as close thereto as possible, is it Major?" There was irritation in the young lieutenant's voice.

"As regards the Quinn ladies, I believe that it just might be." The major raised his left hand. From the brush and trees, six men walked onto the road ahead, eight on the road behind, five on either side, twenty-four men altogether. The mounted cavalrymen quickly drew their carbines and turned to confront the thin, dirty faces of the men surrounding them.

"Major. You and those men are paroled prisoners given leave on a pledge not to bear arms against the Union. I am under a flag of truce. Do you intend to violate your word and the white flag?"

"Those are unarmed men, lieutenant. They have not threatened you or your flag. It would not do for your men to shoot them. You would be responsible for a massacre."

The sound of carbines being cocked by nervous troopers interrupted the debate.

"Stand easy, men!" shouted the lieutenant. Sweat began to appear on his forehead.

"I don't think your men would shoot the ladies too," the major continued, "If they shoot my unarmed men and not the ladies, the latter will make very good witnesses. I bet their story of seeing unarmed, paroled prisoners shot down would appear even in the Washington papers."

"You're bluffing, Major." The lieutenant turned in his saddle and shouted, "Sergeant! Prepare the men to move out."

"Lieutenant, those men withstood all the might of your army. It wasn't Yankee bullets that beat them. They ran out of food, not courage. They're starving, they don't know what they'll find if they make it home, but what you're carrying in that wagon represents the sisters, wives, mothers and sweethearts they hope will still be there. The friends they're leaving behind died defending a dirt bluff. Do you think these men are unwilling to defend the right of a wounded young girl and her mother to go home? Take a good look at them, Lieutenant."

The cavalry officer turned slowly and looked at the gaunt, solemn faces of the silent Grays.

"What do you propose, Major?"

"I suggest you use your prerogative as a commander in the field to declare the wounded young Quinn woman unfit for the long journey to Jackson, and that you order me, as an officer and gentleman to honor your command to see the Quinn ladies safely to their farm. Then carry out your duty to see the other ladies safely to their countrymen's lines." The major looked at the clean, well-fed Union troops and added, "Lieutenant, if your men could spare a little food or tobacco, I'm sure such a charitable act would be appreciated." The major saluted, and moved to the side of the road.

"Sergeant!"

The soldier rode forward. "Sir!"

"The major here is a friend of the young lady that was wounded. He has agreed to escort her and her mother to their home south of here. I don't think she is well enough to travel all the way to Jackson, and I sure don't want anything to happen to her while she is in our charge."

"No sir."

The officer pulled out a note pad and pencil. "Here is a receipt stating the major there accepts full responsibility for the Quinn ladies." He wrote as he spoke. "Show this to them and ask if they wish to proceed under his safe conduct. If they agree, have them and the major sign it. If they do that, turn the Quinn ladies and that woman of color and their baggage over to him, and then get these wagons rolling." He finished writing and handed the note over, "And Sergeant?"

"Sir."

"See if the men can spare some rations and maybe a bit of tobacco for those poor devils. You can tell the men I'll stand good for the tobacco." He nodded to the major who saluted.

The major, his men and the three women stood in the road watching the wagons trundle away in the wavering haze of noon.

"Tom Boatner!" Nannie cried. "How can we ever thank you and all these men?" Major Boatner dismounted. Nannie put her arms around him. "You have done so much for us during these terrible times."

"Nannie," he smiled, "how do you know we didn't just do it for the Yankee tobacco?"

Nannie and Annielise laughed and cried at the same time. Drying their tears, the two women walked up to each of Boatner's men and thanked them. The men took their hats off and seemed embarrassed.

When the ladies were done, Major Boatner faced the men. "You have honored your country and humbled me with your devoted service and courage. I will never know finer men. God bless you and see you safely home." He saluted them for the last time.

Tom Boatner and the women watched in silence as the men walked back into the woods and brush, gathered up what little food and personal belongings they had, and started slowly east.

Leading his horse with the women's baggage tied to its saddle, the major, Nannie, Annielise and Arabella walked into the summer heat and haze on the dusty road leading south toward Natchez. They passed neglected cotton fields overgrown in brambles and broom sedge, rows of abandoned slave cabins, burned barns and houses. Occasional flights of birds twittered overhead while crows mocked them with their rude, arrogant calls. Except for the birds and one rabbit, the foursome saw no living thing as they walked the road. No cows, mules or horses grazed the fields. No dogs barked. It appeared that passing armies, blue or gray, had picked the land clean. A troubled weariness descended upon the travelers with the setting of the sun. After a supper of hardtack and creek water, the women slept on bare ground for the first time in their lives, too exhausted to complain.

It was a long and tiring trek marked by heat, dust, aching legs, blistered feet, pestering insects, occasional rain and frequent rest periods. A good fifteen hours or more by wagon or horse and buggy from Vicksburg, it took two days for the women on foot to make the journey to Shamrock. Late in the afternoon they turned off the main road up a wagon-rutted sunken lane overgrown in weeds to walk the final mile of their journey.

In the golden, soft light of the setting sun, the little group stood silently gazing across weed-choked ground where twin brick stairways accented by rusting, wrought iron banisters curved gracefully up to join a brick arch-supported landing leading nowhere. Beyond, surrounded by leafless, fire-charred oaks, lay a great pile of ashes guarded by four tall, blackened chimneys. Pieces of furniture, bits of clothing, broken china, odd remnants from the pillaged home lay among the weeds on what had been the front lawn.

No one said a word as each tried to reconstruct from memory the way Shamrock once proudly stood, the culmination of the work, sweat and dreams of generations of Quinns in the new world since 1750 and Mississippi from 1806.

Nannie walked over to a scattered pile of books, their covers cracked, their pages curled by exposure to rain and sun. She kneeled and picked through them to find some that were not beyond use and gathered them in her arms. "Worlds do not die as long as they are remembered in the writings of those who knew them. You keep your diary, Annielise. I will help you write of Shamrock, its history and life here the way it used to be."

The group moved down a road to where the barn and workshops had stood. The barn was gone to ashes. A few of the shops still stood; the brick weaving cottage and the carpentry and blacksmith sheds bare of most of their tools.

"What are we gonna do, Mama?"

"Y'all just follow me."

Nannie turned down a foot-worn path and led the little group past what had been a cotton field on one side and a pasture on the other. Tom didn't say a word. He figured he knew where she was headed, figured he'd lead them all to Natchez after Nannie had exhausted all her options at Shamrock. They walked down through a wooded hollow and up to a flat to find a double row of slave cabins that lined both sides of a narrow road. Walking in silence, they reached the first cabin just as a thin, old black man appeared from behind it. Alarmed, he retreated back around the corner to peep out at the strangers.

"Nicodemus? Is it you?" Nannie walked toward the startled old man.

"Miss Nannie!" He took off his hat and walked timidly toward her. His hair and beard were as gray as the once white, tattered, cotton shirt he wore. "Lawd, Miss Nannie! I didn't know if I'd ever see you no more. Ain't nobody left here but ole Nicodemus." He walked a few steps closer. "I'm right thankful to see you, Ma'am. And look a' here at Miss Annielise, and Arabella. Lawd! And ain't that Massa Boatner? I remember you coming here way back fo' Massa Ansel be married even." He frowned a moment and shook his head. "I done heard nearly everybody been kilt in Vicksburg, but here y'all is!" He looked at them and said shyly, "Y'all can come sit on de porch here if you will." He had never invited a grown white person to sit on his little porch before, though Jonathan and Annielise had done so as children.

"Would you tell us what happened?" Annielise asked.

"Them Yankees come, Miss Annielise. De tol' all us we was free, but de took all de food and grain and de animals, horses, mules, cattle and hogs and all de chickens de could catch, and done went and jes' burnt up everything. What de don't burn de jes' break all up. Jes' crazy. Some of us'en try and stop 'em but 'de jes' laugh and say we dumb niggas don't know de done come to free us. De wreck everything and rode off de place. Jes' left. Nobody knowed what to do. Some scared to leave; say de heard rebs would shoot niggas what left de place. Fo' a time dere's jes' a lot a lolly-gaggin' going on round here, but sense dere weren't nothin' to eat, de peoples jes' drifted off de place. Don't none of 'em hardly know where to go. Say freedom mean de jes' go and do like de please. Don't know how de made out. De was hungry. I know dat."

"But you stayed," Nannie smiled.

"Me? I be old; ain't got no place to be going. What I know 'cept dis place? I figure somebody would come back," the old man paused a moment, "but de ain't been nobody 'cept strangers, black and white, looking for food and such. I hides from 'em. Then he smiled, "But I knowed you'd come back, Miss Nannie. I 'jes knowed you would." The old man suddenly frowned. "But where is Massa Daniel? And what about Cap'n Ansel, Miss Nannie, and de boy?"

Nannie was silent for a long moment. She was determined not to cry. It took a while for her to say the words. "Nicodemus, my husband is dead and Grandfather Quinn is in a Yankee prison. We don't know where Jonathan is."

"I be's so mighty sorrowful, Miss Nannie."

She took one of the old man's hands in both of hers. "Oh! Nicodemus, I'm so glad to find you here."

The old man cast his eyes down so he couldn't see the pain in hers. He waited a minute or two before asking what was really on his mind. "Miss Nannie, where is you and Miss Annielise gonna stay, and what is we all gonna do?"

Nannie looked around. "Why, Nicodemus, we're going to stay right here beside you in one of these cabins. Annielise and I will take that one, and Arabella, you pick the one you want. In the morning we'll inventory everything that can be of any use. Then we'll make a start again. That's what we're gonna do. Make a new start here at Shamrock."

"Nannie." Tom Boatner put his arm around her. "I understand that Natchez declared itself an open city. It wasn't shelled or burned. Why don't y'all just come on home with me? You can stay there and rest while you plan what is best. You know my family will be happy to see you."

"Tom, you've done more than enough for us. Your family must be sick with worry. You're needed there. We'll be all right. This place will see us through. Nicodemus seems healthy enough. There must be something to eat here, isn't that right Nicodemus?"

"Well, Missy, all de cabins has a little garden behind 'em, and dere's de big vegetable patch up by de kitchen. All 'em still got a little bit growing what ain't picked by de soldiers or kilt by weeds. I ain't been able to keep up with de weeds by myself." Then he smiled shyly and said, "De root cellar up to de big house were hid when burning stuff done fell on it. I dug it out. De taters on top was all burnt, but dere's a heap of taters left underneath and some dried corn too." He pointed toward the back, "Off yonder in de woods down to a little hollow by the creek I penned up six laying hens and a rooster and got one milk cow de army done missed. And dere's plenty winter greens already started, and sweet water in de well. I reckon we won't starve real soon anyways."

Arabella looked proudly at Nicodemus, "You is one smart old man, I'm here to tell you."

"You certainly are, Nicodemus," Nannie Quinn added. "You see, Tom, we'll be all right. Besides, you look in need of more than a little rest yourself.

Boatner looked at Nannie. *I wonder if she sees through me, that all that's left is a mask, a sham, that I feel hollow, that I don't sleep much and sometimes feel I'm going to come apart like the world around me.*

Tom Boatner was in the grip of a deep, black despair, far worse than the physical deprivation he suffered. He had seen his men give their best and lose the fight; had somehow survived while so many had died. Now he felt shamed by the determined spirit of the lady standing before him.

"Why don't you spend the night here, Tom, and start out in the morning?"

"That's a kind offer, Nannie, but I believe this skinny horse and I can still make a few miles toward home before it's too dark to see. I need to get home and send you help." Tom took one of the pistols from its pommel holster and handed it to Nannie. "I know Ansel taught you how to shoot. I want you to take this and keep it close by you. If any strangers take the time to come off the main road all the way here to Shamrock, they most likely will be looking for trouble. Keep your food and yourselves hidden and don't take chances."

"God bless you, Thomas Boatner." Nannie kissed him on the cheek.

Boatner gave Annielise a hug, climbed wearily into his saddle, and walked his horse slowly in the direction of the lane that led to the main road. He turned and waved. As the little group watched, horse and rider faded into the shadows like ghosts.

Twilight gradually evanesced into the blackest night Nannie had ever known.

CHAPTER 4

Early next morning after a slim breakfast of raw turnips, Nannie Keturah wasted no time organizing the occupants of Shamrock. The little group spent the first two days collecting anything of use they could find—tools from the ruins of the barn, blacksmith and carpentry shops, dishes, cups, a few pieces of china and utensils raked from the ashes of the big house. From the kitchen out back, its brick walls standing but its roof collapsed in charred ruin, they dug out pots, pans, jars, crockery plates, mixing bowls and a few jugs. The third day, they started the real work. Using the serviceable hoes and shovels they had collected, they set to chopping weeds from the vegetable garden behind the ruins of the kitchen and the small gardens behind the slave cabins.

Nannie soon determined that it would be more productive to chop out a new big garden near the cabins where they could transplant all the surviving young plants and tiny sprouts to one nearby site rather than trying to care for all the scattered little gardens. For a week they toiled hard with hoe and shovel. The work went painfully slow. The women, who had never done such work, struggled with blistered hands and aching backs. They tried wrapping their hands in rags, they had no gloves, but it was of little value. Nicodemus told them the only cure was time—their hands would toughen eventually. That was little solace to the Quinn ladies. Suffering the pain of blisters was hard, but the notion that they would soon have callused hands was worse. No Southern lady had callused hands.

Nicodemus's hands were gnarled by a lifetime of work, but at his age, the results of a day's work was little more productive than that of any one of the women.

Late one afternoon after a hard day's work, Nannie felt the need to be alone. Doubts about her determination to stay at Shamrock had begun to nibble at her. She walked the path toward the ruins of the big house. *I can't afford doubt. I will not lose faith. It's hard, but we can hold on here. We must. This land is all we have left. What else can we do? Become beggars? I'll die first. This is Quinn land. I won't see it lost without a fight.*

Returning from deep thought, she found herself standing before what had been her joy; a formal garden that had been laid out just beyond the brick terrace behind the big house. It had once been graced by geometric symmetry, brick paths enclosing carefully arranged shrubs, flowers and herbs. Now she wondered if the slaves who had done the work at her direction had suffered blisters on their hands as she now had. In the silence before sunset, she walked the ruined paths that once offered beauty and solace to the Quinns and their guests. Everything had been trampled by horses, the rose trellises and gazebo knocked down, the planting beds covered in weeds. All that remained of camellias, gardenias, azaleas and roses were blackened stalks seared leafless and dead by the intense heat from the burning house.

Annielise found her mother standing quietly clutching a handful of small flowers from border plants that had somehow survived. "I thought you told me not to waste time on anything we couldn't eat, Mama." She smiled. "We aren't going to eat those are we?"

Nannie's eyes were fixed on the delicate blossoms held in her raw, dirty hand. "Somewhere I read in the works of a philosopher, Chinese I think, words that only now hold meaning for me. I cannot remember his name, but I remember his words. 'If I had but two pennies left in this world, I would spend one on bread to sustain life and the other on a flower to provide a reason for living.' Before the war, I suppose I had too much of everything to take more than passing notice of those profound words. Holding these little flowers, I now understand." Tears ran down her cheeks.

"It's getting late, Mama." Annielise put her arm around her mother. In the fading light of dusk, the bone-tired women walked toward the path that would lead them to their little cabin. Just past the remains of the potting shed Nannie stopped. "Look here!" She pointed at a garden plow lying on its side in the weeds just off the path. It consisted of a small, rusted iron plow point mounted on the end of a forked wooden frame which in turn was fixed to a single iron, spoked wheel. It was meant to be operated by gripping the twin handles of the fork and pushing it along by hand. "How did we miss this?" Nannie asked. "It's just what we need to help with the new garden." She set the little plow upright, grasp the weathered handles, lifted the point off the ground and rolled it along to the row of little cabins.

The next morning they discovered that not one of the four inhabitants of Shamrock was strong enough to use the small push plow to break the dry, hard ground at the site they had picked for the new garden.

"Have you ever plowed Nicodemus?" Nannie asked.

"I has with a field plow behind a mule, Miss Nannie," he answered.

Nannie nodded her head. "Nicodemus, you take up that ole carriage harness salvaged from the blacksmith shop and fashion two slings from it. You are going to be the plowman and Arabella and I are going to be the mules."

"Aw, Miss Nannie," he protested, "What I think you got in yo' mind ain't gonna work. Ain't fittin' nohow."

"Just do it, Nicodemus."

Annielise added, "Make three slings, Nicodemus. I'm well enough to help."

The small man, whose hands were as dried and cracked as the strips of old leather, did as he was told. He fashioned scraps of harness into loops, each with a lead attached to the little plow.

The next morning the three women bent their shoulders to the slings and waited for Nicodemus to take up the handles of the plow. He didn't. The women looked back at him.

"I ain't gonna do it, Miss Nannie. You can whoop me, but I ain't gonna do it. It be a sin to make womens pull a plow."

"Nicodemus, you're the only one of us who knows how to guide a plow to make straight rows, the only one who can do it. There's precious little left growing 'round here to carry us through the winter much less into next summer. Either you steer that plow to break up this earth or we'll all starve."

Nicodemus changed tack and broached a subject that worried him as much as starving. "Miss Nannie, de first white man what comes along and see me plowing white womens dis away gonna shoot me dead on 'de spot.'"

Nannie pictured how bizarre such a scene would appear, and laughed out loud. "You're right, Nicodemus. If some southern gentleman finds you using white ladies as beasts of burden he'll most likely shoot you before I can explain that we're all volunteers trying to keep ourselves from starving to death. I'd be suspicious of his honor if he didn't. Now pick up that plow, Nicodemus. None of us has a choice if we want to live."

The Quinn ladies had never had their fair skin burned by the sun, never had calloused hands, dirt-caked fingernails much less harness bruises on their shoulders. Neither had Arabella, for that matter. She had always been a valued house-servant trained for the duty since girlhood. She had never labored in the fields.

At first, short rows were the best they could manage, but they were straight and the women were proud of them. With all three women pulling the little plow with determined agony, the work went ten times faster than using hoes and shovels, especially on days when the earth had been softened by rain.

The freshly-turned rows were soon planted with potatoes, young turnips, collards, cabbage and mustard greens; "winter" vegetables which had randomly seeded from scattered, unharvested plants in the abandoned gardens.

The inhabitants of Shamrock daily endured aches and pains, blisters and hunger and when alone, quiet tears. Beyond the hard work of plowing and planting and tending the gardens, their survival demanded the gathering of fire wood, wild berries and nuts, sifting piles of ashes for useful items, washing what clothes they had in a creek that ran through a wooded area a quarter of mile behind the slave cabins, carrying buckets of water from the well near the kitchen ruins to the cabins for drinking, cooking and sponge bathing, milking the cow and gathering precious eggs from the hens Nicodemus had managed to save from the scavenging Union army. The work was more than Nicodemus and Arabella had done as slaves and the hardest labor the former mistress of Shamrock and her daughter had ever imagined. There was toil and sweat but no complaints. Black hands and white shared in the labor from sun-up to sun-down. That was a first for Shamrock.

The two white women were digging new vegetable sprouts from among the weeds in the old vegetable garden near the fire damaged kitchen when Annielise whispered "Someone's coming." She stood looking toward the meadow. Shielding her eyes against the sun's glare, Nannie saw a wagon with a saddled horse tied behind it rolling into the sunlight from the shadowy lane. The driver's face was shaded by the wide brim of his straw hat. Nannie dropped her hoe and started toward the spot where she had set down Thomas Boatner's pistol.

"Wait, Mama!" Annielise shouted, "It's Doctor Ted."

The wagon, rattling toward them across the field of axle-high weeds, scattered up a covey of quail. Standing up and waving his hat, Ted Perkins shouted, "Hello Ladies!" He pulled the mule up as Nannie and Annielise ran toward the wagon.

Ted was shocked to see the condition of the mistress of Shamrock and her daughter. They were barefoot, their faces sunburned and sweat-covered, their dresses soiled, wet with perspiration, their hands rough, fingernails dirty.

Arabella and Nicodemus, both with hoes over their shoulders, came across the field to join the gathering.

Looking over the sideboards of the wagon they were like children gawking through the window of a candy shop. "Three Sacks of flour, cornmeal, three, no four smoked hams," Nannie called out the treasures. "Sugar, dried beans, two sides of bacon, salt, and bless you, real coffee. Oh Ted! Are those real store-bought bars of soap? And look at the sun bonnets! My face might not turn to leather after all. What's that wrapped in the blanket?"

"That's Daniel's double barreled fowling piece. I sneaked it out of y'all's house befo'e the Yankees could take it. Had to sneak it out'a town, too. I figure y'all could shoot a little game with it—rabbits, deer and such, and birds like those quail I scared up back yonder, maybe use it to keep varmints out of your garden. There's powder, caps and everything from bird shot to buck shot there under the wagon seat. Anyone here know how to load and shoot it?"

"Nicodemus can shoot dat thing," Arabella said. "He hunted with Massa Daniel."

"That right, Nicodemus?"

"Sho' nuff is, Doctor, sir." Nicodemus grinned. "Only I ain't never heard dat fancy name, fowling piece. Massa Daniel, he call dat a shotgun. Anyway, we gonna have meat on de table now."

"All right, Nicodemus, you're the keeper of the shotgun. Ted handed down the gun, bags of shot, a tin of powder and a box of caps."

Nicodemus took them with great care. "I done carried and loaded Massa Daniel's guns, and those of Massas' Ansel and young Jonathan, and been allowed to shoot one occasionally." He didn't add that he had never been allowed to keep one. "I be mighty proud to take care of dis here gun foe Massa Daniel and de ladies," he said.

"Where on earth did you get all this, Ted?" Nannie asked.

"Miss Nannie, you shouldn't ask, but since you did, I have to say that I came by some of it honestly, trading my medical services to the Yankee occupation forces, and a little of it I liberated. It's Yankee army supplies. I took a Yankee ambulance down to the dock and told the quartermaster to fill the hospital requisition. I admit I added a little extra to the order, but I told them the truth, that it was for the wounded and the sick. Which is the other reason I'm here; to see my wounded patient."

Ted climbed down from the wagon and gave Annielise a hug, lifting her off her feet. "Well now, I do think farming must be good for what ails you. I believe you're picking up a little weight."

"That's not a nice thing to tell a young lady. Anyway, it's my thin mama I'm worried about."

"How did you even know we were here?" asked Nannie.

"One of your many admirers sent a message upriver from Natchez. Seems there is no limit to the number of gallant knights who carry your colors, Lady Quinn."

"That Tom Boatner is our guardian angel." Nannie told Ted how Major Boatner had rescued them.

"I don't know if I'd call this a proper rescue," Ted said, looking around. "You should have gone on to Natchez with Tom. You'd be a lot better off."

"Tom tried his best, Ted, but you know how stubborn we Quinns can be. Besides, we aren't doing so badly. We're eating better than we did during the siege anyway. And now with this priceless wagon load you have brought, we'll do just fine. How are things in Vicksburg?"

"Pretty awful. Folks are no longer quite starving, but they don't have much left. The banks are closed, the army takes over any property it wants to house soldiers. A lot of families have left. The place is overrun with freed slaves not knowing what to do or where to go. They've started a shanty town and the army feeds 'em. There's a lot of sickness. Scallywags and strangers from up North showing up like vultures. I reckon y'all aren't doing so badly, but you're alone out here. Lot of desperate people on the roads nowadays. Some of 'em could be dangerous, Nannie. I'd feel better if you went on in to Natchez or return to Vicksburg with me."

"This is home, Ted."

Ted drove the wagon on down to the slave cabins followed by the inhabitants of Shamrock. While they unloaded the wagon's contents into one of the empty cabins, Nannie insisted on recording every item on scraps of paper, pages torn from ruined books.

"Ted, please bring us a proper account book if you come again so we can keep tally on all this. We aim to reimburse the good doctor when times get better."

Ted smiled. "I'm not worried about that, Miss Nannie."

"Well, you know us Quinns. We pay our debts."

While everyone was busy unloading the wagon, Arabella caught Doctor Perkins sleeve and whispered to him. "Doctor Ted, I be worried sick over Annielise."

"How so? She looks good to me, Arabella. What do you see that I don't?" Ted whispered back and motioned Arabella a few steps away from the wagon.

"I'll tells yo' what I sees. I sees a young lady hardly more 'en a girl all healed up on de outside as far as de bullet wound goes, but what is sick near about every morning and tires easy. 'De truth is, if I didn't know no better myself, I mean she ain't never spent one minute alone with no boy, I can swear to dat 'cause I been wit' her all her life, including dances and parties. I mean if I didn't know no better, I'd say she be act'en like a woman what was aspectin', sho' nuff, and I been round plenty what was."

"Have you discussed this with Miss Nannie or Annielise?"

"Naw, Suh, I ain't. Dere's been 'nuff worry put on 'em. But I been hopin' you would come so's you can tell fo' sure. Scares me to death. Be de most strangest thing ever happened if dat child be spectin'."

After the wagon was unloaded Dr. Perkins spoke to Annielise. "Darling, while I'm out here, I'd like to follow up my surgery properly by giving you a thorough checkup. Would you mind if I did that? I've talked to your mama and she says it's all right."

"After all I've been through," Annielise replied, "I don't think I have any secrets from the doctor who saved my life."

He escorted her into the cabin she and her mother shared. It was clean, but sparsely furnished with two old handmade cots with moss-stuffed mattresses and worn quilts, a table with an oil lamp, two chairs, two small trunks, a tin pail of water on a wash stand made of rough lumber, a piece of broken mirror on a shelf and a pile of books in one corner. Clothes hung from pegs on the wall. There was a small fireplace.

"How have you been feeling?" he asked after he had examined the healed bullet wound.

"Oh, I'm all right, just a little tired, and sometimes I'm a little sick at my stomach, but it goes away. Mama says I don't have any fever."

"How about that time of the month when you ladies don't feel too well?"

"To tell the truth, I haven't been that way since I was shot, but you told me I might not be regular for a while because of the bullet wound and all. I haven't thought about it really."

"Well, let's do a little examination. It won't take long. Don't be embarrassed. More women should have these examinations, and especially when they have had a wound such as you've experienced."

The examination revealed that his Godchild was a healthy young virgin, hymen intact, no signs of infection or disease, her wound all healed. He probed her lower abdomen and found a slight swelling. Although he didn't examine them, and it might have been his imagination, her breast seemed to be a little fuller than he remembered, but then she was a growing young woman. He figured a little over three months had passed since he had treated her bullet wound.

"Well, Annielise darling, I find you very healthy, considering. I'll be back directly to check on you and your mama. You both ought to rest a little more."

Although embarrassed by the examination, she thanked her godfather-doctor, for looking out for her and her Mama.

Ted walked out to the horse tethered behind the wagon and tied his medical bag to the saddle. Arabella sat on the porch of her little cabin, watching him. He returned her gaze and put a finger to his lips before walking back to say good-bye to the ladies.

"I'd like y'all to keep my mule and wagon here for a spell if you won't charge me too much livery. The mule is a little long in the tooth, but ought to earn his feed. He's plow broke." The doctor paused, "And another thing. I noticed the walls of the brick kitchen behind the big house survived the fire pretty well. Nicodemus told me the saw mill is wrecked, but they didn't burn all the lumber stacked for drying. It's rough sawn, but it will do. I'll see if I can find some carpenters to send out to clean out the wreckage, build a new roof and put in some window glass and a new door. You'll need a good warm kitchen this winter. I'm afraid Daniel will need it the most. I'm told he isn't doing too well, Nannie. I've petitioned the new army provost to allow him to come home early."

Ted grew silent and it seemed to Nannie that he was looking at Annielise in a most peculiar way.

"I almost forgot," Nannie said. She went into the cabin and returned with two letters written on tablet paper. "I don't have envelopes. Would you mind mailing this letter to Daniel. You can post it with the Yankees. This other one is for Jonathan. You'll have to address it in care of the Navy Department in Richmond. I don't know where else to send it. There must be a way to get it out of Vicksburg to Confederate couriers." Nannie held out the letters. "We haven't heard from Jonathan, but I've got to believe he's alive, Ted."

Preoccupied, Ted took the letters, nodded, mounted his horse, and set off toward Vicksburg.

The dull gray of false dawn was nudging the night away by the time saddle sore Doctor Perkins arrived in Vicksburg. He drew the drapes over his bedroom windows and tried to sleep. After an hour, Ted threw off the covers, put on his robe and went downstairs to his office located on ground level beneath his raised cottage. He poured himself a liberal portion of bourbon, lit a cigar, gathered a dusty stack of medical books and began to search them for an explanation he knew he would not likely find in any medical library. *How the hell can my virgin godchild be pregnant?*

He ignored Luky when she showed up with his lunch. Luky, so named because her mama came from Louisiana and her daddy from Kentucky, had been his house servant since well before his wife died of yellow fever contracted on a trip to New Orleans in late April of 1853. He had never had more than one or two slaves. Now he had none. Like Arabella, Luky had chosen to stay on as a freed servant after emancipation at the fall of Vicksburg. The doctor paid her what he could: food, shelter, and now and then a little money when he had any.

At three in the afternoon, Ted slammed shut a medical book on obstetrics published in 1850, the latest one he had. *Damnit! There just is no answer in the medical books or anywhere else—nothing to explain how that young virgin is pregnant, if she is and I think so.*

I reckon we'll know for sure soon enough.

Mentally and physically exhausted, he collapsed into bed after an early supper.

When Doctor Perkins wasn't making house calls in town at all hours of the day and night, he could be found at the hospital. Many citizens were in such poor condition from lack of food during the siege that they fell seriously ill to even the most common mild diseases. Head colds lingered and drifted into pneumonia, consumption (tuberculosis) was on the rise, dysentery was common and there were a few cases of malaria. At the end of each day, Ted said a little prayer of thanksgiving that no cases of cholera, typhus or yellow fever had showed up.

Many people were suffering from a general malaise that seemed to have no physical basis. Doctor Perkins figured such melancholia was caused more by having endured daily bombardment through the long siege and the loss of friends, relatives, homes and fortunes than from physical ailments. He did the best he could for both the sick and the sick at heart.

His patients always tried to pay, tried to hold on to a little pride, couldn't bring themselves to accept charity, but Dr. Perkins wouldn't take what he knew they could not do without. He was mostly paid with vegetables, chickens, an occasional dressed brace of rabbits, a basket of eggs, once in a while in the fall a smoked ham or side of bacon, firewood, an occasional wild turkey or venison and IOU's. Such was the currency of the day. There was no money. Almost all commerce in Vicksburg was conducted by barter. Now and then Ted earned a little Yankee money from the military government for treating prisoners too sick to parole or acting as coroner for the ones who died. The Provost paid him little more than a pittance for serving as administrator of the hospital.

Walking from his house to the hospital one afternoon, Ted was confronted on the street.

"Doc! Doc Perkins!"

Ted turned to see a lean man dressed in worn army pants, a white shirt, black suspenders and wearing a high-crown straw hat coming toward him with his hand outstretched. "I know you don't recognize me cleaned up without a uniform, but you saved my arm that day we sank *Cincinnati*. I don't mean to trouble you none, but you're the only familiar face I've seen in town." He shook the doctor's hand.

"I patched up a lot of arms, son. What brings you back to Vicksburg?"

"Well, Doc, I ain't got a mule or horse on the place, and I ain't going to make it with just a hoe and shovel. My wife is 'specting so I don't want her doing field work no more. I was hopin' I could make a trade with one of the Yankee mule skinners. I got a pure silver picture frame and this here gold locket what belonged to my mama. It's all I got. Do you think it'd be enough? I ain't got a Yankee dollar to my name."

"Let me give you a man's name." The doctor took a pencil and pad from his coat pocket, wrote a name on it and handed the note to the ex-soldier. "This man handles the transport for the hospital and the Yankee stockyard. He might do you some good, complains he has more mules to look after than he can handle. Of course, trading government mules isn't exactly Yankee legal, but neither is the mule skinner. I caught him selling government supplies. I found it convenient not to turn him in and he finds it convenient to help me now and then when some patient of mine is in dire need of medicine or food. If you mention my name maybe the rascal won't take your trade and then turn you in to get the mule back. Try to get one that doesn't have a U.S. brand on him or you might not get it out of the city. You keep your mother's locket, son. That silver frame ought to be enough. And son, I never told you all this."

"Yes, Sir, I mean, no, Sir. You can count on me. Thank you again, Doc. Thank you very much."

"I'm just glad to see one of my former patients looking fit. By the way, son, what's your name?"

"Sam Tunnard from Warrenton. I used to be a sergeant." The man shook hands again and moved off toward the stockyards down by the river.

Doctor Perkins had gone barely half a block when he stopped dead in his tracks, turned around, and to the surprise of those in the street, began to run. He was completely out of breath, his lungs burning when he caught up with the man.

"Tunnard! Sergeant Tunnard!" he yelled.

Tunnard turned in astonishment to see the doctor puffing down hill after him. "Sergeant, I just remembered you and something you told me that day."

"Something I told you, Doc?"

"Let's sit down a minute and let me get a little wind before my legs give out." Holding his side, the Doctor sat heavily down beside the road. "Sit here with me a minute," he motioned to the sergeant. "Son, you the one who told me about a boy git'en his balls shot off?"

"Well, I reckon I must be. Happened to a kid all caught up in the excitement of sinking that ironclad. Jumped up on the parapet and waved a flag in sight of every Yankee sniper within half a mile. They must'a all been a shooting at him. A second shot kilt him."

"Look here, sergeant. I know you've got business to take care of, but I would be most grateful if you could show me exactly where all that took place. That's got to sound like a peculiar request, but it's important to me."

Tunnard took a moment. "Doc, that trench up on the bluff is about the last place I figured I'd ever go back to. It's a place haunts my sleep some nights." He paused, but when the doctor didn't reply he said, "I reckon I owe you."

The two men climbed back up the hill and turned onto a street that paralleled the bluff. Directly, the sergeant turned off the road toward the river. After walking through knee-high weeds and scrub brush fifty or so yards, they climbed down an embankment and stepped into an eroding trench. While he followed the sergeant down the line, Ted Perkins tried to picture men living there day and night, rain or shine, weeks without washing or changing clothes, with slim rations, all the while suffering the fury of battle, shot and shell, the sudden rending of flesh and bone, the cries of the dying, the smell of the dead competing with the unwashed smell of the living. The remnants of an army could still be seen—a tattered piece of cloth, a broken rifle stock, a dark-stained bandage half buried, an empty whiskey bottle, a canteen with a hole through it, rusting bits of shrapnel everywhere. The doctor realized he had asked a lot of the man he now followed along the trench.

The doctor recognized pain in the soldier's gaze fixed first on one spot then another along the way. "If we'd of had food and ammunition, they never could a' taken us, Doc, not even with half again as many troops, not up this bluff in front of my men."

Down the line, Tunnard stopped again. "Right here where the line bulges out toward the river a little is where Zeke went down with his flag. He mostly waved it from behind this parapet where the Yanks could only see the flag. Drove 'em crazy. They would waste a bucket of bullets trying to shoot it down. Did once, I think. We all got a laugh out of young Zeke taunting them Blues." The sergeant looked down at the river. "When our guns sank that big ironclad, I reckon Zeke went a little crazy. He jumped up there on the breastworks and waved that flag in front of the whole Yankee army." Tunnard pointed down to the flats below. "Down yonder is where the snipers hid." Perkins could see several shallow depressions, what was left of shooting holes exposed by erosion. The sergeant continued. "Young Zeke claimed to be part Choctaw. He was a good-looking kid with shiny black hair. He died right here, Doc. I lost so many, so damn many." After a minute, he turned and shook the doctor's hand. "You know Zeke's folks, Doc? I think they was from Georgia. That the reason you come up here?" Perkins, lost in thought, didn't answer. "Well, if this is what you wanted, Doc, I guess I better go on back and find that mule skinner."

"Thank you, sergeant. You go on along now. I plan to be here a little while. Just want to do some thinking."

If Tunnard thought it odd, he didn't say so. He never looked back.

Perkins surveyed the muddy river below. Up river, toward the far bank, a pair of black smoke stacks marked *Cincinnati*. A salvage barge was along side. *Looks like they might try to raise her.* Ted turned around. Standing in the trench, his line of sight revealed only a rise of shell-scarred, brush-invested ground mostly clear of trees. The doctor climbed up on the parapet and stood at the forward edge where the sergeant said the boy died waving his flag. He turned to again look up toward the town. His heart began to thump like a hammer on an anvil.

There, angled to the left, clearly visible over the rise and brush, was a slate roof crowned by the distinctive weathervane, a large copper fish, on top of the cupola. The unique weathervane defined it as the Tillman house. For a moment Ted couldn't catch his breath. Below his line of sight, he knew, was the gallery where Annielise was standing when a bullet struck her. Ted turned toward the river and stepped to the forward edge of the parapet. He spread his legs wide the way the boy must have done to steady himself as he waved the long flagstaff from side to side. He looked below from where the bullet must have come. Then he got down on his knees at about the height of a man's testicles and looked up the bluff at the angle he estimated the bullet would have had to travel to tear away the boy's manhood. He could see only the cupola of the Tillman house topped with the copper fish.

That would be right. The bullet, slowed and deformed by its flight through the boy's scrotum and maybe part of his fleshy buttocks would have reached the apex of its trajectory and begun to fall as it lost energy, a trajectory that would carry it below the line of sight, below the roof line, down to the balcony where the girls were standing. Still warm from its flight and slathered in the boy's semen and blood, the flattened, nearly spent

Minié ball would have started to tumble, making that ragged hole in Annielise's flesh, carrying the sperm of a dying boy into her reproductive organs. Yes by damn! That would explain what has happened to that child.

Ted had to sit down. "My God!" he said aloud. "A bullet's baby!" It was the only possible explanation. He believed Arabella about Annielise having never been alone with a boy. He had seen himself that she was still a virgin. *Lord help me! A virgin birth!*

Dr. Perkins went home, sat at his desk in the study, and reviewed the careful notes he had made describing his goddaughter's wound and surgery and the results of his examination of her at Shamrock. Then he added his two encounters with Tunnard, his theory and every detail he had discovered at the trench to support it. *How in the hell can I explain it all to Nannie and Annielise, explain the whole thing to anyone if my Godchild is indeed both a virgin and pregnant. Hell, some folks will want to lock me up in a loony bin, or maybe burn me at the stake as a heretic. And, God help her, no one will believe the story no matter what Arabella says. Who will believe a black woman? Annielise will be cruelly and scandalously accused of fornication.*

Ted got up, walked to his liquor cabinet, poured a little bourbon into a glass, looked at it, then poured a lot and walked back to his desk. There he sat sipping the golden liquid while he pondered the matter. Finally he took up the pen again and wrote a letter to a Natchez address.

Toward the last of October there was a knock at Doctor Perkins' door. A voice he had not heard for three years announced that his letter had gotten through.

"Theodore, I'm telling you right now if you have made all this up as a joke, I'll be sorely tempted to put a bullet through yo' testicles. In the mean time, I hope fo' yo' sake you have some decent bourbon," Doctor Jefferson Jay Little walked past Ted, sat down and ordered. "I'll have two fingers in a glass to start with. Don't suppose y'all have any ice."

Ted got a bottle, poured generous measures into two glasses, and handed one to his old friend and colleague. "We haven't had a boatload of ice down from St. Louis since '60.

Little took a sip from his glass. "Yo' letter constitutes the wildest explanation of the craziest damn theory I have ever heard of in the annals of medical history."

"It puts me in a hell of a predicament, Jay. You're the only one I felt I could talk to about this case. I want you to confirm that my godchild is both a virgin and pregnant."

"Well, Ted, if I do, you gonna have the second hardest announcement to make in the history of mankind."

"What was the hardest, for Christ's sake?"

"You just named it. The angel that had to explain to Joseph that Mary was both a virgin and pregnant. And Ted, you don't look much like an angel."

"That ain't funny, Jay. To tell you the truth I have thought about that, and wondered how hard it was for Joseph to accept the explanation. I wonder if anyone will accept my explanation. I wonder if even Annielise and her mother will."

"Have you told them what you think?"

"Not yet. If you confirm what I believe you will, I don't quite know how I will tell them. Arabella already thinks the girl is pregnant, and I guess by now her mother does, too."

"Well, Ted, why don't you start at the beginning? Just don't run out of bourbon in the telling." Doctor Little listened through supper and into the evening.

"Ted, do you realize the storm your theory will stir up? You'll have every Bible-thumping parson in the country and probably the Pope in Rome accusing you of being the Devil himself. If you are right, it will be one hell of a report in the medical journals. No telling what it might do to that poor girl and the baby."

"Jay, I've already thought about that. I'm not about to put any of it in print, at least not for a long time. If I ever do submit anything publicly I'll probably word it so the medical community will think it was written tongue in cheek, a joke. That way, I'll have given an idea science can play with if it strikes someone's imagination. I'd rather die with the reputation of a humorist than be labeled the second Doctor Frankenstein for seriously claiming a child was fathered by a bullet."

"Ted, I been thinking about that. If you're right, it means that it's possible to artificially impregnate a female."

"I suppose that's what it means, Jay, but if you talk like that the preachers of the world will rise up and burn us both at the stake in the name of God and womanhood."

"Hell! I ain't talking about women! No profit in that. I'm talking 'bout cows and horses, man. You could produce a whole herd of champion stock in one generation instead of breeding generation after generation for a handful. Figure that out and by God I'll become a veterinarian, and a damn rich one at that."

"Now you listen here, Jefferson Jay. You're gonna keep a tight lip on this. I mean it, damnit! Besides, just how in the hell would you keep sperm alive long enough to plant it in reproductive organs in the first place? If that boy's sperm did impregnate Annielise, it's cause it was carried to her in the folds of a warm, deformed bullet in less than a quarter of a second. And how're you gonna get a quadruped's sperm in the first place, much less handle it? By God, I'd pay a pretty penny to see you try and milk a ton of bull, or see the look of surprise on a stallion's face just before he turns around to bite your fool head off. And how about the cows and fillies? Never mind. I don't want to hear about that. What I want is for you to help me take care of my godchild, and her child, God help us. I want you to try and confirm my theory before I start thinking I truly am crazy."

Jefferson Jay sipped his whiskey in silence, pondering all his friend had revealed. Finally he stood up. "Well, Teddy, you sure as hell got my scientific curiosity at a fever pitch. I want to see that trench and the view of the Tillman house before we start for Shamrock. And Ted, I b'lieve I'll have one more bourbon to take to bed. Listening to you all evening has brought on a terrible thirst."

"Nannie, may I present Dr. Jefferson Jay Little, an old friend and colleague. Dr. Little, Mrs. Ansel Quinn."

Doctor Little took the lady's offered hand. "I'm pleased to at last meet the lovely and courageous Mrs. Quinn Dr. Perkins has told me so much about." Dr. Little noticed the roughness of her hand and the strain of hard physical labor reflected in her sunburned face. *Still, after all she's been through, she is a remarkably attractive woman.*

"Dr. Perkins sometimes displays a silver tongue that should be taken with a grain of salt." She smiled at Ted. "I would prefer that you just call me Nannie."

"I'll be honored to do so, Miss Nannie. I happened to be visiting Ted when he told me of your daughter's terrible experience. He said it was time for him to check on her condition, and has asked me to take part in the examination, with your and your daughter's permission, of course."

Nannie looked at Ted.

"Nannie, I'm concerned that Annielise does not seem to be fully recovered. I want Dr. Little's opinion. Where is Annielise, by the way?"

Nannie hesitated a moment before she spoke. "Arabella and I have both talked to her about . . . well, she will tell you. She's resting in our cabin. Y'all go on over there, Ted. I'll see how Arabella is doing in the kitchen. The men you sent out did a fine job of cleaning away the burned timbers and giving us a new roof and window glass. It's a real kitchen now and will do us fine this winter." She paused and looked at Ted, started to speak, thought better of it, and turned toward the kitchen.

The two physicians walked down the lane to the row of slave cabins, two of which had been recently whitewashed. Nicodemus was chopping kindling beside his weathered cottage.

"Good day, Nicodemus. I see you don't prescribe to the fancy new neighborhood look," Doctor Perkins said, and nodded toward the bright white wall of the cabin next door.

Nicodemus stopped chopping and took off his hat. "Afternoon, Doctor Ted. And to you sir." He nodded to Dr. Little. "I reckon it's a mite too late for whitewash to do me or dis here cabin much good," he smiled, "but 'dem women folk gots to have things just so. If dey don't git things like dey wants 'em, ain't gonna be no peace 'round here and maybe no cookin' neither."

"You are a wise man, Nicodemus."

When the doctors reached Annielise's cabin, she was standing on its small porch. "I heard y'all talking to Nicodemus. I'm so glad you've come, Uncle Ted. I'm doing better, but I'm not doing better, I mean . . ."

Tears welled in her eyes. She looked at the stranger, and dropped her head a little. Then she ran to Ted and threw her arms around him, unable to hold back sobs that shook her body. "I'm scared and embarrassed and confused by all what Mama and Arabella asked me. They think I'm with child. Mama thinks I . . . she thinks I got pregnant in Vicksburg." Annielise clung to Ted like the frightened child she was.

Dr. Little discreetly walked a distance away and stood with his back to them.

"Doctor Ted, I haven't even been kissed by a man, I mean really kissed, like Daddy kissed Mama, like you read about in books. Please tell Mama I can't be pregnant, please. It's just that bullet wound that's messed up my insides. Tell 'em Uncle Ted."

Dr. Perkins held his godchild until her sobs subsided. He gave her his handkerchief, put his arm around her. "I want you to meet my friend. He's here to help me help you." Ted walked her over to Dr. Little.

"Annielise, this is Dr. Jefferson Jay Little. He is a fellow physician and lifelong friend. I've asked him to help me examine you like I did last time. Please don't be embarrassed, we're both doctors and are here to try and solve this mystery."

"Did Mama say it was all right?"

Doctor Perkins answered with a nod. Annielise turned without a word and walked into the cabin followed by the two doctors.

That evening in the old kitchen, the Quinn ladies and the two doctors gathered for supper around a rough, pine board table with picnic-style benches on both sides. The table was set with an eclectic collection. Some plates were tin, some enameled metal, a few were china, pieces that had survived the fire and been dug from the ashes. The utensils were just as varied. There were a few salvaged silver pieces, but most were tin or steel. There were three-tine forks and knives with naked shanks, the original grips burned away. Tin cups and canning jars were filled with water. Cut squares of flour sacks served as napkins.

Arabella did the cooking in a fireplace equipped with two pot cranes, a rotisserie and a couple of spider tripods that held shallow pots over hot coals raked onto the hearth. This night she served up helpings of greens, potatoes, one piece of bacon and a small wedge of skillet-cooked cornbread on each plate at the big table. She then served a plate for Nicodemus and one for herself at a bench near the fire.

Annielise and Nannie Quinn sat on one side of the table, afraid to ask questions, the two doctors on the other, unsure how to begin. The only sounds in the room were the ticking and scraping of utensils against plates and an occasional pop or crackle from the fire.

The last rays of sunset provided the only light in the room besides the flickering flames in the fireplace.

When the plates were emptied, Nannie was the first to break the silence. "I apologize for not having brandy and cigars to offer you gentlemen, but times at Shamrock are not what they once were."

Ted answered, "I too wish you had a little brandy, Nannie. I think you will need some when I finish what I am about to say."

Nannie looked very tired, but said nothing. Annielise folded her hands in her lap and stared down at them while she waited for some terrible judgment to fall upon her, some awful disgrace she could not begin to understand.

Ted cleared his throat and began. "Both Doctor Little and I believe, without doubt, that Annielise is with child."

"Oh, God! I knew it, but I didn't want to believe it possible. Annielise, how could you have done this in the midst of all our trouble and pain? Who is the boy?"

"Mama, I didn't do anything. I haven't been with a man, Mama. I swear it."

"Annielise! Do you think us all stupid? I know you understand where babies come from. Do you know what you're saying, what you're asking us to believe? There's been only one child born to a virgin on this earth." Tears of anguish filled her eyes.

Ted reached across the table and took both of Nannie's hands in his. "Your daughter may have the second."

"Lord God! Have you all gone crazy? How can such a thing be?" Nannie pulled her hands free and stared incredulously at the two doctors sitting across the home-made table, their faces but shadows in the failing light.

Dr. Little answered first. "Mrs. Quinn, what Dr. Perkins is going to tell you, what he told me, is a most unusual theory I admit, but he has convinced me that it is a viable explanation, the only explanation for your daughter's condition if we are to believe her chaperone and our own examination of this child. I, for my part, after thoroughly examining your daughter, can say without question that she is a virgin, and that she is pregnant. Both you and Annielise should listen carefully to Dr. Perkins and hear him out completely before you ask any questions. You are fortunate to have so dedicated a friend and so qualified a physician."

Annielise could not contain the question that burned her with fear and consternation. Before Dr. Perkins could begin, she cried out, "But if I am pregnant, who is the father?"

In dying fire light, Ted Perkins looked at her tormented, questioning face. He took a deep breath and answered. "The father of your child is hanging around your neck, at least the messenger who brought the child to you is hanging there."

There was stunned silence while the listeners tried to make sense out of what they had just heard.

Dr. Perkins looked at four appalled faces staring back at him. He figured they thought he was mad. Nicodemus wanted to run, convinced it was all the work of the devil. Arabella thought the same thing, but was more frightened for her child, Annielise, than for herself.

"I assure you that I am of sound mind, and that what I just told you does not represent some kind of black magic or voodoo, or anything except an extraordinary set of circumstances that have resulted in a remarkable event. It began with a boy waving a flag from the ramparts on the bluff the day that ironclad was sunk."

"I saw a flag waving from the bluff, all the girls saw it, but we couldn't see who was waving it." Annielise spoke as if in a trance.

"I know that, Darling." Dr. Perkins began at the beginning and no one in the room spoke for a long time after he had finished.

Suddenly, Nannie Keturah cried out, "That cursed Yankee bullet!" She reached over to her daughter, clutched the bullet in her hand, and breaking the gold chain, threw it at the fire. Annielise was too shocked to move.

"Who in the world will ever believe it?" she asked out loud, "Tell me that, Uncle Ted."

"I think maybe we shouldn't ask anybody to believe it. It would be best for the child if no one knows the real story. Can you imagine what people would say? Maybe we should just plan on saying the father was killed in the war, which is the truth . . . just not all of it. Better a child be born fatherless than looked upon as some kind of freak, or worse, the work of the devil. I suspect there are a lot of young women in a family way whose betrothed have fallen never to come home to marry them. It's another sad legacy of war."

Annielise sat quietly, tears running down her cheeks. Nannie put her arm around her daughter while she fought to absorb the incredible explanation her family friend and doctor had presented. Not a word was spoken as the last soft edge of twilight lapsed to darkness.

"We best be light'en a lantern, Miss Nannie. I b'lieve hit' be mo' better to have a little cheery light in here than sit'en in de dark thinking 'bout all we done heard." Nicodemus got up and lit an oil lamp, illuminating a circle of faces frozen, masklike, in tormented perplexity.

Ted Perkins broke the spell. "I almost forgot," he reached in his coat pocket, "Here is a letter for you. I picked it up at general delivery." He handed Nannie an envelope.

Nannie moved the lamp a little closer, opened the letter, and began to read aloud.

Office of Provost, U.S. Army

Subject: Daniel H. Quinn, prisoner, Fort Jefferson.

To whom it may concern:

The U.S. Army, at the request of the prison doctor, has agreed to parole the above-mentioned prisoner due to the onset of arthritis, and in consideration of his age. You may expect his arrival at Vicksburg via packet boat on or about the first week in December.

By Order of: George P. Andrews, Post Commander Fort Jefferson, Dry Tortugas

"Granddaddy is coming home!" Annielise cried, the first happy words she had spoken in a month. Then her face fell with despair. "But what will he think of me?"

"He will think of you as we do, Annielise," Doctor Perkins took her hand, "He will think you are a very brave and loving granddaughter."

"Well, I'll tell y'all what I thinks," Arabella said, "Ain't gonna be no peace 'round 'jere. Bullets making babies. Us workin' can'til—can't to keep from starvin'. Now here come Massa Quinn stove up with arthritis. When he see dis place and find out what de done to his granddaughter, he gonna commence cussin' ever' Yankee on dis here Earth. Voodoo or de Devil his self be mo' easy to b'lieve than all I done heard dis night."

"Why Arabella."

"Can't hep it, Miss Nannie, dat's de way it gonna be. Nicodemus, you stay here and clean up de kitchen and bank de fire foe you leave. I's fixin' to go make de beds in de guest cabin."

"We ain't got no guest cabin, woman."

"We does now. You don't 'spect de doctors gonna lite out fo' Vicksburg this late does ya?" She lit another lantern and left in the direction of the lane that led to the cabins.

"And she talking 'bout Massa Daniel wreckin' de peace." Nicodemus said to no one in particular.

Everyone around the table burst out with laughter, a rare and welcome commodity at Shamrock. It was the cue Jefferson Jay Little had been waiting for. He reached down beside the table to his medical bag. "I think it's safe and proper for me to break out a little medicinal alcohol which I thoughtfully included in my kit, just as a precaution, don't you know."

"Why, Dr. Little," Nannie said, "you are a crafty devil."

"Yes, Ma'am. I must confess I am, especially since I requisitioned this fine elixir from the hidden stores of an even craftier ole devil."

"You stole my liquor?" Ted asked.

"I prefer the term, requisitioned."

"I bet you got into my cigars as well."

"A petty complaint, sir," Little replied as he handed Perkins a cigar. "Now, Nicodemus, if you can find a few mo' drinking cups, hand 'em round, including one for yo' self, I'll pour."

One surviving crystal wineglass had been found miraculously unbroken in the ashes of the big house. It was offered to Nannie who handed it to Annielise. "I think under the astonishing circumstances it is fitting for Annielise to join us," Nannie said. "Just a little sip for her, now Dr. Little."

J. J. Little poured a measure in each of the collection of cups and jars.

"To the newest Quinn. May he be as strong, brave, and handsome as his kin."

Annielise choked on her first taste of liquor. "How do people ever learn to like this awful stuff?"

There was laughter and then the room grew silent once more. The fire had absolved itself of angry flame leaving behind the warm and friendly glow of embers.

Nannie broke the silence. "You gentlemen must excuse us. I think it may be a long night."

By the light of a lantern, mother and daughter walked arm in arm toward their cabin.

"I'm scared, Mama. Do you believe Doctor Ted?"

"I have to. You're my daughter and I love you. We must keep all we heard tonight to ourselves for the child's sake. You are going to have that baby and we're going to love that little child. Just think, a new Quinn. That will brighten things here at Shamrock."

"I love you, Mama. You are the bravest woman in the world." In the little cabin Nannie and Annielise lay awake long into the night, each pondering the evening's startling revelations.

In the glow of the embers the two doctors lingered silently passing the bottle of bourbon between them. Directly, arm in arm, they staggered off to find the guest quarters down a worn path fortunately illuminated by a full moon.

Stretched out on a lumpy cot in the chilly dark of the cabin, Jefferson J. said, "Theodore, you have involved me in the most unbelievable, bizarre damn medical situation I ever heard of."

"Unbelievable but true, Jefferson J. You confirmed it yourself."

"You do realize if this gets out we'll have our sanity questioned. Hell, we'll wind up in a loony bin and the girl and her baby in a circus freak show."

"All true. Now shut up and go to sleep."

In the first gray light of dawn, Nicodemus hitched up Doctor Little's buckboard. The physicians, afflicted by the common malady of overindulgence, found the simple act of carrying their heads on their shoulders a heavy and painful burden. The long throbbing ride to Vicksburg passed mostly in silence except for the rhythmic clopping of the horse's hooves, the squeaking of the buckboard and occasional grunts, groans, farts and choice expletives in reference to the evils of drink.

CHAPTER 5

On a cold, overcast December afternoon Dr. Theodore Perkins walked out of his medical office with his last patient of the day, Miss Jessie Lee, on his arm. Miss Jessie, eighty-two years old and only four feet ten inches tall, had gained an infamous reputation among the occupation troops. Not even the most campaign-toughened, blue-uniformed soldier could stand up to a whirlwind of gray hair, jabbing parasol, and implications that blasphemer, thief, arsonist and molester of the innocent were all appropriate appellations for Yankees. As a result, martial law or no, Miss Jessie went where she pleased when she pleased unhindered by men in blue uniforms except for an occasional innocent newcomer who either accidentally encountered her or was put in harm's way by more knowledgeable friends who would gleefully retreat to watch the mayhem from a safe distance.

Miss Jessie visited the good doctor once a month feigning frailty of the heart to get a proper amount of attention and what was more important, her monthly *prescription*, a pint bottle of medicine that strangely resembled peach brandy.

The good doctor helped Miss Jessie wrap her crocheted wool shawl snugly around her tiny shoulders to ward off the chill of the winter day. Her black wool dress may have been frayed at the elbows and her gloves worn thin at the fingertips but she carried her head high. He watched her leave and whispered to himself, "Give 'em hell Miss Jessie!"

As Ted turned back to his house, he noticed a man walking toward him with the aid of a cane, his jaw set against the pain every step cost him. Ted swallowed hard, put on the best smile he could muster and walked to meet the man. A fresh gust of wind carrying the damp chill and muddy scent of the river swirled around them, stirring the dry leaves carpeting the rutted road.

"Hello, you old curmudgeon," Ted said to the thin, shabbily dressed individual. "I've got the last bottle of Napoleon brandy left in Vicksburg, maybe the South. I was saving it to celebrate victory, which don't seem likely. I think it will do just fine for your homecoming."

Slight quivers at the corners of Daniel Quinn's mouth and a watering of his eyes were hardly noticeable except to the old friend who watched him struggle to gain control of his countenance. The two stood facing each other for a long moment before Daniel spoke. "I reckon I sorely need a brandy, Ted."

They climbed the steps at Quinn's painful pace, Ted just behind in case his friend needed help. He could have used a little, but wouldn't accept any.

"Well, I see you're still the hardheaded bastard they hauled off to Dry Tortugas.

I was hoping they might tame you down just a mite, make you a little easier to put up with."

"Can't say they didn't try. Now, where's that brandy?" Daniel lowered himself into a wingback chair near the fire, resting his cane against his knee.

Doctor Perkins left the room, spoke with Luky, and returned with a dusty bottle and two brandy snifters. He poured a generous measure into the bowl of each glass.

Daniel spent a long moment staring into the fire while savoring the first sip of brandy. "I've let those down who depend on me the most, my family, and you old friend, who's been burdened by my foolish absence. Nannie wrote me about all you've done for them. God knows, they wouldn't have made it except for you."

"Oh, horse shit! You're selling the Quinn women short, and yourself. You're simply suffering the infirmities of age, you old cuss. You're finally facing the fact that Daniel Quinn is a mere mortal after all. That's a let down, all right. You're still the same man, Daniel, only the critter you inhabit is wearing out. As much abuse as you've laid on it all your life, I'm not surprised. As for the Quinn women, they're a lot tougher than you or me. You'll see. Now, after you finish that brandy, I'll pour you another one to take back to the bedroom there at the end of the hall. Luky is filling that copper tub with hot water for you and she's laid out some clean clothes. When you're ready we'll have supper and I'll bring you up to date on matters of importance."

"Damn if you wouldn't make a fine wife," replied Daniel. Leaning heavily on his cane, he struggled out of the chair, held out his glass, which the doctor refilled, and moved stiffly down the hall.

Luky set a plain meal of potatoes, gravy, cornbread and baked chicken. Daniel was too intent on eating to engage in conversation. Ted sat silently, watching his friend eat as if he would never get another meal.

When Daniel was finished, he took the napkin from his lap and put it on the table. He was ashamed to notice how soiled it was with gravy stains and crumbs and looked down to see food droppings on the front of his clean, borrowed shirt. Daniel picked up the soiled napkin and did the best he could to clean himself. Finally he looked at his host. "I want you to know that was the finest meal I've ever tasted. Tell Luky that. And I want to apologize for sitting at your table eatin' like a swamp hog. It would appear they nearly turned me into an animal. I won't forget my manners again."

Quinn paused a long moment and then looked at his friend. "Ted, I don't have the slightest idea of what to do. I've got no cotton, no money. What's left of my town house is now home to a bunch of Yankee troops. They left me one trunk of old clothes. Everything else is gone, even the portrait of my wife and son. I got a burned and looted plantation with debt and taxes owed, and now I come home so stove up I can only be an added burden." Daniel realized his friend was staring at him. "Ted, I apologize again. You don't want to hear all this crap."

"You're damn right! I don't ever want to hear any self-pitying crap out of you again. I sure as hell haven't heard any out of the Quinn women. They honor you by their courage and determination to hold on no matter what it takes. They got that from you. You've still got plenty to contribute. There's not a smarter business mind in the state. You have a family to be damn proud of and, you old bastard, you're goin' to be a great-grandfather."

Daniel Quinn was struck dumb. He sat at the table with his mouth open.

"Well, get that droll look off your face and come with me to the parlor. There's plenty of brandy left and at least two cheap cigars. Damn Yankee officers get all the good ones that come upriver. You gonna need the brandy, Daniel. We didn't write you about it acause we figured you would think us all mad."

Luky found them the next morning in the parlor sound asleep in their chairs, cigar ashes down the fronts of them, empty glasses on the floor and a near-empty brandy bottle lying on its side.

Just look at 'em. Gone and done got ossified. If dey ain't dead, de gonna sho' wish de was when de wakes up to pay de devil his due. I gots too much to do round here without nursing grow'd men what 's'posed to know better.

She went to the kitchen and fixed a strange concoction of baking soda, buttermilk, castor oil, herbs and a lot of other things too horrible to mention—a potion of equal halves of African medicine and Christian retribution designed to make even the heaviest of imbibers keep their hands off liquor for months. As bad as a hangover could be, it was nothing compared to Luky's cure for one.

Both men spent the entire day getting intimately acquainted with the hand-painted thunder-mugs in their respective rooms. Daniel piously voiced his disgust at the shameful drinking habits of the good doctor.

They left well before dawn the following day. Doctor Perkins rented the softest sprung carriage at the livery to ease the rough and frequent jolts on the road to Shamrock. It was well past nightfall, too dark to see anything of the place, when Daniel arrived at his plantation. It had been almost eight months since he, Nannie, Annielise and Arabella had traveled to Vicksburg and been trapped there when Grant crossed the river at Port Gibson and laid siege to the city. Daniel had been forewarned of what to expect, but the fact that former slave cabins offered the only shelter available to him and his family brought reality heavily upon him.

The ladies gave him a loving reception, taking care not to hug him too hard for fear of paining him. Ted had told him of the hard work his daughter-in-law, granddaughter, Arabella and Nicodemus had been doing to make a new beginning.

Daniel did not speak of the despair and heartbreak he felt. He told everyone how proud he was of them. Bone tired from the long trip, he said good night after a late supper of cornbread and beans.

"We goin' to take it nice and easy Massa Daniel, Sir. It be a long time since you walked dis here path." Nicodemus, carrying an oil lantern, led Daniel down the long path to the slave quarters and on to the cabin prepared for his homecoming. Daniel refused any help getting up the foot-worn steps. Nicodemus opened the door and saw the senior Quinn safely inside. He hung the lantern from a hook on a rafter and put a log on the small fire.

"I thank you, Nicodemus. I'll be just fine now."

"Ya suh Massa Daniel. We sho' glad to have you back home." Nicodemus left

Daniel standing in the middle of the cabin and faded out the door into the wintry night.

By the light of the lantern, Daniel could see that the little cabin had been furnished as best his family could provide. Warmed by a cozy fire, the room was clean and there was a soft, moss-stuffed mattress upon which to lay his aching body. Best of all, he thought, there were no bars on the windows. Welcomed with love and "too much fuss," he was ashamed that he had cried a little, and perhaps held too tightly to Nannie and Annielise, heavy with child, and then to Arabella and old Nicodemus each in turn.

It was a simple slave cabin, but he was home on Quinn land where he had been born seventy-four hard years ago. Daniel Quinn, lying under a worn, hand-made quilt, felt like a lost child found. It rained all night.

Christmas Eve everyone gathered in the old kitchen bright with candles and decorated with holly branches.

Gifts were presented as IOU's, their descriptions written on scraps of paper rolled into tiny scrolls tied with string and fastened to a small cedar tree decorated with bits of broken glass, shards of china, whitewashed pine cones, and strips of rags tied in bows.

Nannie plucked the *gifts* from the tree and handed them out one at a time so the recipient could read them to the crowd. There was fun and laughter, the first at Shamrock in a long time.

When things calmed down a bit, Arabella announced, "We got a surprise for y'all don't we, Nicodemus?"

"We sho' does, but we better feed these folks first."

They laid out a Christmas dinner of wild rabbit, potatoes and collard greens, and for dessert, cornbread covered with wild honey.

After the meal, Nicodemus got up from the bench in the corner and announced, "Now I is gonna bring in our surprise." He went out the door and returned a few minutes later leading a big billy goat and a pregnant nanny goat.

"Where on earth did you get that fine pair?" Daniel asked.

"Well, suh, Arabella noticed 'em whilst she was down to de creek doin' de wash. We spent two weeks tryin' to catch 'em. Arabella took to spreadin' potato peeling out foe 'em, a little closer each time 'til she had de nanny goat eatin' out'a her apron. She slipped a rope 'round her neck and dat's all there was to it. Big ole' Billy, he just follow along."

After a round of applause, Nicodemus continued, "Now dis here pregnant goat limps a little on her back leg. Looks to me like she been grazed a while back by some hungry fellow what don't shoot too good. Billy here is missing half a horn what maybe got shot off by the same fellow. 'Dey ain't wearing no brands, and I figure de good Lawd sent 'em for Massa Daniel's Christmas present."

"Amen," added Arabella.

Daniel had never received a Christmas gift from a slave, former slave he reminded himself.

I used to be the giver: time off at Christmas, pigs and steers to roast, tobacco, bolts of cloth for dresses, pants and shirts, candy and fruit for all the children. Now two of my former slaves are the givers.

Although he was thankful to them, he felt shamed. He was now the needy one who had so little left to show for a lifetime of work. Two goats from former slaves was more than he could contribute to the well-being of Shamrock.

Daniel realized everyone was looking at him. He struggled to his feet. "I admire your industry, Arabella, Nicodemus. Why, in no time at all we'll be taking goats to market, not to mention roasting a nice tender kid for ourselves now and then. I am most grateful and very happy to receive this wonderful gift."

Nicodemus and Arabella couldn't hide their pride upon hearing Daniel's slow thoughtful words. Daniel, sincerely thankful, felt he had no pride left.

The lamps and candles, scarce commodities at Shamrock, were extinguished after dinner. Everyone lingered a while by the dying fire, its light reflecting off their silent faces.

Finally, Arabella broke the spell. "We all best go to bed now and let sweet Jesus rest tonight. He gonna start out on his birthday morning with a sorry world on his shoulders."

Nicodemus helped Daniel to his cabin, talking softly to himself, "Ole Massa Daniel gonna need mo' than a cane and dis here old nigga to get him around foe long."

"What's that mumbling, Nicodemus?" asked the senior Quinn.

"Oh, I's jes thinking 'bout how old I's gittin', Massa Daniel. What I wouldn't give fo' a good bottle of whiskey and a fine young gal and a body what could handle both 'em like I used to could," he chuckled, "If you don't mind me talkin' out like dis."

For the first time in more than a year, Daniel Quinn found himself laughing. "Hell, you're right, Nicodemus. Here we are, two emancipated men, you from me, and me from the damn Yankees, and both of us nearly too old to enjoy it."

Nicodemus looked right funny at Daniel Quinn and then grinned, "I reckon we sho' nuff is, Massa Daniel. Yes sir. Too damn old to enjoy it. I been on dis place wit you nigh on to fifty years and I can't think of no other place to be. You been fair, Massa Quinn, but the Lawd knows it be better me choosing to stay as a freed man. Dat's de truth brave as I done ever spoke it. I don't mean no disrespect by it neither."

"None taken. I'm resentful as hell about what's been taken from me and mine, but I'll lay none of it on your head, Nicodemus. I'm very grateful you stayed." Daniel nodded goodnight and walked on alone to his cabin.

In nearly fifty years it was one of the few conversations the two men had ever exchanged that did not concern horses or cotton. This one would rest comfortably between them, recalled by a look of the eyes, a nod of the head, maybe a smile.

Nicodemus thought to himself, *Ole Abe done said we was free, but them words with Massa Daniel done made it so. Ain't no black really gonna be free less'in white folks lets him be. Dat ain't gonna be no easy road to travel. Plenty black folk gonna find dat out. Dat's de truth, Lawd, and you can tell 'em ole Nicodemus done said so.*

He peed off the side of his porch, blew his nose, one finger holding each nostril closed in turn and stood listening for a few minutes like always, seeing if he could hear anything amiss, hoping he wouldn't. He went inside, stripped down to his longjohns, rinsed his face and hands from a water bucket, said his prayers kneeling and crawled into bed, pulling the worn quilts over his gray head. *B'lieve it gonna freeze tonight.*

January and February passed cold, wet, and quiet. The small cabins were a little drafty, but cozy enough. Filled with the musky fragrance of unpainted cypress and yellow pine, damp wool clothing and oak wood smoke, they were a refuge from the dank Mississippi winter. Sometimes the stillness grew so heavy that the soft patter of falling rain seemed loud.

There was work of course, animals to look after, game to shoot or trap, clothes to mend, firewood to gather and meals to prepare—mostly potatoes and greens. Often after supper when everyone was gathered in the old kitchen, Nannie would read aloud from one of her beloved books. It was a time of peace.

Daniel spent much of his time close by the small fire in his cabin. One cold night he sat watching the flickering firelight reflect off the pine board floor that had been polished with the sweat and oil from the countless barefoot steps of slaves. Their former owner couldn't help wondering where they all were now, and what in the world they were doing to get along.

The major winter project was cleaning the weaving cottage which, along with the carpentry shop, had not been burned. It was a fifteen foot square, brick building framed with heavy timbers where cotton and wool had once been carded, spun into yarn and woven into cloth. The long unused spinning wheels and looms were set in one corner while a homemade bed, wash stand, table and two mended chairs were moved in. The last item was a small wooden crate that had been cut down and padded with quilts to serve as a baby crib. By the end of February the cottage was ready for Annielise and the arrival of a new Quinn.

Doctor Theodore Perkins knew exactly the day the bullet carried the flag boy's seed to Annielise. Calculating the approximate day of delivery was easy. He notified the hospital and his private patients that he would take a fortnight off beginning the second week of March. After all, he told them, he had not had a vacation since before the war reached Mississippi.

Perkins made arrangements to rent a mule and wagon from Benton's Livery. Actually, he was never charged for rentals. During the siege, all of Benton's livestock, and that boarded by town folks like the Quinn's carriage horses, had met an untimely end. Most that hadn't been killed by the shelling had eventually been shot and butchered to fill cook-pots during the siege. Claiming that Union shelling had killed every horse and mule, the doctor talked the military authorities into "lending" a dozen mules to the local livery. The army mule skinner had been delighted. He picked out the twelve most ornery critters in his care, happy to be rid of the beasts. Benton was glad to get them, and grateful to the doctor.

Leading a large gray mule, Benton said, "Doc, I'm gonna hitch up General Grant here for you 'cause he don't kick none."

"I appreciate that," the doctor replied.

"On the other hand," Benton continued as he hitched the mule to a wagon, "he'll bite the ever living hell out of ya if you give him a chance, and if that don't work he'll try and fart you to death. He ain't hard to catch, and he don't seem to mind being harnessed up. That's what'll fool ya. Every once in a while he'll just up and nip a plug out of ya. I can't figure out if he does it cause he didn't like his Yankee handlers or 'cause I named him after that jackass, Grant. Have a pleasant journey, Doc."

The doctor and the mule eyed one another. The mule looked docile as a cow. As Ted walked past General Grant to the wagon, the mule, quick as a rattlesnake, stretched his neck around and nipped at the Doctor's arm, snagging his coat sleeve at the elbow.

"See that, Doc? I think he likes you." Tobacco juice dripped from Benton's grin.

The doctor climbed up, took the reins, released the brake, and headed the wagon down the street to load a few supplies he intended for the Quinns.

He was examining the damage to his coat sleeve when General Grant lifted his tail and fired the first of many loud bursts of odoriferous flatuses in his direction. The ride to Shamrock seemed longer than usual.

Ted found his Godchild in surprisingly good condition and credited her health to outdoor work, fresh milk, and the fact that she came from good stock. He presented her with a large, somewhat worn, loosely woven, wicker trunk filled with quilts, baby clothes, diapers, a small enameled tin potty, and other infant paraphernalia which had been donated by friends in Vicksburg. He also unveiled a pair of items he figured he would catch hell for bringing. He was right.

"What the hell did you bring that pair of crutches for? We have no invalids here at Shamrock unless it's a certain moronic person claiming to be of the medical profession. You aim to share any of this whiskey you brought me you better just leave all that cripple's gear in the wagon."

For emphasis Daniel threw down his cane and walked over to the wagon to prove he was perfectly mobile. The first several steps were uneventful. The last two brought forth a "goddammit" as Daniel barely kept himself from falling by grabbing hold of the mule's harness. Just as he got himself straightened up, showing some degree of pride at his achievement, the mule whipped around and took a quick nip at the senior Quinn's rear end. Arthritis or not, Daniel Quinn jumped forward like a flash, landing abreast of the U.S. brand on the mule's hind quarters. The air turned purple with rhetoric concerning Yankees and their mules. In spite of his concern for his friend's painful condition, Ted Perkins could not control his laughter. In response, Quinn reached into the wagon, grabbed the crutches, and hobbled off to his cabin. Ted was elated to see Daniel using the crutches until he saw him returning with a colt pistol tucked into his pants. It took the doctor and both the women to keep the senior Quinn from shooting the mule. Nannie, now holding the pistol, had barely calmed him down a little when Ted referred to the animal as "General Grant."

"What the hell you call that mule?"

"General Grant. That's his name."

"Goddammit! Nannie, give me that pistol."

The whole ruckus began again.

After things calmed down for the second time, Ted appealed to his friend. "Daniel, I know what you're thinking. Don't you sneak out here later and shoot that thing. I'll have to pay for it. It's not mine. Benton Livery lent me this nice mule."

"Nice hell. That animal is a malevolent, carnivorous menace."

"All right you two, that's enough," said Nannie. "If I hear one more cross word about mules or anything else, neither one of you will get a mouthful of cooked food for a week, and I mean it. And furthermore, I'll hide the liquor, which any Christian woman ought to do in the first place."

Daniel and Ted immediately became remorseful. Nannie, the unequivocal victor, lifted the hem of her skirt and gracefully walked toward the kitchen still carrying the pistol.

At three o'clock in the morning Doctor Perkins was in deep, dreamless sleep when he awoke to the flickering light of a candle and the not-too-gentle shaking of his shoulder. "Miss Annielise 'bout to have her baby. Miss Nannie say if'en you don't want a miss it, you better come on."

He found Annielise in hard labor, every oil lamp on the place burning brightly in the one-room cabin. Nannie and Arabella were completely in charge.

"Damn if I haven't been invited as a spectator," Ted grumbled. It was almost true. He found himself sitting beside the bed wiping the sweat off his Godchild's forehead. "Everything's going fine, Darling. Quit trying to be so brave. You can yell if you feel like it," he told her. "It's almost over."

It wasn't, of course, but eventually the newest Quinn child came into the world announcing its presence with a fine pair of lungs. The child had the bone china complexion of the Quinn strawberry blonds, mother and grandmother alike, but it had raven black hair, lots of it for a newborn, which, the doctor was convinced, had to have come from the part Choctaw, flag-waving boy. "Here you are, Annielise," Ted said. He placed the child in her mother's arms. "You have a beautiful raven-haired daughter."

Daniel came in from the porch while Nicodemus stood outside and peeped in through the door.

"All right now," Arabella said, her arms full of fresh bedding. "Dis child is exhausted and so is her baby. Dey both need rest, and dey is gonna git some cause all you men folk," and she eyed Doctor Perkins to let him know he was included, "is leaving while I freshens de bed and gits Miss Annielise into a clean nightgown."

"Well before we go," Daniel Quinn asked, "what's that little bullet baby's name?"

"Now don't you start that bullet baby business," Nannie said. "I won't have it."

"Well, Annielise?" Daniel persisted.

Annielise fought to keep her eyes open. "Mama, I've had lots of time to think of names. If it had been a boy, I WOULD have named him Bullet, but this little girl is Beverly Bethany Quinn."

"That's a pretty name," her mother said, relieved. "The idea of naming a child Bullet."

"But Mama," Annielise replied weakly, "her initials are B. B. for 'Bullet Baby'." Annielise winked at her grandfather and faded into sleep with a smile on her face.

Nannie took Grandfather Quinn's arm and helped him out of the cabin and into the chill of the night. "I think your grandchildren must have gotten their rebellious nature and mule stubbornness from you, Daniel," she said with a chuckle.

"I reckon you might could blame that on me, Nannie darling, but I think their courage comes from you."

Nannie reached up and kissed him on the cheek. "No, Daniel, they got it all from you Quinns. I'm just a woman who worries all the time about her children, and, mercy, I better add a grandchild to that list. Thank God Annielise and the baby are all right."

Nannie stopped and looked up at Daniel, tears forming in the corners of her eyes, her lips trembling slightly. "My courage fails me when I think of Jonathan. We don't even know what ship he's on. I've got to believe that he's alive, but where, Daniel? Where in God's name is my Jonathan? I can't lose him too. I just can't. I couldn't go on."

Daniel put his arm around his daughter-in-law. "That headstrong young grandson of mine is gonna come home to us, Nannie, you'll see."

BOOK TWO

JONATHAN

PART TWO

JONATHAN

CHAPTER 6

"Monsieur Quinn? Monsieur Quinn?"

Vaguely a voice reached through the sea of swirling, sweat-soaked dreams induced by fever and heavy doses of morphine. Slowly, with great effort, he surfaced into consciousness. At first his eyes hurt from the glare of mote-filled sunbeams reflecting off white walls. The brightness was pouring through windows spaced along a hospital ward lined with mostly empty beds. The walls, the beds, the sheets, everything in the ward was white except the blue painted ceiling.

Jonathan turned his head toward the voice and was rewarded with a stab of pain. Gradually, he was able to focus on a plump, rosy-cheeked nun standing over him with a tray. *Why do I see only through one eye?* He lifted his hands to his face and felt thick bandages covering most of his head and half his face.

"I know your head hurts, but pain or no pain, you must eat if you are to get well," the nun intoned cheerfully. She helped him sit up, and put pillows behind his back.

A dull pounding assaulted his head and brief flashes of light shot across his brain. "Where am I, Sister?"

"At Hotel Dieu in Paris, of course. Every day I have to tell you this," the Augustine sister replied in heavily accented English. "Now here, I've brought you warm broth to make you strong." She began to feed him.

Gradually taken off morphine, he began slowly, painfully, to return to the conscious world. Weeks later most of his bandages were removed. A nurse finally allowed him to see his face in a mirror. Self-pity and depression ruled his isolated world for a while, but the more he remembered, the more he began to realize, *It is enough that I am alive.*

One day, when she brought his lunch, the plump little nun sternly insisted, "Monsieur Quinn. Eat! Don't you want to grow strong enough to go home?"

"Home? Yes, if I can get there without being captured and maybe hanged."

"Oh, Monsieur, not hanged! Certainly no one would do such a thing."

"I don't know, Sister. Yankee newspapers referred to the crew of my ship as pirates."

"Pirates! I refuse to believe it."

"Well," Quinn replied, "I'll tell you a sea story and let you decide."

The little nun pulled up a chair. "I would love for my patient to tell a story. It means you are healing."

"This one has to do with a French girl. A pretty one."

"Oh! Monsieur, you seafaring men are all alike," the nun smiled and added, "This better not be naughty."

"We were huntin' Yankee ships off the eastern tip of Cuba when the large steamer *Ariel* hauled into sight rounding Cape Maize. We could see her passengers crowding the rail under her bright colored awnings. Captain Semmes ordered a blank shot fired. *Ariel* immediately unfurled a Confederate flag and increased her speed. 'Mister Quinn!, the captain shouted at me, 'Go forward to the pivot gun and tell the master gunner to fire a shot over her, high so as not to endanger life.' The shot arched over *Ariel* and plunged into the sea dead ahead of her. She hove-to and we swiftly came alongside her.

"Our boarding party found a hundred and forty Union officers and men aboard bound for a new Yankee ship-of-war being built in England. Our men quickly disarmed them. I was still aboard *Alabama* when it was reported that the ladies aboard *Ariel* had screamed in alarm at the sight of our boarding crew, fled to the main salon and locked themselves in.

"Captain Semmes was furious to learn that the women truly believed the stories describing him and his crew as pirates and plunderers, and that the ladies were hysterically apprehensive of the worst consequences to their persons. Unbeknownst to us midshipmen, the Captain ordered Lieutenant Knell to collect the youngest officers aboard his ship and pick a handsome one to report to him immediately.

"When Lieutenant Knell lined up several of us midshipmen and repeated the Captain's order I couldn't help but laugh. I thought it was a joke. The Lieutenant said if I thought it so funny I could fill the strange request. I dutifully reported to the Captain. I'm here to tell you, Sister, Captain Semmes was not in a joking mood. He looked me up and down, nodded his head and informed me, 'It's going to fall upon your shoulders, Midshipman Quinn, to rectify the terrible impression the news vermin have apparently given women all over the world that this ship is manned by barbarians. By God! Mister, you are going to restore my honor as an officer and a gentleman, and the honor of this ship and the men who sail her! You've got ten minutes to dress in the best uniform you own and get back here. If I hear another feminine shriek from the decks of that ship I'm liable to hang somebody.' I rushed to my quarters, dressed, and returned to the captain's cabin for inspection.

"Semmes gave me his own gold braid sword knot and sent me to draw the best sword in the ward room. After a final inspection I was rowed across to *Ariel* where I reported to her captain and respectfully requested to be shown to the ladies' salon, which I was. There I found a scene of dismay, confusion, and whimpering women. It was awful. All those women silently gaped at me like I was the devil himself. The room grew very silent except for occasional sobs and sniffles. I was so embarrassed I had to clear my throat twice before I could speak. Ladies, I said, Captain Semmes of *CSS Alabama* has heard of your grave distress and sent me to allay your fears. I told them, you all have fallen into the hands of Southern gentlemen under whose protection you are entirely safe. We are by no means the ruffians the Northern press has led you to believe. You all have nothing to fear. Upon the word and honor of my captain you can rest assured that you will be treated with every courtesy.

"Well the sobs ceased, but the ladies still eyed me askance so I picked out a pretty young woman and began chatting nonchalantly, asking about her home and how the voyage had been. Others joined in and presently a petite, dark-haired young lady took hold of one of the gold buttons on the front of my best uniform and with a lovely French accent asked if I would permit her to have the button as a memento to her adventure with *Alabama*.

"Mademoiselle, how could I refuse? I replied in French. For the first time in my life I was thankful for all the lessons I had suffered under the French tutor at Shamrock. That's my family's plantation back home. Anyway, a pair of scissors was produced accompanied by shy feminine giggles as pleasing to the ear as the bell tones of fine cut crystal.

"Later, while walking down a passageway in the company of several young ladies, not a button left on the front of my uniform, I noticed several male passengers hiding valuables taken from their pockets. I turned to the ladies and in a voice loud enough to be heard up and down the deck declared, 'These fellows obviously think we are no better than the Northern thieves who are burning dwelling houses and robbing our women and children in the South.' The ladies gave these Yankee fellows a look of disdain. I laughed and bid adieu to my charming company, returned to my ship and reported to Captain Semmes that all was well. That pleasant sojourn did not change the opinion of the Northern press, sister. They still label us with the insinuation that we are pirates."

Remembering having to explain to his captain why he had returned with no buttons on his uniform, Jonathan smiled.

"Oh! Monsieur Quinn! I am delighted to see you smile. It is the first time."

"I was just thinking about this face of mine. It will win no lady's favors now, I'll bet . . . but what the hell, Sister, I'm alive. I'll win them with charm. It will take more than a little, I suspect."

"You shouldn't use profanity, especially since you are nothing short of a miracle," the sister scolded him sternly, but silently thought, *Praise be to God! This boy is healing.* "But if you know French," she asked, "why don't you speak it to me?"

"I don't speak it as well as you speak English, Sister. It would be a struggle and make my poor head hurt."

"Well never mind, but you must finish the story. Tell me, what happened to this *Ariel* with all those adoring ladies."

"Not much I'm afraid. We didn't have room to take aboard 500 passengers, crew, and Yankee prisoners. We waited several days hoping a neutral ship would come along to take them so we could sink *Ariel*. She was a Yankee ship, don't you see, but that didn't happen. Captain Semmes had her captain, in the name of her owner, a Mr. Vanderbilt I believe, sign a ransom bond and let her sail away."

"That was a very noble and Christian thing to do," smiled the little nun. "Pirates would never have done that. I'm quite confident God won't let anyone hang you when you go home." The sister nodded her head as if to say, 'So there!' She picked up Jonathan's empty soup bowl and walked rather regally down the long ward as if she had just handed down a safe conduct proclamation from God, which perhaps she had. A few moments later, the happy little nun returned with a bedpan.

No longer sedated with heavy doses of morphine, memories of the last moments before the darkness of his long sleep flooded into Jonathan's dreams and waking thoughts; memories so real he could hear the roar of cannon, the screams of men torn asunder, taste salt spray and smell the caustic odor of spent powder.

He must have screamed out in his dream for he awoke in a sweat sitting bolt upright in his bed. A sister, the ward night nurse, appeared at his bedside. The only light in the room emanated from the dim lamp at her station.

"I'm sorry, Sister, did I do it again?"

"I think it is time for you to talk about it. Get it out of the corners and crevices of your mind and let it go with the coming of the dawn."

"You speak English!"

"Yes. My father was English, my mother French. I attended Catholic school, was orphaned, and stayed with the only home and family I had left. That is my story, so why don't you tell me yours about the last battle of your *Alabama*?"

"It would bore you, or perhaps shock you. It was not pretty."

"I served at a French hospital in Algeria in the 1850's. That was not very pretty. So I doubt you can shock me."

Jonathan feared the dreams sleep might bring. Glad for the company, he began to talk.

"I wish you could have seen her, Sister. *Alabama* was a handsome vessel. She was very fast when launched, fast enough to overhaul every Yankee merchant ship that crossed her path from the Caribbean to the North Atlantic to the Pacific and Asia. But by June of this year, as we approached the coast of France, she was sea-worn, her bottom fouled, her gunpowder deteriorating, her crew fatigued. Captain Semmes docked his ship in Cherbourg harbor because he knew excellent dry dock and repair facilities were there. When we asked permission to place the ship in dry dock for repairs, French officials insisted that they would have to consult Emperor Louis Napoleon III before permission could be granted. The news of *Alabama*'s arrival did not go unnoticed by the Yankee Navy. They had deployed warships across the world's oceans but never could catch us. Anyway, we were not surprised when SS *Kearsarge* arrived. Captain Semmes sent ashore all the ship's gold, payroll records and the ransom bonds he had issued. It seemed everyone but us thought the upcoming battle was gonna be a gala affair. Trainloads of spectators came down from Paris. We heard tell that all the hotels were sold out. There's nothin' gala about a naval battle, Sister. I was scared fo' we left the dock. I don't mind tellin' a nun that. God already knows how scared I was.

"It was a lovely Sunday morning when *Alabama* steamed out of the harbor. My battle station was near the helm. I remember lookin' back and seein' a whole floating parade steaming out of the harbor behind us. There were several pilot boats loaded with spectators. I especially remember a lovely, trim, steam yacht flying a British ensign. There was a French warship leadin' 'em, I guess to ensure French neutral territory wouldn't be violated. I reckon we resented all those people making a holiday out of watchin' men kill each other. You sure you want me to go on?"

The sister nodded her head and took his hand in hers.

"Captain Semmes steered straight for *Kearsarge* waitin' some six miles offshore. We knew we were out-gunned. *Kearsarge* had been built for war; *Alabama* for speed to take merchantmen, not to fight ships of the line. We knew with *Alabama*'s bottom fouled, she no longer had the advantage of speed. Still, a copy of the *Federal Ship Registry* classified *Kearsarge* as a wooden gunboat. We all looked through the ship's glass at *Kearsarge* when she first stood off Cherbourg harbor but saw nothing to dispute the *Registry*'s description. I guess we thought we were sailing into a fair fight. We were dead wrong, Sister.

"*Alabama* closed on *Kearsarge*, both ships maneuvering for advantage but neither got any. We ended up on opposite sides of a circle rotating clockwise facing starboard to starboard, and commenced firing at a thousand yards. For maybe six or seven full turns of the circle we exchanged broadside for broadside gradually closing to 500 yards. It was murderous, Sister. Captain Semmes, standing fully exposed on the horse-block abreast the mizzen mast, glass in hand, saw our explosive shells hit the enemy's side and fall into the water. I reckon he assumed the problem was due to the deteriorated state of *Alabama*'s gunpowder cause I heard him yell at Mr. Knell to change to solid shot. He thought our shells were faulty, but when some planks were torn off *Kearsarge*, we saw that she had false planking covering up a blanket of anchor chain draped down her sides. Our shells were bouncing off cause they were hittin' steel.

"The enemy's 11-inch guns wreaked terrible damage. The aft pivot gun took three direct hits. The first swept away the gun crew. They were replaced. The second cut one man in half and wounded others. The third hit the gun-carriage and fell spinning on the deck until it was pushed overboard by one of the survivors. It exploded underwater behind the ship.

"*Alabama*'s hull was punctured and taking on water and she began to list to starboard. Captain Semmes shouted to Lieutenant Knell, 'Pivot her to port when next the bow comes round toward the French shore!' He turned to me and ordered, 'Master Quinn, have as many cannon as you can moved to the high side. Maybe we can right her long enough to reach the shore.' We did what he asked. Lieutenant Knell then ordered me to transfer the men from the aft 32-pounder to the larger pivot gun, putting me in command. The deck around the gun was encumbered with the mangled trunks and limbs of the dead, pieces of humans, Sister. We grabbed up bloody slick hunks of flesh and limb and tossed them like garbage over the side. I pray for those men's forgiveness now, but there wasn't time then. My gun crew and I had to steady ourselves on anything available to keep from slipping on the thick blood that covered the deck."

There was sweat on Jonathan's brow. "Maybe I shouldn't be tell'en so factual, Sister."

"You just keep talking, son. Tell it all out loud. It will leave you alone after this." The sister's voice was calm and reassuring.

"Well, ma'am, moments after I took command of the pivot gun, the ship's engineer came topside. 'Captain, Sir!' he yelled to be heard over the roar of cannon. 'The boiler fires have been drowned below. We can make no steam.'

"Captain Semmes shouted to Knell, 'Go below, sir, and see how long the ship can float.' Knell returned and yelled, 'Sir, we will not float another ten minutes.' I heard Captain Semmes shout, 'Cease firing and strike the colors. It will never do for us to go down with the decks covered with our wounded.'

"The order to cease fire was sounded and immediately I had my crew silence the gun. As was the custom when the colors are struck, men all up and down the line, men with powder-blackened, sweat streaked faces, some of 'em bleeding . . . we all stood up at our posts to show the enemy the battle was over.

"But it was not over, Sister." Jonathan said in anger. "*Kearsarge* fired a whole salvo into us. 'Stand by your quarters, men!' Semmes ordered, 'Quartermaster! Show a white flag over the stern!' Sister, I saw the quartermaster frantically do so. I remember *Kearsarge* firing another salvo into the midst of us and one of her shells hitting the oak railing in front of our gun. Something hit me and when I woke up I was in the water, the ship trying to suck me down with her. I was hurtin' and strugglin' and growin' weaker, but I didn't know I had lost an eye and my ear and cracked my skull. Although it was a sunny day, darkness descended over me and I could no longer see. I was drownin' I reckon. All I remember is somethin' bumpin' me and pull'en at me. I thought of sharks. I thought sharks were goin' to take me. It was terrifying. It's still terrifying, Sister. That's the last I remember. I don't know how I got here."

"You got here through God's grace my young Confederate sailor. For you to recover, for you to live, it is a miracle." The sister tucked the covers around Jonathan. "Now go to sleep and don't let all of that frighten you ever again. And Mr. Quinn, don't forget to say your prayers." The sister smiled and faded quietly away, like a holy spirit it seemed to Jonathan.

Eventually his surgeon, Doctor Paul Andre Courbet, told him his cracked skull would mend. He would recover, function again, be almost whole except for a right eye, and half an ear.

"When can I go home, doctor?"

"We will talk about that next week, my hardheaded Confederate. By the way, your captain is in England, rescued by an English yacht I understand. He sent his compliments and your pay, which is in the hospital safe."

"Bless my Captain. Now I can pay you."

"Your stay here has already been taken care of, a debt repaid so to speak."

"A debt repaid? I don't understand. Who in France could possibly be indebted to me?"

The doctor reached into his pocket and held out a closed fist. "I have been waiting to show you. It was paid with this." He opened his hand to reveal a shiny gold button. "My daughter and other French young ladies had been on a chaperoned tour of our French islands in the Caribbean and were returning to France aboard the steamer *Ariel* when your *Alabama* captured her. A handsome young man from your ship gave her this as a memento before your gallant captain sent *Ariel* safely on its way and my daughter home to me." Jonathan held the button in his hand a moment, then returned it to the doctor.

"Now I, too, owe that young man a debt I cannot repay. I'm sad to inform you that he died with his ship. As grateful as I am for the care you are giving me, I would ask just one more small favor. Please don't tell your daughter and spoil her pleasant memory of the voyage."

The doctor patted his patient's shoulder, put the button back into his vest pocket and walked out of the room.

That evening the good sister brought pen, paper and ink along with his supper. "Never mind your headache," she said, "No supper until you write a letter to your mère." She stood over him, waiting.

Dear Mother,

By the time you receive this letter you may have heard that Alabama was sunk. I can at last tell you that she was my ship, but I want you to know that I am fine. I received a minor head wound which is of little consequence except for giving me a bit of a scar, you know, the kind that adds to a seaman's mystique, that lends character as Granddaddy Quinn would say. I am in Paris recuperating under the best of care. I have sufficient funds, and will begin making preparations for travel home. Don't worry. I'll make it back to Shamrock.

Love to all, Jonathan

Weeks later as a restless ambulatory patient, Quinn received an unexpected message.

Southampton, England, September 15, 1864

J.H. Quinn, Midshipman, Hotel Dieu, Paris, France

Dear Mr. Quinn,

By the noble kindness of an English gentleman, John Lancaster, a number of the crew, including myself, were rescued aboard his yacht, Deerhound. He delivered us out of the hands of the Yankees here to Southampton. Like yourself, I have been delayed due to a wound and the need to complete my final duties as concerns Alabama. I invite you to join me for travel to our Confederate States. If you are well enough to make such a journey, join me at the port of Southampton no later than the evening of October 2 aboard the steamer

Tasmanian. She sails on the morning of the 3rd. I emphasize your being well enough to travel. Reaching friendly forces at home will be a risky and arduous journey. Not a single port is left open to us.

Yours faithfully,

Raphael Semmes, Capt. CSA

Captain Semmes rose from his desk to greet the young man whose handsome face had once calmed the fears of ladies aboard the captured *Ariel*. That face now had dark puncture marks left by stitches outlining a raw, jagged seam that began at what was left of an ear, led under a black eye patch, and coursed on above the bridge of the nose, up across the forehead to end high above the good eye where a new growth of hair was beginning to cover the shaved portion of his skull. Semmes made an unsuccessful attempt to hide his distress as he walked to Midshipman Quinn and shook his hand.

"Welcome Mr. Quinn. It would have been a long, dull journey without the company of a shipmate. Will you have a brandy with me?"

"Thank you, sir." Quinn accepted a glass from Semmes.

The captain motioned his guest to a chair and seated himself at a small desk.

"I heard you had a serious wound, son, but I didn't know about, well, the extent of your injuries."

"It's all right, Sir. Shocked me too." Jonathan smiled to put his captain at ease.

"When did it happen? You were all right when we struck the colors. I recall seeing you."

"Sir, I don't remember a thing after that until I woke up in a hospital in Paris."

"Well, son, all things considered, you look tolerable to me," replied Semmes.

"They say the scar will improve with time. At least I'll not suffer the ridicule of being chosen for any more assignments with the ladies." Jonathan smiled.

"Well hell, son, you looked too pretty to be a fighting man then. By God! You look like one now."

"I may look like one, Captain, but to tell the truth, when their eleven inch guns began to tear us apart, I nearly killed my pants, if you know what I mean."

"No different from any man aboard, including your captain, but you stood fast and did your duty. That's the definition of a warrior, son."

The two men talked into the night until their tongues grew heavy and their memories light from the brandy.

Jonathan awoke unable to remember exactly how he got to his cabin. It was ten in the morning when he carried his aching head to the dining salon for black coffee, plain toast, and more coffee. He was in no mood to face an egg.

Weeks after their departure they reached the island of St. Thomas rising like a green jewel from the clear, coral-shadowed waters of the Caribbean. There, hardly pausing ashore, they boarded a vessel named *Solent*. She carried them past Puerto Rico, down the north side of Santo Domingo into the old Bahamas Channel and eventually, under watchful Spanish eyes peering down from ancient Moro Castle, glided smoothly into Havana Bay. While awaiting arrangements to be finalized for the next leg of their trip, Jonathan ventured into Old Havana and was able to locate several of his Cuban acquaintances, shipping agents from his days of blockade running aboard *Virgin*. One of them told him rumor had it that Captain Jones had escaped aboard his ship during the confusion at the battle of Mobile Bay, and was now somewhere in the Bahamas.

Jonathan laughed, "That sounds like the old devil. If he shows up in Havana, tell him I'm alive and headed home. If he wants to contact me, tell him not to use my name directly. Hopefully the Yankees think I'm dead. Tell him to address any correspondence in care of my mother, Mrs. Ansel Quinn, general delivery, Vicksburg, Mississippi." He wrote out the address and asked that the information be given only to Captain Jones.

Semmes and Jonathan boarded a small schooner which set a west by northwest course from Havana directly across the Gulf of Mexico.

No Southern port on the Gulf was open to them. Their destination was a Mexican village called Bagdad located at the mouth of the Rio Grande. Upon arrival at what could hardly be called a proper port, they discovered that Bagdad was a boom town of hastily constructed shanties thriving on illegal commerce carried on mostly by Yankee traders who received Southern cotton across the border from Texas for export in exchange for all kinds of goods, including medicine and arms sold to the Confederacy at outrageous prices.

"So much for Yankee allegiance," Semmes remarked.

The pair traveled by donkey cart a distance of thirty bone-jarring, dusty, desolate miles to the border town of Matamoros. Following instructions Semmes had received in England, they went to a mission in town and asked for a priest by the name of Father Fisher. As directed, they arrived at a cantina filled with cigar smoke, the smell of sweat, spilled whiskey and beer. A few unsavory looking Mexican men turned to look at the pair of gringos as they entered. Semmes deferred to Jonathan, who knew a little Spanish from his blockade running days aboard *Virgin*.

Quinn walked to the bar and asked the cantinero, "Por favor, adonde es Padre Fisher?"

The bartender nodded toward a door leading out to a patio in back. The air was fresher there. A portly man dressed in a cassock was sitting with a Mexican officer at a table shaded by a weathered market umbrella.

"Father Fisher?"

Fisher stood. Speaking English with a heavy European accent he replied, "I am Father Fisher, a humble servant of the church. This officer is Coronel Mejia."

That correlated with the information Semmes was given during a briefing by Bulloch in London, information that described Father Fisher as far more than a "humble servant of the church." A German who emigrated in his youth to Mexico, he was a cultivated and vagarious intellect who spoke half a dozen languages. He had served as Emperor Maximilian's confessor and trusted counselor, a position that earned him a fortune. Fisher had been described to Semmes as a spy who sold information and certain services to the highest bidder. At the moment he was in the pay of the Confederacy.

"You must be the famous Captain Semmes," Fisher continued. "And who is your companion? We were expecting only yourself."

Semmes answered, "This is Midshipman Quinn." Quinn nodded.

"Ah! Well, Captain Semmes and Midshipman Quinn, won't you please join us?"

After the four were seated, The Mexican officer turned toward the door and in a commanding voice shouted, "Cantinero! Cuatro aguardientes aprisa!"

While the drinks were set before them, the good father explained in English that Coronel Mejia provided "security" for the transportation of Southern cotton from across the Texas border. The coronel explained that he provided the service out of "admiracion por los Estados Confederacion," and added with a sly smile, "e dinero oro."

Thirsty, Jonathan took a large sip of the drink set before him. He thought he had poured fire down his throat. It was his first experience with tequila. His eyes watered as he gasped for air, much to the amusement of his hosts. *By God! I think I just melted my tongue.*

Fisher held his glass in toast to Jonathan and emptied it in one swig, smiled, ordered another, and pulled a letter from his cassock. "This is for you, Captain." He slid the envelope across the table.

The letter was addressed to Semmes and carried the Confederate seal. There was no postmark. It had obviously been delivered by courier. Semmes excused himself, walked a few steps from the table, broke the seal, opened and read the correspondence. When he finished, he burned the document, ground the ashes into the dirt floor and returned to his seat.

"Father Fisher, can transportation be arranged to as far as Shreveport, Louisiana?"

"I anticipated your needs, Captain. Arrangements have been made with your Confederate forces. You and Midshipman Quinn will cross the Rio Grande to Brownsville in the morning where you will take a carriage for the long journey to Shreveport."

"Why don't we begin immediately? There is still time enough to cross to Brownsville this afternoon."

"There is no hotel in Brownsville, Captain. You should make the most of your rest in a soft feather bed tonight. Once you leave Mexico, you will be sleeping on a blanket roll with no roof over your head for many days. The exploits of *Alabama* and you as her captain are well known. It will not do for you to stop where hospitable people along the way would gladly put you up for an evening. They surely would brag to relatives or neighbors that the famous Captain Semmes had spent the night in their abode. I know from experience that such news could quickly gain the ear of spies. I am afraid, Captain, you and Quinn are on a clandestine adventure. Your capture would make the front page of every Northern newspaper and I would lose the confidence of my Confederate paymaster. You must do your best to avoid even casual contact. People are always curious about strangers."

The next morning, Fisher supplied the two travelers with bedrolls and sacks containing hard tack, smoked ham, dried fruit, simple rations that required no fire to prepare, and jugs of wine. Drinking water would be scarce. For his services, Father Fisher would submit an outrageous bill to the covert Confederate paymaster.

On the east side of the Rio Grande, Semmes and Quinn were met at Brownsville by a Confederate agent dressed in civilian clothes. He supplied them with a wagon hitched to a pair of horses. He apologized for not providing a carriage but said such fancy transport might attract unwanted attention. For the next fourteen nights Semmes and Quinn would sleep on the ground.

Their rough passage from Brownsville took them across the Nueces River at San Patricia, the Guadalupe at Gonzales, through the small towns of Houston, Hempstead, Navasota, Huntsville, Rusk, Henderson and Marshall, Texas without incident. On the 27th of November, they reached Shreveport, the temporary capital of Louisiana since Baton Rouge had fallen to Yankees.

At a dinner in their honor, the two special guests were seated on either side of Governor Henry Watkins Allen. They were dressed in plain clothes. Neither Captain Semmes nor Midshipman Quinn had presentable uniforms to wear for the occasion. Theirs had been soiled with blood, spent gunpowder, rips and saltwater. Even so, the guests made quite a fuss over them.

There was a package on the table in front of Governor Allen. With the help of crutches, the governor struggled to his feet, tapped his glass to quiet the room and addressed his guests. "Ladies and gentlemen I received a communication from Richmond several weeks ago alerting me of the expected arrival of our distinguished guests and authorizing me to make the following presentations. The governor untied the package and took its contents in his hands. He turned to the former captain of *Alabama*, "I am happy to have the honor of presenting to you, sir, the well-deserved promotion to the rank of Admiral. May I be the first to congratulate you?"

Semmes stood. The Governor handed him a pair of new shoulder boards of sky blue cloth edged with black and bordered with an embroidery of gold upon which were five stars. There was enthusiastic applause.

Governor Allen, braced by his crutches, asked the new admiral to say a few words to his guests.

"Admiral is it?" Semmes said. "I was expecting a reprimand for losing my ship." Semmes was serious, but his remark was received with laughter from an audience who were well informed of the exploits of *Alabama*.

Allen then turned to Quinn who stood. "Mr. Quinn, Richmond has confirmed your promotion to lieutenant, granted upon the recommendation of your commanding officer." After another burst of applause, Governor Allen presented Jonathan with similar shoulder boards with the exception that his had only one star. Jonathan thanked the Governor and sat down, proud but a little embarrassed.

After dinner, Governor Allen, who had suffered terrible, crippling leg wounds at the battle of Baton Rouge while leading a Louisiana regiment, gathered up his crutches and led Admiral Semmes and Lieutenant Quinn to the privacy of his study.

"Gentlemen, I'm afraid your visit with us must be a short one. It's urgent, Admiral, that you continue your journey in the morning. The command of the river squadron at Richmond awaits you. We have made arrangements that should get you safely through. It will be a toilsome journey. You will be in the hands of a relay team made up of the very best and experienced scouts we have. They know every foot of ground you will cover, the position of enemy lines, camps, pickets and outposts. They will get you through, Admiral. That reminds me. No names will be used. Not yours and not your guides. And no salutin'. There's still Yankee eyes along the way. Someone sees a salute they'd know you're officers. Gittin' picked up in civilian garb will likely git you shot as spies."

Before dawn the next morning, Admiral Semmes and Lieutenant Quinn left in a light, closed carriage. No names were exchanged. Unknown to Semmes and Quinn, their driver was a Confederate cavalry sergeant named Calvin Jessup. All three men were dressed in civilian clothes.

Calvin assured them, "Thar won't be no Yankees on this here part of the route. General Kirby and General Taylor done run ole General Nathaniel Prentice Banks and Admiral Porter clean out the valley and off the Red River up in these here parts. They ain't agonna be a problem fer ya 'til you git nie on to the Mississippi. You'll meet some of our boys thar what can git ya cross the river and on your way."

Raphael Semmes and Jonathan Quinn had done their fighting on the world's oceans far from Southern soil. They had seen men die, but the ocean cleans itself of man's folly. Until they departed Shreveport, neither had seen the destruction war had strewn across the Confederate States. Their route followed the Red River Valley for a while before turning directly for the Mississippi. Both men were appalled by the devastation they could see from the road. The Union had lost their Red River campaign, but they had left the countryside in ruin. The travelers passed what was left of rotted animal carcasses, hastily butchered cattle, horses, a few still in harness or saddle, sun-shriveled hide and bleached bones, the leavings of what dogs, opossums, foxes, ants, flies, larvae, worms, beetles and humans had left behind. They passed oblong lumps of earth, eroded by rain, where hardly a blade of grass had caught . . . unmarked graves where the dead had been hastily buried.

When Semmes remarked on the sorrowfulness of such field expediency, sergeant Jessup told them, "That ain't nothin'. Over yonder a little to the west around Mansfield there was fierce fightin' . . . so many dead you couldn't count 'em, buzzards so thick they damn near provided shade for the grave details. It took several hundred men to dig a long trench, I mean far as you could see. They just laid the dead head to toe, maybe three across, sometimes doublin' up. Just thrown 'em in dressed like they was and covered 'em over. Had to do it that way, just so many of 'em. We caught some niggas and whites too out thar thievin' the dead, blue and gray alike. Should of shot 'em, but made 'em tote bodies to the ditch instead. It was pretty awful but the best could be done at the time. Them diggers should of made the ditches a might deeper, but they was wore out same as we was, I reckon. Anyway, them graves was too shallow, maybe only two or three feet a' dirt on 'em in places. The ground must a heated up like a fermentin' manure pile do cause it swole up them bodies 'til a week or two later the ground over 'em heaped up some. Looked like a giant mole run. The ridge of it cracked open some. It was like them dead resented not having a proper burial, no one saying words over 'em, no one knowin' who they was even, just throwed in thar and covered like it was a trash pit. Some said them boys was a trying to git out. You get close and you could smell 'em, and that bucked up ridge . . . all up and down . . . it was shiny green with them bottle flies."

Every few miles they passed the charred remains of a dwelling where some family had been unhoused and turned into the fields. Semmes remarked, "What we're seeing, Mr. Quinn, is the result of an enemy that is writing new and horrible rules of war concerning the treatment of unarmed civilians. This whole Red River Valley laid waste, all burned and pillaged. No cause for that. I'd like to think that all this was done by disorderly, drunken soldiery with no officer to raise his hand to stay the conflagration of the land, but I know better. The officers in blue had to order or at least approve for there to be such wanton destruction."

They occasionally saw little bands of freed slaves who had been left to wander purposelessly.

"What will they do?" Jonathan asked.

The sergeant answered. "I reckon they'll beg or thieve where there's somethin' to thieve, somethin' to eat. No different from a lot of whites, women and children and old men mostly, burnt out by the Yankees. 'bout twenty thousand of them Yanks come through here on the way to fight, then back again retreatin' after we put a whoopin' on 'em. Comin' and goin' they done foraged most ever' thing. You ain't seen a single chicken or cow or pig have you? Hell, we ain't even heard a dog bark. The fields all been stripped. We ain't carrying much to eat ourselves, but it gotta do us cause we won't find nothing along the way. Ain't uncommon hereabouts for folks to go two or three days with noth'en to eat, soldier or civilian. Thar's plenty famishing. If'en they don't find food or get help somehow, plenty gone jest give up, lie down and die. I seen it happen."

Just after dark one night, they pulled up at a road junction. A figure emerged from the shadows of a large oak leading a saddled horse. Sergeant Jessup pulled a pistol from his belt, pointed it at the man and asked, "You got any whiskey in them saddlebags, stranger?"

The man, whose face was hidden under a wide-brim hat answered, "I reckon I do, but I'm saving it for a sailor."

Jessup nodded, lowered the pistol and put it back in his belt. "That's the right answer, pard', only we got two sailors here." He turned to his passengers. "Sailors, this here fellow will take you on the next leg of yo' journey. He just soon you not know his name and he don't want a know yours. He knows the territory from here to the next relay. Thar's some Yanks here abouts, but this fellow knows where they at. Ya'll can trust him same as me."

Jessup got down from the carriage, took the reins of the stranger's horse and swung into the saddle. "Nice meeting you." Jessup smiled, nodded and rode into the darkness back the way they had come."

The stranger walked back to the oak, picked up a burlap sack of food and put it in the carriage boot. He nodded to his passengers, climbed up on the driver's seat, took up the reins clucked up the pair of horses and starting them eastward up the road.

Some twenty miles or so west of the Mississippi, they were turned over to three mounted men, one of whom led two saddled horses. The men belonged to the unsung Confederate mail service whose job it was to cross enemy lines at great risk to deliver important official dispatches as well as the letters of ordinary citizens and, when they had room, as many firing caps as they could carry.

The small amount of personal gear Admiral Semmes and Jonathan carried was carefully tied to their saddles in such a way as to make no noise. There would be no rattling of canteens, pistols or spurs.

The leader, a tall wiry man with tobacco stains in his beard, told the two travelers, "I didn't know there'd be two of you. We usually carry an extra horse just in case. Looks like we won't have no extra this trip. We gonna be making our way through enemy territory. From here on out, you gentlemen are not to speak, not a word. We only gonna use hand signals. Nobody smokes. No fire at night. We ride single file, two of us ahead of ya'll, one behind. With no spare this trip, a horse goes lame the rider walks.

"If we run into trouble, meaning shoutin' and shootin', it's ever man fo' himself. The man behind you will try to lead you two out. Us two up front will try to draw 'em away. We know you're important or you wouldn't be a'going with us. Ain't gonna tell what our names be, don't want'a know yours. Anybody git caught, won't have noth'en to tell. We gonna be on a rough trail hardly fit for a hog. You fall off your horse or git hit by a limb, you don't holler or cuss, you don't make no sound. You git back in the saddle, hurt or not. We'll do you the best we can. Remember, the only thing that will git you to the river is silence. I hold my hand up like this, you stop. I motion like this, you come on. I motion like this, you turn quietly and backtrack. Don't worry none 'bout these horses. They woods broke. You got any questions let's hear 'em."

Semmes and Quinn shook their heads.

"All right. No talking. Let's go."

The group of five moved eastward through woods, fording creeks, skirting farms and towns, almost always at a walk. At intervals the leader would signal a halt to listen a while, then signal forward once again. First night, they slept on the ground in a well hidden hollow. No fire. They ate jerky and hardtack. The next day, nearing the river, they entered into swampland following cattle and hog trails where they existed. Noticing highwater marks on trees, Jonathan felt fortunate that the water level was seasonally low. He was also thankful it was winter. In warmer weather, the mosquitoes would have eaten them alive, there would be plenty of snakes to contend with and you wouldn't be allowed to shoot them. There would also be the possibility of surprising a gator. He didn't envy the couriers their jobs. They rode on, slopping through mud and marsh, ducking under low limbs, crossing shallow bayous and taking advantage of the cover provided by thickly wooded hammocks where sunlight, probing the leaves of gum, cypress, water oak and pine dappled the shaded riders with green and yellow flecks. The silence of their passage was broken only by the clop of horses' hooves on dampened earth and occasionally by startled birds that flitted and fussed in the branches above them.

After dark, as planned, the clandestine party reached the Mississippi. The Union army had contracted anything that would float to be used as an armed picket boat, one anchored every three miles along the entire southern stretch of river. Most were manned by river rascals who, besides making a sport of shooting at anyone who tried to cross the river, fattened their pokes by trading Union supplies at highly inflated prices to desperate civilians.

In a slough off the west bank, the couriers uncovered a well-hidden skiff and placed the mail and travelers aboard.

The leader whispered, "We got to git 'fore the moon come up." They were the only words spoken during the entire leg of the trip.

Two of the men, using muffled oars, rowed quietly out of the slough into the river while the third man attended the horses. The skiff crossed within a half mile of a picket boat anchored upstream. The skilled oarsmen worked hard to cross before the current could carry them down on the next picket boat. They slipped the oar blades silently into the water on the power stroke and never touched the feathered blades to the surface on the back swing.

Upon reaching the east bank, the exhausted oarsmen let the boat drift slowly along in the shallows. One of the men softly mimicked an owl's call every few minutes. A hundred yards downstream the signal was answered. A man stepped from the shadows and helped pull the bow of the skiff onto shore. With mail pouches exchanged and passengers safely on the east bank, the oarsmen cast off, pulling hard against the current for the west bank.

Three horses were brought up by a second man. They had been told to expect only one traveler. The men gave Semmes and Quinn each a horse. Before either one could protest, one of the couriers whispered, "We can pick up another horse on up the way a couple of miles." He swung up double behind the other courier on the third horse.

Jonathan knew Shamrock was only a day or two ride upriver. Still he whispered, "I can go with you, Admiral. I'm fit enough."

Semmes shook his head and whispered back, "Son, you've done about as much as any man could for the cause. Even if I make it all the way to Richmond, which is doubtful, it will be to make the obligatory and senseless last stand, maybe buy a little time to negotiate better terms of surrender. Mr. Quinn, you made your stand on the deck of *Alabama*. Go home. Find your family if you can. If you don't get captured or shot, you can make it before Christmas. Besides," Semmes smiled, "you look so damn mean with that scar and patch I doubt if anyone will mess with you."

Raphael Semmes returned Jonathan's nod in lieu of salute and disappeared following the couriers into the woods. The date was December, 22, 1864.

CHAPTER 7

Nicodemus liked to combine his nightly call to nature with his habit of "checkin' fo' any strange doings 'round de place." Before the Quinn ladies moved in next door, he used to pee off his porch and stand there a while listening for any sound out of the ordinary. He was always relieved to hear only normal sounds of his night sentinels, the call of an owl, the fidgeting of some coon or fox passing through, and in warm weather, cicadas, crickets and frogs. If such sentinels suddenly fell silent, he would know something was scaring them and couldn't go to bed until he knew what it was. Only when satisfied all was well could he go inside and sleep peacefully. But since the ladies moved in next door, Nicodemus felt obliged to change his nightly habit a little. He would walk up the trail toward the old place a ways where he could pee out of hearing and sight of the ladies and still do his nightly surveillance.

On this night, Christmas Eve, the moon was playing hide and seek ducking in and out from behind ragged clouds driven across the winter sky. Other than the wind rustling through the treetops, the night seemed ordinary. He was just before turning back to his cabin when he heard a faint sound, a clunk like that of a horse's hoof striking a rock. That got his attention. He walked a little distance on up the lane and stood still to listen. Drifting on the night air was the unmistakable sound of a horse approaching from the ruins of the big house. Nicodemus rushed down the lane to get Daniel Quinn.

"Massa Daniel!" he said breathlessly. "Wake up Massa Daniel! A horseman coming, already close."

Nannie heard Nicodemus urging Daniel out of his cabin. She joined the two men, giving Daniel Tom Boatner's pistol and sending Nicodemus to fetch the shotgun. Dressed in longjohns and propped on his crutches, Daniel waited where he could see down the lane toward the ruins.

The racing moon would break from a cloud to light the lane ghostly white, then disappear behind another. The rider came into view like an apparition, faintly visible in moonlight one moment, disappearing in darkness the next.

Daniel raised the pistol, "That's far enough, stranger. You best identify yourself and state your business 'fore I blow a nice big hole in your belly."

The stranger laughed. "You better shoot that thing or put it away. I'm too tired and cold to stand around wait'en for you to make up your mind."

Daniel recognized the voice. "Jonathan, is that you, son?" The rider swung down from the saddle. "The Shamrock I remember was always lit up like an opera house. You people are hard to find in the dark."

Nannie rushed from the shadows and threw her arms around her son, "Oh! Jonathan! Thank God."

"Mama," was all Jonathan could manage. A tear escaped his good eye and trickled down his cheek.

Daniel stood absentmindedly holding the gun pointed as before. Annielise, frightened that a stranger was approaching, quieted her baby daughter as she and Arabella peered from the doorway of her darkened cottage trying to hear the muffled voices coming from the head of the lane that led toward the slave cabins. Then she heard her mother cry out, "Jonathan!" Annielise handed the child to Arabella.

The moon broke out once more and Jonathan saw the figure of a girl running down the lane, her hair and night clothes streaming behind her in the soft lunar light.

"Sister! By God you're all grown up." He grabbed her in his arms, lifting her off the ground. He hadn't seen her for over four years, not since he had left home for his last year at Marion. She had been barely thirteen at the time.

"Well, time has passed all right, Brother, and there comes the proof." Annielise pointed to Arabella coming toward them carrying a baby. "Old Uncle Jonathan, meet your niece, Bethany."

"My niece!"

"All right," growled Daniel. "The devil with standing out here in the cold. Although I'm a mite disappointed I didn't get to shoot anybody, getting ready to do it has made me hungry. Come on, Arabella, my grandson is home. Let's have a celebration."

"We gonna celebrate all right. We gonna celebrate you not blowing yo' grandson's head off. Dat's what we all gonna celebrate." Arabella started for the kitchen.

"Woman!" hollered the senior Quinn, "You gonna git too smart with me one of these days and I'm gonna throw you off the place." Arabella kept walking with the baby in her arms. "Child, yo' gots about the meanest, sweetest great-granddaddy in the whole world. He could scare the Devil his self, but not the peoples he loves."

Nicodemus went ahead to the kitchen to stoke up the fire and light an oil lamp to guide the group walking at Daniel's slow pace.

Once inside, Arabella turned to Jonathan, the baby in her arms. "Here, take yo' niece and get acquainted while I makes coffee."

Jonathan backed away. He had seen his mother try to hide her shock at seeing his face in the kitchen lamp light and was not ready to frighten children. Arabella insisted. Beverly Bethany Quinn reached her small hands out to him. He took her in his arms and they looked at one another. The child was beautiful. Her coal black hair was set off by the same fair complexion as her mother. She had a serious expression on her face which Jonathan took as a signal that tears would soon follow. Bethany raised the index finger of her small right hand and touched the black eye patch. Then she ran her finger along the deep scar, tracing it up his forehead and back around to the damaged ear. Jonathan did not move. Neither did those in the room who traced the same path with their eyes. When the child reached the half ear, she felt all around it, and then felt her own ear. Jonathan laughed at her inquisitive comparison. Bethany looked at him, grabbed his half ear again and laughed with him. It was a moment that would bond old Uncle Jonathan to that baby girl for life. Arabella took the baby to carry her back to the cottage for bed, but she would have none of it. She screamed her protest and to the surprise of everyone stretched out her arms to Jonathan.

"It's just my universal appeal to women," he smiled.

"Oh, let her stay awhile, Arabella," Annielise said.

Everyone had questions. Jonathan was totally perplexed by his sister having a child named Quinn. "Who is the father, and where is he?"

"The father used to hang mounted in gold around my neck," Annielise said, "but it got thrown in the fire, melted away to nothing I guess."

"Sister, I'm too tired for riddles. Who is, or was my brother-in-law?"

Jonathan was astounded by the story of the little girl called "Bullet Baby" by his sister and grandfather to the obvious irritation of his mother and Arabella. He was amused when he heard how his sister got marched out of town. Grandfather Daniel was not.

"I should have shot that son of a bitch provost marshal."

"Now, Grandfather," Annielise said, "watch that kind of language in front of this child. Besides, they'd have hanged you."

"By God, they'd have hanged a contented man." Jonathan laughed out loud.

"Nicodemus," Arabella said, "move de lamp to the table so I can serve a little somethin' to these folks."

Everyone took a seat and Arabella served up a slice of cold cornbread spread with a portion of precious honey and poured a cup of even more precious hot, black coffee. As the conversation turned to more current subjects, Jonathan listened quietly to his family talk proudly about the hard work they were doing to improve their living conditions. He began to understand the reality of the hardships his family was suffering. He took a closer look at the faces reflected in the lamp light and was shocked to discover that his mother and sister had the sun baked skin and the rough hands of field workers. Before the war, no Southern lady would allow her skin to be tanned by the sun. His private thoughts were interrupted. It was, he discovered, his turn to entertain the listeners. He began with Deuteronomy Jones. Those at Shamrock were enthralled by the stories Jonathan told of his travels around the world, and as appalled by his account of the last battle of *Alabama* as he had been by their descriptions of the siege of Vicksburg.

It was one in the morning when Jonathan carried the sleeping baby to her homemade crib, hugged and kissed his sister, and followed Nicodemus to the "guest" cabin. Once inside and alone, he stripped down to his longjohns, blew out the lamp, and crawled exhausted into bed. It had hardly been the glorious, triumphant homecoming he had imagined almost four years ago when he ran away from school to go to war. Lying in the chill of the little cabin, he didn't know whether to cry over all that had happened since, or to laugh at the naive boy he had been that day. Almost too tired to sleep he remembered it was Christmas Eve.

Jonathan opened his eyes in the dim, false-dawn that portended the lifting of a darkness that had cloaked his homecoming and filled his fitful sleep with mournful thoughts of the death of his father and the obliteration of the life his family had known before the war. In the stillness he dressed and walked up the frost laden lane toward the ruins of Shamrock. The creeping sunrise banished the shadows slowly as if they were reluctant to unveil before him the barren piles of ash and tall, blackened chimneys that stood testimony to a grandness that was finished. There, alone in the chill of a Christmas dawn, the boy-returned-scarred-warrior thought, *At least on the sea, war leaves no mark. The waves roll on, their beauty undiminished by the events of man.*

"Merry Christmas, everyone!" Ted Perkins arrived, half frozen just at sundown. When he saw Jonathan he jumped down from the wagon. "Jonathan Hillary Quinn!" Ted Perkins grabbed the boy and hugged him. "What a wonderful Christmas this is. No wonder your mother looks so radiant."

Ted had driven half the cold winter night and all day to reach Shamrock in time for Christmas dinner as he had done every year since his wife died. He arrived in a wagon instead of his buckboard. The doctor fetched a basket of food stuffs from under the seat and handed it to Arabella. He didn't disturb a tarpaulin covering something bulky in the wagon bed and refused to answer questions concerning the mysterious cargo.

"I'm about frozen stiff. Ya'll quit askin' questions and git me in that warm kitchen." The family and their guest sat down to a feast of potato soup, baked opossum, turnips, hoe cakes, homemade scuppernong wine, and afterwards, hot, black coffee.

Ted had fidgeted all during the meal and could sit still no longer. "Never could turn down Christmas dinner at Shamrock, especially not this one." With a big grin he announced, "I have a surprise. Nicodemus, I'll need your help out at my wagon."

Everyone in the kitchen exchanged questioning glances. A few minutes later Ted and Nicodemus returned pulling a green, freshly-painted goat wagon complete with harness. The wagon, too wide to squeeze through the doorway, was positioned just outside the kitchen entrance. Everyone gathered to see what surprise the wagon held concealed beneath a blanket. With a flourish Ted jerked the blanket away. There followed astonished silence.

Sitting in the wagon, brightly reflecting lamplight spilling through the doorway, was a silver punch bowl eighteen inches in diameter at the thick, decorative rim that was inlaid around its circumference with inch high, green cloisonne shamrocks. Ted Perkins lifted the heavy bowl in his arms and carried it inside to the table.

The Quinns stood silently around the splendid piece. It looked incongruous sitting on a table made from rough sawn lumber surrounded by tin plates, enameled cups, chipped china, and canning jars; the only place settings available for guests or family.

Ted expected his surprise to garner approval, but as he looked at the expressions around him he wondered if in returning the beautiful bowl to its rightful owners he had made a mistake.

Nannie expressed everyone's thoughts, "Oh Lord! Did we ever really live like that? Have things like that? I dream of the way it was, and when I wake, I know it would be easier to face the day if it all had only been a dream." She reached out and touched it as if making sure it was real. "Daddy Quinn gave this to Ansel and me as a wedding present." She was afraid to wipe away the tears in the corners of her eyes, afraid Ted, with his wonderful surprise, might see the pain it had brought.

"By God! Where on earth did you find it?" Daniel asked. "And how the hell did you pay to get it back?"

All eyes turned to Theodore Perkins.

"Close the door and stoke up that fire a little, open that bottle of bourbon I brought, and I'll tell you the tale." The men all took a slash of bourbon. The ladies declined.

"All right, Ted, out with it," Daniel commanded.

"I saw that bowl sittin' in the window of a carpetbagger's buy-and-sell store across from the marketplace in Natchez. I was there to visit Jefferson Jay Little. By the way, both he and Tom Boatner send their best. Now, I knew there was no other silver bowl like it, Daniel. I knew that you had ordered it custom made from England just for the wedding. No doubt where it came from, so I brought it back to Shamrock."

"You mean to tell me the shop keeper just smiled and gave it to you?"

"He gave it to me, but I don't remember a smile."

"Come on, Ted, tell the story."

"Well, I walked into the shop. The owner saw me lookin' at the bowl. He offered, 'That's a mighty fine piece, ain't it?' To his delight I agreed it was indeed a pretty piece. 'These days, I don't see many well-dressed gentlemen such as you, sir,' he smiled at me through rotten teeth. I was wearing the best suit I own for the medical meeting Jay and I were attending, all about epidemics, fevers and such that usually follow wars, you see. River towns usually git 'em first. Anyway, I nodded in agreement. Because of my clothes and my black bag, I think he took me for a prosperous scallywag out bargain huntin'. He stroked his beard and said it would be worth not a penny less than eight hundred dollars in Philadelphia, but recognizing that the marketplace in Natchez wasn't boomin', he'd let me have it for a mere two hundred in gold or Yankee dollars. I raised my eyes and remarked that the price seemed a little high taking into consideration how much of that kind of stuff thievin' Yankee soldiers were pawnin' as they got tired of carrying it. 'I don't know nothing about thieving,' he countered, 'but I'm fair as I can be with soldiers and darkies alike. Yes, Sir. Why, I come down here on account of slavery is an abomination. I come here with a Bible and a cash box. The way I look at it, paying 'em for that stuff they done found laying round abandoned is a way of supplementin' them brave soldiers' pay. As for them poor darkies, you ought to see 'em smile when I give 'em the first cash money they ever had. Yes sir! Doing business with them soldiers and darkies is akin to charitable work. I'm going to tithe the Lord's share out of my profits, give it to the church when I get back to Pittsburgh, yes sir. To the glorious victors of a righteous cause go the spoils I say, and I'm going to give the Lord his fair share. You can trust me on that,' he said.

"I started to leave to keep from killing him, but he didn't know that. He wanted to make a sale. He asked me where I was going in such a hurry. Said to make him an offer." Ted Perkins looked around the room.

"Well? What did you say?" asked the senior Quinn.

"Now, you know me, Daniel, a kind and peace-loving physician. I smiled and told him I was leaving to go fetch the Yankee provost marshal to come hang him for receiving stolen property. You know that fellow drew himself up and looked downright insulted, said he was a good and loyal Union citizen trying to bring commerce to a war-torn country and righteousness to the poor, newly-freed masses. 'Yes Sir,' he said, picking up his Bible, 'Those pagan darkies are God's children just the same, and I give 'em good Yankee money in fair trade fer what they brung in here same as I treat soldiers and poor folks selling belongings. It ain't my business to know where they got the stuff.'

"That was when I shoved the hypocritical little bastard onto a table with one hand, and slammed my black bag down beside him with the other. Holding him fast by the throat, I took my bone saw out of the bag. 'Now you greedy little self-righteous fraud, listen carefully to me,' I told him. 'I'm goin' to take that punch bowl back to the rightful owners just as soon as you polish it for all you're worth, and furthermore, I snarled at him, you aren't gonna say one word to anyone, or do you see this?' I pressed my shiny steel bone saw down the ridge of his nose. He looked cross-eyed at it. I told him he could give me that bowl to return to its rightful owners or have his choice of either getting sawed in half from his crotch on up, or getting his prissy, pharisaic self hanged before God and everybody by the provost marshal of Natchez. That's when, in spite of my not wanting to damage my surgical instrument, I took two good noisy strokes cutting into the table between his legs, just for fun, don't you know. I think that's when he peed his pants."

The doctor fell silent and took a sip of his bourbon. "I've gotten a little carried away with the language, ladies, and do apologize." The room was silent.

"Well, Ted?" Nannie said, "Don't stop now. What happened?" Ted grinned, "Don't you know that little weasel went right to work polishing that thing. I couldn't stop him for the next half hour. He got it shiny too, don't you think?"

"Damn, if you don't still amuse the hell out of me, Teddy," said Daniel, "When we gonna go up there and saw the little bastard in two? Tell him I'm the nurse."

"While I'm amusing you, Daniel, let me explain your Christmas present."

"Sounds to me like you don't think I'll like it."

"Well, just let me explain." Ted continued, "The bowl, which cost me nothing, is a present to Shamrock. Your present is the wagon."

"Wagon? The goat wagon? Looks like one old goat pulling a trick on another old goat to me. What's the punch line?"

"Well, from one old goat to another, it's no joke."

Daniel looked at his friend questioningly and the doctor continued. "I don't intend for you to pull it, Daniel. I intend for you to ride in it. You'll notice it's padded nicely, has a chair back, and is easy to get on and off of even for an ornery, stiff old curmudgeon like you, easier than trying to climb up on a real wagon. You got a big billy goat to pull it, thanks to Nicodemus' and Arabella's present last Christmas. It's a lot better way to cover activities on this place come spring planting than that pair of crutches, Daniel."

"Damnit to hell, Ted, if you don't have the most twisted sense of humor of any half crazy quack ever practiced medicine. It will be a cold day in hell before you see Daniel Hillary Quinn, master of this plantation yet, by God, riding in a child's goat wagon. (*It was a cold day in January, to be exact.*) Daniel continued, "I ought to hit you with this crutch for joking on me like that."

"You already did last Christmas when I brought the pair of them out here."

Daniel Hillary managed to look chastised and angry at the same time.

"All right you two, that's enough. It's my turn now." Jonathan stood up holding two packages. "Neither of you deserves them, but here is a box apiece of the finest Cuban cigars direct from Havana." He handed his grandfather and Ted Perkins each a package. They handled the boxes as if they had just been given the Holy Grail.

"And now for the rest of you children," he said, "Close your eyes and hold out a hand. That includes y'all, Arabella, Nicodemus. No peeking now."

He placed a twenty-dollar gold piece into the hands of his mother and sister, and ten dollar coins into the outstretched hands of Nicodemus and Arabella.

"You can open your eyes now."

They did, and were as surprised at the shiny coins in their hands as any child on Christmas morning. Before they could comment on the gifts, Jonathan pulled a leather pouch from inside his coat and noisily emptied its contents of gold coins into the Shamrock bowl. Everyone in the room was startled wide eyed.

"My God, Boy, what did you do, rob the Yankee treasury?" roared Grandfather Quinn.

"It's Yankee gold all right, taken from the prizes of war captured by *Alabama*, but it came to me as honest pay. I didn't have much of anything to spend it on, so I asked Captain Semmes to keep most of it for me in the ship's safe. Captain Semmes had the good sense to send the ship's gold and payroll records ashore before the last battle.

"Now I want you all to use the gold in your hands to buy something special for yourself and for no other purpose. As for the rest, I figure if you sell that bowl and add the proceeds to the money I dropped in it, you ought to have just enough to stave off the wolves for the first year, feed yourselves, and maybe put in a little cash crop. That's how I would like to see it used."

"But son," Nannie protested, "what about you? We can't take all your money. What are your plans?"

"His plans?" Daniel said, "Why, he's gonna stay right here and rebuild Shamrock like me and his daddy before him. That's right, isn't it, son?"

"Part of it is, Granddaddy. I'm going to help rebuild the best way I know how. I've been a lot of places, listened to a lot of smart men talking; Englishmen, Frenchmen. They've learned a thing or two about the financial aftermath of war, both from the losing and winning side. What Shamrock must have is capital. Without it we'll just be working the place for the tax man, the carpetbaggers and scallywags who'll buy it for the debt and taxes we can't pay. People like us with land down here will likely be forced to borrow money from the Northern bankers.

They are gonna come down here, smile, and lend money to a land owner like us knowing we can't pay it back. They'll say how sorry they are to call the loan and take the land. Those who don't borrow money are gonna lose their land to tax sales. Yankees and scallywags will buy it for pennies on the dollar. We've lost the war and that's the way it's gonna be."

Everyone waited for the senior Quinn to explode in rage at hearing anything about losing 'The Cause'. Instead he sat back in his chair and lowered his eyes.

Jonathan continued, "I never had a chance to learn much about farming, but I know the sea. There's trade to be had and money to be made there. I'll stay and work to get in spring plantin'. Then I'll try to find Deuteronomy Jones or some other ship owner who will give me a berth. I'll send every penny I make back here. Otherwise, we'll wind up having to sell the place off a piece at a time until there's nothing left." The room fell silent.

Annielise picked up Bethany and set her in the punch bowl. The baby laughed and swished the gold coins around. "I remember getting in trouble for sneaking a cup of punch out of this thing." Annielise laughed. "It was a little strong for a six year old."

Daniel Quinn perked up. "Look at that great granddaughter of mine already taking to gold and silver. She's a Quinn alright. Aren't you darlin'?" Bethany giggled.

The bowl became Bethany's favorite plaything. She would crawl around it trying to pick the green shamrocks off its rim. Arabella used it to hold the baby's bath water.

Jonathan didn't have to find Deuteronomy. On the fifteenth of March 1865 the good doctor picked up a letter addressed to Mrs. Ansel Quinn, General Delivery, Vicksburg, Mississippi, and sent it on to Shamrock. Crudely written in pencil, it read:

Santiago de Cuba, January 2, 1865

J.H. Quinn,

Can't handle everything by myself much longer. Been waiting fer yer. Knowed you'd get through the war with only a piece or two missin'. The sea has you now boy and a ship of your own is waitin'. A certain English scoundrel, name of Jeremy Wright, has business representing yours truly in Vicksburg. He will explain things to you when he arrives the first week in April. Will expect you to proceed to Nassau with him by way of Cuba. This ain't no invitation. It's an order.

D. Jones

Jonathan would be leaving Shamrock and soon. If he was to help Daniel manage the planting before he left, there was no time to waste in hiring help and procuring the seed and tools necessary to get the job done.

* * *

Among the occupation troops there was a trio of misfits who had passed through myriad cracks and rat holes to be assigned, by caliginous chance, to the same mess tent in Vicksburg. All three shared one thing in common; they had been given their choice of joining the army or going to jail.

McKenna was from Philadelphia. He was a big man, sloppy, unkempt. He had killed a man in a bar room fight. McKenna liked to bully smaller men but didn't care much for fighting at the front. Some officer finally had sense enough to make him a mess sergeant and leave him behind with the occupation forces.

McKenna wound up with two particularly despicable miscreants as cooks. One was a little caitiff from Peoria named Wylie Weaver. He had a stumpy build, weak chin, close-set, pig eyes and bad teeth. Weaver had been a merchant of sorts, sold things which didn't belong to him. Wylie got to be a cook the second time he was found playing dead as his unit advanced under fire. They would have shot him, but were short a cook.

A slim, clean, neat soldier named McNamara completed the trio. He looked more like a chaplain's assistant than a mess cook. McNamara's offense was different. He liked to play with little girls; liked to undress them and rub his hands all over them and make them play with his 'dolly'. A Boston district police captain locked him in the basement of the jail and beat the ever-loving hell out of him with a billy club. Then he told McNamara, "You're not going to be here come dark. As much as I might like to, I can't kill you myself, but that crowd of angry fathers out there in the street is likely to storm my jail come nighttime. I'm not having a lynching in my district. I'm going to turn you loose, say you escaped. You better be gone clear out of Boston 'cause you turn up around here again, you'll be a dead son-of-a-bitch."

McNamara had no money and no place to go. He figured the army might be a good place to hide. He was right. With a war on and riots breaking out over the draft, the army wasn't asking too many questions of volunteers. Unlike McKenna and Weaver, the baby-faced McNamara took to killing; especially when things got up close. After one particularly savage engagement an officer stopped him, concerned that he was hurt. "That's a lot of blood on you son, don't you need to go to the aid station?"

McNamara smiled, "No sir. It ain't mine; came from Johnny Reb. I got in real close and used this on him." He drew a twelve-inch knife from his belt and smiled up at the officer. Killing with a knife, he had discovered, gave him visceral pleasure akin to sex.

McNamara got to be an army cook for practical reasons. He not only knew how to cook, he knew how to bake bread, cakes and pies. His overbearing mother had taught him. He was a soldier's dream; he could bake just like mom.

Assigned to McKenna's cook tent, McNamara missed the killing but found other diversions. He discovered that leftovers, especially anything sweet, would bring the town's children out in droves. They were always hungry. The army had orders to feed the freed blacks, but not the Southern white population. The children called him Baker Man and gathered around the minute they saw him coming. He hadn't gotten a chance to get any of the little girls alone yet, but he sometimes was able to put his hands on them.

BOOK THREE

SHAMROCK

CHAPTER 8

Daniel figured that with the mule Theodore had left them and a second mule and plow bought in town, they could put in a field of vegetables and maybe two hundred acres or more of cotton for a cash crop with the help of a few hired hands. For the first time since he had returned from prison, Daniel showed real enthusiasm.

"We can pay for a mule, plow, seed, supplies, and hired hands with about a quarter of the money Jonathan brought home. The silver shamrock bowl and the remainder of the gold can be held in reserve to add to whatever cash the cotton will bring to pay taxes, interest and supplies for next winter. If we have to, we can sell off a little of the land."

"Hiring won't be easy," Ted Perkins had told them. "And you can't expect to hire the same bunch of freedmen for the whole season. Soon as you pay the first group for plantin', they'll take off and y'all will have to hire another bunch to work the cotton and pick it. That's freedom to 'em. The damn Yankees are turning hundreds of thousands of the poor devils out on their own in a defeated South with no money, no credit, nothing. The Union won't feed 'em forever, will they? Land owners can't hire 'em all. I never liked the idea of slavery, you know that, but the way things are now, some of those poor people are gonna wind up worse off freed for a while than they were as slaves."

Neither Jonathan nor Annielise could go into town. Jonathan had no parole papers and could be arrested. Annielise couldn't leave the baby and might be recognized as one of the young women exiled by General McPherson's order. The senior Quinn wasn't fit to make the long, bumpy wagon ride to town. That left Nannie the chore of making the trip to hire freedmen to do the spring planting. Nannie would carry enough of the gold coins to pay for supplies and convince the hired hands that the Quinns had money with which to pay them. Nicodemus would handle the wagon and provide protection of sorts. Even before the war a Southern lady never went anywhere alone. Now that Vicksburg was occupied by Yankee soldiers and freed black men, Daniel Quinn insisted it simply wasn't safe for any white woman to be alone on the town streets much less on the road.

They left at three in the morning. Nicodemus put the shotgun, a jug of water and a basket of food under the seat, loaded lap robes and a gutta-percha gum blanket in back, and helped Nannie up on the wagon. After a few hours on the road it turned chilly and began to rain. Rapped in the lap robes and shielded from the rain as well as possible with the gutta-percha gum blanket, they road in silence for a long while. The steady clop of the mule's hooves, the squeak and rattle of the old wagon and the pitter-patter of light rain on the gum blanket played a syncopated rhythm in the dark stillness before dawn. The rain stopped as gently as it had begun, leaving gossamer tendrils of mist scattered over the road. They could smell the moldering leaves on the forest floor as they descended into wooded hollows, smell the damp clods of earth turned up by the mule's hooves. Occasionally they scared up roosting birds that fluttered noisily away, some squawking in protest at being so rudely disturbed. Once a great owl swooped low over their heads to snatch up some small, unfortunate creature they could not see in the darkness ahead. The clouds moved on south-eastward leaving a clear velvet night sky. There was only a sliver of moon, but the crystal starlight was sufficient to outline the road.

"Nicodemus?" Nannie was on the wagon seat beside him.

"Yas'm," he replied.

"Tell me about what happened when the soldiers came to Shamrock."

The old black man sat up straight as a board. "Aw, Miss Nannie, you don't want to hear 'bout dat. I don't know much nohow. Jes' tried to stay out de way."

"Now, Nicodemus, don't be scared to talk about it. You need to tell it as bad as I need to hear it. You can't go into an attic and resign yourself to living there until you know what's in the dark corners. Help me get rid of my dark corners, Nicodemus. I need the truth, to know everything the way it happened. Can you understand that?"

"Yas'm," was all he said for a while, the mule walking slow, the rough road jarring the hard sprung wagon seat he shared with the mistress of the place where he had lived as a slave most all his life. The old white-haired man sat wrestling with the conflict inside himself. Nannie could sense it, he knew she could. *There's nothin' fo' it, I reckon.* Looking straight ahead he began. "Massa Daniel took you and Miss Annielise to town wit' Arabella. Den de war done come close and got y'all stuck there when de Yankees done cross de river to fence in Vicksburg. We done hear all about dat. Weren't no time foe de overseer, Massa Bates, he heard 'bout Yankees comin' down de roads tearing up ever'thing. Directly, a whole bunch of black folk come by down yonder on de main road and says de Yankees was camping close and would be here and free us just like dey done already freed dem. Some was dressed funny, all in silk and finery and hats come from the bighouse of dey's plantations. Some carried things what been took, all kind of stuff, jes' crazy.

"Well, we is happy to hear we gone be freed, but maybe scared some. Massa Bates, he scared too, frettin' and yellin' at everybody git near him. We seen dat. Now you and Massa Daniel been good to us at de bighouse, but Massa Bates could be rough on de field hands. He done whoop mens and womens without y'all knowing noth'en 'bout it, without telling Massa Daniel or Massa Ansel. Whoops 'um, he says, for working too slow pulling cotton. Says dey gonna cost him his bonus if dey slacks off and don't meet what he calls de quota. Massa Bates tells 'em what gots whooped, if dey tells Massa Daniel he'll sell 'em off to de cane fields in Louisiana. Dem cane fields is meaner than cotton, Miss Nannie."

Nannie hadn't known about that, wished it wasn't true, but said nothing, fearing Nicodemus might stop talking.

"Anyway, Massa Bates, he jes' up and loads two wagons with his stuff and some of ya'lls stuff from the bighouse and left de place.

"Nobody did much a nothing. Jes' waiting fo' to be told what to do. We always been told what to do. Massa Bates, he ain't say stay, ain't say leave, ain't say nothin' foe he go. Everybody scared to leave. Some say dey hear Rebs shoot niggas what leave dey place. Next day from de top of the big ridge we could see smoke way off yonder. Folks on de road say Yankee soldiers was burning all de plantations dey come to.

"Wit' Massa Bates gone, everybody figure us done be free already. 'We is free!' dey shouts and commence to singing and dancing, all kinds of foolishness. Folks goes to de big house hollerin' and carryin' on. Dey says might as well not leave nothin' foe to burn and starts takin' what fancy 'em. It be a sight I'm shamed of. Dem field niggas gits into Massa Quinn's whiskey and start taking things saying dey was gonna sell what all dey was takin' and maybe go up North. Course nary a one of dem field hands knowed what nothing was worth. Most of em don't know where de North is even, or how far 'tis.

"Jes' fo' soldiers come up to de place next mornin'. We 'speck dey gonna look all fine like picture book soldiers, but dey is dirty and soiled, same as de Grays, jes' look better fed than our boys, I mean de Rebs, and all of 'em got shoes. Dey seen ain't nobody 'round but black folks. Ole Rattler and Bonaparte take after 'em and them Yankees shot them po' dogs. Laugh 'bout it. Directly, lots mo' soldiers come on de place. Dey rides 'round lookin' and noddin' to us'en saying we is all free to go. Don't say go where. Didn't even make no suggestions. I's thinkin' jes' where in de dickens was I gonna go old as I be?

"Anyway, dem soldiers, most of 'em, dey done rode up to de bighouse and went in to get what dey wanted. Weren't no officer wit' 'em I could see. Dey done commence to bust up everythin'; push de piano out de music room right off de veranda, bust it to pieces. Laugh 'bout it. Dey throwed all de books out de study windows and cusses the blacks foe takin' stuff dey wanted.

"Directly, I wandered through de bighouse myself, looking at de mess done been made. I heard shoutin' and looked off de gallery to see 'bout two dozen soldiers commence to ridin' all over de place setting near 'bout everything on fire. Two of 'em rides up to de house lookin' up at me. 'Hey! Ol' nigga!' one of 'em hollers. 'Yo' better get's down from yonder less'en you want's to burn.' Dey throws torches right in de front doe. Foe I leaves I looks around real quick, and Miss Nannie, I done took some of Massa Daniel's clothes. Dis here shirt I's wearing be de best of 'em. I'm wearin' it so I be dressed proper foe taking you to town. And, Miss Nannie, I done took a plate and a cup and a fork and spoon and knife, like what I done always set out on de table foe all y'all. I eats wit' 'em in my cabin foe ya'll git hea'. I'll give 'em back. Wouldn't took nothing 'cept it was all gonna burn."

He turned his head toward Nannie dropping his eyes, "I sho hopes yo' ain't gonna run me off or tell Massa Daniel."

"I told you, Nicodemus, I wouldn't tell anyone. Those things are yours to keep, but tell me the rest and then I can let it be."

"Yas'm." Nicodemus focused back on the mule's rump. "Mo' soldiers come and loaded up all de food dey could find, took what was gathered and picked all what was still in the field, what de army could eat and what dey horses could eat. Loaded all dat in army wagons and Massa Daniels wagons too. Dey took all de livestock and chickens 'dey could catch, and done left. Everybody done party dat night by de light of all de fires. Next day folks start leaving, said de army gonna feed 'em all dey wants. I stayed on de only place I knows. Be's too old to take to no road."

The old man paused. "Miss Nannie, dat's the whole of it, 'cept I got two mo' shirts and a pair of pants of his'en what I will give back, but he sho' might be mad wit' me. I done told you de truth. You was right, my soul done feel mo' better fo' tellin' it."

Nannie didn't look at him, didn't want to show the tears streaming down her cheeks. "I thank you for it, Nicodemus. I just had to know all of it if I'm to put it behind me. We all have to look to tomorrow now. Can't look back, Nicodemus, mustn't look back. You keep the clothes and don't worry about Mr. Quinn. I'm glad you're here with us and so is he. Bless you for staying."

Nicodemus nodded but didn't look at her. He hadn't told her quite all of it, hadn't told about the field hands spitting and stomping on the family portraits, or how they shouted 'Hallelujah!' when the bighouse started to burn, or the cheering as the windows burst like cannon fire, or how the grand old oak and magnolia trees that shaded the house exploded in flame from heat so intense that it was painful to the skin from more than a hundred yards away. He had told her enough, he reckoned. *She too fine a lady to have to hear any mo' 'bout all dat.* He would say no more about the fires of Shamrock that would forever burn in his memory.

The first rays of sunrise foretold a fine spring-like day. Lark and mourning dove winged across fields of dead cotton stalks overtaken by weeds, scraggly brush and pine saplings spreading from adjacent woodlands. A red fox raced across the road in front of the wagon and disappeared into the brush. On down the road a blurred whirring of winged flight heralded a flushed covey of quail.

The morning sun chased the chill from the two figures riding silently in slow, lonely passage down the rutted, sandy-clay road. Occasionally they could see the ruins of burned plantations. Once in a while they passed standing farm houses abandoned and gone to ruin, claimed by creeper vines entwining the porch railings and climbing up the board siding. On a few places they saw families working small gardens. None paused to wave. The only farm animal they saw was one swayback mule hitched to a plow with a young boy struggling behind.

"You did good saving that cow, Nicodemus. Looks like one army or the other has taken just about every horse and cow."

"Sho' does, Miss Nannie."

"Used to be a dog or two would run out to the road to herald the passage of strangers, but there hasn't been a one this morning, not the bark of a feist nor the bay of a hound. What do you reckon happened to them all?"

"Dey gone wit dey families, I reckon, or starve wit no one around to feed 'em. Likely some done been ate."

"We're doing a little better than most around here aren't we Nicodemus?"

"I reckon we is. Miss Nannie."

Nannie grew silent in thought. *Four years ago even the poorest of these places made do. Look at them now. Their men all went to war, husbands, sons. Like my Ansel, so many won't be coming home. Dr. Ted says many of those who do return will be too crippled to do farm work. Where have they gone; the women and children and the old folks from all these cold, gray, burned out farms? What will they do? God, could all this be your wrath over slavery? Is that what it is, God? Did you send Moses back down to set the black people free, or is it just punishment for stupid Southern pride and arrogance? Did you just turn your back on us, God, and let all this happen, or did you make it happen, retribution like in the Old Testament?*

When they arrived in Vicksburg, Nannie made arrangements to stay with the minister of the Episcopal church and his wife. Staying at Ted Perkins' home wouldn't be proper, she decided, though she gladly accepted his invitation for dinner. She put on her best dress, the one she had a seamstress make after receiving news of her husband's death. It was one of only two decent dresses she now owned. All the others were worn and patched, ruined by field work. The widow Quinn's black dress did not stand out in public. It was rare in Vicksburg to see a woman in any other color.

When Ted Perkins called for Nannie at the Reverent W. W. Lord's home, he was pleased to see that for the first time since the siege began, Nannie was wearing a touch of rouge on her lips and cheeks. It softened her lovely face, once light as cream, now deeply tanned by the daily demands and travails of Shamrock. Her hair, gold streaked with silver, neatly pulled back into a pinned roll at the nape of her neck reflected a lambent sheen in the soft light of the hotel dining room. Their table was surrounded by Union officers and a few Northern businessmen. Many glanced in Nannie's direction. She ignored them coldly.

"Can't say I blame 'em for noticing you," Ted smiled, "You are a beautiful lady, Mrs. Quinn. When it's proper for you to wear something besides black, I hope you will let me present you with a pretty new dress, the very best that can be found."

"You are the dearest and sweetest man I know, Ted, but I'm not at all sure that day will come."

"Well, Nannie, I'll wait patiently while I keep an eye out for a red ball gown."

"Red! You are a scandalous rake, Theodore, but I love you for the thought, and I thank you for bringing me out to dinner. I had almost forgotten such treats. How I miss the parties, the dancing, the laughter, and . . ." she paused.

"You were going to say Ansel." He took her hand, "I miss him, too, you know."

"It's nice for a lady to have such a good friend, Ted."

"Even if he is a scandalous rake twenty years your senior?"

"Even if he is a very handsome Southern gentleman who is generous and honorable and kind." She raised her glass to him.

Nicodemus set out early to recruit contract labor. He wasn't sure what contract labor meant, but he knew it wasn't slavery. He gathered a dozen or so freedmen around him on a street corner. To convince those who were interested that Shamrock could pay wages, Nicodemus showed them several five dollar gold pieces Miss Nannie had given him. A few passing citizens paused at the back of the group to see what was going on. One was a Yankee sergeant.

Later that day, Nannie walked to the Quinn townhouse thinking she might find a few personal items to take back to the farm. When she saw the house, she didn't stop, afraid of her anger, afraid if she unleashed her feelings it could lead to another Quinn confrontation with the provost. They couldn't afford that, not with Daniel's early release from prison and Jonathan's presence at Shamrock. She turned and walked away full of bitterness. Union troops were billeted in her family's townhouse. *At least they've fixed the roof and replaced the broken windows. I wonder if they'll leave any of our china or a single piece of silverware or furniture. It will probably go in a tax sale before we have enough to save it.*

She met Nicodemus at the appointed time and hired six out of the ten black men Nicodemus brought around for her to see. She told them to meet at Benton's Livery by three o'clock the next morning. Nannie deferred to Nicodemus' judgment to select the extra mule, used plow and harness they needed. She paid for them out of the money Jonathan had given Shamrock.

In chilled darkness, Nicodemus secured the plow to the side of the wagon and tied the spare mule off the back. The newly hired workers piled in with their meager belongings. Nicodemus then helped Nannie up on the seat, handed her the lap robe, climbed up next to her and took up the reins.

"Git up dere, mule!" The wagon jolted forward toward dawn and a long, bone-racking ride to Shamrock.

Jonathan was plowing when he saw a buckboard turn into the field and head straight for him. He turned the mule over to one of the hired hands, a tall, thin, rather sullen man who went by the name Blue David. As the buggy drew closer, Jonathan recognized Nicodemus up on the seat beside a stranger.

"Massa Jonathan, dis here gentleman says he has bidness wit' you. I done told 'em you busy, but he say you knowed he was coming."

The stranger held out his hand. "Jeremy Wright. I've come a long way to find you, Lieutenant Quinn."

"It's all right, Nicodemus, I've been expecting Mr. Wright." Jonathan took a rag from his back pocket and wiped the sweat from his face. "Why don't you water his horse in the creek and tie him in the shade over yonder."

"I 'speck you could do with a drink of water yourself, Mr. Wright. Sorry I can't offer anything better." The two walked across rows of newly turned rich earth to the shade of a large oak where Jonathan handed Wright a jug filled with well water.

The man was dressed in a fashionable suit, expensive polished boots, ebony cane, gold watch chain, broad-brimmed, white Panama straw hat. He was neat as a pin even after the long trip to Shamrock. He spoke with an impeccable English accent. Jonathan took an immediate dislike of Jeremy Wright.

"Suppose you tell me what Deuteronomy Jones has in mind." Wright took a long drink of water. "Captain Jones got the *Virgin* out of Mobile, made for the Bahamas and began picking up business transporting this and that among the islands, South America, Mexico, and Cuba. I was introduced to him in Havana by a mutual friend, a Cuban shipping agent. I had a contract to supply certain cargo and was in need of a ship to fetch it. Captain Jones was in need of business. We struck a deal in a rather specialized trade. He now transports lumber, machinery, food, salt, rum, whatever, and special cargo."

"Special cargo? Sounds like contraband. Just what type of cargo are we talking about, Mr. Wright?"

"Captain Jones says he trusts you completely Lieutenant Quinn, so I assume what I tell you in confidence you will keep strictly to yourself."

"Where Captain Jones is concerned, you assume correctly."

"All right, Lieutenant. The 'special cargo' we handle consists of arms, mostly rifled muskets and ammunition. It's a very, very profitable trade. There appears to be no shortage of unrest in Latin America and the Caribbean these days. Seems the natives are restless. And on my side of the Atlantic there is a market in the Balkan states, Africa and as far as the Middle East."

"Why do you and Captain Jones need me?"

"Captain Jones is getting old, tired. He wants to put ashore, enjoy some of his newly acquired wealth. He insists that you are the only man he will trust to look after his interests and sail his ship. Captain Jones knows how to make money in the shipping trade. I am quite good at negotiations, terms and conditions, that sort of thing as concerns the 'special cargo'. Most important, I have valuable contacts that help me find sources for such cargo and customers for same. For instance, I have found some opportunities due to this civil war you Americans are having. But to get back to your question. I hate crossing oceans, stay sick the whole time at sea. Captain Jones tells me that with you, he can run operations from this side of the Atlantic. I'll mostly run things on the other. That should make a very profitable partnership.

"Now weigh this carefully, Lieutenant. There's an astonishing amount of money to be had, but not without risk. I must tell you that. The powers against whom the arms we deliver are to be targeted are never amused. If we are suspected, things will get unpleasant. If caught, I expect we would meet the hangman. But there are rewards to balance the risks."

"I think that you mean *I* would meet the hangman, Mr. Wright. You don't make deliveries, if I understand you correctly. I'm to be the one in danger during pickup and delivery, danger that can come from an unscrupulous seller or buyer on one side or their enemies on the other. Those are the risks I will face, Mr. Wright. The same ones Captain Jones has been facing. Suppose you give me an example of the rewards. What would be my part?"

"I was coming to that, Lieutenant Quinn. I have an order for the purchase of as many as ten thousand captured Confederate weapons stored in Vicksburg. Never mind how I will arrange such a deal. That's how I earn my share. The point is this. We have a buyer who has the cash to pay for the merchandise. We only deal in cash . . . gold, Yankee dollars, English pounds. On this particular transaction, I estimate our cost at four dollars a rifle. In addition, a certain Union Major will receive one dollar per weapon for his cooperation. We will add two dollars and fifty cents per rifle for brokerage and shipping. That makes the cost to the customer seven dollars and fifty cents per rifle. A fair deal, you will admit. It allows us up to twenty-five thousand dollars gross, and a net profit of as much as sixteen thousand, give or take a little.

"Now for your part. Although I strongly objected, Captain Jones insists that you will be a full partner. One third of the profits will be yours should you come on board in time to handle delivery of the transaction I just mentioned. Captain Jones must think a great deal of you. There are a lot of ship's captains on the beach who would come much cheaper."

"Why don't you just hire yourself one of them and find another ship?"

"Captain Jones is honest, reliable—rare and valuable commodities in this special trade. With Captain Jones as a partner, I don't worry having my throat cut. That sort of thing has happened between partners in this trade, in any trade as lucrative as this one. Why compete? Why leave a partner proven trustworthy for a new, unknown one? Besides, I don't think Captain Jones is the sort to take a double cross lightly."

"And how about you, Mr. Wright? Can Captain Jones trust you?"

"I always deliver exactly what I've agreed to, Lieutenant Quinn, no more, no less. You can confirm that with Captain Jones."

Under the circumstances, what Jonathan thought of Mr. Wright personally didn't enter into the matter. He knew he had no choice. His family needed money and what was promised was far more than he could earn even if he could get a berth as a ship's officer.

"If I accept your offer, there is a problem. I'm not a paroled prisoner. I've not surrendered. Don't intend to. And drop the Lieutenant Quinn. The Union would love to capture an escaped member of *Alabama*'s crew. I have no papers. The river, not to mention New Orleans, belongs to the Yankees."

Jeremy Wright produced a sealed packet. "We have thought of that, Lieu . . . ah, Mr. Quinn. Here are papers to prove that you are a paroled infantry sergeant headed for home in Mandeville on the north shore of Lake Pontchartrain. You will also find a small amount of money and a steamship ticket for the river packet *T.L. Beauchamp* leaving Sunday week. Your trick will be to get past the pickets into Vicksburg. These papers will get you out. I'm afraid you'll have to travel on the cargo deck with the riffraff. Wouldn't do for you to reserve a cabin. You might have to explain how a paroled Confederate could afford such luxury. There's one more thing, Mr. Quinn. I'll also be aboard that riverboat. You and I must show no signs of recognition or communicate in any way. Wouldn't be able to explain that, would we? In New Orleans there'll be Union soldiers all over the docks. You simply walk off the boat. Before you've traveled a block, a Cuban by the name of Lopez will contact you and lead you to a safe place to stay until we are ready to sail for the Bahamas. Are you on board, Mr. Quinn?"

Jonathan nodded his head and took the packet from Wright.

"Excellent. Captain Jones said we could count on you. Do you have any questions?"

Jonathan had none. His mind had already shifted to the hard task of once again leaving his family. They needed him at Shamrock, but they needed money more. He called Nicodemus to fetch Wright's buggy and walked off toward the field where the man called Blue David was plowing.

"Suh, reckon you can find de way to de main road on yo' own?" Nicodemus asked.

Jeremy nodded and climbed into the rented buggy. On the way out he noticed two women, one holding a child, watching as he passed the ruins of what he imagined to have once been a beautiful manor house. He tipped his hat to the ladies. They did not wave.

As the steamboat *T L Beauchamp* got underway, Jeremy Wright lit a cigar and walked forward on the boiler deck for a view of the Mississippi. Watching muddy swirls and eddies slip under the hull, the river seemed as restless and unpredictable as the country it divided. He glanced down at a handful of rough looking, unshaven men lounging on the forward cargo deck below. They were dressed in combinations of civilian garb and ragged gray or butternut uniforms. One among them, a shabbily-dressed man lounging on a wooden crate, looked up at him. The man's right eye was covered by a black patch.

CHAPTER 9

April 1865 brought news of Lee's surrender. The Confederate government fled Richmond to Danville, Virginia, then to Washington, Georgia where the last cabinet meeting of the Confederate States of America was held.

By the first week in May it was official, the fighting, the bleeding, the dying was over. Church bells in the North rang gaily; those in the South, the ones that hadn't been melted down to make cannon, rang mournfully.

At Shamrock there was too much work to hold a requiem. Planting had to be completed without Jonathan. Still reluctant to admit he needed the goat wagon, Daniel put it to good and frequent use. He thought it fitting to name his goat Blue Belly. He now had a mule named General Grant and a goat named after his troops. The senior Quinn claimed he was "only paying proper respect to the Yankee sons of bitches." Each morning after Nicodemus harnessed Blue Belly to the goat wagon, Daniel loaded it with his crutches, a lunch pale, a jug of water, a lap robe and his shotgun, the latter item for the chance to shoot one of the deer that occasionally crossed his path, or a quail or two if he flushed a covey as he returned from the fields at dusk. The elder Quinn never complained about pain. His enthusiasm had returned. He was happy to see his land, even a small portion of it, under cultivation. He loved the smell of the rich turned earth, his earth. *This is a beginning. If Jonathan can send just a little money home we can hold on. Shamrock will prosper again.*

The long days spent supervising the hired hands were hard on his health. Blood circulation to his lower extremities was so poor that even in warm weather he carried a blanket to spread over his arthritic legs.

With planting done, the hired hands were paid. They left, just as Doctor Perkins had predicted. Daniel and Blue Belly continued to check the fields every day. Looking down the tilled rows as he passed, he could see young leafy crops emerging. He also noticed sprouts of grass and weeds breaking through the soil in the furrows. *We'll have to hire a few hands to chop cotton foe long. Can't let the weeds choke the new crop.*

Nearing the old place, Daniel saw Annielise carrying his great-granddaughter toward the kitchen. The baby was already walking, and talking enough to get what she wanted, enough to say 'Granddaddy'. Annielise was barefoot, her dress a faded print. Her blond curls, teased by the afternoon zephyrs, contrasted with her baby's shiny, raven hair.

"Whoa there, Blue Belly, dang you. Whoa!"

"Ladies," he called, tipping his hat, "Y'all just grow prettier all the time. I tell you the first thing we're gonna do when that money arrives from your brother is to go to town to buy you, Nannie and the baby new clothes. I'm gonna show off all three Quinn ladies." He reached up and tickled the baby's bare feet. She giggled and held out her arms. Bethany loved to ride in his little green cart.

"I'll hold you to the dress, Daddy Quinn, but I'm not sure about going to town," Annielise said, handing the baby to him. "I've thought some about that. There'll be a lot of talk 'bout me and this baby."

"Long as I'm around, honey, won't but one person say anything."

"Who would that be, Granddaddy?"

"Oh that'll be the first one, Sugar. When I get through with the first one, there won't be a second volunteer."

Annielise laughed, but she didn't want to go to town.

"War over or not, Granddaddy, we are still under martial law. The military might not let me back into Vicksburg. I'm still an exile."

"They will unless they want a new war," he replied. Annielise walked on toward the kitchen with Daniel and the baby rolling along beside her in the little wagon. When they reached the doorway, Daniel handed Bethany to Annielise, got out his crutches and struggled up from the shiny green cart, the only thing on the place with new paint. He made his way through the door to a seat at the table.

Bethany ran over to Arabella. "Ride Granddaddy, Bella."

"Child, I know you ride with yo' granddaddy. And yo' is smart to be talking so." Nicodemus, Arabella and the baby sat at a small table in a corner to one side of the fire place. Above them the Shamrock bowl rested on a wide shelf Jonathan had installed before he left.

At the big table Annielise asked, "Father Daniel, what's gonna happen now that the war is over?"

"I don't know, darling," Daniel answered. "I've put some thought to it. With Lincoln killed, the damn Yankees will probably hang Jeff Davis and come down here and punish the rest of us—make us pay for the war."

"They won't be vindictive in victory, surely."

"They still got an army. We don't. With that kind of advantage, I reckon they can do what they want. The best we can do, Honey, is look after ourselves and Shamrock."

"Sho' seem peaceful round here with them field hands gone," Arabella said from the corner. She'd had the extra work of cooking the meals for the six hired hands.

"Well, Arabella, it may be peaceful, but I wish some of 'em had stayed. Give 'em some money and they're gone. Doc told me it'd be like that, no steady labor. A lot of owners say they gonna offer share cropping to whites and blacks alike."

"How does that work, Daniel?" Nannie asked.

"Owner puts up the land in plots the size one man and his family can handle, provides the seed, tools, mules, shelter and such. The share cropper puts up the labor. Owner gets half the crop, share cropper gets half. Nobody gets anything 'til the crop is in."

"Will it work?"

"I don't know. Owners don't have money to hire enough labor to work their land and workers, white or black, don't have money to buy or rent land outright. There's just no money and no credit to be had in the South. What would we have done without Jonathan's money? Thing is, there's a bigger market for cotton than ever. Share cropping might be the way to get land back into production. One thing's for certain. No cotton, no money; no money and Yankee bankers and carpetbaggers will get the land by foreclosure and tax sales like Jonathan said. With martial law, and keeping white Southerners from votin', they can dictate anything they want, and what they want is what little we got left. We never wanted a damn thing they have up North, not a foot of land. We just wanted to be left alone."

At their separate table in the corner, Nicodemus and Arabella exchanged glances. Arabella, holding the baby, leaned over and whispered, "Lawd! White folks lives de whole life not seeing us'en at all less'en de needs somethin'. De all wanted to be left alone all right, left alone to own and order black folks till Angel Gabriel blow his horn. And Massa Quinn being one of de good ones. Lawd! I likes my white folks here, dat's de truth, but if'en you and me was younger, reckon we be out on dat road seeing how's freedom takes you anywhere yo' feets can walk."

"Hush up, woman, and give me some mo' beans," said Nicodemus holding out his plate while glancing to see if those at the big table might have heard.

"Get 'em yo' self, old man. Can't you see I'm feeding dis here child?"

With the war over, the Union was left with a vast and purposeless army. The great majority were mustered out wherever they happened to be. Most headed north to homes and businesses untouched by war and crying for workers. In Vicksburg, there were three soldiers with a different plan: Sergeant McKenna and Corporals Weaver and McNamara. McKenna was the one that came up with the idea. "The way I see it, we got here late after all the good pickin's in town was over, after things was organized and a soldier couldn't just walk in where he pleased and take what he wanted. Ain't that right? We got left out of the good times, boys. But see here. Maybe there just might be a little left to get."

Weaver and McNamara were willing to listen.

"A few months back I was on the street when this old nigger came around recruitin' coloreds to work at a place called Shamrock. Now here is the interestin' part. He was showing 'em gold coins and telling 'em this Shamrock place had plenty more to pay wages. That give me an idea, see. I done some checking, found one of the blacks that went out there for planting and got paid in gold. Says he can show us how to get there. Says the only people left on the place are one old man, two women, and maybe the old nigger I was telling you about. I was thinking that before we go upriver to catch a train back East, we might take a little trip out there and relieve 'em of that gold. Might check on some other places, too. Now that the war's over, I bet folks around here are digging up all the stuff they hid when they knew us Yankees was coming. What do you say? You want to come along for a cut of easy money? Could be we get lucky. Ain't nobody out there to stop us, and I ain't planning to leave nobody behind that can put the law on us, know what I mean? We'll be long gone foe anybody knows what happened. Now what you say?"

"You're talking about killing, McKenna, killing women," Weaver sniveled.

"Well, Weaver," McKenna replied, "what the hell do you think the army did shelling this here town?"

"Killing for the army didn't pay much," McNamara said, "I'd just as soon get a little real money for a change. Killing is killing. I'm in."

They both looked at Weaver. He had enough sense to figure his choices were going along or dying. McKenna had already said he wouldn't leave anyone behind to squeal. "Let's go get us some loot," he said with what he hoped would pass for callous enthusiasm.

McKenna met briefly with the freed slave who had been among those recruited to do the planting at Shamrock. The tall, thin, black man spoke in a whispery, high-pitched voice. He said his name was Blue David. Said he would show them how to get to Shamrock for twenty dollars, said he needed a mule, and twenty dollars would get him a good one, said he would meet them beyond town on the Jackson road after dark.

Late that night McKenna and McNamara slipped four horses from the army corral while Weaver collected saddles and bridles from a large pile that had been thrown into a wagon. The horses and saddles would hardly be missed among the several hundred waiting to be shipped upriver to Saint Louis where the Army planned to sell them off as surplus property. The three ex-soldiers moved the mounts out of town and up the road a mile or so where Blue David was waiting. It was near midnight under a full moon when the four horsemen set out for Shamrock. The ex-soldiers rode side by side with Blue David following behind. To pass time in the saddle, the three told raunchy jokes and bragged about how much loot they were going to get.

A little after sunup, they asked Blue David how much further it was to Shamrock. "'bout eight mo' hours, I reckon."

Around noon they stopped for lunch and to give the horses a rest. Sitting in the shade, McKenna broke the silence. "Hey, Blue David, you want to throw in with us? You'll get lots more than twenty dollars."

"Naw suh. I figure I can hire out with a mule and plow. Be's on my own wit' nobody tellin' me do dis or fetch dat." The black man spoke barely above a whisper.

"Aw, come on, Blue David. Wouldn't you enjoy putting down slave owners? Tell you what. After we finish with this Shamrock place, we'll go see what's at your former owner's place."

McNamara joined in the fun. "You can beat the hell out of your old master. We'll tie him up and you beat him. How about that for fun, Blue?"

"I ain't never going near 'dere. You'ens does what suits ya. I don't gives a damn what white folks does to white folks. Ain't my bidness. Ain't gonna remember nothin' about y'all, never say nothin'. You give me my money like you say and dat's de end of it."

Ignoring Blue David, the trio begin to speculate about the kind of loot they might find: silverware, jewelry, gold, rings, watches, any treasure small enough to fit into saddlebags. When they got bored talking about all the riches they would find, they turned to telling how they might spend their new found wealth. It was pretty unanimous that women and whiskey would be at the top of the list. They had just about worn out the topic of women when Weaver had an idea. He turned to the black man. "Hey, Blue, you ever had a white woman?"

Blue David looked as if the question had struck him a physical blow.

"Well, have you?" McNamara asked.

"Naw, suh."

"Aw, come on, Blue, you bound to have heard about some black buck gittin' a little white pussy. I could tell when Weaver asked you that he hit a nerve. You know some stories now don't ya? I heard there was plenty fancy white planters had their fun with colored gals. Bet you know about that, huh? That's where all them high yellows come from, ain't it?"

"Yeah, Blue David, fair is fair. Bet you know a story or two about young bucks getting the attention of some of them bored, lonely white farm gals." Weaver added.

"Y'all don't know nothin'. Don't know how it is down here."

"Why don't you try us? I doubt you can tell us anything we ain't heard before," Weaver replied, "Come on tell us about it."

"Yeah, Blue, we'd like to hear all about that," McNamara said, "Maybe it would give us a slant on technique. Huh, boys?" Their laughter was sneering-mean, the kind Blue had heard from low-class white men all his life.

McKenna added, "You don't tell us a good story, you don't get your twenty. But if you tell us, we'll make it thirty."

Blue David was silent a long while. "Mr. McKenna, you made a deal wit' me foe twenty dollars."

"Well, I'm changing the deal, paying you more money, but you got to tell us a story or you git nothing." McKenna grinned at the others. "Don't make noth'en up neither. We want to hear the real thing."

Silently, Blue cursed them. After brooding about the situation a while, he knew he had no choice. He needed the money. "I never heard tell but one such story."

"You just tell us, Blue, we listening."

Blue had a change of mind. "I don't want to talk about none such. Please Mr. McKenna. I just want my twenty dollars."

"You tell us or you get nothing," McNamara growled.

"If I does, I's to be paid jes' like you said; thirty Yankee dollars?"

McKenna nodded. "That's what I said, Blue. What's the matter, don't you trust us?"

"Alright. What I gonna tell yo' gonna most probably be mo' 'en you wants to hear." Blue David was silent again for a while, his eyes cast down.

"I reckon Blue here don't want his money," Weaver said.

"You gonna tell us or not, Blue? You make somethin' up and lie we gonna know."

Blue David, still looking at the ground began. "On dis one place, de Massa, he has two daughters. One of 'em was real pretty, de young one, real nice, too. De older one weren't as pretty, didn't have no beaus hanging round much, not like de younger one.

She was mean, too. She whoop her maid foe nothing sometimes, then gives her sumpin' to make up fo' it, clothes, trinkets. She was a good horsewoman. Ride sidesaddle. Go over jumps better'en de mens do. Beat 'em racing, too. She spend most all her time down to de stable. Foe it be burned by Yankees it be like some fancy house, floor all polished stone, stalls made out'a fine wood all hand rubbed and oiled. De fittin's was brass, polished every day, and de lamps, dey was crystal hanging lamps jus' like in de big house. In dat stable was fine horses, I mean fine as dere be's anywheres. De names be on de stall doors in real silver. Dem horses live mo' better than black folks and po' whites, too."

"Get back to the white gal," sneered Weaver.

"Dat's what I's talking 'bout. De older daughter, dat was her stable. Place had another barn fo' de regular work animals. She spent all her time near 'bout at dat stable. Got six stable boys works 'dere. When she go out in her carriage, or has a party she dress 'em fine too. De all be wearin' white stockings, silver buckle shoes, white shirts and fine blue coats."

"Get to the part we want to hear, boy," McKenna urged.

"Yas suh. One day she say to one of de stable boys for him to stay while she told de others to go. One of de fancy stalls be empty. She brung him into it and closes de bottom part of de door. She tell him to take his clothes off. Well dis boy, he afraid. He heard de hang a nigga even raise his eyes up to a white woman. She tell him if he don't, she gone whoop him and sell 'em off de place.

"He done what she say. She have 'em turn all around so she can look on 'em, and 'den goes and close de top part of de stall gate. Now hit's dark in de stall, but she tell him keep his eyes shut tight or she have 'em blinded. He hears clothes rustling and 'den her naked body be touching his, hands on him. She say he don't keep quiet about it she have his tongue cut out. Dis boy plenty scared. He do what she say."

"See boys," Weaver smirked. "I told ya." Blue David grew silent.

Weaver spoke up again. "That ain't all is it Blue David? You got to finish the whole tale to get your money."

"I told ya'll 'bout it like yo' asked."

"That ain't all of it. We can tell. You scared nearly white just thinking on what happened, ain't he boys?" Weaver chided.

McKenna growled, "Finish the story, boy, or get no money." Staring darkly ahead, full of loathing for vile, low down whites, Blue David begged, "Don't make me say no mo'. It be mo' than you wants to hear 'bout."

"Didn't you hear me, boy? Not a penny 'less you tell all you know on that white bitch fucking that nigger."

Blue David, looking at the ground, began in a voice barely audible. "One day de's doing it when de hears da overseer's voice call de missy. She told de boy, 'Be quiet!' Dey both trying not to breathe, not to make no sound. He call de missy again, say her daddy want her up to de big house. She don't answer, 'fraid to answer. 'Den de hear boots walking down de stone flo', steps coming closer. De missy she start shakin'. All a sudden she reach down and tear her dress what's lying on de flo' and commence to scream and holler. De stable boy, he jump back in de corner trying to git his pants on. De stall gate done flung open and de light come in on 'em with Massa Raymond, de overseer, standing dere. De missy, she crawl to him thanking him for saving her, begging he don't let on to what done nearly happened to her, what dat nigga done tried to do to her. She say she be ruined if'en he tell. He say he won't tell de Massa, say he gonna handle things so no body gonna know. 'Course, he mean nobody but de black folks, and de don't matter none cause de don't never tell nothin' to white folks."

"Quit bitching and get on with the story," McNamara interjected.

"Massa Raymond, he puts chains on dat boy and rounds up all de black mens and boys down to fo'teen years and has em all take dat boy out to de woods. Has em cut down a gum tree."

Blue David's voice got a little stronger with anger. "De lays de trunk out on de ground and takes wedges and splits dat green log open 'bout three inches. Den de overseer makes all de blacks stand 'round in a circle and has four big mens strip de pants off dat boy, him screamin' and fightin'. Massa Raymond told them four big mens to sit de boy on de log and stuff his balls in de split of dat green log. When dey gits 'em like dat he tells de two wood cutters to take up de sledge and knock de wedges out."

"Goddamn!" Weaver said.

"Shut up and let him finish," McKenna ordered.

Blue David looked far off into the woods and was quiet a moment. When he spoke they could hardly hear him.

"Dat green log done close up like a steel trap on dat boy. De say he went to hollerin' like no such sound ever come from no human, say de boy commence making animal sounds like dogs and bears fightin'. All de shit come out of 'em, his legs a quivering, head jerking. The overseer, he step up and slap him three, fo' times 'til de boy see through his pain what de man holdin' out to 'em. De boy, he grabs dis big ole rusty knife Massa Raymond holdin'. He took up dat knife in both hands and hack at dat log trying to free his self, but can't hardly dent dat green log. De boy commence to screaming fo' somebody to kill 'em, fo' the Lawd' to kill 'em. All to once he commence to hack at his self, cuttin' 'tween his legs, blood coming, screaming and cuttin' 'till he come up off de log. He stop hollerin'. Stood looking down at the log, blood all running down his legs, den' falls to de ground. De mens, dey jes' gawk at 'em, 'fraid to move."

Tears were streaming down Blue David's face. McKenna had to clear his throat before he could ask, "Did the overseer kill him then?"

"Naw, suh'," Blue said, tasting the bitter salt of his own tears, "Cauterized de bleedin' with a hot iron and doctored 'em up, kept 'em alive, put 'em in the fields cross the river to work where de missy never see'em. Drag 'em out when ever new slaves first come to de place. Line 'em up and have dat boy stand in front of em and drop his pants, tell em dat what happens to niggas even look at a white gal."

The three whites were silent. They got up and mounted their horses.

"Come on, Blue, we got business up the road."

Late afternoon Blue David stopped at a trail leading off the main road.

"Y'all go on up dat road yonder. Dat's Shamrock. Y'all find it 'bout half a mile on. Now I wants my money, thirty dollars like you said. I done brung ya' here, and I done told you de story you asked me about."

"That you did. Didn't he boys?" McKenna smiled, turned to McNamara and winked. "McNamara, count out thirty gold dollars for ole' Blue here. And Blue, besides the money, you can have that horse, but you best not be caught riding him with that U S brand on his rump."

"Naw' sir. I gonna turn him loose when I gets close to home. Now I wants my money."

McNamara held out a twenty dollar gold piece and two five dollar coins in his outstretched palm. As the black man reached for them, McNamara eased a leg back and spurred his horse. The animal jerked forward, spilling the money from his hand. "Whoa! Damn you, horse. Sorry about that Blue."

"Dat's all right, I'll git it." Blue climbed from his horse. As he reached down for the money, he felt just the slightest movement across his throat followed by the sharp pain of severed nerve endings. He tried to cry out, but a soft gurgling was the only sound he made. Blue slumped toward the ground, his neck sliding on down the full length of McNamara's blade. Blue's body twitched in the dirt as his blood clotted in a mat of dead leaves. McNamara wiped his knife blade on his saddle blanket and grinned at McKenna.

"Weaver, pick up the money and drag his dead ass off in the woods there," McKenna ordered.

"Me? How come McNamara don't do it. He's the one done him," Weaver complained.

"You refusing an order?" McKenna moved his hand to his pistol.

"No, I ain't," Weaver sniveled. He got down from his horse and started dragging the body into the woods.

"Hold up a minute." McNamara called to Weaver. "How you reckon he knew so much about that story. How did he know the name of the overseer and all? Weaver, pull his pants down."

"Pull his pants down?" Weaver whined, "You some kind of pervert?"

"Get smart with me you rotten-toothed little bastard and I'll cut yours off and feed it to you."

"McKenna," McNamara said, "I'll bet you ten dollars Blue David, with that high, soft voice of his, is the boy with no balls."

"I'll take that easy money. Come on Weaver, do what he says." Weaver did and stepped back. "I'll be damn. Look at that." The other two rode over to stare down at the mutilated black man.

McKenna reached in his pocket and flipped McNamara a ten-dollar gold piece. "Hell, that's a story worth ten dollars. Come on boys. There's lots more than ten dollars waiting up this road."

"Weaver," McKenna said, "Pick up that horse. We might need a spare."

Weaver, leading Blue David's horse, followed McKenna and McNamara up the tree-canopied, overgrown lane. They startled a brace of crows picking at a snake carcass.

CHAPTER 10

Near midnight, on a calm, flat sea, a barely visible shape ghosted out of the moon-less black. Sails furled, no lights showing, the boiler carefully tended so no sparks escaped the stack to give away her presence, *Virgin* eased quietly toward shore. Overhauled, her rigging altered, her hull painted flat black, she was now registered out of Nassau, the capital of the British colony of the Bahamas. The Union Jack hung limply from the staff on her stern. Ranging on two shielded signal lanterns set on land, Captain Quinn eased his vessel toward one of the few stretches along Cuba's southern shore where *Virgin* could get close in to the beach. Taking soundings with a lead line, the bow lookout signaled four fathoms. Jonathan raised the engine room on the brass speaking tube, "Slow astern." The engineer reversed the engine until the ship lost all way. "All stop." The anchor was eased overboard. At Quinn's order, a hand-held signal lamp on the bow was opened for one brief second and shut down. The range lights on shore were immediately extinguished. No further signals would be exchanged. Cuban nights had Spanish eyes.

Down below, grimy-faced stokers rested on their shovels, sweat streaming riv-ulets of coal-dust down their bare chests in the 120-degree heat of the boiler room. On deck, the crew quickly turned-to, quietly removing hatch covers, hoisting ob-long wooden crates up on deck, and lowering away two boats in preparation to ferry five hundred cases of rifled muskets to the beach. The hoisting tackle was well oiled and all oar locks padded to make as little noise as possible during the transfer of the "special cargo"; surrendered Confederate weapons Jeremy Wright had obtained by bribing a Yankee major in Vicksburg.

A calm sea lapping softly onto the beach made landing the heavy-laden boats easy work, but the lack of surf meant the sounds of transferring rifle crates from boats to complaining donkeys would carry dangerously far. Seven Cubans were in the first boat to return from shore. Some were white, some black, some in between. Once aboard, it was evident that a large, muscular mulatto was in charge. The six men with him quickly formed a protective screen around him. Jonathan, speaking Spanish, introduced himself to the big man.

"Your name Maceo?"

The huge man, offered his hand, "Si Capitán, Antonio Maceo." The bronze-skinned Cuban stood silently studying the young, scarred captain.

Maceo's men interrupted the transfer of cargo to pry open one of the cases on deck. A long object wrapped in oiled paper was picked at random and handed to Maceo. The big man asked to go below where a lantern could be lit.

Leaving all but one of his bodyguards on deck, Maceo and a Cuban carrying a leather satchel followed Capt. Quinn below. Jonathan lit a lamp in his cabin. Tarred canvas flaps covered the portholes to ensure no light would leak into the night. The Cuban leader laid the long object on a small table, carefully unrolled the paper and exposed a rifled musket covered with a protective coat of grease. The big Cuban nodded approval.

"You have packed them well," he said to Jonathan. "That is important. They will have to sleep in the mountains a while until we are ready."

Jonathan brought out a bottle of Cuban rum and a box of cigars. While the cargo transfer continued, the three men passed the time sipping rum and smoking. The Cuban with the satchel remained silent while the sparse conversation between Jonathan and Maceo focused mostly on matters of security, contact procedures and payment terms for possible future deliveries. In this trade, Jonathan knew, one asked few questions. He knew nothing about Maceo. He had been given his name and description, nothing more. That would have to do for the moment.

Informed that the last case had been tallied, Maceo told Jonathan, "Capitán Quinn, you have delivered what was promised at a fair price. We will look to you for more shipments when we have the money to pay for them."

"Speaking of payment," Jonathan smiled.

Maceo nodded to his assistant. The man placed his satchel on the table and counted out full payment in Spanish gold as had been agreed to previously. Business done, the Cuban closed his satchel. Jonathan nodded to Maceo and the three men left the cabin to return topside.

Just before climbing over the side and down the rope ladder to the waiting boat, the Cuban paused and pointed up in the rigging where two barely visible crewmen sat with rifles in hand. Maceo smiled. "I like a man who is cautious. Capitán Jones told me you would do. We shall meet again, Capitán Quinn."

Sunrise caught *Virgin* running for sea room, her sails set, her boiler cooling. Coal cost money. Wind was free. She resumed her original course for Montego Bay where she was expected with a cargo of general merchandise. Captain Quinn, satisfied that they were free and clear, turned the ship over to the first mate and retired to his cabin. His first delivery had gone well. He drifted to sleep thinking of the tidy sum of money he would send home to his family.

It was a rare lazy afternoon at Shamrock for everyone but Arabella. She was washing clothes 'down to de creek'. Nicodemus sat upstream in the shade doodling for bream using a cane pole and fresh dug worms for bait. Annielise and the baby were taking their usual afternoon nap while Nannie, grateful for a little quiet time to herself, sat at the kitchen table reading a book of poems by Browning. The book's cover was warped, the pages curled but readable.

Daniel, restless and pained by his arthritis, got in his cart and, as he often did, went up to the ruins where he sat dreaming of a new Shamrock. Blue Belly was the first to notice the strangers. He lifted his head and took a few quick steps forward. "What the hell you doing, Blue Belly? I didn't tell you to get up and go anywhere . . ." Daniel saw them, three mounted men, one leading a fourth horse with an empty saddle. He shaded his eyes against the low afternoon sunlight. They wore Yankee uniforms, two of them sloppily; shirt tails out, suspenders hanging loose. The tall slim one was neat as a pin, looked ready for inspection. A chill crawled up Daniel's spine.

Wylie Weaver, anxious to improve his standing with McKenna, moved to the front when they reached Daniel. "Well, look at this, boys. What we got here? Ain't you a might old to be playing in a young'ens wagon?"

Daniel eased his hands under the lap robe covering his legs.

"Now hold on Weaver," said the big man, looking down at Daniel. "Can't you tell this gentleman is the master of this place come up here in his fine carriage to survey all his wealth. Why, just look at all them ashes Grant and Sherman done left him."

"You sons of bitches, get off my land! There's nothing left here to take unless you want my goat here, but I doubt he would lower himself to such company."

"You're a right smart-mouthed old bastard, ain't you?" said Weaver, "Ain't he, now, boys?"

Daniel hoped he was cussing loud enough to warn Nannie and Annielise of trouble.

Annielise heard him, picked up her sleeping baby and stood watching from the shadow of the cottage doorway. Her mind raced. If she tried to slip out, would the baby cry and give them away? Should she stay put and hope Granddaddy could handle things? Either way was a risk. The cottage was clearly in view of the strangers.

Nannie had heard Daniel, too. She put down her book and moved quietly to the mantelpiece over the fireplace, lifted Tom Boatner's heavy revolver and carefully made her way from the kitchen to conceal herself behind one of the fire-blackened chimneys not far from the group of men. The air was still. A quail called in the distance. Nannie looked down at the pistol and with both thumbs, cocked the hammer. She noticed her worn shoes were covered with soot from the ashes of Shamrock.

"Now listen, old man," McKenna said, "I know you got some gold stashed here. I saw some of it when the old nigger come to town hiring hands."

Nanny closed her eyes. *How foolish*, she now realized, *to have shown money in town.*

"You verminous horse turd. You're an insult even to a Yankee army. They've thrown you out haven't they? And you two," he motioned at Weaver and McNamara, "you follow this fat slob all the way out here 'cause he told you there was gold?" Daniel laughed. "He saw a few gold coins all right, but that's all there was. It's all gone to pay for seed and labor for planting. It was the last we had. You bastards took a long ride for nothing 'cept to be out-cussed by an old man." Daniel lowered his voice and hissed like a rattler set to strike. "Now get off my land!"

McNamara eased his knife out, "You're wasting my time you carping old bastard. You'll tell where the gold is, tell me anything I want to know, beg to tell me."

Weaver, eager to show McKenna he was smarter than McNamara, dropped the lead to Blue's horse and swung down from his saddle to stand in front of the old man. He smiled, showing tobacco yellowed teeth, then backhanded Daniel, splitting open his lower lip. "We don't need your damned knife, McNamara. Knife's all you know, ain't it? Just use your brain. Look at them crutches in the wagon. You ain't got sense enough to see this old man is plum eat up with arthritis. This here is all you got to do to make him talk." Weaver grabbed Daniel's left boot and twisted the leg.

Daniel screamed. The excruciating pain shot all the way up to his hip. There were two audible clicks as he raised his double barreled shotgun beneath the lap robe. Weaver stumbled back against his horse's front legs, reaching for his gun. The shotgun fired with a startling blast. It was Wylie Weaver's turn to scream. He was slammed under the horse as two loads of buckshot carried his belly and lower spine away and nearly severed the animal's right leg at the shoulder. The horse fell on Weaver and the two of them writhed screaming in the muck of Weaver's guts while jointly bleeding the ground red. Weaver died while everyone was frozen in place by the bizarre horror of the moment. Weaver and his horse stopped struggling and lay in shock, bleeding-out.

Except for the startling moment when the shotgun fired, Blue Belly didn't seem to give a damn. The goat had gotten used to Daniel shooting from the wagon. Slightly up wind from the blood, Blue Belly continued to graze.

Daniel had not meant to fire both barrels, had done so in the madness of pain. McNamara and McKenna fought to hold their frightened horses. Dead Blue's horse bolted. McNamara managed to draw his gun while Daniel was desperately still fumbling to reload. Nannie, overcoming her shock, stepped from behind the chimney, raised Tom Boatner's pistol in both hands and fired just as McNamara pulled his trigger. She hit the slim, neat, child molester in the right thigh, but not before his shot caught Daniel Quinn full in the chest. The bleeding McNamara and McKenna both wheeled their horses to face the new, unknown marksman. They saw a woman standing by a brick chimney with a pistol held in both hands pointed full at them. Nannie fired again. The forty-four caliber ball caught McNamara in the throat. For a brief moment he sat rigid in the saddle, mouth open, surprise showing on his face, then fell backwards off his horse. McKenna's first bullet missed. Nannie cocked her pistol once more. Before she could fire, McKenna's second shot hit her in the left shoulder, knocking her to the ground. Lying on her back, she struggled to raise the pistol with her right hand as McKenna rode toward her.

At the first shot Bethany awoke, afraid but silent. Annielise was quick to calm the child. "Granddaddy is playing a game, you know, boom, like Uncle Nicodemus hunting squirrels." There were two more shots. "Now Mama is gonna hide you right here." She sat the child on a folded quilt at the bottom of the wicker trunk in the corner of the cottage. "Won't this be fun?" She dropped the child's rag doll in with her. "We'll play peek-a-boo. Don't make a sound. Are you ready? I'll go out and get everyone to start looking for little Bethany." She smiled at the baby. Bethany, unsure, rolled her big green eyes up at her mother and clutched the rag doll as Annielise lowered the hinged, wicker lid and said a silent prayer for the safety of her child.

Annielise arrived at the cottage door to see McKenna fire into her fallen mother. Losing all reason, she ran out across the open ground. "NO! Not Mama! Not Mama!"

McKenna wheeled his horse to face the new threat in the terrible melee that had so quickly erupted around him. He fired at the running figure and missed. The bullet hit the ground in front of the girl.

Annielise suddenly remembered the burning pain of the bullet that had struck her that day in Vicksburg; Bethany's bullet. She stopped. *I've got to save my baby!* she screamed silently and stood frozen with fear staring at the vile killer coming toward her.

McKenna, still pointing his gun, hand shaking badly, got down from his horse.

"Well now, this place has no end of surprises." He looked cautiously in all directions. Satisfied, he turned his attention to the slim young woman standing in front of him. Annielise tried to break and run. McKenna grabbed her arm and jerked her roughly to him. Ignoring the terror and grief that showed in her twisted face, he told her, "Your mama is dead. You don't want to look at her just now. That crazy old man is dead too, he's the one that caused all this. We just wanted the gold. Bet you know where it is. Me and you are gonna have a little fun and then you'll tell me."

Annielise said nothing, just stared ahead. She was not there. She could not let herself be there. She shut her mind down. There was no big man dragging her into the cottage, throwing her on the bed. She dared not look at the wicker trunk. *Be still Bethany. Please don't cry.*

"Come on Honey, fight me a little, you're gonna enjoy it more if you fight me."

Don't scream, she told herself, *don't frighten the baby. Please, God, don't let my baby cry out!*

The heavy weight of the horrible man's fat body pressed down on her, his unwashed smell gagged her, his foul breath invaded her nostrils. For an instant she was paralyzed by stark, raw fear. Then revulsion and hatred took over her soul. She bit his cheek, hard, drawing blood. He growled like a bear and let go of her arms to get away from her tearing sharp teeth. She went for his eyes with her fingers. He slapped her, hard.

"So there is fire in there after all. I like 'em to fight. You like it rough don't you honey? All of you do." She freed a hand and clawed his face again. He hit her with his huge fist. The small girl beneath him went limp.

It had happened in a matter of minutes, all of it. He finished the thing, never knowing that a pair of eyes stared out at him from the wicker trunk in the corner. They were big, innocent eyes, confused and frightened. Bethany, like all very young creatures, obeyed the primeval instinct to remain still and quiet in the presence of danger. Through the tiny spaces in the wicker she saw boots walk past, heard the door close. Then everything was quiet.

McKenna's first concern was to catch his horse. Nothing had gone according to plan. He was filled with fear. Like all bullies, McKenna was a coward. What would happen if he were caught? The Army might hang him. God knows what some mob of Johnny Rebs would do to him. Blue David's story flashed across his mind. Run! He knew he would have to travel long and fast. He would need food. Couldn't be stopping for food. He quickly picked out the kitchen building behind the ruins. Pulling his horse behind, he ran to the building. Inside McKenna grabbed what he could find—two loaves of fresh bread, baked sweet potatoes, a smoked ham. He no longer thought of gold. He thought of escape.

Then he saw it, the heavy silver punch bowl sitting on its shelf. He took it down and inside, in a cigar box, he found nearly four hundred dollars in gold coins. "Well now, Mr. McKenna," he said out loud. "The luck of the devil." He stuffed the coins in his pockets. The bowl was large, awkward to handle, but he would have it. He dumped what was left of fifty pounds of flour on the floor and put the bowl in the empty sack. With his pants and boots white with flour, he tied the sack to his saddle and stuffed the ham, bread and potatoes in the saddlebags.

McKenna mounted, rode across the field to retrieve McNamara's horse, and leading it behind, galloped for the main road. His plan was to ride hard north until his horse dropped. Then do the same with McNamara's. He figured by the time he rode the second horse into the ground he would be far enough north to safely catch a boat upriver to St. Louis. From there he could take an eastbound train and leave the South behind for good.

Nicodemus was nodding off when the first shot faintly echoed down the hollow to the creek. "You hear somethin', woman?" he asked.

Arabella was standing with her mouth open when the unmistakable sound of more gun fire reached them. "I hear shootin', Nicodemus. Our folks is in trouble!"

"'Dem folks is in trouble," Nicodemus corrected. "We is our own folks now. Maybe we better wait here a while, see if it don't gits quiet. It most probably be Massa Daniel shootin' dat goat like he been saying he's gonna."

It did get quiet. "See woman," Nicodemus said, "things is all quiet."

"You do what you wants, old man," Arabella said over her shoulder, "My baby's up dere and I'm going."

"All right, Woman. We both going, but when we gets up dere, you let me take a look foe you runs into de open not knowin' what's happenin'." They left the laundry beside the creek.

It was nearly a quarter mile to the cabins and another quarter of a mile from the cabins to the ruins of the bighouse. Arabella held her skirt high so she could move as fast as her bones would carry her. They reached the cabins, then slowed, cautiously walking up the lane leading to the ruins.

It had taken over twenty minutes for the pair to cover the distance. They heard the faint sound of galloping horses fading toward the main road. Out of breath, Nicodemus struggled on toward the ruins while Arabella turned to the weaving cottage. The child was sitting on the ground just off the cottage steps playing in the dirt with a spoon. Arabella stopped, her heart pounding, not so much from the struggle to reach the cottage as from what she saw. Bethany's white gown and her small hands and bare feet were covered with blood. The dark-haired child looked up at Arabella. "Mama hurt, Bella."

Inside, Arabella found Annielise on the bed, her clothes torn open, her small perfect breast exposed, her legs spread to reveal her most private parts. Her lips were blue, her skin ghost-gray except where deep bruises marked her jaw and cheeks and arms. Her eyes were closed, her golden-red hair spread on the pillow. There was blood, lots of blood. Her throat was slit open from ear to ear. Small bloody hand prints were on her face where the baby had tried to awaken her. From a thick pool of blood on the floor, tiny footprints mixed with the tracks of large boots led to the door.

Arabella tried to scream, but no sound would come. She wanted to run, but her feet would not move. Slowly she reached out and touched the child she had looked after for eighteen years. Weeping and murmuring, "Oh baby! Oh baby!" over and over, Arabella smoothed Annielise's hair, folded her arms, and covered her with a quilt.

Sobbing, she walked up from the cottage carrying the baby. Nicodemus stood looking down at something in the tall grass near one of the chimneys. She could see Daniel Quinn slumped half out of the goat wagon, face dragging on the ground as the goat grazed slowly across the grass near the bodies of a man and a horse. Another man's body lay a few yards further on.

Nicodemus waved his arms, "Don't come dis' a'way, don't bring dat child dis' a'way. Go round de other side. Oh Lawd! Arabella, what done happen here?" Nicodemus was scared and crying and chastising God for letting such a terrible thing happen. "Ain't no cause fo' dis, Lawd, no cause a'tall."

Arabella was already close enough to see that it was Miss Nannie's body that Nicodemus was standing over. "Miss Nannie! Oh Lord! Not Miss Nannie too!"

She cried as she carried the baby the long way around to the kitchen and sat her on the table to keep her out of the flour scattered over the floor. She stripped the bloody clothes off the child, bathed her with water from a bucket, wrapped her in dish towels made from flour sacks, and started packing what food she could find.

Nicodemus went back down to the slave cabins and returned with blankets. He cut Blue Belly loose, rolled Daniel Quinn out of the cart and wrapped him in one of the blankets. Then he went to where Nannie lay. He looked at her pain-twisted face, her lifeless eyes staring up at him, the pistol in her right hand. As gently as he could he wrapped her body in the second blanket. *Oh, Miss Nannie, I be so terrible sorry.*

While Nicodemus tied Nannie Quinn's body in the blanket, Arabella stepped out of the kitchen door and hollered, "Po' Miss Annielise is in de cottage, yonder. Be gentle wit' her . . . and bring some baby clothes and a blanket foe dis here child."

It took a while for Nicodemus to catch the mules and harness the team to the wagon. He bundled up what little personal belongings and clothes he and Arabella had and put them and a little sack of baby clothes and flour sack diapers fetched from the weaving cottage under the wagon seat. He picked up the quilt wrapped body of Annielise and laid it in the wagon. Then he drove the wagon over to collect the bodies of Miss Nannie and Massa Daniel.

Nicodemus loaded the dead headfirst onto the back of the wagon. The feet of all three bodies stuck out of their blankets. It was the best the frail old man could do. Finished with the mournful task, he called for Arabella to bring the child. He put the small bundle of food Arabella had packed into the wagon with a jug of water. Then he helped Arabella and the child up on the seat and handed them a quilt. Finally he gathered up Daniel's shotgun, powder and shot and Nannie's pistol, climbed up on the seat and took up the reins.

"What you got 'dem guns fo'?" Arabella whined. "Dey been used fo' killin'."

"We gonna be on dat road all night, woman. Maybe dere be mo' mean white trash like what come here. We talking about our lives and dis here child's. I'm loadin' de guns and keeping 'em right up here, Bella. Now you dress dat child and don't let her look back at them bodies."

Arabella said nothing, did what she was told and tucked the quilt around herself and the child. All through the night they rode without speaking. The wagon groaned and swayed, jiggling the feet of the bodies hanging just off the back edge of the worn planks of the wagon bed; bodies Nicodemus and Arabella dared not look upon. The steel-rimmed wagon wheels crunched the gravel encrusted dirt beneath them and jarringly thumped in and out of potholes on a road that hadn't been graded since the war began. There were no signs of human life along the way, not so much as the light of a single candle. Mosquitoes were a dreadful bother. They had a small bottle of oil of pennyrile to smear on their skin but it did little good. In the moonless dark, progress was noted by the steady clop of the mules' hooves and the rattle of the triple tree hitch and trace chains. Occasionally the sounds of nocturnal creatures drifted from the fields and woodlands; the cry of night birds, the scurrying of creatures across the road. Such sounds scratched at the suppressed terror trailing just behind the two former slaves. It was a fearful, dark passage.

As dawn gentled the night away, Nicodemus asked the question that had been bearing heavily on his mind all night. "What we gonna do when we gets to Vicksburg?"

"We got to find Doctor Ted, bless him. All dis gonna 'bout kill 'em. Ain't nothin' else we can do." They rode on in silence.

After a while Nicodemus spoke. "Dere was three of 'em Bella, Yankee soldiers. Two of 'em is dead. Looked like Massa Daniel got one with the shotgun and Miss Nannie got de other 'ern with Massa Boatner's pistol. De last one of 'em rode off. Done got away. I seen the tracks. He done took Miss Nannie's wedding ring, cut her finger off to get it."

"He took de Shamrock bowl, Nicodemus, and Jonathan's money and my fresh baked bread and de smoked ham we been saving. He done 'kilt Shamrock and all its people, all 'cept 'dis po' child."

"We was doing so good, Bella, but Lawd, it be a most sorrowful place now. I ain't goin' back 'dere, Bella, not ever."

"Think of po' Massa Jonathan." Arabella cried, "Him out 'dere from home, gonna send money, gonna save de place, and he don't even know. It's gonna kill 'em, it's jes gonna kill 'em."

Nicodemus asked a question that had suddenly, frighteningly occurred to him. "Bella, reckon dey'll take de word of black folks 'bout all dis?"

Arabella pondered on that. Then she said with conviction, "Doctor Ted will. I ain't gone worry about 'dem others."

Bethany awoke and clung to Arabella. Once in a while she asked for her mama. "Yo' mama be sick, child," Arabella would answer. "She gonna be a while, but Bella loves you, Bella be here with you. We gonna take care of you, Honey." She fed the child small pieces of biscuit.

Two former slaves with a white baby in a wagon carrying three white bodies picked up a crowd of both Union soldiers and Vicksburg citizens as Nicodemus drove the team into town. His intent was to follow Arabella's directions to Doctor Perkins' house, but word had quickly spread to the provost office that "two niggers got three white bodies in a wagon and are telling the crowd Yankee soldiers kilt 'em'."

A mounted officer appeared. Nicodemus explained he wanted to go to Doctor Perkins place.

"I don't care what you want, ole nigger. You follow me." The officer led the wagon directly to the town morgue where the bodies were quickly taken off the street.

Arabella, Nicodemus and the baby were escorted to the provost headquarters. Frightened, they asked for Doctor Perkins. The provost marshal said he would send for the doctor "after you blacks tell me your story." As it turned out, he didn't have to send for Ted Perkins.

Word reached the hospital that two blacks and a white baby had arrived with three bodies in the back of a wagon. The news was all over town. When Ted was told that the driver's name was Nicodemus he left the hospital immediately. He was told on the street that the coloreds had been taken to the provost headquarters.

Perkins ignored the office personnel who tried to stop him and barged into the provost's office. The officer was sitting behind his desk with Nicodemus and Arabella, holding the confused baby in her arms, standing before him. His assistant was taking notes while an armed soldier stood behind them.

When Perkins barged through the door, Arabella cried out, "Doctor Ted! Oh Lord! Doctor Ted, some Yankee soldiers done come and kilt everybody but Nicodemus, this baby and me. We was down to de creek when we heard shootin' and we runs fast as we can but they all dead when we gots to 'em. What we gonna do, Doctor Ted? Look at dis po' baby. What we gonna do? Dis here Yankee don't wants to believe us'en."

After Arabella and Nicodemus told their story again, the provost marshal released them into the doctor' custody with the admonition, "None of you will talk about this incident. There is no proof yet as to what really happened. I order you to be silent on this matter until this office completes an investigation. I don't want to hear a thing about Union soldiers involved in this."

Ted guided the two blacks and the baby through a curious crowd gathered outside and took them to his home where he told Luky to see to them and the baby. From there he went to the morgue where he found the bodies of the people he loved most in the world. Ted had seen every kind of grisly wound and dismembered body, but what he found at the morgue sundered his heart, almost brought him to his knees. The room, shades drawn, was stifling in the summer heat. The bodies were laid out on pine boards supported by trusses and illuminated by one oil lamp. Rigor mortis had set in and the odor of morbidity was already upon the flesh. The door, propped ajar for ventilation, let in flies. The gaping slash across Annielise's throat was black with them.

The undertaker had grown used to charging inflated prices to prepare Union dead and pack them in salt for shipment to their homes up North. He voiced his main concern. "Who's to pay fer my mortician services and caskets and the grave diggers? I done ask and was told the government ain't gonna pay fer no civilian arrangements."

Ted grabbed the man by the throat, shook him, told him, "You merciless, scallywag bastard. You'll get your money, but you are going to do the most decent and respectful job you have ever done in your miserable life or I will personally see your sorry remains fed to hogs. Do you clearly understand me?" The man shook his head like he was bobbing for apples. "You call me to see 'em before you close their caskets, you hear me?" The man bobbed his head again. Ted let go of his throat and walked out.

Using the power granted him under martial law, the Provost had prevented any mention of the murders in the local paper. It mattered little. Everyone in town knew by word of mouth what had happed at Shamrock. Fearing the story might be true, the Provost refused to begin an investigation based upon the wild ravings of two ignorant niggers about Union soldiers killing people out in the country. He told the locals, "It was most probably renegade Rebels that did it." It was the intervention of Doctor Perkins backed by a large contingent of citizens who convinced the provost marshal to investigate the scene of the crime. A citizen's committee told the provost they were going to send representatives out to Shamrock to see what happened there whether or not the army sent official investigators. The provost agreed to send his deputy with a detachment of soldiers, and allowed Dr. Perkins and a committee of four other Vicksburg citizens to accompany them. He had little choice if he didn't want a riot in town.

At Shamrock they found what was left of the two bodies Nicodemus and Arabella had described. Their eyes had been pecked out by crows, noses, lips and cheeks gnawed off by animals, probably opossums and raccoons. A host of grunting, hissing turkey buzzards argued over what was left of the torn flesh and innards of the human remains and the carcass of a dead horse still bearing a McClellan saddle with U.S. markings. Green flies were swarming about and maggots and carrion beetles had joined in the abundant feast. The stench was overwhelming. By their uniforms, and papers found in their pockets, there was no doubt that the dead men had been Union soldiers.

Ted Perkins walked to the old kitchen where he had spent so many pleasant hours with the Quinn family. Field mice, rat tracks and droppings stood out against the white of the flour-coated floor. Ted noticed that the Shamrock bowl was missing.

Against his will, Perkins was drawn to the weaving cottage and stepped just inside the doorway. The bed and floor were stained dark black by thick, clotted blood, Annielise's blood. Flies and beetles were feasting on it. From a small window at the opposite end of the room, sunlight beamed through dust motes drifting in the stuffy heat of the room. Ted wanted to leave, leave quickly, but something caught his attention, something reflecting sunlight from a small, crudely made table by the window. He walked over the blood coated floor, scattering flies and crunching beetles and maggots under his shoes.

The source of the reflection was the shiny brass clasp on the leather bound diary Ted had given Annielise. He lifted the small, thick book from the table. *I will finish this journal for you, Annielise, put down the terrible ending of your young life and those of your mother and grandfather, finish and preserve it so that your baby will someday know the truth of her birth and what happened here. She deserves that. She'll know you, Daniel and Nannie from these pages.* Ted put the book in his coat pocket. *If Jonathan will let me, Annielise, I will take care of your baby girl. I promise you that.* Ted would never be able to erase from his memory the blood soaked little cottage where his godchild died.

Dr. Perkins made it clear to the Deputy Provost that he dare not bury the vile vermin at Shamrock. The bodies of the two ex-soldiers were not carried into town. The Provost truly feared a riot. He already had his hands full without attracting more attention to what was officially termed "the incident at the Quinn place." He gave special orders and instructions to soldiers assigned the grave detail. The two dead corporals would join the thousands of Union troops listed as missing. Their remains, what was left of them, were buried in unmarked graves well off the Natchez road miles from the Quinn property.

The provost, given the report of what was found at Shamrock, had no choice but to dispatch a number of cavalry detachments to comb the countryside for the third killer. They had no name, no description, only that the man may have taken a silver bowl with him.

By the time a search was launched to track down the mysterious third member of the trio that purportedly had murdered the Quinn family, the trail was cold. The detachments checked many discharged Union troops on the roads, all moving east and north toward operating railroads. The telegraph was used to deliver messages up river to ports where boats transporting homeward bound troops might stop. After a week the search was called off. The Army never made public any report concerning the affair. As the Provost said, "It wouldn't look good in the Northern press."

The Quinns were buried in the wrought iron fenced family plot at Cedar Hill cemetery in Vicksburg. The whole town turned out for the burial. Even some Yankee army officers attended standing in the back of the crowd, not speaking and not spoken to.

There were no living Quinns at the service. The baby was with Luky. Daniel's brother, Judge Bill Quinn, was imprisoned with Jefferson Davis at Fort Monroe, Virginia and said to be dying in the prison infirmary. Doctor Perkins had sent a message to Jonathan in care of Captain Deuteronomy Jones, New Providence, Nassau, Bahamas. It stated only that Jonathan's mother, sister, and grandfather had died. No details were given. No one knew where Jonathan was or how long it might take for him to receive the message.

Nicodemus had to help a heartbroken, sobbing Arabella from the cemetery. Long after they and the crowd of mourners had drifted away, two men lingered at the grave side. Both had seen death many times, but the sudden, violent death that had been visited upon the Quinn family was bitterly hard for them to comprehend.

Two Negro grave diggers approached, nodded respectfully to the two men and began laboring to close the graves. Ted Perkins and Tom Boatner stood close to one another like two lonely, lost little boys as shovelsful of loose earth thumped onto the caskets. The air around them was filled with the musty smell of fresh turned earth and the sweet scent of honeysuckle blooming on the rusty, wrought iron fence enclosing the family burial plot. For the rest of their lives, the scent of honeysuckle would remind them of the excruciating sorrow of friends lost.

Doctor Perkins' household finally settled down to a state of truce with Arabella generally staying out of the doctor's office and rooms, and Luky leaving all matters pertaining to the baby to Arabella. Nicodemus tried with little success to stay out of their way.

Nearly six weeks later, Jonathan finally arrived in Vicksburg. Doctor Perkins found him to be calm but distracted, unable to finish a conversation. On the first morning after his arrival, he visited the graves briefly, placed flowers upon them, and spent the rest of the day playing with his black haired, green-eyed little niece. He couldn't tell whether or not the child remembered him, but she paid no attention to his eye patch and scar. Several days passed before he sat down with Ted Perkins and for the first time said he was ready to be told the details, the whole story. "I think I can take it now, Ted."

Dr. Perkins, who had performed the awful tasks of verifying the identity of the murdered Quinns and writing their official death certificates, omitted as many details of that awful day as he could. Ted watched Jonathan leave the house and walk toward the cemetery two miles away. Townspeople would recall seeing him visit the graves every day that he was in town. One lady told friends that she had seen him kneeling beside the headstones talking to them.

Late one night, the doctor was awakened by pleading voices coming from the servants' quarters.

"Please don't make me tell mo', Massa Jonathan. Nicodemus and me done told all we can. It's too hurt'en to tell, too awful to even think about no mo'."

"Damnit. I've never struck either of you in my life, but I swear to God if you don't tell me what was done to my family, everything you know and saw, I'll beat it out of you."

"Why you doing dis, Massa Jonathan, why? Can't help 'em now. Can't do nothin' but drive you mo' crazy with pain. Let it be! Oh, please let it be!"

"I'll never let it be! I want it to hurt, to burn with the fire of hell. Look at me! I should have been there to protect them. I left for money, damn my soul! Money! And now they're all dead. I should never have left. You tell me, all of it, or I'll end it here."

Arabella knew he meant it, could see it in the wildness of his eye. "Aw right! I gonna tell you, tell you all of it. Gonna drain it from my soul so you can live de nightmare I does ever night. You can stow it all in a black heart loaded fo' vengeance. But first you gonna promise me on yo' mama's grave dat you will love and care foe yo' sister's child. Dat precious baby Bethany need you, de last of her blood kin. I don't know how you and Doctor Ted gonna do it, but ya'll is gonna do it. Now you swear it to me."

They told him how his granddaddy, fighting from a goat cart, killed one of the intruders with his shotgun, how his body was found hanging out of the little wagon dragging face down as the goat grazed its way across the yard, how Jonathan's mother came to Daniel's aid, killing one of the men, how she looked lying in the grass still holding a pistol in her right hand, eyes wide open, her left hand missing its ring finger, the finger itself thrown on the ground bare of the wedding ring her husband had given her, and about his sister and what the last one did to her, how the pitiful baby had looked up and said, "Mama hurt, Bella."

Doctor Perkins, dressed in his nightshirt, met Jonathan in the hall as he returned from the servants' quarters. "I'm sorry you insisted on hearing all of that. Don't let it destroy you, son. Live for them, Jonathan, for the baby."

Jonathan didn't say a word. He put his arms around the doctor and held him for a long moment. Then he walked away toward his room.

The next morning he was gone. The doctor found a package and a note on his desk.

Dear Uncle Ted,

Once again my family and I become a burden to you. I know you loved my mother. She knew it too, and held a place in her heart for you second only to the memory of my father. Now I leave you with her granddaughter for there is no place for a baby where I must go. Together we will provide for her. Take the money I have left as a down payment for all the supplies you furnished my family and for the care of Bethany and the coming taxes on Shamrock. More will follow. I am indebted to you beyond all means of payment on this earth, but I will continue, on behalf of my family departed, Bethany and myself to try to find a way to thank you for your kindness, generosity , and loyalty to the Quinns.

Your loving godson, Jonathan

The package contained five thousand U.S. dollars, an unimaginable fortune at the time.

Captain Quinn was two days drunk by the time the river boat reached New Orleans. Filled with deep brooding, self-imposed guilt, he aimlessly drifted from one waterfront saloon to another finding little solace in whiskey or the false compassion of sporting ladies. He was sitting alone in a saloon on the riverfront called La Casa de los Marinos when a sailor, to the amusement of his companions, slapped a tray of drinks from the hands of a waitress. She fell to her knees cursing him while picking up the broken glass and wailing that she would have to pay for the spilled liquor. The sailor lifted his boot and pushed her rump, sending her sprawling on the whiskey-slick floor. He thought that was funny. The one-eyed man at the next table didn't.

Jonathan knocked the sailor out of his chair. The sailor drew a knife from his boot and came off the floor at Jonathan. Quinn beat the man senseless with a broken chair leg, nearly killed him, would have if others had not pulled him off.

Jonathan might have gone to jail if the waitress had not calmed him to a point where the men holding him were no longer afraid to turn loose the one-eyed demon. She barely got him out the back door and down the alley before the police arrived.

Her name was Grace O'Connell. She was a forty-year-old dolly that could pass for a sad and broken sixty in the harsh light of a noonday sun. By the light of an oil lamp in her little loft on Decatur Street, she studied the sleeping drunk who had so fiercely come to her aid. She had struggled to keep him on his feet long enough to stumble up the stairs to her room where she lay him on her fancy brass bed, the one piece of furniture in the room that was not second or third or fifth hand. Now sadly tarnished, she had bought it new from a store on Royal Street years ago when she made a living on her back instead of sloshing whiskey at drunks. She no longer rolled with naked sailors in her glorious bed. Instead, she rolled fully dressed, drunk ones in alleys, relieving them of money earned on their latest voyage. Only those too drunk to manage it actually invited themselves to bed with her, and if they sobered enough to do it, they usually changed their minds. Never pretty, she now had stringy hair and a nose that had been broken by some brute long ago.

"Well, Grace," she said to her shadow thrown on the wall by the light of the oil lamp, "this here one ain't no beauty," but the more she looked at the one-eyed man on her bed, the less she was certain that in a way, he wasn't so bad looking. In fact, from the profile of the good side, he was handsome. On the bad side she could see the ugly gouged pit where an eye had once rested. As for the rest, she had seen ears bitten off and spit on the bar room floor and jagged scars from broken bottles slashed across faces. Cleaned up with an eye patch in place, the scars probably gave him a certain mystery, she decided, the kind that could entice, teasingly frighten perhaps, but still attract women, excite the secret uncontrollable places deep inside.

"Hell," she admitted with a smile, "The longer I look at him . . ." More out of curiosity than charity, she took his filthy clothes off and bathed him with sponge and soap from her plain, white china wash basin. His body was beautiful, still young, lean, strong. Looking at it kindled distant memories of a time she didn't want to remember, a time when she was not then what she was now. She covered him and began to pick through his clothes. They were, under the soil of an extended running drunk, the rather fine clothes of a gentleman, all of them, shirt to shoes. She went through the pockets of the pants and laid the contents on a small table under the lamp.

She smiled. There was a gold locket that opened to reveal ambrotype photographs of two pretty women, perhaps mother and daughter, perhaps older and younger sisters. She was too experienced to take the locket even though it was gold. She set it aside. There was a deadly looking instrument clipped to the back of his belt. She put that in her purse. Next, there was a pocketful of change including a twenty-dollar gold piece. The other pocket held only a pen knife. She picked up the vest. There was a short section of gold chain hanging from a button hole. The watch to which it was once attached was gone, lost in the fight. A vest pocket held several cards engraved with the name, Captain Jonathan Hillary Quinn, and a company, Jones Shipping with a Nassau address. She turned to the coat. In one pocket she found a ticket for a boat to Nassau that had sailed the day before. In another, she found what she was looking for. She counted the bills as she pulled them from the leather fold. Six hundred fifty-three dollars. It was more money than she had ever seen in her life.

Jonathan awoke just before noon feeling worse than vile with no idea of where he was. Finding himself naked, he got up to look for his clothes. All he found behind the doors of a battered armoire were a few sagging, threadbare dresses. He felt bile rise in his throat, ran to the opened window and let go the putrid contents of his stomach onto the alley three floors below. After the dry heaves left him, he washed his face with water from the washstand and looked around for some whiskey. There was none. On the table he found the opened locket with the ambrotype pictures of his mother and sister dressed in silk, lace and pearls. It was, as Grace had guessed, his most precious possession. He ignored the loose coins and picked up his billfold. It contained fifty-three dollars and the outdated ticket to Nassau. Jonathan poured a glass of water from the pitcher, drank most of it, splashed his face with the remainder, and crawled back in the bed, covering his lower parts with a once white sheet gone yellow with age and too many washings, or too few.

The door opened. Grace walked in carrying his freshly cleaned suit, starched shirt, stockings, underwear, and a new collar and eye patch. She also had a basket containing French bread, butter, orange marmalade and a crock of hot, thick, chicory coffee. Jonathan didn't see all that. Sober for the first time in days, he stared at the bent-nosed, stringy-haired, painted woman standing in the middle of the door smiling at him. *Great God!* He pulled the sheet up to his neck. Grace hung his clothes on a hook on the back of the door and set the basket on the table.

"Well, ain't we proper this morning?"

Jonathan fought to keep from being sick again. "We are feeling close to death this morning," he replied. "What did we, that is, what did I do last night? What day is it?"

"Oh, you tried to kill a Greek sailor, that's all, Captain Jonathan Hillary Quinn," she replied. "And it's Sunday the fifteenth of November. From that ticket it seems you missed your boat."

"What else . . . I mean, well, what else?"

"You didn't spoil my virginity or yours for that matter if that's what's worrying you." He immediately looked relieved she noticed. "That ain't no compliment to the lady what saved you from going to jail?"

Jonathan felt much better. "What's your name, princess?"

"It's Grace, not that you care."

"Well, Grace, my darlin', is that hot coffee I smell?" Over breakfast Jonathan asked how much money was in his wallet the night before.

"Just what's in it now, honey. You wouldn't accuse your saving Grace of stealing after she brought you home and cleaned you up? You must have been hanging around some pretty rough women to be thinking that."

"Dear saving Grace, like Hamlet, I think you protest too much."

"And just who the hell is Hamlet? You know, after all I done for a one eyed, hacked up dandy, you got some gall to accuse me of thieving. Some gratitude. I should have left you to the police."

"I'm very grateful. That's just the point. There's only fifty dollars or so left. Your kindness to this one eyed, hacked up dandy deserves more. I feel bad that's all I have to share with you."

"Oh, all right. There was a hundred dollars more, but I only took it for expenses. Gittin' your clothes cleaned, breakfast, I have to get all the bedding cleaned, I paid your damages at the bar and ordered myself a new dress. The one I wore last night was ruined." She held out ten dollars, "Here, this is all that's left."

Jonathan smiled, "Grace dear, you didn't have to tell me all that. I know how much money I had a week ago upriver, but I don't have the least idea how much I had last night. Why it might have been six hundred dollars for all I know." Grace's mouth dropped open. "I thank you for looking after me, and I hope the new dress is as attractive as your honesty and charity."

"Honest as the day is long. That's why I'm so poor, that and the fact that I got a soft spot for fellows in trouble."

"There is one other thing you might do for me, Grace."

She brightened up, moving the hair out of her eyes and giving her most eager smile. "Anything at all, my dandy." The stack of bills tucked in her stocking felt warm against her leg. Leaving the fifty in the wallet along with the gold locket was a keen trick she told herself.

"While I get dressed, would you go to the bar again now that you have paid my damages," he smiled, "and see if you can find a very special possession of mine. It's a knife in a tooled leather scabbard with a metal clip on it. The knife was a gift to me from an old sea captain. I would reward the barman who finds it twenty of the fifty I have left. Could you do that? You can have the rest."

Grace took the money and put it in her purse beside the knife. "I'm not sure he will have it, what with all the crowd and the fighting, but I'll go and see." She turned at the door, "Tell me something. If you had a knife, why didn't you use it? The Greek had one 'till you knocked it away with the chair leg."

"Chair leg? Yes, I think I remember that now."

"Well? Why didn't you use the knife?" she asked again.

His expression changed, darkened, and the way he spoke frightened her.

"It's a virgin blade," is all he said.

Grace quickly closed the door and went downstairs to wait a proper length of time before returning with the knife. She opened her purse and carefully slid the wicked looking weapon out of its sheath. It had a five-inch doubled edge blade, thick in the middle but with both edges hollow ground like a straight razor. A shamrock was engraved on one side of the blade. 'A virgin blade' He didn't have to say more. She knew what he meant. *I wouldn't want to be whoever he's saving this for.* A shiver ran through her at the thought. As if touching a tool of the devil, she quickly put the blade away.

Jonathan was fully dressed when she returned. "You're in luck," she told him. "The barman wanted more money, but I convinced him he wouldn't want the owner to come for it. He took the twenty." She lay the knife on the bed.

Jonathan clipped it to his belt at the small of his back, picked up the change and locket, and put on his coat. "Hereafter, be more careful of dandies." He gave Grace a smile and was gone.

Grace went to her mirror and spun around. *You ain't pretty, old girl, but you got enough money to start a place of your own. Damn if you ain't goin' to be a prosperous madam in your old age.*

Jonathan passed a few vaguely familiar bars on his way to the riverfront. By late afternoon he had arranged to work passage on a lumber schooner bound for Key West. He would have to find a way to Nassau from there.

Deuteronomy must be looking for me by now. He'll give me a good dressing down when I show up.

He didn't. Captain Jones asked no questions. "Welcome back, son. We got work to do."

It was true. They had a great deal of work to do. Cuban nationalists were gathering a force to conduct what would be called the Ten Years War. Jones Shipping was increasingly called upon to perform the dangerous but highly profitable task of clandestinely assembling and delivering cargos of arms, ammunition and medicine to the Cuban rebels. Jonathan sent much of the considerable amount of money he made to Doctor Perkins in Vicksburg for payment of taxes and debt on Shamrock, and the care of his murdered sister's child. He traveled to see Bethany when business allowed, which wasn't often. On those rare occasions, he stayed with the good doctor and spent all his time with Bethany. He never visited Shamrock, nor checked on the books Ted Perkins had set up to account for the funds Jonathan provided. On each visit, just before his departure, he would go alone to the cemetery to place flowers on the graves of his slain family.

Jonathan hired the Pinkerton detective firm to conduct a search for the third killer who had escaped. Their offices reviewed army records of soldiers discharged or furloughed from Vicksburg and surveyed the South, the North East and even as far as California for any scrap of information, any barroom or jail rumor, any clue at all that might lead to the identity of the third man who had murdered the Quinn family and stolen the Shamrock bowl. No Pinkerton detective ever uncovered a clue. The final Pinkerton report stated . . .

Having exhausted all available avenues of investigation using the fullest extent of resources in manpower and professional experience within this company, we, in good conscience, must discourage any further pursuit of this matter. It is our belief that any additional time spent on our part would prove futile.

Jonathan could not accept that so brutal and cruel a crime would go unpunished. Haunted by the guilt he felt for not having been at Shamrock to protect his family that terrible day, he vowed, *I will find him . . . either here on Earth or in Hell.*

BOOK FOUR

BETHANY

CHAPTER 11

Vicksburg, 1875

Mrs. Butterworth came up the walk dragging her twelve-year-old son, Tommy Lee, behind her. Mrs. Butterworth was the sole piano teacher in town and wife of the Methodist minister. Ten-year-old Bethany saw the visitors coming and made a bee line out the back door and up a tall magnolia tree.

Luky showed Mrs. Butterworth into the doctor's study. From behind his desk, he looked up at them over a pair of gold-rimmed spectacles perched on his nose. He stood, removed a cigar from his mouth and put it in a green glass dish filled with ashes.

"Good afternoon, Mrs. Butterworth. Please have a seat and tell me what brings you and young Tommy Lee out this afternoon?"

"That little ruffian of a godchild of yours is what. It would be bad enough if she were a boy, but the very idea of a little girl acting the way she does. It's just disgraceful. Look at what she's done to my boy here."

The boy, hanging his head down, stood behind his mother. She shoved him toward the doctor and lifted his chin with her hand.

Doctor Perkins sat back down at his desk and motioned the boy to come around so he could have a close look at him. "Tommy Lee, do you mean to tell me that you had a fight with Bethany and she gave you that shiner?" Tommy Lee nodded his head. "Well what brought on this pugilistic contest? She didn't just walk up and blind-side you for no reason at all did she?" Tommy Lee seemed to put some thought to the question. While he was pondering his answer, Doctor Perkins called out, "Bee Bee!" There was no answer. "Luky!" Luky appeared at the door. "Luky, where is that child? She was here just a minute ago."

"Dat child done seen trouble coming. My guess is she out yonder up to de top of de magnolia tree like always when somethin' amiss 'round here."

"Well, go get Arabella to get her to come down, tell her I want to see her."

Luky resented the fact that only Arabella could control the child, but she admired the child's spunk long as it was directed somewhere out of Luky's area of responsibility. Directing it at Mrs. Butterworth was just fine as far as she was concerned. From the doctor's study they could hear the goings on in the back yard. "Bee Bee, you come down from 'dere right dis minute! You hear me? One a 'dese days you gonna fall and bust yo' head wide open. Now I done told you a hundred times not to climb so high in de first place. You listenin' to me?"

Bethany was too high in the thick glossy greenery to be seen from the ground. From her perch she could see over the houses clear to the river. It was her castle in the sky, her sanctuary unattainable by others. The young were afraid to follow her so high, the old, not about to.

Arabella decided it was time to use her full authority. "All right, Miss Beverly Bethany Quinn. Yo' better git down out'a dat tree and in de house to see yo' uncle Ted, and I mean now!" Silence followed. "Alright, Missy. I'm gonna cut me a switch and have it ready to give de doctor when he come out his self, which he gonna do when I tells 'em you ain't comin'. Is dat what you is wantin' me to do, go fetch him and embarrass him in front of visitors? Huh?"

Directly there came the rustle of leaves from somewhere above. After a while Arabella caught sight of a slim, ivory skinned child with long black hair and green eyes climbing down one limb after another with the grace of a cat. She dropped to the ground and stood barefooted wearing a soiled dress with a torn sleeve.

"My! Yo' is a mess, child. What have you done dis time?" Silent, Bethany marched past Arabella, past Luky holding the back door open at the top of the wooden steps, and down the hall into the doctor's study. Tommy Lee moved just far enough behind his mother so the adults couldn't see him stick his tongue out at her. She ignored him and came to a halt at the doctor's desk.

"All right Bethany, since Tommy Lee here hasn't told us what started the argument, suppose you do."

"He started it, Uncle Ted."

"I did not!"

"Did too!"

"Did not!"

"Yes he did. He started saying bad things and got the other children to say them too."

"What did he say, Darling? You tell us the truth. Don't go making anything up."

She looked up at him. "I don't want to say what he said. I just told Tommy Lee that if he didn't stop saying it I would lick him good, and that's what I did. And I'll do it again, too." She was looking straight at Tommy Lee.

"Why, what she needs is a good spanking to get some of that sass out of her, Doctor. I would never tolerate a child in my house talking like that." Mrs. Butterworth raised her nose just a little higher in the air.

"Bee Bee, Honey, just tell me what started all this. Mrs. Butterworth is correct in saying that a pretty little girl shouldn't go around picking fights with boys. It isn't ladylike. I want to hear it, and hear it now."

Arabella and Luky were standing in the back hall just out of sight listening.

Tears welled up in Bethany's eyes and she looked down at the floor. "He said I didn't have a daddy 'cause my mama took up with a no-good Yankee who left her fo' I was born. I told him it was a lie; that my mama and daddy were killed by no'count Yankees, that my mama was as brave as a soldier and never would even speak to a Yankee, not ever. Tommy Lee, he wouldn't stop teasing and saying things about my mama, so I beat the daylights out of him and he better not do it again." She eased around the desk while she was talking until her face was hidden against the doctor's shoulder while she clung to his arm.

"Tommy Lee, did you say those things?"

"Of course he didn't. Where would he get such an idea?"

"Mrs. Butterworth, why don't we let Tommy answer?"

"I said 'em cause it's true," Tommy Lee said defiantly, "Everybody says so. She had no right to jump on me 'cause I wasn't the only one saying it."

"And where did you hear such stories, Tommy Lee, or did you just make them up?"

"I didn't make nothing up. I heard all about it when I was in my mama's kitchen one day. The church ladies were having a sewing in the dining room and talked all about it, didn't y'all, Mama?"

"That's quite enough, Tommy Lee. We don't have to sit here and listen a minute longer. I don't want you to say another word. Good day, Doctor." Dragging Tommy Lee, she turned toward the door.

"Good day, Mrs. Butterworth. Please tell the Reverend Butterworth hello for me, and oh yes, give all those nice ladies in the sewing circle my regards."

Mrs. Butterworth nearly yanked Tommy Lee's arm out of joint hauling him from the house.

Luky and Arabella walked into the room.

"My, my," the good doctor said. "A real genteel, Christian lady that Mrs. Butterworth."

"Come on child," Lucky said. "Doctor's got work to do. Me and Arabella jes happen to have some cookies hid out in de kitchen. Let's go git some. 'Den Arabella gonna git you a bath fixed while I see if I can mend dat sleeve on yo' dress."

Ted kissed her on the forehead. "I guess I would have hit him, too, Honey, but never pay any mind to trashy gossip. Only weak people with nothing better to do talk about others. Besides, we know the truth. You come from the best people east of the Mississippi river and I'm very proud that your Uncle Jonathan decided to let you live with your Uncle Ted 'til you're old enough to join him in the islands. I have the prettiest little girl in Mississippi right here and we all love you just like we loved your beautiful mama and grandmama. Now run along and have a cookie, but don't forget to save one for me."

Bethany rubbed her sleeve across her tear filled eyes and followed Arabella to the kitchen. While the little girl was taking her bath, Arabella came back to the doctor's study and asked to speak to him.

"You and Captain Jonathan gonna have to do somethin' 'bout dat child, and I don't mean teach her more men stuff. She can out shoot, out ride, and now I reckon, out fight nearly any boy in her school, and she can sho' climb higher up a tree. Now all them ain't exactly de talents a proper young lady should be having. What dat child needs is a mama, or a school to make her want'a be a lady 'stead a copy of you and Captain Jonathan, or Lawd hep us, her great granddaddy Quinn what she acts mo' like ever day. Now I ain't saying you and Captain Jonathan ain't give her love and nearly ever thing she wants, including being allowed to run all over de place. Lawd! She done raced her pony down main street last Sunday causing church folks to scatter every which a way. Folks is talking 'bout dat wild Quinn child what ain't got nobody to look after but an old doctor and two old black women what can't keep up wit' her. I knows acause I hears what folks say. Sooner than you think, dat little tomboy gonna be growed into a young woman . . . 'bout five quick mo' years I reckon. Den you gonna have real trouble."

"You're right." The doctor picked up his cigar, struck a lucifer match on the bottom of his desk and relit it, puffing a cloud of smoke to fire it up.

"Course I is. And what's mo', you, me, and Luky ain't gonna be round here fo' ever. Nicodemus done already kicked the bucket last January, bless his old soul. You and Captain Jonathan better sit down on his next visit and figure out what to do 'bout dis child."

"Uncle Jonathan!" Bethany called as she ran to him from the back yard.

It was June 1875 and Captain Quinn had arrived for another visit. He came two or three times a year and regularly sent money for his niece's support and to pay the ever increasing taxes on Shamrock and, against the doctor's protest, a generous management fee for taking care of Quinn family business. In spite of the doctor's denials, Jonathan knew he needed the money. Every Mississippian needed money. Whether they held out in paint-peeling mansions with patched roofs and sagging eaves, or clung to weathered, unpainted shacks, the people of postwar Mississippi all shared a single endeavor . . . survival.

Jonathan stood on the back steps, arms open, waiting to hug the girl running toward him. Her dark tussled hair flowed about her shoulders, her bare feet danced across uncut grass and scattered leaves. Jonathan no longer noticed the neglect common to the yards and once-splendid homes of Vicksburg. The doctor's house was stained by brown runs from rusting iron grillwork, but looked no worse than the rest of the town.

"How's my girl?"

"Look how tall I am!"

"Tall and dirty doesn't mean grown and ladylike." He picked her up. "Whoa! You are growing. Let me look at you. Uh-oh, I see sweat beads under your chin, and you smell a little like your pony. Arabella, take this ragamuffin in and see that she gets a good bath."

"Oh, Uncle Jonathan," she protested.

"Oh, Uncle Jonathan, nothin'," said Arabella. "Yo' done heard de Captain. Now git, or yo' ain't gonna have de present he done brung ya."

Still with her arms around her uncle's neck, her green eyes opened wide. "What present, Uncle Jonathan?"

"A new Sunday dress made in Paris for a very ladylike young girl. I thought one lived here, but all I see is a dirty stable boy, or could there possibly be a young lady under those overalls?"

"A dress from Paris! That's in France, Bella. My mama and grandmama used to have dresses from Paris. Isn't that right, Uncle Jonathan? I bet nobody in Mississippi has a new dress from Paris." She looked at Arabella. "Is my bath ready?"

"Is yo' bath ready? Since when did you take to goin' peaceably to a bath? And talkin' 'bout fancy dresses, seems to me it's hard enough to git you outta dem disgraceful overalls. Ain't no young lady s'posed to go 'round in pants nohow."

"How could I ride bareback unless I wore pants?" Bethany argued as she and Arabella went up stairs.

"Young ladies ain't s'posed to ride bareback. De s'posed to ride side-saddle wearing a dress."

The doctor and Jonathan moved to the parlor. "Now you see what I'm up against with a house full of women. Damn if I don't miss the army."

"You're doing a fine job, Ted, but what concerns me is that each time I return, damn if things around here don't look worse instead of better. The war has been over for years. Tell me about the way things are here."

"I'm not sure you'll want to hear it."

"Suppose you hit the high spots."

"There haven't been any. When you were a boy, Mississippi was the fifth richest state in the Union, probably had more millionaires than any state this side of New York, your granddaddy being one of 'em. The trouble was that her capital was tied up in land, cotton, and, God forgive us, slaves. Emancipation meant the loss of two hundred and fifty million dollars worth of capital investment. All the warehoused cotton held by the banks as collateral was confiscated. With the slaves and cotton gone, and no money to pay mortgages, the banks failed. I think Lincoln would have prevented such suffering if that damn drunken fool Booth hadn't killed him. Am I boring you, son? I tend to get my vinegar up about all this."

"I'll tell you if you do."

"All right. Where was I?"

"Your vinegar was up."

"Damn right. Seventy eight-thousand Mississippians went to war. Only 28,000 came home and they were in such bad shape that one fifth of the entire state budget in '66 went for artificial limbs. There wasn't enough black cloth in the state to make dresses for all the widows."

"I'm ashamed I didn't know all this, Ted. I guess I was too grieved by my own troubles and I left the country. But that was years ago. Things should be getting better."

"Well they ain't. Goddamned reconstruction is nothing but deliberate oppression. The South was divided into five military districts, all under martial law and occupied by Federal troops. The only people allowed to vote in Mississippi were blacks, scallywags, and carpetbaggers. No ex-Confederate could vote. That ought to tell ya' what kind of sorry legislature we had running the state. In Jackson you could buy a vote for a bottle of whiskey, pass a law for the price of a new suit. Carpetbaggers got them to raise taxes. They knew folks couldn't pay, had no cash, couldn't get a speck of credit. They bought up land cheap at tax sales. Damn near all business was done by barter and still is. The average farmer here is lucky to see twenty dollars cash in a year. Some say the state has lost more than 80 percent of its economic base. Eighty percent! It'll take a hundred years for Mississippi to even begin to recover. That's the sum total of Reconstruction."

"I feel guilty for leaving, Ted, but there's no other way to hold on to Shamrock."

"I don't know why you keep it if you mean never to come back to it."

"It's where my heart is buried."

Both men grew silent, lost in their own thoughts of the past and the present.

In 1881 Beverly Bethany Quinn celebrated her seventeenth birthday. Jonathan returned to Vicksburg to keep his promise. He would take Bethany to live with him in Nassau before taking her on to Europe where she would join other wealthy young ladies at an exclusive finishing school in *la ville lumiere*, Paris.

In the kitchen, Arabella stood over the sink fussing with the dishes while she talked to Jonathan. "I don't see no reason to send dat child off way over de 'Lantic Ocean foe schooling nohow. Yo' sister and you weren't sent off dat way."

"Before the war we had tutors at Shamrock, a teacher from Atlanta who taught us English, Latin, mathematics, literature and history, and another from France to teach us French and art. You know that. Those days are over. Her mother and grandmother would be pleased to see her get this opportunity. You told me she needed to learn to be a lady. Well that is why she is going to join other young ladies at finishing school, the very best. I'll be damned if I'll send Bethany to a Yankee school up North. You should be glad I can afford to give her such an education. If Deuteronomy had not sent for me, we would all still be hooked to a plow, digging potatoes to live. Besides, I've asked you to go with her."

"I's too old fo' to pack up and cross no ocean to some land I ain't never set foot in. I love dat baby, but I's tellin' de truth. I's jes' too old to get on no boat." Arabella dried her hands on her apron and turned to Jonathan, "I gonna miss her so much, and worry 'bout her, too." She looked up, tears in her tired eyes, and put her arms around Jonathan. "I ain't gonna see her again, Massa Jonathan. We all jes so old now—me, Doctor Ted, Luky . . . been so much change, jes woe us out I reckon." She let him go, wiped her tears, and said, "You de one got to look after her now. Don't never let nothing harm dat child, you hear? She yo' child now."

Jonathan hugged her. "I'll look after her, Arabella. She's going to be quite a lady. And what's all this talk about not seeing her again? You're not that old. She'll visit Vicksburg from time to time. You'll see."

Later upstairs, Arabella had almost finished packing a steamer trunk when Bethany walked in to see her stuffing a small package down into one corner. "What is that you just put in my trunk, Bella?"

Arabella jumped like she was hot. "Lawd! You shouldn't sneak up on me like dat. Make my heart stop."

"But what is it?"

"Child, yo' is growing up and 'dere are things . . . things 'bout yo' mama, and, well, yo' self, things ain't nobody ever done told you cause maybe you was too little to understand. Doctor Ted, me and him talked last night. He done kept yo' mama's diary all dis time, and some'em else too, some'em yo' grandmama throwed at a fire what everybody thought was burnt up, but what I done picked up and put in my apron pocket. Doctor Ted, he done wrote down things in yo' mama's diary help 'splain de whole story. Time you had dem things, read yo' mama's and Doctor

Ted's words. Even yo' Uncle Jonathan ain't never seen 'em. But you jes leave 'em be in de trunk 'til you get's where you's going. It done kept all dis time. It'll keep a mite longer." She buckled the leather straps across the trunk and snapped the lock. "Besides, it's time we called dem carriage mens up here to tote yo' things down. You got goodbyes to do and a riverboat to catch what ain't gonna wait."

"But what is all the mystery? What's in the package with the diary? Why am . . ."

"Now I done told you it's time to git. So git!"

Bethany's excitement for the adventure that lay before her was tempered by the emotional distress of leaving a familiar and loved place and the people who made it so. It was a tearful and hard exchange of farewells.

Jonathan understood the potential finality of such goodbyes. He had said them to his family before leaving Shamrock. More recently before leaving on a routine trip to Cuba, he had said a casual farewell to his aging partner, mentor, and friend, Deuteronomy Jones. He returned barely in time to bury Deuteronomy at sea, as was his wish. The salty old captain had died quietly in his sleep.

Captain Quinn, waiting beside the carriage, looked at the frail, white-haired man who had been his grandfather's best friend, who had been ever loyal and caring to the Quinn family, and was reminded of his father and grandfather, of a different time, a world that would never be again.

Arabella's voice rescued him from his thoughts. "Cap'in Quinn, you better take dis here child fo' we all changes our minds. She ain't nothing but trouble and fuss, but we all reckon to miss her mischief 'round here."

"This child, if you haven't noticed, Arabella," Bethany said, "is a grown young lady, and the world awaits."

"Grown lady my eye. Yo' uncle gonna turn gray as de doctor here jes trying to keep up wit' you."

Doctor Perkins held Bethany in one long, last hug and helped her up into the waiting carriage. Luky and Arabella stood back dabbing their eyes with handkerchiefs. Jonathan and Ted shook hands in silence, their eyes saying the emotional goodbye their voices left unspoken. The carriage pulled away, everyone waving.

CHAPTER 12

From the landing below the great bluffs of Vicksburg the riverboat turned out into the muddy, roiling current and headed downstream for New Orleans. Bethany stood at the port railing looking back as the city on the bluff faded into the distance. She was leaving behind the only place she had ever known. Standing there, Bethany was torn between feelings of profound sadness and excited anticipation of the new adventure before her.

When they could no longer see Vicksburg, Jonathan and Bethany inspected their adjoining, outside cabins on the boiler deck, checked to see their trunks had been delivered and then went into the lavishly decorated grand salon. To Bethany it was all so new, so exciting.

That evening after dinner, Bethany excused herself saying all the excitement had worn her out. She disappeared into her cabin, retrieved the mysterious package Arabella had stowed in her trunk and quickly unwrapped the parcel. It contained a leather bound diary with her mother's name embossed in gold on the cover and a very unusual pendant with a gold chain. Bethany set the pendent aside and opened the diary. In the delicately penned hand of her mother, it began with a detailed narrative history of Shamrock the way it had been before the war. There followed Annielise's account of the siege of Vicksburg, her father's death, their worry over Jonathan, and details of the day Annielise was wounded. Then came the fall of Vicksburg, daily life after the surrender, Annielise' defiance of martial law resulting in her exile, the trip to Shamrock, and how they began the hard work for survival there.

It was almost two in the morning when Bethany came upon the explanation of her own conception. A cold shiver ran down her spine. *Oh, dear God! I was not fathered by a man at all, but by a bullet! What is that Latin word in one of Doctor Ted's medical books for a freak of nature . . . lusus naturae? Yes! That's it, that's what I am, a freak. Doctor Ted, Arabella, Luky, Jonathan, they all told me my mother and father had been killed by Yankees. They had not lied, exactly, but they had not told me the whole terrible truth.*

Bethany sat trying to absorb the impossible, what it meant. Why had they never told her? *They were trying to protect me. They were afraid to tell anyone. Couldn't tell a child, not and keep it a secret. How could they? Who would believe it? God! People would put me in a freak show. Write about me in medical books. God help me! I must keep this secret all my life.*

She put her mother's diary down, felt trapped in the tiny cabin, wanted to run out, thought of jumping into the river. For a long while she sat facing the door. She could faintly feel the rhythmic movement of the steam driven beams below turning the great paddlewheel. It called to her. Bethany slipped out of her cabin and walked aft to stand watching the powerful paddlewheel churn a foamy wake that stretched into the moonlight to fade in the distance like a sad memory . . . like her mother and grandfather and Doctor Ted and all she had known.

It's good that I am going away. Yes, that's what they want, those who love me. A new life far away where I'll never have to explain that I am a freak of nature . . . no a freak of war. That's what I am. What would my life be if everyone knew I was a bullet's baby?

Following the account of her conception and birth there were daily entries in the diary describing events in her life as a baby. The last entry written by her mother the day before she was killed read, *She is such a happy little baby. She is the one joy of the Quinns here at Shamrock, and I love her so.*

There followed the heavy script of Doctor Perkins handwriting that revealed the terrible facts of the brutal murders of her family, Arabella's and Nicodemus's descriptions of how they found the bodies of her mother, grandmother and great grandfather that terrible day at Shamrock.

On pages dated much later, the doctor, with obvious love, affection and humor, told of the trials and tribulations of raising the baby girl fate had placed in his hands, of the tomboy who had *grown into a loving, beautiful child.*

Old Shamrock Plantation 1915

Still sitting at her desk in the Shamrock Cottage well past midnight, Bethany closed her mother's diary.

Over the years I had forgotten much of that, but not the courage of my family, not the warm and loving home Uncle Ted and Arabella and Luky provided for me, and certainly not the fact that I exist as a consequence of war, a bullet's progeny, a freak.

Bethany looked at the second diary, the one with her name hand-written on the plain, cloth cover. She touched it, took it in her hands.

My life is written in your pages, most of it anyway. Your pages begin with the words of a young, immature girl and end, I suppose, with the secret, world-weary confessions of a lonely woman.

She absently rubbed the cover of her own diary while looking through the window into the night. The sweet scent of flowers mixed with the smell of woodland pine wafted into the room.

I wrote you, but no one has ever read you, not even me. Perhaps I should do that now. No one else will 'til after I'm gone. I wonder what the boy will think of me when he reads it.

Well Jonathan, since you've put me back in the 'special cargo' business, I guess it helps to remember what is written in these pages. God! I was so young and naive when I first found out who I really was, where I had come from.

It was fun for a while, my new life. And I know, Jonathan, you never meant for me to be hurt. It was my choice, my doing, wasn't it?

Bethany took the last sip of bourbon in her glass.

Are you playing a joke on me, Jonathan, or are the gods of war using me as a plaything one last time? Whatever the case, I will finish it. Hell, I have to if it's to be done, don't I? Machinery parts from Cuba to New York to England; I can do that. Cuba and America would not be pleased to discover private weapons moving from Cuban soil through an American port into English hands would they? It will be a little illegal I think, a violation of their neutrality. Think of that, little ole me creat'en a international incident. Why President Wilson might have a hissy fit.

Our old agent, George, will have to help. He and the British bastard will know but they won't tell. George will try and talk me into letting him handle it all, collect payment on delivery, but I will do it myself. Yes, I will do it; a fitting and final ending for auld lang syne. . . . for Jonathan and Louisette, Mannela, Henri and Felipe.

Besides, it will give me an excuse to check on the boy while I'm over there, try one more time to talk him into giving up the Army and coming home where he belongs.

Bethany opened the diary to the first page. It was yellowing with age but the ink stood indelibly sharp in her clear, delicate handwriting. The short written descriptions of times and events evoked full and clear memories. Some of them made her smile, some were sweet, some opened wounds, some were torture. It started with the departure from Vicksburg.

Mississippi River, 1881

In her cabin, seventeen year old Bethany closed her mother's leather bound diary. Through her cabin window she could see a gray, rain-swept dawn washing the night away. For the first time in her life, she felt close to her mother. *My poor, brave Mama, You died to protect me, didn't you?* Emotionally exhausted, sleep at first eluded her. Lulled by the soft, puffing rhythm of the steam engine below and the faint vibration of the paddle wheel slapping the muddy water as it rippled from beneath the flat bottom of the boat, sleep came at last.

Jonathan checked on his niece in her adjoining cabin and was surprised to find her still asleep. He quietly closed the door and went to the dining salon for coffee. It was after ten when a solemn young woman approached his table. Jonathan rose to seat Bethany and noticed the odd piece of jewelry she was wearing. He immediately knew what it was, had heard his sister describe the pendent and the night their mother threw it in the fire. He stared at the deformed lead slug enfolded in delicate gold hanging from the chain around her neck.

"Not many young women can wear their father around their neck, can they Uncle?"

She placed her mother's diary on the table and patted the leather cover on which her mother's name was embossed.

"For the first time, I know who I am, what I am." She pushed the diary across the table. "I think she would want you to read this. Do you realize she was only my age when all of it happened?"

Bethany was more reserved than Jonathan had ever seen her. For the rest of the journey down river they settled into a quiet routine of strolling the deck, sipping coffee and reading in the grand salon. Neither mentioned the contents of the diary. Surprisingly, Bethany wanted to hear all about the business of Jones & Quinn Shipping.

Jonathan made a vaguely disturbing observation during the trip down river. His niece, dressed in her new travel attire, received admiring glances from more than a few male passengers. *Arabella was right*, he thought to himself.

They wasted no time in New Orleans. While Jonathan took Bethany to dinner at Antoíne's, their baggage was taken from the riverboat directly to J & Q Shipping's three-masted schooner, *Barca Vela*, docked a few blocks away at the foot of Toulouse Street. Sunrise found the schooner under tow by steam launch headed down river for the Gulf of Mexico, a twisting ninety-five river miles away. She was bound for the Bahamas with a cargo of wire rope, cotton caulking, oakum, marine hardware, kegs of nails, farm tools, kitchen wares, dry goods and several tons of sacked Louisiana rice.

The first day out on the Gulf, Bethany wore a dress and played the part of a perfect lady, strolling the deck, staying out of the way, careful not to crowd the bow where she might catch spray. By the next morning she had had enough of doing nothing. She appeared on deck in a pair of pants, a long sleeve shirt, and a straw hat held firmly to her head with a chin strap fashioned of red ribbon.

Jonathan smiled. "All right, Bee Bee, where did you get those clothes?"

"I folded them into one of my quilts before Arabella packed them. She thought she had thrown out all my 'ragamuffin' clothes, but I saved a few of my favorites. Don't worry, uncle. In public I will not embarrass you. I'll mind my manners no matter how bored I get, but in private I intend to do and learn what I please, and some things can't be properly done or learned in a dress."

"I can't say I wasn't warned."

"No, you can't. Now to business. I want to learn to handle this schooner, know her from stem to stern below deck, topside and aloft, and how to navigate her across the Gulf. I intend to be Captain Bee Bee by the time we make Nassau. After all, I could hardly be a partner in J & Q if I couldn't handle one of its boats."

"Partner?"

"Yes, a working partner when I get out of school. I intend to earn my share."

Jonathan thought about that a moment. "We'll see."

The crew was made up of black Bahamians except for the captain, Jorge Lopez, a Spaniard born in Cuba. Bethany took an interest in each of the crew members and the jobs they performed. It took her a while to understand the elegant, rich patois that flowed from the tongues of the English speaking Bahamian crew. It was completely different from that spoken by Arabella and Luky and the freed slaves in the South.

With Jonathan's nod of approval, the crew taught her every inch of ship, sail and rigging while he taught her navigation and weather, how to read the sea, wind and sky. The schooner had not been chosen for her cargo capacity. In the arms business one didn't need a lumber schooner or coal collier. What one needed was speed. *Barca Vela* was built for it. She was one hundred-seventy feet in length and carried

12,600 square feet of sail including topsails, staysails and jibs. Jonathan showed Bethany just what the graceful vessel could do, how to get the most out of her. He drove her on a close reach in a fresh breeze, topsails set, windward rigging taut, lee rail boiling the sea into effervescent foam. At times, her speed touched thirteen knots. Bethany rotated watches at the helm by day and by night, in fair weather and foul, always with her uncle at her side.

He loved her brightness, her enthusiasm. Her joy in learning was infectious. The crew laughed with her when she made mistakes and sang out their approval when she accomplished some new task. They had only one complaint. Captain Lopez conveyed to Captain Quinn that the crew was concerned because he allowed her to climb aloft. They did not want their pretty young apprentice risking a fall. She climbed anyway. Up the rat lines she would climb to sit on the crosstrees at the top of the mainmast where the topmast was stepped. From her high, rocking perch she scanned the cloud-fluffed horizon and watched the bows cleanly slice the warm, clear Gulf water. She had seen the color of the Gulf change from the brown turbid mix at the mouth of the river to green further offshore and then, as if crossing a line drawn on a map, to a deep cobalt blue. Watching her from the deck below, Jonathan remembered his own feelings when first he went to sea. *Oh, Deuteronomy, I hope you can see this. You would love her you old sea dog.*

They sailed east, south-eastward down the Gulf. Early one morning Bethany spied what looked to be a patch of tiny white streaks on the horizon off the port bow. Using Captain Lopez's glass, she could make out low, flat islands and a large, flat, brick structure that appeared to float on the water. "What is that sitting so alone on the sea?" she asked her uncle.

Quinn looked to port. His expression changed. For the first time Bethany saw a different Jonathan, one with a coldness in his eye accented by the tightening of his jaw. She would not see that expression often, but she would learn to respect it as a storm warning.

"That's Fort Jefferson sitting on a sandy, coral reef called Dry Tortugas. It's the hell hole where Grandfather Quinn was imprisoned. They took an old man trying to defend his granddaughter and put him in that place. It broke him physically, almost broke his spirit." Jonathan's expression changed when he looked back at Bee Bee. "Grandfather Daniel loved you Bee Bee. Do you remember him at all? You were two or so when he . . . when they all died."

"I feel I know him from all Uncle Ted and Arabella and old Nicodemus used to tell me. I don't know if I really remember those times, or if I just remember what I have been told about them and what I read in Mother's diary. I dream about my mama sometimes, but never clearly." She did not tell him about her childhood nightmares, vague dreams she didn't understand. Bethany frowned. "I can't remember my mama's face."

"I've been keeping something I was given when I went off to school, something I want you to have now," Jonathan said. "Perhaps one day you will put away the bullet and wear this instead." Jonathan pulled a gold locket from under his shirt and took its gold chain from around his neck. He opened the locket and placed it in Bethany's hand.

"These were taken when your mother was only twelve, but you can see how beautiful she and your grandmother Nannie both were."

Bethany looked at the two Ambrotype photographs for a long time and then closed the locket. "This must mean so much to you, Uncle."

"It rightfully belongs to you, now." Jonathan put his arm around her. "I no longer need it now that I have your bright eyes and pretty smile to remind me of them."

They left Dry Tortugas and the ship-killing reefs of Marquesas Keys behind. Just before sundown they docked at the sleepy, mosquito-ridden little village of Key West. The settlement was comprised of a general store, a saloon, a few houses, a row of waterfront shacks, and a group of buildings adjacent to large piles of coal that constituted a fueling station for U.S. Navy ships.

The local saloon owner greeted the boat and personally invited one and all to his establishment. He informed Jonathan that one day a railroad was going to be built from the mainland across the chain of small islands to the Key for the purpose of supplying the coaling station, and that a ferry was planned that would link Key West to Cuba when the railroad was completed. "Make this place a boom town," he predicted. Jonathan declined the saloon keeper's invitation. He didn't want his niece in the company of rowdy sailors, nor did he intend to depart the next morning with drunken hands.

He set the crew to off-loading the marine supplies and dry goods consigned to Key West. Once that was done, he gave his crew two hours leave under the strict supervision of Captain Lopez. He knew none of the crew had enough money to get into trouble. They had spent all they had in New Orleans waiting for Bethany's arrival from Vicksburg. After a quiet dinner on board with his niece, he passed the time teaching Bethany about bills of lading, how to tally the loading and offloading of consigned cargo and record credits and debits in the ship's book. *Barca Vela*, with a reasonably sober crew, was back at sea shortly after sunrise the next morning.

When Bethany first saw the Gulf Stream it was running hard against both wind and tide. She climbed aloft to see more clearly this mystery of the deep. Marked by a change in color, it had the distinct appearance of a great river in the middle of the ocean. The famous current had its own peculiar and uncomfortable wave pattern seemingly indifferent to the sea state on either side.

Under clear skies they had a rough, wet crossing, but once free of the great ocean current there was smooth sailing. Prior to reaching Bahamian waters, the American flag was struck and the English Ensign flown. Although J & Q, Ltd. was registered as a British company operating from British territory, its expatriate Southern owner casually flew whatever flag was convenient, especially where port officials were or could be persuaded to be lax when examining a ship's papers and cargo. J & Q found such arrangements necessary to commerce in the Caribbean where absentee English, Spanish, French, and Dutch Governments jealously protected their national economies with punitive tariffs on foreign imports to their island possessions. The colonial islanders resented such restrictions and welcomed the opportunity to obtain the products they desired at the best price however they could get their hands on them. J & Q Shipping thrived in such an atmosphere.

Jonathan patiently educated his niece about such matters during the voyage from New Orleans to Nassau, New Providence, Bahamas. J & Q Shipping was now his, and Bethany was all the family he had. She did not yet know just how special she was, but Jonathan knew. He had watched her grow. He had no doubts that she would keep to herself all he confided to her. *She is, after all, a Quinn.*

Instead of resenting taking orders from a young woman, the crew was grinning-proud at journey's end as the green-eyed girl navigated Barca Vela down the narrow channel leaving Long Cay and Silver Cay to starboard and Hog Island to port to enter the anchorage of Nassau Harbor. There she brought the schooner sharply into the wind. The vessel quickly lost way. She ordered the anchor let go and the sails hauled down in proper sequence. Captain Quinn had stood at her side as she navigated through the coral passages and had not found it necessary to interfere. He repeated Deuteronomy's words from long ago. "You'll do, Miss Quinn, you'll do."

As they rowed *Barca Vela*'s tender toward the dock, the heat of the afternoon sun melted the bright colors of the village into a wavy montage of pastels accented by the white cotton awnings of market stalls.

"So this is home," Bethany said. "It looks like a toy town sitting on blue-green crystal. I've never seen water so clear."

"You can see your anchor thirty feet down. Just remember, it's hard to judge depth and coral will rip the bottom out of the strongest ship and skin a human to the bone. We'll go swimming so you can see its beauty and touch its sharpness. With a glass-bottomed bucket you'll see tropical reef fish wearing colors not yet dreamed of by artists."

Before they reached the landing, Bethany asked, "If I'm old enough to be a partner, Uncle, then you consider me grown, don't you?"

"I no longer consider you a child, but you do have a few years of school before you. Suppose we let Nassau decide the question of just how grown-up you are."

"Let Nassau decide?"

"The Governor is giving a lawn party the twenty-fourth of May to celebrate Queen Victoria's birthday and the forty-fourth year of the old girl's reign. I have an invitation. I'll escort you to the party and introduce you to the society of the island. If they treat you as a grown-up, so will I. Of course, they won't think too much of a barefooted ragamuffin in work pants, an old straw hat, a suntan like a field worker and rope-burned hands."

Bethany looked at her rough hands and tanned skin. "Oh, I think by the celebration this ragamuffin just might change herself into the grown young woman Arabella warned you about."

"You seem very sure of yourself."

"Well, Captain, I am a Quinn."

Jonathan and Bethany were rowed ashore in the tender, leaving orders at the dock to have their trunks delivered to J & Q living quarters after the crew transferred *Barca Vela*'s remaining cargo to shore.

"Uncle," she said as they walked along the wharf, "I really need a new dress if I am to attend a royal lawn party."

Jonathan smiled. "I suppose if I don't agree you will show up in your ragamuffin garb claiming you have absolutely nothing to wear."

"Perhaps." Bethany smiled.

"I'm not much help in selecting dresses. You will find a very nice shop downtown."

"Uncle! You're not a mean ole' pirate after all."

"No? What am I then?"

"A sweet ole' pussycat."

"Please don't tell anyone. It would ruin my reputation."

As they neared the steps of the J & Q building, Bethany found herself in a tug-of-war with a small Chinese man over the small valise she was carrying.

"Let go, Missy!"

"Uncle! This man is trying to steal my bag."

Jonathan turned around and laughed. "Let him have it. That's Billy Wong, my number one house boy, cook, and waiter. You will make him lose face if you don't let him have it." Billy Wong took the luggage and ran up the steps leading to the second floor.

"Lose his face?" Bethany said quizzically.

"Lose face . . . it means lose his dignity, his pride, all the rank of his position. It's an oriental thing; very important not to have him lose face. If he does, we may not get a cooked meal for a week."

When they reached the second floor gallery, the little Chinese man was holding the door open for them. Bethany smiled at him. "I'm very proud to meet Captain Quinn's number one man, Billy Wong."

The small man bowed gracefully. "Thank you, Missy."

J & Q Shipping was housed in a two story wooden frame building on the Nassau harbor front next to a row of small warehouses. The first floor consisted of the shipping company office and a marine hardware and supply business. The second floor was divided into living quarters for J & Q Shipping's owners. It was roomy, comfortable, and convenient for bachelors, though totally void of anything feminine. At the last moment before he left to fetch his niece, Jonathan was inspired to order lace curtains for the windows, potted plants for the gallery overlooking the harbor, a new, hand painted chamber pot, a fine china wash basin and pitcher and a second copper bathtub for his niece's quarters.

Bethany was given the bedroom and adjoining parlor formerly used by Captain Jones. His naval sword, the Confederate ensign, a painting of a ship under full sail and various nautical mementos decorated the walls, book shelves and table. The bed looked heavy, as if made from ships timbers, the chairs large, their cushions threadbare. Jonathan's quarters across the common area was even more lacking of decorative considerations.

Separating the two private living areas was a long open room. One end, comfortably furnished, faced the harbor, while the opposite end, overlooking the courtyard, served as a dining area. An open pair of French doors at both ends invited cooling breezes. Large galleries ran the width of the building, front and back. A small separate kitchen occupied one corner of the courtyard.

"Jonathan, as successful as you are, I would have thought you would have a house by now."

"Just never got around to it."

"Surely you haven't entertained here. I mean you wouldn't bring a lady friend here?"

"Some of my lady friends like this place just fine."

"I can't wait to meet them, Uncle."

"I should have listened to Arabella."

"I did listen to Arabella and she instructed me in the ways of bachelors, especially seagoing bachelors. She also said I was not to be too critical of you because you have not yet had the opportunity to be properly civilized by a good woman within the state of matrimony."

"I don't think I like the drift of this conversation. I admit these quarters are not suitably decorated for the habitation of young ladies, but as for my private social life, well, it's private, and not subject to debate by a seventeen-year-old."

"Fine! Yours will remain private, and mine will remain private."

"But you don't have a private social life."

"Yet," replied Bethany with a very coy smile.

"I wish Arabella had agreed to come." Jonathan retreated from the room.

Government House was a stately structure built in the typical West Indies style of architecture; raised to take advantage of the breezes, wide steps leading up from the street to a broad veranda, tall windows that opened like French doors, high ceilings, all designed for cool living in a tropical climate. The party was held outdoors on the back lawn where gaily striped canopies shaded long tables covered with white linen tablecloths set with splendid buffets laid out on silver salvers. Guests had a choice of Indian or Chinese tea poured from large silver Hayne and Cater tea sets into Minton bone china tea cups. A crystal bowl filled with rum punch beckoned the more daring. Servants walked among the guests with trays of canapés, sliced fruit, cheeses, biscuits and petit fours.

Guests from surrounding islands and cays had come to attend the gala celebration, the most prestigious and popular social occasion of the year. Among them were government bureaucrats, bankers, merchants, shop keepers, British naval officers, a doctor or two, a few stiff collared representatives of the Church of England, the diplomatic community, a goodly number of wives, and a smattering of young gentlemen and ladies; all the expatriate types found in the Empire's far flung colonies.

The party was underway when the Quinn's carriage arrived. Heads turned as the couple made their way across the lawn to pay their respects to the Governor. Jonathan was not surprised. He had been stunned when his niece walked out of her room ready for her debut to island society.

Bethany wore a white, high-necked lace dress over a silk chemise, white shoes, lace gloves and matching purse. Her face was framed by a broad brimmed straw hat trimmed with a green ribbon that trailed halfway down her back. Her suntan had faded into the healthy look of youth and was accented by a touch of rouge to her cheeks and lips, the first she had ever used. There wasn't the slightest hint of the tomboy who had played in the fields and woods of Mississippi. Some openly stared at the incredibly beautiful, raven-haired, emerald-eyed young woman who walked through the crowd on the arm of Captain Quinn.

Bethany noted that her uncle was acquainted with many of the guests, especially the ladies. She had never thought of him other than as a loving uncle. For the first time she looked at him as women might see him. Although still young, he had a light touch of gray at his temples. The facial scar had faded with age and the black, silk eye patch, if anything, lent a measure of dignity to the tall, slim sea captain. He dressed impeccably for social occasions, and his manners in the presence of ladies were ever those of a Southern gentleman. She concluded that indeed ladies might find her uncle, if not handsome, certainly interesting, even mysterious.

It was true. Women found him attractive in ways most could not explain. With some it was the frightening aspect of the violence that had marred his once hand-some face. With others it was the tragedy of the scarring. Some experienced an unexplainable feeling of fear in his presence, sensing, perhaps, raw animal virility.

Men, on the other hand, knew him as an honest man in business dealings, but one never to cross. Local rumor had it that he was always armed.

"Governor, may I present my niece, Miss Beverly Bethany Quinn."

The host was so impressed that he insisted upon leading her a few steps up the veranda staircase. There they turned to the crowd.

"Ladies and gentlemen," he began, "Guests of good Queen Victoria."

"Here! Here!" several gentlemen responded.

"I have the most delightful honor of introducing a new visitor to Nassau. May I present Miss Beverly Bethany Quinn, niece of Captain Jonathan Quinn."

"Why, Jonathan, dear, you never cease to surprise the island folk." It was the husky voice of Mrs. Anthony Warren. She was standing on the lawn just behind the Captain.

"And I was sure I had no surprises left for you, dear Jessica," he replied without turning to look at the attractive, red-haired, brown-eyed lady dressed in yellow, carrying a matching parasol to shade a shocking amount of bare shoulder and cleavage.

"I hope I'll have the chance to see if that's true, Captain," she whispered, "You have been away a long time." She moved away, waving her ivory fan to a couple across the way, "Freddy dear, where have you and Clara been? I haven't seen you all spring."

On the way home Bethany said, "Now, Captain, tell me who is that beautiful woman with the lovely bosom almost covered in yellow taffeta."

"I was hoping you wouldn't notice."

"It's all right, Uncle, I won't tell."

"Tell what?"

"Let's change the subject. I had a wonderful time. The ladies weren't always friendly, but the men were charming. Nassau has accepted me as a grown woman, so you can quit sniveling about Arabella."

"Now damnit, Bethany! There is a lot you don't know. I mean about men. I mean, well, didn't Doctor Ted have a talk with you about the birds and the bees and that sort of thing?"

"Why, Uncle, I do believe you are blushing."

"I'm doing nothing of the kind."

"Yes, to answer your question."

"Yes what?"

"Yes, you are blushing, and yes, I have been quite schooled in the subject of social behavior between men and women, where babies come from, me being an exception of course, and what is considered acceptable behavior on the part of a young lady. I have also been informed by Doctor Perkins that in the case of men, young or old, sea captains and sailors being the worst of the bunch, they tend not to abide by what is referred to as acceptable behavior for gentlemen in mixed company when the mixed company dwindles down to a party of two."

"Great God! No wonder Ted has aged so."

"Now that we have had that little discussion, Uncle, I think you should know that several nice gentlemen asked if they may call upon me while I am here." Jonathan opened his mouth to speak, but Bethany continued, "I, of course, told them they would have to have your permission. Some of them looked a little pale when I explained that."

"By damn, they're gonna look a lot worse than pale if they come hanging round wanting favors from my niece."

"That's not what I'm talking about. I just want some interesting company, someone besides my uncle, as much as I adore him, with whom to share social activities."

They arrived home where Jonathan spent half an hour in silence. Finally he walked out on the gallery where his niece sat viewing the sunset. "What kind of social activities?"

Bethany laughed, stood up and hugged him. "You, who have faced cannon and death, storms at sea, and the ever present risks of your special business, are terrified by the sudden imposition of having to care for a young woman."

"Damn right!"

"I love you, Uncle. I will not disgrace or publicly embarrass you, but you should know that I don't intend to waste my life knitting, quilting, going to church socials, or with the idle do nothing activities of typical, snooty ladies of society. Now quit worrying, and teach me some more about the business."

"Not until I get a bourbon." It was the only rebuttal he could manage.

CHAPTER 13

Early the next morning, Billy Wong set out on a mission for 'Captain J', he could not pronounce Jonathan.

"Billy, I want you to scour Nassau for a neat, Christian native lady with references to be Miss Bethany's maid and chaperone. Full time, Billy. I want her to be with my niece at all times. Do you understand?"

"Oh, yes, Captain J. Just like honorable young ladies in China. No hanky panky!" Billy Wong laughed and hurried off.

"You heathen," Jonathan shouted after him. "Deuteronomy should have left you down in that boiler room where he found you."

Her name was Mannela Wombi. She was tall, slim, with smooth skin the golden color of almonds. Wavy, glossy-black hair spilled out from under a yellow bandana and flowed down her back. Her attractive face was without wrinkles save those at the corners of her eyes; eyes that were dark chocolate pools of unflinching brightness. She wore long dangling earrings and several necklaces, some made from shells, some from bone and ivory and one bearing a cross, the Christian symbol having been given her by Billy Wong as a condition of employment.

Jonathan had prepared a list of instructions for the position and rehearsed a speech of stern warnings of dire consequences should any liberties on the part of young men be allowed in the company of his niece. However, upon meeting Mannela Wombi, Captain Quinn decided to refrain from giving any detailed instructions to a woman who obviously didn't need, and might not tolerate, too much advice on responsibilities he didn't know much about in the first place. He simply explained that he expected her to, above all, protect his niece from the carnal desires of men and any other dangers she might encounter in the islands, and that should a problem of any sort develop, she was to immediately report it to him. A wage was settled upon. A storage room at the back of the first floor facing the courtyard was converted into quarters for Mannela.

Jonathan's concern now was whether or not his headstrong niece would accept a guardian of her virtue thinly disguised as a personal servant. He needn't have worried. Bethany had lived her childhood in the watchful care of Arabella, the closest thing to a mother she ever had growing up. She would find in Mannela not a replacement of Arabella, for there could be none, but an extension into adulthood of a companionship, perhaps peculiar to the South at the time, between a servant of color and a younger white mistress, an alliance often based more upon mutual trust and respect than the simple relationship of employer and servant.

Mannela Wombi was not an avowed Christian, nor was she a Voodoo queen as some islanders thought. It was her great grandmother who had been a voodoo priestess and slave in Haiti during the period between 1791 and 1804 when more than fifty thousand French colonials and soldiers were massacred in a slave uprising instigated by a voodoo priest that eventually resulted in the creation of the Republique d'Haiti. Along with other household slaves, she was taken to Fort de France, Martinique when her owner abandoned his plantation and fled Haiti. The voodoo practice was secretly passed down two generations to Mannela's mother. She was said to have been so attractive in her teens that the owner's son, who inherited his family's sugar and banana plantations in Martinique, took her as his mistress when she was only fifteen. Mannela was the issue of that affair. The French planter never granted freedom to her mother for fear of losing her, but Mannela was given the status of a free French Creole by her French father the day she was born. She was educated in a Catholic school, learned the secrets of Voodoo from her mother, and refused both confirmation in the Church and the birthright of becoming a Voodoo priestess. Instead, she ran away with an Englishman to the Bahamas when she was sixteen, more to escape the advances of her incestuous father than for love of the Englishman, who, a few years later, went home to his wife and children in Liverpool. Afterward, she adopted her great grandmother's African name, Wombi.

The rituals of the French and Spanish Catholic Church; candles, incense, what appeared to the Africans as spirit worship of statues and relics, and priests who conducted religious rites in a secret tongue (Latin), were easily blended into old West African beliefs in the minds of many island slaves. To them, the blood rites and magic of Voodoo and its variations didn't seem so different from the ceremony of consuming Christ's blood and flesh at communion and the spiritual power of religious artifacts, not the least of which were the rosary beads carried by devout Catholics. While Voodoo tended to fade away among slaves under the influence of the predominant Protestant services of most Southern states, the practice of Voodoo was easily absorbed by island natives who misunderstood the rituals of Catholicism in the French and Spanish controlled islands of the Caribbean and the city of New Orleans where it remained a powerful influence among the African population. Mannela Wombi grew up knowing how to use that influence. She found she could make a living by practicing native herbal medicine resulting from hundreds, perhaps thousands of years of trial and error handed down from one chosen practitioner to another. It was this mysterious practice, taught to Mannela from childhood, that gave her the reputation and fearful respect of one who possessed the power of Voodoo.

Mannela hid none of these facts from Bethany, both of whom recognized, with some delight, that such would appall Captain Quinn. The two formed an easy relationship based upon mutual recognition of the free spirits and strong wills possessed by each. Mannela did take her duty for the protection and care of the captain's niece seriously. She was surprised to admit to herself that this was due more from her growing fondness and respect of Bethany than from the captain's generous pay.

Mannela found Bethany an interested and willing student of native herbal remedies. In return, Bethany taught Mannela what modern medical practices she had learned from her godfather's teachings and medical books. Sometimes, when Jonathan was on business trips to Cuba or other voyages, Mannela took Bethany to small communities in the islands where whites seldom, if ever, ventured.

The first time the two returned from such an excursion, Billy Wong wanted to know where they had been and threatened to tell Captain J. Late that night, Mannela went into the little hut where Billy lived. She was dressed head to toe in white, her face powdered. She lit a candle. In the flickering light, the little Chinese man woke up to a startling apparition standing before him with a covered basket in one hand.

Mannela spoke in a low voice. "If you so much as tell Captain J a single word about Bethany's trips, I will turn you into a frog. If you don't believe me, look closely at your would be relatives." Mannela dumped the contents of the basket onto his bed. Frogs, dozens of them, crawled about the covers. "Unless you want to join them, seal your lips or this will be you." She opened her hand. In it was a large frog wearing black pants, a white coat, and a small black skull cap from under which hung a tiny pigtail. She quickly blew out the candle and disappeared, leaving a very startled Billy Wong in darkness with a bed full of frogs.

The next morning Mannela casually strolled into the kitchen as if nothing had happened. The little Chinese man was indignant. "Billy Wong no 'fraid you!" he said. Mannela looked directly at him and opened her mouth. A frog jumped out and landed on the kitchen table. Billy Wong ran out the door and did not return to cook for three days, nor did he ever mention a word to Captain J about the women's trips.

On their visits to remote native communities, Mannela and Bethany applied healing techniques, Bethany using the medicine of western civilization, Mannela that of Africa. Darkness and light, white and black; it was strong medicine to the super-stitious islanders who had never seen a white Voodoo woman. Bethany in turn was introduced to rites and practices few, if any whites in the islands, had ever witnessed.

On one occasion they stayed quite late at a small settlement. After dark they were given seats of honor on the porch of a small cottage while islanders gathered around a bonfire in the yard.

Mannela whispered, "You must show no fear."

Bethany had never seen anything like what she saw that night. To the accom-paniment of drums, the people chanted and danced with strange disjointed move-ments. Suddenly a young woman began to gyrate wildly. Cries emanated from her; frightening, inhuman sounds. The other dancers sat down on the ground around her. A chicken was taken up and its throat cut and the bird thrown at the feet of the girl. The headless bird leaped into the air, its blood splattering the dancer's white dress as she imitated the frantic, spastic movements of the dying bird. The girl col-lapsed writhing in the dust, twitching, her eyes rolling from side to side.

"Fear is a great power," Mannela had said, and fear is what Bethany experienced as an outsider watching the girl, watching the effect the ceremony had on the people gathered there.

Twenty minutes later the same crowd engaged in loud talking and laughter as if the frightening ceremony had never taken place. The *magic* was done for the evening. The drums began again, but this time with a gay tattoo that brought many to their feet dancing. A young woman entered the circle and by the light of the fire began to dance in a way Bethany had never seen a woman move; slowly, deliberately in a sensuous undulating manner, her body's movements gracefully locked to the pounding of the drums. Others stopped dancing and sat down to watch as she circled the fire, pausing in front of one male then another, her skin gleaming in the light of the fire, men's eyes glowing in the heat of her body. She lifted her skirt so her legs could move more freely and began to shake her shoulders and breasts to the rhythm, tossing her head from side to side as her hips moved in and out. Bethany's excitement grew as the tempo of the drums increased, an excitement she could feel inside her, growing, crawling down her spine, pulsing to the beat of the drums. She was embarrassed to discover that Mannela was watching her, smiling.

The tempo reached a crescendo as the girl suddenly stopped in front of a young male. The man stood and took her by the hand. The crowd cheered as the couple disappeared into the darkness beyond the fire.

On the carriage ride home, Mannela explained the purpose of the different rituals, those that were harmless, those that were not.

"But how can a ritual of killing a chicken or sticking pins in a doll harm someone?" Bethany asked.

"How does fear of Hell and the guilt of conscience influence the minds and actions of Christian believers?" Mannela asked in return.

"But that's different," Bethany protested.

"Because whites are civilized and blacks are savages?"

"No. Because Christians teach love and tolerance and don't go around placing curses on people."

"They teach love and tolerance, but history has shown they often fail to practice either. Christians were slaves to Romans, yet they made slaves of Africans. They make war on each other in the name of their God. What is 'damning someone to hell' if not a curse? The seeds of fear and hatred can be cultivated in all people. Faith can be used for good or it can be twisted for selfish and evil purposes. Among its believers, Voodoo can induce fear so intense it can kill. There are evil practitioners, but not all Voodoo is evil. Some is looked upon as good. You appear to them as a practitioner of good Voodoo. Good Voodoo is the stronger medicine, as sunlight is stronger than moonlight. We practice healing as we know it, you and I. If these people want to accept it as Voodoo, what do we care? We might not be allowed to help them otherwise. You certainly wouldn't have been allowed to see the things you have seen tonight. Besides, those who think they are cursed will come to me, and I will remove the curse." Mannela's eyes brightened in the moonlight as she smiled and added, "For a fee, of course."

As far as Captain Jonathan was concerned, Mannela carried out her duties toward Miss Quinn in a most satisfactory manner. In truth, with no fear of misplaced trust, Mannela allowed Bethany to discretely do as she pleased. There was no man willing to cross either Captain Quinn or Mannela Wombi.

It was a summer of passage for Bethany. She learned more of the shipping business, and for the first time, the details of J & Q's trade in "special cargo".

"Guns, Uncle? We deal in death?"

"I make no excuse for trading in arms, it is very profitable to us. If it helps your conscience, we try to sell to those who wish to win or protect freedom from those who rule unjustly by force. We've pretty much stuck to that I think. We let the competition sell to despots and tyrants."

"I have never seen war as you have, Uncle, but I can't very well be a hypocrite about J & Q Shipping's business, can I? After all, I was born because of a bullet. How many can say that? I am the daughter of war. How fitting that I join a business that promotes it."

"That's pretty cynical, Bethany."

"Perhaps, but it's not directed at you, Uncle. I understand you are trying to maintain principle in an unprincipled business, a business that you fell into by chance more than choice. It was for the salvation of your family, only now you and I are all that's left of the Quinns. I'll stand with you Uncle, and J & Q."

Jonathan was silent for a long moment spent looking at his niece, weighing her words against his own conscience. He had sworn to take care of her, the only family he had left. Was he preparing her for the future, or putting her in harm's way or both? Her eyes were steady on his, calm and steady.

"All right, Bethany. There are three cardinal rules you must remember. The first is never say a word to anyone about our 'special cargo'. I am still in the business, perhaps still alive, because no one outside myself, Jorge Lopez, trusted crew members, Jeremy Wright and certain J & Q customers, and now you, who know that occasionally, along with conventional cargos, J & Q buys, stores and ships arms. Lopez, certain crew members and Wright keep silent for the money and their own safety. 'Special cargo' customers and suppliers do so in their own interest. The second rule is that we must never become directly involved in conflict. We will deliver arms, but never use them except, of course, in self defense. That brings up the third rule. The arms trade is as risky as it is profitable. Because of me, even if you knew nothing and never took a direct part in handling our 'special cargo', you could be at risk by association. You could be a target, your welfare a lever to use against me. I am ever mindful of that fact. It is one of the reasons I waited so long to bring you here. Now that you are here . . ."

"Yes, Uncle?"

Jonathan opened a desk drawer and took out a polished wooden box with brass hinges and latch and laid it on the desk top. "This is for you. I am away so much of the time. I'll feel better knowing you have this. I'm confident you can handle it."

Bethany opened the box. It was lined with green velvet and held a small, nickel-plated pistol with ivory grips engraved with the letters B. B. Q. in a delicately embellished style. The pistol had two barrels, one over the other, and a slim, folding trigger. Also in the box were ten short, fat, 41 caliber, rim-fire cartridges. The pistol was small enough to be concealed in a woman's hand.

"Thank you, Uncle." Bethany didn't know what else to say. She had been taught from the age of ten to shoot rifles and pistols, had even hunted, but it had never occurred to her that she needed to be armed. She took the little pistol out of the box. It was actually very pretty, almost jewel-like. "Why does the trigger fold?"

"Well, it's a lady's pistol," her uncle replied with what seemed to her a boyishly-shy grin.

"Yes, go on."

"Well, do all your dresses have pockets?"

"Only a few of them do."

"Well then, there you are."

"Where am I, exactly, Uncle?" she teased him.

"The trigger folds so it can be carried in a lady's garter or pocket without snagging when it's withdrawn."

"I don't wear garters, Uncle. Under my dress, pantaloons hold up my knee stockings just fine."

"Well, a lot of women do these days. I mean I assume a lot of women do," he corrected himself, "or they wouldn't call this a garter pistol. You won't go around wearing girl's pantaloons forever. These days women wear stockings and garters . . . so I've been told. You can wear garters if you like, or carry this in your hand bag, or whatever. I would just feel better if you have it with you. In the first place, there are always a lot of rough sailors around this town you know."

"Yes, I know. According to gossip hereabouts, I have an uncle who's one of them. By the way, you didn't get this idea by finding such a pistol on a lady yourself did you?" Before Jonathan could answer, Bethany continued, "And what is the second reason for me to carry this deadly little jewel? You said in the first place there are sailors in town."

"I don't want you to be frightened by all this, but in my, that is, our special business, we could have enemies, primarily the enemies of those who buy from us. Someone could try to get to me by threatening to harm you. I want you to always have that pistol with you, either wearing it or in your purse. Don't let me catch you without it." Jonathan fell silent, frowning with genuine worry.

Bethany came around the desk, leaned down and kissed him on the cheek. "How nice to have an uncle so thoughtful of my safety. I will get myself some beautiful garters trimmed in lace, of course, and wear this rather adorable little pistol on my thigh just to put your mind more at ease when you are away."

"Good," he said. "Don't let me catch you without it. Now go check the store's books for yesterday's sales figures and see that the stock is replenished. That should keep you from distracting me long enough to finish whatever work I sat down here to do, if I can remember what it was."

"You should be glad you have a distracting niece. I could be silly, fat and demanding instead of charming, intelligent and adorable."

"I couldn't be that lucky. Now out of here!"

* * *

Bethany marched into the Cachet Boutique on Bay Street and boldly asked to see their selection of garters and stockings. Several older women in the shop appeared shocked at so young a woman asking for such unmentionables as were usually associated with 'women of the daring sort'. She was shown what the clerk heralded as the very latest from Paris. Bethany purchased six pair of each. In her quarters she experimented in wearing the weapon and finally decided the inside of her left thigh halfway above the knee was best. There the pistol wouldn't bulge her skirts, it wasn't too uncomfortable to get used to, if it started to slip she could catch it between her legs and when she raised her skirts it was easy to withdraw with her right hand.

Mannela had never handled firearms. The first time she saw Bethany don the pistol she rolled her eyes, but said nothing. Bethany grinned, "Captain's orders." She left Mannela standing in the room with her mouth open.

As the summer drew to a close, Jonathan was convinced he was being outsmarted again.

"I think Mannela should go to Paris with me," Bethany stated. "The good sisters will look after you. That's one of the services for which the school will be paid."

"Uncle, I know I promised to go away to school for two years, but I didn't know it would be a Catholic school and I would have to live in some old walled prison with nuns. Besides, I'm an Episcopalian. They will probably start the inquisition all over again the minute I arrive."

"That is not the way it will be."

"Why can't I attend some nice school for young ladies as a day student?"

"Bethany, you are only seventeen. I can't put you in an apartment in Paris."

"You can if Mannela is with me. And Uncle, I'll be eighteen when I arrive at school," she reminded him. "Mannela speaks perfect French, you know. Her father was French. She is a free French citizen by birth. Now I said I would go, and I will, a Quinn keeps her word. But I am not a child, and I am not like the other girls who go to such schools, most of whom won't have been anywhere or done anything outside their family's watchful sight in their entire lives. I could sail myself across the ocean if I had to. I already keep books and run a store. I hardly think any of them will have a pistol in their garter, do you? If you sent Mannela with me as a chaperone and housekeeper it would be both respectable and safe for me to reside in an apartment near some school. Your man Jeremy Wright can look in on us and verify my progress at school. He is in Paris a lot according to the outrageous record of expenses he sends us. Besides, if Mannela and I live in our own respectable apartment, you can come over at least twice a year and stay with me. You can't stay with me if I live in a convent, now can you?"

Jonathan felt the screws turning. "This is probably a wasted exercise anyway. Mannela likely won't go even if I can find a proper school and agree to such a plan."

"That's a chance I'll have to take." Bethany replied.

"The purpose of sending you to a young ladies' finishing school is to put you in the care of genteel women for the first time in your life. You will have the opportunity to learn all the social graces and knowledge expected of a lady: how to manage a household, give parties, be a successful hostess, wife, mother, home-maker, all sorts of things Ted Perkins and I admittedly have not been too good at teaching you. Your mother and grandmother will come back and haunt me if I turn you loose in Paris alone."

"My Mother was younger than I am now when she was impregnated by a bullet and had me. My grandmother died, gun in hand, defending her family. That is my legacy from the Quinn women. They would expect me to take care of myself, which I am capable of doing. Doctor Ted and you have certainly taught me how. Besides, Mannela will be at my side. I will give you my word that she will know exactly where I am every moment."

"No school in Paris, in all of France, will hear of such arrangements for a young lady attending their institution."

"I am sure, Uncle, that there are schools which accept day students as well as those who board."

"Perhaps, but those students go to and from home under the supervision of their parents."

"It is not my fault that I have no parents. Mannela will act as my guardian and chaperone. That's the best an orphan can do."

"Now don't think a sentimental tack claiming orphan-hood will steal the wind from my sails, young lady. I like you better when you fight fair."

"Uncle, a woman never fights fair against a man. How else could she win? You think about it for a while. I'll talk to Mannela. If she won't go, then I won't say another word about it. I will board in some dark old convent and waste away into a subservient, dependent, shy young lady submissive to the boring rules forced upon the weaker sex by stuffy, know-it-all old men."

"I am not a stuffy old man."

"Of course you aren't, Uncle, or I wouldn't waste my time trying to carry on a logical debate with you. You are my Uncle, the intelligent and brave Captain Quinn who will decide this matter in a fair manner. And I will abide by your decision because I know it will be based upon your confidence in your niece."

"Thank you for not smiling during that speech, young lady. It is bad enough that I am knowingly being coerced. It would be intolerable for you to laugh while you do it."

"I'll let you know what Mannela's decision turns out to be, Uncle," Bethany said, and left Jonathan sitting at his desk, a totally defeated authoritarian.

"My God!" He thought out loud, "And to think some men have three or four daughters."

Mannela, though never out of calling distance, did occasionally allow Bethany time alone with a young man for a walk or to sit and talk. It was on such occasions that Bethany discovered there was much more to kissing than a mere peck on the cheek. She understood the difference in the physical aspects between men and women and the process of procreation of the species, but her knowledge was strictly clinical, obtained from the texts and drawings of her godfather's medical books. The books did not treat the subject in terms of physical feelings and human desire which, she was now certain, were the real and inseparable causes of the whole process.

She held many long discussions with Mannela about such subjects. Mannela, for her part, determined that her young friend and charge should be thoroughly prepared to handle men and rebuff any advances. Bethany proved an attentive student, neither shy nor shocked by the revelations, graphic descriptions, and philosophy passed on to her by the exotic, almond-skinned mulatto.

Mannela did not give such instructions lightly. She stressed responsibility on the one hand and made clear on the other that only silly women were inclined to be taken in by men of no consequence interested only in satisfying the needs and pride of manhood. Wise women, she said, especially beautiful wise women, had the power to rule any man. "After all, wasn't the great empire of England ruled by a woman? Didn't Cleopatra change the history of Egypt and the Roman Empire? Was it not Helen who caused the downfall of Troy? Had not Catherine the Great ruled Russia?

"You are a very educated woman for a . . ."

"For a person of color, you were going to say," Mannela interrupted. "It may surprise you to know that in the days before I left my French father I was schooled with his legitimate children in language, history and literature. On the other hand, I admit that you, who came from the slave states of America, surprised me. I was prepared to despise you."

"Well, Mannela, we may not change history," Bethany smiled, "but woe be unto he who messes with us." Mannela threw her head back and laughed.

Jonathan called Bethany to his office. "All right, you will have it your way. Jeremy Wright is making the necessary arrangements. You and Mannela have two weeks to pack. *Tropic Bird* has cargo consigned to Philadelphia. We might as well sail that far aboard on one of our own ships. We will take a train from there to New York to board a ship for Liverpool, England then cross the Channel to Paris. Now, young lady, France is far away and two years is a long time. Are you sure this is what suits you, Bee Bee?"

"Oh, yes! I look forward to the adventure."

"Damnit! There's to be no adventure about it. You're going for the sole purpose of obtaining a classical education, which, I remind you, is an opportunity not many young ladies get. I expect you to remember who you are at all times and to take full advantage of school, especially languages. You'll have to learn French, of course, Mannela can help there, but Spanish will be important to the development of our investments in Cuba. Now, here is your American identification paper and a letter of introduction from the British colonial governor of the Bahamas. Don't lose them. Last, but not least, if I get any reports from the school or Mannela that are the least questionable, you're coming home." A smile broke through the stern countenance he was trying hard to maintain. "Bee Bee, I'm gonna miss you."

Bethany ran from the office. "Mannela! We're going to Paris!"

CHAPTER 14

Jonathan, Bethany and Mannela boarded the J & Q ship, *Tropic Bird*, a swift steamer that had been purchased new in 1875. Saturday the first week of August 1881, *Tropic Bird* docked in Philadelphia and began unloading her cargo of rum, cigars, hemp and sugar. She would return to the Caribbean carrying furniture, hardware, flour, bolts of cloth, glassware, lanterns and machinery. Bethany's crated household goods were loaded on a dray and sent to the railway freight office with instructions for shipment to the White Star Line in New York. Mannela was sent ahead to the hotel with their travel luggage and steamer trunks.

With business done, Jonathan was free to act as Bethany's tour guide on her first visit to a great Northern city. They began, at Bethany's insistence, with the harbor district before going downtown.

The busy waterfront was fascinating. There were great ships, both sail and steam, docks crowded with cargo and streets busy with carts, carriages and drays. All around them, hurrying to and fro, was a mingled assortment of longshoremen, sailors, well-dressed businessmen, fashionably-dressed women, teamsters, trades-men, merchants, peddlers, and painted ladies of obvious trade. Shouting street vendors, the cries of fish mongers, the clatter of horses' hooves and steel-rimmed wagon wheels on cobblestones, the puffing and clanking of ships' machinery and steam-whistles all blended into a cacophony of sound, a symphony of commerce.

They walked past great brick warehouses and explored side streets filled with shipping offices, marine chandlers, saloons, hardware and mercantile shops, cheap waterfront hotels and boarding houses catering to seafarers. More accustomed to the fresh air of the Bahamas, Bethany's nostrils were assaulted by the smell of coal smoke, raw fish, human sweat, oiled canvas, dried hides, tanned leather and horse manure. She thought it all wonderfully entertaining.

Jonathan had seen it all before. "Aren't you about ready to take a cab to the hotel?"

When his niece did not answer, he turned to see her standing several yards behind him staring at something across the brick-paved street. He walked back to her, amused to see a brow-wrinkled expression of perplexity on her face. He slipped his arm around her shoulder. "What is it, Bee Bee?"

"I have the strangest feeling I've seen that before, but I have no idea where."

"What are you talking about?"

"That," she said, pointing.

Jonathan glanced across the street. "A saloon?"

"Not the saloon. That bowl painted on the sign above it," Bethany replied.

Jonathan looked up at the top of the building's two-story facade. A faded sign displayed the words, *PUNCH BOWL SALOON*. Above the lettering there was a large painted likeness of a silver bowl, its perimeter decorated with green shamrocks.

Jonathan turned and flagged a taxi. "Bethany, I want you to take this cab to the hotel." He helped her into the carriage, gave the driver instructions and paid him.

"But why, Uncle? What's the matter?"

Without answering, Jonathan quickly crossed the street and entered the saloon.

Disconcerted by her uncle's sudden change of demeanor, taunt facial muscles, set jaw, the fire in his eye that had always foretold anger, and his abrupt order for her to go to the hotel alone, Bethany told the cabby to wait. What had she done to cause such a change in him? She climbed down and tried to catch him, but he was too quick in stride. She followed into the saloon and caught sight of Jonathan moving through the crowd. Bethany had never been in such a place. It was filled with a lunch crowd standing four deep around a long table piled with sliced meat and bread under a sign that read, LUNCH 10¢ WITH THE PURCHASE OF A QUART OF BEER. The sound of raucous laughter, loud talk, shouted arguments and the clatter of glass beer mugs was deafening. The bar was doing a brisk business in hard liquor, mostly from seafaring men egged on by saloon girls. The smell of stale beer, whiskey and unwashed bodies assaulted her nostrils. She had to push through the crowd to catch up with her uncle moving toward a bar at the back of the room.

When she caught him, her uncle stood staring at a large silver bowl sitting on a wooden pedestal on the back counter. It was black with tarnish and flanked by rows of whiskey bottles reflected in the back bar mirror. The bowl had a band of emerald-green, cloisonne shamrocks garnishing its circumference. It was filled with oranges.

"What's wrong, Uncle?" Bethany asked.

Jonathan wheeled around, his eye blazing wildly. "Bethany, what are you doing here? Where is your cab?"

"It's waiting outside, Uncle. What did I do? Why are you acting so strange?"

"Bethany, I'm not asking you, I'm ordering you. Leave! Take your cab and go to the hotel. Now!"

Bethany looked at a Jonathan she did not know. His lips were drawn thinly apart and the flexing muscles of his jaw distorted his face into a cold, hard expression she had never seen. It was, she thought, a look that would frighten the Devil.

Bethany turned toward the door. Confused, in tears, she wondered what in the world she had done to transform her uncle into someone she didn't know.

"Wait!" Jonathan called. Bethany froze. "Do you have your pistol?"

"No, Uncle, I didn't think I needed it when I'm with you," she said lamely.

"Don't ever let me catch you without it! Do you hear me? Now get the hell out of here!"

"For God's sake, Uncle Jonathan, what is wrong?"

"Bethany!"

For the first time in her life, he frightened her. Bethany backed away, bumping the people behind her. She turned and pushed through the crowd to the street and the waiting cab.

Struggling to gain control over his emotions, Jonathan bought a whiskey off a waitress's tray and tossed it down. *If a man is to live through battle, he must control his anger as well as his fear*, Deuteronomy had preached to him. *You have to think clearly, boy, control your emotions if you are to do your job and survive. Remember that, learn it, practice it.* The raw cheap whiskey burned his throat. He walked to the bar and edged a place to rest his elbow.

"What's your pleasure, Captain?" The barman called every customer Captain.

"I'll have a whiskey, a real whiskey, not that raw swill served out on the floor." Jonathan put a twenty-dollar gold piece on the bar.

"The best we have for a gentleman like yourself." The barman selected a bottle from the back bar, poured a measure into a glass and set it in front of Jonathan.

"While you're at it I'll have an orange out of that fancy bowl you have there. What's the story on it?"

The barman retrieved an orange from the bowl and put in on the bar. Quinn absently picked it up and began to peel away its skin with his fingers.

"Been here since the place opened, so I'm told, not long after the war. Pure silver it 'tis. Needs a shine. Used to keep it shined some. Too fine to be appreciated by the likes that hang out here, yourself excepted."

"Do you think the owner might sell it?"

"Kind of doubt that, it being the name of the place and all." The barman paused to wipe down the counter top. "On the other hand, he likes money enough to sell his own mother."

"What can you tell me about him?"

"He ain't one to cross. Watches every penny. He's a big, mean bastard. Had a wife once, said she was his wife. Beat the hell out of her a while back, called her a thieving whore and threw her out. She ain't even come back to get her stuff. Afraid of him she is. But like I said, he likes money. You want to make him an offer, the office is at the end of that hall over there." The man moved away to tend others along the crowded bar.

Jonathan left his hat, the half-peeled orange and his nearly-full glass on the bar, eased through the crowd into the empty hallway and knocked on the door at the end.

"It's open," came a growled response.

The man sitting behind a cluttered desk was big with a belly to match. He wore a stained shirt that pulled at its buttons. Tobacco juice dribbled from the corner of his mouth. He needed a shave. His fingernails were dirty, but he wore a diamond ring on the little finger of his right hand.

"Who the hell are you?"

"Name's O'Brien, Captain John O'Brien," Jonathan answered. "I saw that piece of Irish silver behind the bar out there and thought to myself it would make a fine present for my Irish bride, impress the family, don't you know, those shamrocks around it and all. Thought maybe you might sell it for the right price, Mr?"

"Name's McKenna."

"Well, Mr. McKenna, what will you take for that Irish trinket?"

"First place, it ain't Irish. Made in England. Says so on the bottom. Second place, it's the one thing I got ain't fer' sale. You'll have to get that Irish gal of yours something else. Hell, give her some gold, them Irish women will do anything fer' it."

"Well, you think on women like I do, McKenna. Some might get offended hearing talk like that about their bride to be, but to tell you the truth, I just need me a wife at the other end of my sea route. I got one at this end."

McKenna grunted a laugh. "Sounds like you're one of the few men left knows what women are good for, all they're good for. Come on, Captain, I ain't selling my bowl, but I'll buy you a drink, something I ain't in the habit of doing for paying customers." He got up, walked around the desk, and was out in the hallway before Jonathan could stop him.

"Wait a minute." Quinn said, "I want you to tell me something before we get out in that noisy crowd where I can't hear a word." McKenna paused. "If you won't let me buy the thing, at least you can tell me the story behind it. Got to be a story. Where did you get it anyway? Hell, I'll pay you twice what it cost you."

McKenna faced Jonathan across the narrow hallway. "In the first place it's the trade mark of my business, kind of classy you know. It come to me as a gift, you see, a sort of prize." McKenna hesitated, looking Jonathan over closely. "Was you in the war?" he asked, "You sound kind'a Southern-like. You get them wounds in the war?"

"Not me," Jonathan answered. "I was in California. Sailed out there as a bosun. Jumped ship to try my luck prospecting. Then worked a crew of Chinamen building on the railroad. Takes a bunch of damn fools to fight a war. When I fight it's for me. Like when I got this." He pointed to his eye patch. "Mescalero Injun surprised me while I was prospecting. Tried to slit my throat but I moved fast, traded him a bullet for this eye. You in that war?"

"I wore a uniform, if that's what you mean. Drafted I was, like a damn livery mule. I saw to it that the others did the fighting. I did the fucking."

He was getting into his story now, leaning back against the wall, his belly hanging over his trousers, thumbs tucked into his suspenders. Jonathan gave him a knowing smile, like he couldn't wait to hear more. A little interest was all McKenna needed.

"That's why I asked about you being in the war. Some Southern bastards would take offense about how I got that bowl. All them Southern women was without their men too long, see? The dumb bastards were all off fighting someplace else. Shit, them neglected women was in some need, most of 'em. Know what I mean?"

Jonathan froze a smile on his face. "What's that got to do with the bowl?"

"That's what I'm trying to tell you. There was this little southern gal on a place out 'a Vicksburg give me the bowl 'cause I done pleased her so well. I mean she was one of them screaming hollering kind of gals, hadn't ever got enough till McKenna here showed her his stuff. Course I was younger then, see. She give me the bowl out of appreciation so I wouldn't never forget her. She liked it real good, begged me not to go."

Inexplicably, Jonathan could smell the choking odor of spent gunpowder, hear the roar of *Alabama*'s guns, hear the screams of the dying, but the screams weren't those of sailors in the midst of battle. They were the screams of women, his mother and sister. Temples pounding, all reason and control fled his mind and soul.

Jonathan pinned McKenna to the wall with his left forearm against the big man's throat. In one flowing motion his right hand moved under his coat to the back of his waist, slipped the short, razor-edged blade out of its scabbard and swung it down and forward in front of him. It took less time than the blink of an eye.

It was the Spanish Toledo blade Deuteronomy had given him, the blade he had sharpened to a surgical edge absently honing it on lonely nights when he awakened from haunted dreams of his murdered family, nights when he was afraid to go back to sleep. It was a virgin blade, its sharpness kept solely to sustain the improbable dream of finding the third man who had killed Shamrock that lazy Southern afternoon. Now, fifteen years later, Bethany unknowingly had found her mother's killer.

Jonathan deftly moved the razor sharp edge upward between McKenna's legs. The steel cut past the cotton trousers, slid off the pelvic bone and up the bulging, hairy belly, parting waist band and shirt, skin and fat, until its smooth passage was finally stopped by McKenna's breast bone. Jonathan stepped back, never taking his eyes from McKenna's, pulled the knife away and returned it to its place at his back.

McKenna initially felt only the strange sensation of something coursing a line up his body. Then the sharp-burning pain of nerve endings from cut flesh raced up the front of him faster than a shriek of terror could reach his lips. His hands instinctively grasped for his belly as he felt the sickening shift of that which was inside him. He looked down at the crimson ooze. His first attempt to speak was feeble. "What the hell?" were the words he managed.

With both hands, Jonathan grabbed McKenna by the hair, pulled the man's massive head down and whispered in his ear, "It was my grandfather, my mother you killed that day in Mississippi, my little sister you raped, whose throat you slit, you vile murdering lump of putrescent scum."

There was relatively little blood pooled at McKenna's feet. The strong, short, hollow ground blade cut through skin and fat, opening the great cavity of McKenna's trunk without cutting into the entrails inside.

McKenna, wild-eyed, mumbling fear-stunted curses, pressed his hands against his abdomen trying to hold the terrible wound closed.

Jonathan turned to leave, but the ferocity of unleashed vengeance refused to release him. He spun back around, and with one quick movement, slipped the fingers of his left hand into McKenna's opened belly. McKenna felt himself being emptied. Quinn let go in horror that which he had drawn from McKenna's hollow. He stared at his bloodied hand, quickly put it in his pocket and moved from the dim hallway back to his place at the end of the bar where his hat, drink and little pile of orange peels waited. Hardly more than forty five seconds had passed between the time

Jonathan had unsheathed his knife and he once again stood at the bar, trembling, unnoticed by the rowdy crowd.

Out on the noisy saloon floor where the odor of spilled beer and tobacco-smoke mixed with that of bad breath and unwashed bodies, the throng couldn't hear McKenna's whimpering cries. Their attention was focused on a loud argument between two drunken sailors. The crowd, eager for a little entertainment, was about to get more than it bargained for.

A woman screamed. No ordinary scream, this was a siren from hell. The startled patrons, suddenly silent, turned toward the horrific sound.

Open-mouthed, sucking gasps came from those gathered closest to the specter shuffling toward them. The crowd surged back in a single wave as McKenna emerged into the room. He came slipping on that which oozed from inside him like some endless coiled serpent. His pants and shirt hung open exposing the full length of the awful wound. The great opening widened and narrowed with each gulping breath he took. He continued to move forward, viscera dragging over the floor between his legs. He finally found voice and began screaming, more from terror than from pain.

Some diverted their eyes. Most could not. For an indelible moment no one moved, could move, dared move. Then the crowd began to out scream McKenna, to back against the bar, against the far wall, to flee toward the door.

The bartender at last overcame his shock. He ran from behind the bar, a pistol in one hand, a stack of bar towels in the other. He reached McKenna who, recognizing a familiar face, sensed help and sank to the floor. "Roy! Oh! Goddamn! Roy, you got to help me," McKenna gasped.

Roy spread all the towels he held over McKenna and over what spilled from him.

"Who done this, Boss, who done this?" Roy kept asking in a frightened, whining voice.

McKenna wheezed "I'm cold. Christ! Get a doctor!" Then he suddenly screamed, "Vicksburg!"

Every time McKenna screamed, Roy grabbed up his pistol and looked frantically around as if the horror that had struck McKenna might visit upon him. It didn't occur to Roy that the one-eyed gentleman could have done it. He was standing at the bar when the woman screamed.

"Look what he done to me! Jesus! Look what he done, Roy!" McKenna grabbed the barman by his collar and pulled him close. "We were just having fun. Tell 'em I wouldn't have killed the girl if the others hadn't shot the old man. That's who caused it, the old man." The voice grew weaker, further away. Roy bent down, had to strain to hear him.

In a rasping whisper McKenna said, "Didn't leave no witnesses. How the hell did he find me? Weren't no witnesses."

Roy clutched the pistol and looked wild-eyed into the crowd. He didn't want to hear any more, afraid knowing would call the terrible avenger down on him, too.

McKenna pulled on Roy's sleeve and mumbled something that sounded to Roy like 'ball' or 'bar' or 'bow'. It made no sense.

"What ya' trying to say Boss?"

A living, eviscerated body stared up at the barman, moaning, jerking, dying hard.

Some in the crowd got sick, vomiting trails toward the door.

Some stayed, immobile, their eyes frozen to the horror. Most ran.

After the crowd had fled, after McKenna's body was taken away, after the police had asked all their questions, Roy closed and locked the front door and absently began mopping up the globules of offal and blood befouling the floor. Then, he had a flash of inspiration. *The cash box!* Roy ignored the aggravation of stepping among the oranges littering the floor behind the bar while he stole a dead man's money.

Bethany and Mannela stood on the upper deck of the White Star liner, *Britannic*, as she steamed out of New York Harbor. Passing under a giant web of wire rope and iron suspended above the East River, they looked up in wonder at what would become the Brooklyn Bridge. Workmen perched precariously high above waved down as the ship passed beneath them. Mounted on the most forward of her cream and black funnels, *Britannic's* whistle sounded an all-clear signal as she steamed from under Roebling's engineering marvel. Startled by the unexpected blast, Bethany and Mannela grabbed one another, then laughed at their foolish alarm.

Bethany thought how amused Jonathan would have been to see her jump, but then realized she had been thinking of the old Jonathan. She did not know the Jonathan who now stayed secluded in his cabin. Something terrible had occurred that first day in Philadelphia. She knew by the appalling look of him when he finally arrived at the hotel. He had come into the salon of their suite without a word and stood staring at Bethany and Mannela.

"Jonathan! My God! What happened?" Bethany asked.

"It was the Shamrock bowl you recognized," he said coldly. Bethany had never heard of the bowl. There had been no reference to it in her mother's diary. "You mean like the sign on the building, the one I puzzled over? Tell me about the bowl, Uncle."

"It's safe aboard *Tropic Bird*," was his only reply to her question.

Jonathan turned and reached for the door knob to his bedroom. Bethany and Mannela both saw that the cuff of his shirt sleeve was stained crimson with what appeared to be blood. Bethany started to follow him, but Mannela caught her arm and motioned 'no' with the turn of her head.

They left for New York by train that night. Jonathan refused to leave his private compartment except to escort his niece and Mannela to the dining car where he sat in silence picking at his food.

Bethany's enthusiasm for the trip evaporated. She never mentioned her disappointment in not touring Philadelphia or in knowing there would be no gay tour of New York City. The trip had held such anticipated joy for her. Now she was overwhelmed by her own confusion in the wake of her uncle's unexplained behavior. As the sleeping car swayed and click-clacked over the rails into the night, she lay awake wondering how a bowl could have transformed Jonathan into a stranger.

Now, aboard *Britannic*, Jonathan remained distant, leaving his cabin only late at night when the weather deck was devoid of other passengers. Though he allowed Bethany, always in the company of Mannela, to stroll the promenade deck and take meals in the first class dining salon at their assigned table, Jonathan insisted on taking his meals alone in his cabin.

Bethany could not begin to understand the depth of his agony. She tried to breach the impenetrable shell of silent brooding that had engulfed her uncle, but could not.

Slowly, after several days at sea, the dark, disconsolate shroud that had entombed him began to slough away. Perhaps it was having a ship beneath his feet with a clear horizon and clean salt air in his lungs that began to restore his sanity, or perhaps his wretched brooding had sorcerously subdued recall of the savagery of vengeance taken. As the days passed, Bethany sensed that Jonathan's spirit was beginning to heal. After she begged him one morning, he reluctantly joined her for a walk around the promenade deck and allowed her to hold his arm. She rejoiced in this simple gesture.

The day before their scheduled arrival at Liverpool, Bethany asked her uncle if he would take her on a tour of the liner. She had tried everything else to draw him out of his dark mood. He was unenthusiastic but consented to ask *Britannic's* Captain Haddock for permission. Haddock, as a courtesy of one sea captain to another, granted Captain Quinn free rein to tour the ship.

Almost imperceptibly, his interest in the intricacies of the vessel began to grow. For the first time since boarding, he took note of *Britannic's* luxurious first class salon with its fine furnishings: crystal chandeliers, wall murals, marble and gold leaf trim, mirrors and stained glass skylights.

"You might as well see what drives this ship," Jonathan said. He led the way down stairways and finally through a door onto a walkway of metal grating. "Mind your skirts, Bethany, there are men down below."

There in the bowels of the ship lay the huge, steam driven machinery that propelled the vessel. Standing at the walkway rail, they could look down on the engine room's 'black gang' shoveling coal into the glowing, hungry throats of a line of furnace doors spanning the width of the ship. The men were stripped to the waist, their faces black with coal dust, their muscled bodies streaked with rivulets of sweat. One stoker looked up and was shocked to discover a young lady watching them. "Look there," he said to his mate, "an angel come down to hell."

As they stood watching the stokers feed the fires, Jonathan exclaimed, as if talking to himself, "Those boilers drive all 455 feet of her sleek iron hull at a steady sixteen knots." Bethany considered each statement a small triumph, not because of the knowledge imparted, but because her uncle was talking.

The Quinns received an invitation to dine at the captain's table on the last night at sea. Jonathan would have declined but for Bethany's insistence. It was Jonathan's first appearance in the dining salon. Eyes turned toward the striking couple as they walked to the captain's table. Jonathan was dressed in white tie and tails, his black silk eye patch a dashing accouterment to his formal attire, his scar a romantic mark of valor, or so it seemed to many of the ladies present. The attention of the gentlemen was fixed upon the young woman on his arm. She was dressed in green silk, her hair piled fashionably high on her head with little ringlets framing her face. She wore a pair of gold shamrock earrings, each with a small diamond in the center. The earrings had been among the few personal belongings Ted Perkins had retrieved along with her mother's diary from the cabins at Shamrock. A simple strand of pearls graced her slim neck. What couldn't be seen was the jewel-like decoration held firmly to the inside of her left thigh by a white lace garter. Should ever her uncle ask again, she would have the little pistol with her.

Every man at the table rose with Captain Haddock to greet the couple. "May I present the very able Captain J. H. Quinn and his niece, Miss Bethany Quinn, who have been kind enough to join us tonight."

They were seated on opposite sides of the table toward the middle. Bethany was amused to see the ladies vying for a few words with her polite but reticent uncle. He, in turn, not nearly so amused, noted the effect his niece was having on the gentlemen present. In spite of her formidable abilities as a chaperon, he vowed to have a serious meeting with Mannela to review her responsibilities for the care and protection of his niece, who, it seemed to him, received the undivided attention of every man she met, young and old alike.

"These modern steamships are wonderful," someone ventured. "They are," Jonathan spoke to the table for the first time. "They will eventually drive the tall ships from the sea. It's a pity, I think. Most seamen I know would rather be topside running on a fresh, clean breeze than locked down in the grumbling bowels of boiler and engine room with never a view of the sea or sky."

"Understand, Captain," said Bethany, "all Quinns are hopeless romantics."

Haddock replied. "But I agree with your uncle. There's no sight on earth more beautiful than a grand sailing ship with all her canvas flying. But then you know that. Your uncle told me you are a fair sailor yourself."

Those at the table took a greater interest in the young Miss Quinn. "Really, I'm just another young woman going abroad to polish her education. These two sea dogs here are conspiring to ruin my reputation by making me out to be a lady pirate or something just because I've done a little sailing. In any event, I must ask to be excused. I have toured this ship from top to bottom today and I'm worn out. I've had a wonderful day and a delightful evening with you all. Thank you for your gracious hospitality, Captain Haddock." The gentlemen rose from their seats as Jonathan escorted his niece from the table.

Mannela was waiting. She shared Bethany's cabin and, as her attendant, was allowed full access to the first class area as long as she was performing her duties. Her slim build, almond skin, dark eyes, wavy black hair, self-confident manner, and the tastefully conservative new wardrobe Captain Quinn had provided only increased the mystery of 'that French speaking mulatto who so closely watches after the young Quinn woman'. In spite of several invitations and more than one outright proposition, she remained polite, dignified, and aloof.

Jeremy Wright was waiting for them when *Britannic* docked at Liverpool. In spite of his assurance that satisfactory arrangements for Bethany's stay in Paris had been made, Jonathan was anxious to see for himself. He hardly allowed time to tour London before whisking his small party across the Channel to Calais and on by train to Paris.

Paris! To those on their first visit it was indeed *la ville lumiere*, the city of lights, but to Jonathan, it held a different image, far different even from his days of convalescence there in the sixties. In 1870, only six years after the American Civil war ended, Louis Napoleon III, perhaps longing for the glory of his more famous departed uncle, committed France to yet another invasion of Prussia. The Prussians were tired of the French. They had suffered five French invasions since 1785, an average of one every sixteen years. Louie Napoleon III's invasion gave Prussian statesman, Otto von Bismarck, the key he had been seeking to unite the multitude of Prussian states into a united Germany for the first time in history. The French were overwhelmed at Sedan and Paris fell under siege. Not unlike the citizens of Vicksburg, Jonathan recalled, it had been Paris's starving citizens' turn to eat rats.

The Franco-Prussian war provided very nice profits to J & Q. Bismarck had disarmed France and gone happily home with the much disputed Alsace-Lorraine in German hands. Jeremy Wright arranged to purchase all the surplus arms the firm could afford. Jonathan was to provide their shipment to the Bahamas for sale to Cuban rebels, but before he could sail, the ever-devious Wright had sold them to both sides of a French civil war that erupted in 1871 after the Prussians had gone home. The Second Empire of Louie Napoleon III had been replaced by a new French republic, but the working classes, university students and a number of leading French intellectuals, all inspired by the teachings of Karl Marx, had formed the *Commune de Paris* and rebelled against the bourgeois Republic. Fed by class hatred, the violence committed by members of the Commune before their defeat made the Jacobin reign of terror seem tame by comparison. Not only did the French revolt prove shamefully profitable to J & Q Shipping thanks to Jeremy Wright, but when it was over, J & Q bought back many of the same arms for little of nothing in time to sell them to the revolutionaries of Cuba.

Now, ten years later, Jonathan was much relieved to find Paris back to normal. Bohemian lifestyles were again in vogue, the decadent morals of the Second Empire had been replaced by the decadent morals of the Republic. The gas lights of the city once more burned brightly.

Bethany was delighted by the apartment Jeremy had arranged for her, and told him so. It was located on Rue Saint Severin on the left bank of the Seine at the edge of the Latin Quarter not far from the University of Paris. It was comfortably furnished, had a balcony overlooking a small park, and was, Jeremy Wright had informed them, within walking distance of the beautiful Jardin de Luxembourg with its glorious avenues, trees and vistas of seemingly endless flower beds. It was also within walking distance of the Place Saint-Germain where art students, intellectuals and the Bohemian set frequented the many cafes and bars catering to the night life of Paris. Wright failed to inform them of the latter convenience. Jeremy paid a great deal of attention to Bethany after meeting her in London. She thought little of it. He was forty-two years of age. After his arrangements for Bethany's stay in Paris were deemed satisfactory, Jeremy returned to England, promising to "look in once in a while to see that all is well."

"It was very sweet of Mr. Wright to make all the arrangements for me," Bethany said after he left for London. "He seems like a nice man."

"He is not a nice man," Jonathan replied. "I suppose the aging dandy, when sober, is still attractive to ladies of a certain age, but he is not a nice man."

"But he is your business partner."

"I'm not proud of that, but Wright still has the ability to put together profitable deals from this side of the Atlantic. Jeremy jealously guards contacts I lack, contacts spread from Europe to North Africa to as far as China where outdated muskets are still acceptable. In spite of the profitable association, I will not be disappointed to one day end working relations with Mr. J. Wright, Esquire. Now, let's change the subject."

The Paris neighborhood was familiar ground to Jonathan. While in ambulatory convalescence at the Hotel Dieu just behind Notre-Dame, he often crossed the Seine by way of the Petit-Pont, the site where a Roman road had crossed the river. He would walk along the Rue Saint Jacques with his bandaged face and watch the university students going to and from classes knowing that his opportunity for such an education was lost. The Quinns, struggling just to eat, could hardly afford to provide a university education for Jonathan.

Now at least he could give his niece that opportunity. Her school, though not a university, was considered an exceptional institution for young ladies. The Ecole d' Ecouen, a school originally founded by Napoleon Bonaparte exclusively for the daughters of members of the Legion of Honor, was now open to 'young ladies of family', and daughters of the diplomatic community. Certain other foreign students, meaning those with money, were sometimes accepted.

Madame Couperin, the head mistress of the school, received the Quinns formally, speaking French only, while the school's English teacher interpreted for both parties. When Captain Quinn, speaking partly in French, expressed concern that his niece might be handicapped by her lack of proficiency in the French language, he was informed that other foreign students lacking French had been enrolled, including the daughters of several ambassadors. "I assure you, Captain Quinn, that your niece will soon be speaking French perfectly."

To prove the point, she summoned a second year student, the daughter of the Spanish ambassador, to assist Bethany in registration and escort her on a tour of the academy. Maria Simone Cruz-Vidal managed enough English to communicate with Bethany. "You help my English, I teach you Spanish, no?"

The school was an old stone structure stained black by the soot of Paris and protected by high walls. It was better than the convent Bethany had imagined. There were large windows to let in sunlight and small, well-kept flower gardens, but she would have hated living in the dormitory rooms which did resemble those of a monastic institution.

Upon completing the formalities of enrolling his niece in school, Jonathan established accounts in Bethany's name at the Bank of Paris and several boutiques. Satisfied that all was satisfactory he announced, "Now, we have time to tour."

"It must be the influence of Paris," Bethany whispered to Mannela, "He is almost his old self again."

And it was true. Captain Quinn set out to show the whole of Paris to his niece. He led a tour each day in the city where the skill of a French surgeon and the care, or perhaps the prayers of the good sisters had saved his life.

Jonathan wondered silently, *Would the nuns pray for me now, an arms dealer and the executioner of my family's murderer?* The fact that he had killed the bastard didn't bother him. It was his uncontrolled rage and savagery in the doing of it that frightened him.

Though most of the city appeared healed ten years after the revolt of the Commune, ample evidence of their wanton vandalism remained. The once lovely Tuileries, the Palais Royal, and the Hotel de Ville were still fire-blackened ruins. Reconstruction of a burned wing of the Louvre was nearing completion, but the priceless art treasures destroyed in the flames were gone forever. Still, the beauty of the city was more than Bethany had imagined.

"Look at these magnificent boulevards," Bethany remarked as they rode in an open carriage.

Jonathan laughed. "Their great width was designed by Baron Haussmann under Napoleon III to give the government's troops quick access to trouble spots and uncluttered fields of fire against the *classes dangereuses* should civil strife develop. The wide boulevards discourage the building of barricades. They are paved with macadam to deny rioters access to paving stones for use as missiles."

"Oh, don't be so cynical, Uncle. These wonderful boulevards are beautiful."

"I'm not being cynical, just explaining the truth.

"Sometimes, beauty itself is truth enough."

"Did you borrow that from somewhere, or has my partner become a philosopher?"

"A smart woman never answers a question like that. Let's go have coffee and pastry at that little café over there."

In spite of an abundance of summer blooms coloring the entire city, the outstanding perfume of Paris was that of horse manure. Unfazed, Bethany was delighted to find that the Etoile and Champs-Élysées were surrounded by stables and riding schools, never mind the fragrant scent. She was quick to wring permission to patronize a stable of her choice.

"Mannela probably doesn't know how to ride," he offered as a feeble discouragement. "Probably hates horses."

"Then she can wait at the stable for me, Uncle. I'm sure it's quite safe for an armed young woman," she paused to smile at him, "to go riding in the park."

Uncle was not amused.

"And Uncle," she continued, "for propriety's sake, I'll wear a dress and ride side-saddle even though it is an awkward and silly way to ride a horse."

He was, he knew, defeated again.

Jonathan turned Bethany and Mannela loose for a day of shopping so he could visit the Hotel Dieu. In spite of painful memories of his disfigurement, he could not visit Paris again without asking about the good doctor who had saved his life.

Jonathan crossed the old Pont Neuf to the Île de la Cité, walked along Quai des Orfévres, turned at Notre Dame and reached the hospital. Hotel Dieu looked different. The nuns had told the convalescing Jonathan that the 'Hostel of God' had been founded in 660 and rebuilt many times. He strolled along a wrought iron fence and turned through the opened gate. Flowers were blooming in a series of large planters spaced along the building. Adding to the color were clusters of French flags decorating the building's facade. On the arch over the main entrance were carved the words Liberté, Égalité, Fraternité. Inside he learned that yet another restoration had been completed only five years before in 1877. When he asked about Doctor Paul Andre Courbet he was saddened to learn that the doctor had passed away two years before. He started to leave, but on impulse turned to ask the hospital administrator, "By chance is the doctor's daughter living in the city? I would like to at least express to her my gratitude for her father saving my life when others had given up on me."

"Oui, Captain Quinn, she is now Madame Jean Louis Buisson." It had taken only a moment to decide. With the address in his pocket, Jonathan crossed the Seine over the Pont Notre Dame and hailed a taxi. The carriage made its way along the Champs-Élysées to the Place De l'Etoile, past the colossal Arc de Triomphe and on toward the Bois de Boulogne and finally into a quiet residential area. The taxi stopped on Villa Said at house number six. A gray-haired woman wearing a starched apron met him at the door, listened to the explanation of his visit, spoken in not too perfect French, accepted his card, and disappeared closing the door behind her.

Jonathan was wondering if his French, which was more than a little rusty, had been understood when the woman returned to usher him into the house and to a parlor paneled in walnut. The room was sparsely furnished, but the pieces were old and fine. Shelves of books lined one wall. There was a portrait of Doctor Courbet hanging over the marble fireplace and on the mantle below, a silver framed photograph of a handsome man in the uniform of a French officer. Moments later, a demure dark-eyed lady entered the room. She paused a moment at the doorway to study the tall stranger with the eye patch.

Jonathan had no doubt that she had been the young lady aboard the *Ariel* that day so long ago, the first to ask for a button from his uniform. She was no longer a charming young girl. She had become a beautiful woman, but, he thought, a beautiful woman with a sad countenance. The black dress she wore was unmistakably a dress of mourning.

"Captain Quinn?" she spoke in English and offered her hand. "My father spoke of you often. You were, how do I say . . . his miracle patient. He would be very proud to see how well you are today."

"I owe my life to your father. I tried to find him when I visited France on business after your Franco-Prussian War, but I was unsuccessful. Paris was a little confused then." Madame Buisson lowered her eyes. "Yes, those were very bad times. Father and I had to flee from the Commune." She saw Jonathan glance at the picture in the silver frame. "My husband was a captain, first in the army of France under Napoleon III, and then the army of the Republic. He survived the Prussians only to be killed by the horrible *Commune de Paris*, his own countrymen."

"I am so sorry, Madame."

"Yes," she said, and then, "But you must tell me what brings you all the way to Paris, Captain."

She sat down. "Please sit." She motioned around the room. "I'm afraid we haven't replaced much of the furniture we lost in those days. Our home was burned, but enough survived to almost furnish this small house." She smiled, "Would you care for coffee?"

"Yes, please."

He explained that he was in Paris to establish his niece at school.

"The Ecole d' Ecouen! I went there myself. You leave your niece to me. I will see that she is properly introduced to Paris."

Coffee and pastries were brought to them by the same servant who had answered the door. As they talked, Madame Buisson looked curiously at Jonathan, especially the least damaged side of his face. She put down her coffee cup, rose from her chair, insisted her guest remain seated, walked to a small desk and retrieved something from one of its drawers.

"Captain Quinn, you told my father one small lie, did you not?" she asked.

"Why whatever makes you say that, Madame?" He was genuinely surprised at the accusation.

"You told him that the young officer who gave me this died in that terrible naval battle. I have studied your face, Captain. You were that young officer and this," she opened her hand, "is your button, is it not?"

Jonathan saw the sad expression that had veiled her face lift momentarily with a smile.

"I was young and vain then, afraid if you had known the young man in your father's care was the one who had given the button, you might have come and seen him the way he was," he paused. "The way I am."

"Captain, it is true that you are not the beautiful boy I met that day, but forgive my boldness if I say that you are an attractive man, perhaps made more so by the mystique of your scar. I am sure other women have noticed."

"Now you make me blush for the second time, Madame."

"How rude of me, Captain. I must apologize."

Jonathan, shifting to French, said in a quiet but serious tone, "An apology here and now is not sufficient, Madame."

It was Madame Buisson's turn to look surprised.

"How long have you been in mourning, may I ask?"

"Since my husband's death," adding, "extended, of course, by my father's passing."

"I think I could accept your apology, Madame, if it was made over dinner tonight at La Tour d'Argent. You have been in mourning much too long, as have I over the loss of a button." He smiled.

Madame Buisson looked startled for a moment. She started to speak, caught herself, then began again. "I could not possibly do that, Captain. I haven't had dinner in public with a man in so long. And at La Tour d'Argent! It would be scandalous."

The matronly servant peeped around the doorway and spoke in French. "It would be about time, if the Madame would allow me an opinion." It was evident that she had been listening beside the parlor doorway for some time. Jonathan understood and smiled.

"I must apologize for my unruly servant," Madame Buisson said. "Marie here helped my widower father raise me from a child and has failed to ever give me proper respect as an adult."

Marie huffed out of the room, noisily taking the coffee tray with her and speaking French over her shoulder in such an agitated manner that Jonathan couldn't understand a word.

"Marie is right, you know," he said, reverting back to English. "It is time such a lovely lady as you joined the bright and living world."

"It would be hard for me to do," she replied, not looking at him. "It was hard for me to come here today knowing I would see the one person in Paris, perhaps the world, who might remember the way I once looked before a cannon shell exploded in my face." She walked over to him and touched his cheek. "You were a golden young god come to save me that day. We are both scarred, only my scars aren't on the outside." She turned and walked away, then paused for a moment, turned and faced him again.

"All right, Captain Quinn, I accept your invitation, but for tomorrow night. I must have at least a day to find something to wear for the occasion. Everything I own is black."

"What do you mean you aren't dining with me tonight?" Bethany asked, surprised.

"I mean I'm fix'en to go out this evening. Doesn't a man deserve a little freedom around here? After all?"

His niece looked over at Mannela who smiled knowingly.

Bethany caught the idea.

"Why, Uncle, you have an engagement with a lady."

"Confound it! I used to have a private life. Now everything I do is under scrutiny by two prying females. I can't wait to get back to sea."

"Maybe, Captain, but it seems to me that you are in less hurry to do so than you were yesterday," remarked Mannela in her charming island accent.

From the balcony the two women watched Captain Quinn step into a waiting carriage. He refused to look up at them.

"You didn't slip one of your love potions into his soup did you?" Bethany laughingly asked Mannela.

"I think Paris can be a love potion all by itself. Now you better follow me to the table and learn some more French." Mannela laughed, "I believe your uncle is going to have a French lesson himself tonight."

The dress Madame Buisson wore was dark, but it was burgundy, not black, and its high collar was softened by a three-strand pearl necklace with a diamond clasp. She was thirty two years old, slim in stature, lithe in movement, and with the youthful face of the young girl he remembered from so long ago.

They were shy in conversation, awkwardly searching for some neutral topic for discussion. Each carefully avoided the painful subject of family. They conversed in French and English, both having a little trouble in the subtleties of the other's first language. After they had finished dinner, Jonathan suggested a walk along the Seine.

"It has been years since I have walked with a man along the river," Madame Buisson protested.

Jonathan persisted. They left the restaurant and walked along the Quai de la Tournelle, stopped at a sidewalk café and ordered coffee. As the two talked, the cloud of mourning which Madame Buisson had loyally worn into habit, began to lift. It was as if a dull film had been removed from her eyes to reveal a sparkle to match the moonlight on the Seine. Color blushed her cheeks and she laughed. Her laughter was light and timid as if she had almost forgotten how. And then it was time to end the evening.

In the carriage they were very proper, hands in their laps, hardly a word spoken, afraid to look into each other's eyes, afraid of the things they might say, wanted to say, afraid of their own feelings.

On her doorstep, Jonathan said, "I must leave in a week's time. Would you consider dining with me again, Madame Buisson?"

"Please, Captain, my name is Louisette. And yes, I would consider dining with you again. I shouldn't, of course, but yes I will dine with you again before you leave. What evening would you suggest, Captain?"

The captain wanted to take this woman into his arms, but he was afraid the fragile joy of the night might collapse.

"Well, Captain?" she asked again.

"Every evening between now and when I depart. I beg the pleasure of your company every evening."

She laughed, "I do not even know your first name, Captain Quinn."

"Jonathan," he replied, "Jonathan Hillary Quinn, completely at your service, Miss Louisette," spoken with an exaggerated Southern accent.

She laughed again.

"Please," he said, like a school boy without pretense, open and earnest.

"But the neighbors, friends, they will think I have gone mad, or worse."

"All right, bring them."

"Bring who, Jonathan Hillary?"

"Bring the neighbors, the friends, anyone you like. I'll bring my niece, anything, just say yes."

"I would like to meet your niece, but let's not have my neighbors."

"Then you will do it?"

"Yes!"

"Every night until I leave?"

"Oui. I said yes, Captain."

Jonathan took a deep breath, smiled, regained his composure, and said, "In that case I may never leave."

"Good night Captain. I think you are quite mad."

"But you said yes. I will call at eight."

"At eight," she repeated, and went into the house.

To their astonishment, Jonathan rousted Bethany and Mannela out of bed to find breakfast, including fresh bread, waiting in the kitchen.

"Is he ill, do you think?" asked Bethany, loudly so her uncle could hear.

"Mannela!" said Jonathan, ignoring his niece, "I cooked it. You serve it. We'll take it on the balcony."

"Must have been quite a lady," he heard Mannela whisper to Bethany.

"I think he's in love," she whispered back.

"I think you both are in for a heap of trouble if you don't leave me alone. Here I get up early and fix breakfast for y'all, and all I get is torment."

"Well?" said Bethany.

"Well what?"

"Aren't you going to tell us about last night?"

"For the last time there is nothing to tell. I simply fulfilled a social obligation to the family of the deceased doctor who once saved my life here in Paris."

"Oh."

"Oh, what?"

"Oh nothing, Uncle. Just a boring social obligation. We understand."

"Women are the most annoying, distracting, maddening creatures God ever put on Earth. I'm going out for a paper." Jonathan stormed out of the building.

"I tell you that must have been some social obligation."

"Bless him, Mannela, I think it would be wonderful if he found the right lady. No more teasing."

Jonathan and Louisette dined and walked and occasionally talked the nights away. Late mornings, Jonathan would take Louisette on long carriage rides on the boulevards of Paris and lunch at sidewalk cafes where they would talk of all manner of things, of good times and bad, their lives since the day they had met aboard the captured *Ariel* an eternity ago.

Late one morning when Jonathan arrived to pick up Madame Buisson she said, "I have invited a dear friend to meet us for lunch. I hope you don't mind."

"Anything to please Madame Buisson."

They arrived at number 31 Place de la Madeleine and entered a small restaurant of the same name where they were joined by a gentleman Jonathan guessed to be in his late forties. He was not shabbily dressed exactly, Jonathan decided. It was more that his clothes were rumpled, or maybe carelessly fitted. The man kissed Louisette's hand. His receding hairline was offset by a healthy mustache and beard.

"Jonathan," Louisette said, "may I present Monsieur Edouard Manet. Edouard, Capitaine Jonathan Quinn."

The stranger shook hands with Jonathan. His fingers were stained slightly around his nails and the cuff of his shirt had a smear of blue color on it.

Jonathan could deduce by the tone and sweep of Louisette's introduction that the man must be of some renown. "Capitaine Quinn," the man said, "it is quite remarkable to see you again."

"You have me at a disadvantage, sir. I must admit that neither your name nor your face is familiar to me."

The maitre'd showed them to a table by a window. Once seated Manet began speaking so rapidly in French that Jonathan could not keep up. "Please," he said, holding up his hands, "my French is very poor. Louisette, you had better act as interpreter."

She spoke with Manet, who looked at Jonathan with intense interest.

"Edouard is excited. He says he has something to show you after lunch which he thinks you will find interesting."

"In the meantime, Capitaine," Manet said slowly so that the American could understand, "I hope you will forgive me for intruding upon your lunch with this beautiful lady. France should give you a medal for the magic you have wrought in returning her to society. She has been away too long."

Louisette dismissed his remark with a wave of her hand.

"But Monsieur Manet, how could we have met before?" Jonathan asked.

"That question will keep for a little while, Capitaine. Right now, you cannot blame me for wanting to devote my time during this delightful lunch to a lady whom I have not seen in more than a year."

Edouard and Louisette chatted away as old friends are prone to do upon meeting after a long separation. Jonathan patiently listened, not getting all the conversation, but content to see Louisette's lively participation and hear her laughter. Like a butterfly emerging from a cocoon, Louisette appeared to be shedding her long, self-imposed burden of mourning.

After lunch, Monsieur Manet smiled at Jonathan. "And now, mon ami, the mystery of our meeting. But first, a short excursion." Louisette smiled at Jonathan's perplexed expression, took his arm and followed Edouard to a taxi.

"This is all very strange to me," Jonathan remarked, but neither of his companions explained. They took him to an art gallery in Montparnasse. There, Jonathan was led to a painting which immediately captured his attention.

"Edouard Manet is one of the leading impressionist painters of France, Jonathan."

"And this is his painting?"

"Yes," Louisette explained, "He arranged with its owner to bring it to the gallery for you to see. It is not for sale."

Completely absorbed, Jonathan ignored her words. The painting depicted the battle between CSS *Alabama* and USS *Kearsarge.*

"Well, Capitaine?" Manet said finally, "I would be interested in your opinion of the accuracy of the painting. I have had no small amount of complaints arise from American authorities who claim the painting is inaccurate because it shows *Kearsarge* firing on *Alabama* with her colors struck."

"You have it correct." Quinn pointed to his scar. "I carry proof of that fact, but how did you know?"

"I was there, of course. I sketched the battle as it happened. That is when we met."

Jonathan looked at him questioningly.

"I was one of many spectators aboard the pilot boat that pulled you from the sea. I need not describe the way your injuries appeared to those of us on board. To see you now . . . well," Manet paused, "miracle is not too strong a word."

Jonathan looked back at the painting, studying it intently. "There is only one detail."

"Yes, yes, what is it?" the artist inquired.

"*Alabama*'s funnel," Jonathan pointed. "You have it set behind the wrong mast, but that is of no importance. The battle ended as you have painted it. Once could have been excused as an accident, but they fired four salvos into us after our flag was struck. It was deliberate."

"My father saw the painting at a gallery," Louisette explained. "He was furious because it had been sold, but he did meet the artist and we have been friends with Edouard ever since."

"And why not?" said Manet, "All three of us had stories of *Alabama* in common; Louisette, captured by her, I saw her final battle and the Doctor saved one of her young officer's lives. You, mon Capitaine, are the incredible link to all our stories."

"You can see why Edouard had to meet you for himself. Fate placed you in all our lives."

There was silence as the three studied the painting.

Turning to Manet, Jonathan asked, "May I see more of your work?"

"Of course, if you like."

As their taxi moved down Rue Tournon opposite Luxembourg Palace, Manet pointed at a particular house, "Look there, Captain, number 19. Almost a hundred years ago an American hero died there on the second floor, impoverished, forgotten by your country. He too, lost a ship in battle. His name was John Paul Jones."

Jonathan turned to look back at the house. "But he bettered us by far. He conquered the enemy and took their ship as his sank."

"Well, my friend, his crew was more lucky perhaps, but not more valiant. I saw your ship fight that day." The carriage stopped. "But here we are."

Manet ushered Madame Buisson and Captain Quinn into the building. There were several paintings scattered carelessly around the studio. Jonathan looked at them all.

"It's remarkable how you have captured light."

Manet laughed. "You have hit upon the key to all painting. Light is ever there for the artist, but to capture it on canvas as you see it at a single moment in time, that is the trick. Goethe, the writer, perhaps put it best when he said, *Colors are the deeds and suffering of Light.* Color we artists understand, but light?"

Jonathan and Louisette took Bethany to dine with them at 99 Champs-Élysées, a restaurant called Fouquet's. After dinner they toured the fashionable evening clubs, and later, the cafes on the left bank crowded with a delightful mixture of students, artists, intellectuals, and night revelers like themselves. Bethany and Louisette laughed and talked and teamed up to pester Jonathan. Bethany was fascinated to learn that Madame Buisson and her uncle had met briefly during the 'button incident'. The following evening, Bethany turned down an invitation to join them, knowing it would be their last together before Jonathan left for Nassau.

The couple decided on a quiet neighborhood restaurant. Their conversation was light, their thoughts heavy with the weight of an approaching goodbye. After dinner, Jonathan pulled a small box from his pocket. He had spent the morning searching Paris for just the right gift. Louisette opened the box and found a gold brooch in the likeness of a sailing ship.

"Now my reputation is really ruined," she said, "Everyone will know that the mysterious man who has coaxed me out into the world again is a sailor. It will be the scandal of the neighborhood." She laughed.

Jonathan looked at her. "Thank you for the loveliest week of my life."

She reached across the table and held his hand.

They walked in silence down the tree-lined boulevard. Just as they reached the corner of Villa Said it began to rain. Holding hands, they ran laughing like children all the way to the house. Jonathan knocked on the door expecting Marie to open it.

Louisette, water running off the end of her nose, reached in her purse. Smiling shyly, she handed Jonathan the key. He quickly opened the door and they stepped dripping into the entrance hall. She stood shivering, her wet hair coming undone around the edges. She pulled out the hair pins and shook her head like a puppy, spraying Jonathan with droplets of water as the dark hair fell about her shoulders. One minute they were laughing, the next they were locked in an embrace, shivering from the chill of the rain . . . or the excitement of desire.

"But where is Marie?"

"She is visiting relatives." Louisette buried her head on his chest. "You must think me a wicked woman." She looked up at him, embarrassed. "I don't know what has come over me since you walked into this house. I haven't thought of tomorrow for a long time, and then you appeared, a thread from the past, a beautiful week of awakening, and now you are leaving."

Jonathan smoothed the wet hair from her face and kissed her cool forehead. She looked up at him with childlike eyes. He lifted her off the floor, pressing his lips against hers. She clung to his neck kissing him, melting into his chest.

Slowly he let her down until her feet once more touched the floor. She took his hand in hers and without a word guided him up the darkened stairs. It was raining hard now, the window panes streaked with water, thunder rolling across the rooftops of Paris.

They kissed again, his fingers gently feeling for the tiny buttons that ran down the back of her dress. She undid his stiff collar. His efforts, as careful as he tried, were clumsy.

She broke away from his kiss and stepped back, turning so that he could reach the buttons on the back of the dress. When he had undone them, she slipped the dress over her head and let it float to the polished, parquet floor. He let his coat fall and unbuttoned his shirt. She stepped out of her petticoats. He kissed her again and sat with her on the bed. They laughed at the awkwardness of getting out of their high top button shoes. Their laughter ended as they looked at one another. She ran her hands over his firm chest. Illuminated by the glow of the city lights filtering through the rain-ribboned windows, Louisette was the most beautiful, delicate creature he had ever seen. He gently lifted her linen camisole over her head. She looked up at him. Her ivory skin seemed to glow in the soft light, her small breasts, as perfect as a Greek sculpture.

Louisette touched his torn ear and kissed the black silk patch covering his blind eye. Speaking in French, she smothered him in soft words and kisses and arched her body to meet his. Jonathan growled, animal-like, in unfettered release. Their passions sated beyond all anticipation, they lay silently side-by-side listening to the music of the rain until sleep gentled their breathing.

Much later, Jonathan felt Louisette moving in his arms, snuggling close to him. She moved herself up on her knees and slid elfin-like to straddle him. She looked down at him, her long dark hair falling off her shoulders, her mouth slightly open, her eyes half closed.

He was totally in her control, helpless. Slow at first, her movements became frantic, her head tossing from side to side teasing her hair into a blurred sheen of raven wisps until, exhausted in ecstasy, she collapsed upon him.

Jonathan gently pulled the covers over them. Neither had spoken a word, none had been necessary. They fell into deep, untroubled sleep.

When Louisette awakened, sunlight filtered through the window. There was a note on the empty pillow beside her. "Until Christmas, my love" was all that it said. It was enough.

CHAPTER 15

"Welcome back, Captain J," chimed Billy Wong, "You long time gone. Yes, long time. Many ladies be velly glad you home. They give me special letters, smell velly sweet." He ran giggling a few steps ahead with his employer's valise.

Jonathan went straight to his desk and began going over the J & Q accounts posted in his absence. When he finished, he sorted through the mail, wrote several bank drafts, and walked to the post office to mail them. He could have sent one of the clerks, but he wanted to walk through the town himself. It always looked smaller when he returned from a long trip. Perhaps he was getting island fever and beginning to tire of New Providence.

It was late afternoon when he returned to the J & Q building and climbed the stairs to the living quarters. He expected to find the usual glass of bourbon waiting on the table beside his favorite chair. Instead he found two glasses and a lady's hat.

"Hello, Captain," she said in a husky voice from the doorway of his bedroom. Her red hair fell about her bare shoulders accentuating a very attractive bosom. "You are making a habit of such long trips lately. You must be tired." She was barefoot wearing only a single petticoat. "How would you like someone to rub your back?"

"Jessica, you are going to get us both shot. Where is your husband, and who saw you come up here?"

"My, what a worrywart. I came through the back gate and up the rear stairs like I always do, J. Hillary. And you need not worry about my straight-laced husband. That's what you think of him isn't it, that he is the perfect straight-laced citizen?"

"I don't think about him at all, but I am concerned about your reputation. It's a small island."

"It's a boring island. So boring even my adoring husband has been affected. What would you say if I told you he had an island girl, a brown-skinned island girl that he visits quite often?"

"I'd say that it's none of my business."

She walked across the room, stepped behind him and kissed the back of his neck and reached both hands around to unbutton his shirt. He moved her hands and turned to face her.

"You're a damn attractive lady, Jess, but you were right, I am tired." He kissed her on the forehead, stepped to the small table, and picked up both drinks. "Here you are," he said handing one to her. "I toast the prettiest redhead in all the Caribbean."

She took a sip, put the glass back on the table, and kissed him hard on the mouth. He reciprocated lamely. She tried again and this time she ran her hand down to feel his response. There wasn't any.

"Who is she?" Jessica asked as she sat down in his chair, and picked up her drink.

"Who is who?" he answered.

"Come now, Jonathan. I've known you too long for you to deceive me. Before you left, I could merely look at you across the room and see your flame come alive. And I know I'm not the only lady in the islands to do so. Now you return and find a woman of passion waiting in your bedroom and you rebuff her, gently I admit, but without even the hint of a flame." She took a sip from her drink and smiled up at him. "My poor Jonathan. You are in love."

Jonathan felt himself blush. "I told you, Jess, I'm tired."

"What's her name? At least you can tell me that."

"Damn! Are all men so easy for you to read?"

"Of course, Darling. Why do you think I came to you so soon after we met? I can judge any man when it comes to passion. And we have shared such passion, J. Hillary."

"You're an exciting woman, Jessica, dear. I bet you have scared the hell out of some men."

"Why, what a charming thing to say. Are you sure we shouldn't try to test the spell the unnamed lady has placed upon my brave captain?" She looked up at him and slowly licked her lips. "After all, unbridled passion is fun, and you are so good at it." She once more put a hand between his legs. "Love, on the other hand, is an affliction," she said, withdrawing her hand. "I thought by now you would be immune."

"So did I. But damn if I can help it. I don't even know if I can do anything about it," he said honestly.

"Then you are a lost little boy," she replied with all hint of sarcasm gone from her voice. "She must be a very special woman. I hope for your sake she is a sincere one."

"Come on, Jess. I'll rub your back before you get dressed. At least you'll feel relaxed when you leave."

"That's not a good idea, J. Hillary. I would surely lose my pride in failing a second time to seduce you. It's going to be a very dull season."

"You are a fine woman, Jess," he said, and he meant it.

"Yes," she said, "I'm not a bad bitch, just a hungry one."

She dressed, put her hair in place, pinned on her hat and brushed away the tears in the corners of her eyes.

"Don't hate me, Jess," Jonathan put his arm around her.

"I don't hate you, J. Hillary. It's this damn island I hate."

He walked her to the back gate in the high wall that surrounded the compound.

"Billy Wong!" Jonathan called when Jessica was gone.

The small Chinese man appeared at the door, smiling at him. "Billy Wong, don't let any more ladies upstairs. None, do you understand?"

The smile turned to a frown. "Oh, Captain J! Many ladies have breaky hearts. You sick, Captain?"

"Maybe, Billy, maybe."

Lopez brought *Tropic Bird* into port two days later. Her cargo of lumber, slate roofing, kegs of nails and cement was unloaded. She would sail in ballast to Cuba for sugar and cigars, to Jamaica for rum and proceed to Boston to deliver her cargo. There she would load hardware, hand tools, oil lanterns, paper to feed the printing presses of the Caribbean and straw-packed ice to cool the drinks of Nassau.

"Captain Lopez, how would you like to move our operations to your home island of Cuba?"

"I think I might like that, Captain, provided the Royalists don't hang me."

"This letter from Felipe de Alacon arrived while I was away. He says the fighting is over. The island is quiet. Both sides have suffered too much to continue, but this is the interesting part. The combatants have signed an agreement called the Pact of Zanjon. The most significant item of the Pact is the encouragement of United States investment in return for supporting Spain during the insurrection. American interests have already moved on the sugar industry. He says money is pouring into cattle ranching, tobacco, fruit farming, ore exploration, and utilities. I have an interest in several thousand acres of good land in partnership with Alacon. What do you say, Jorge? Come with me and I'll give you command of the marine operations and six percent of J & Q profits. The chief accountant can handle the scaled back operations here in Nassau."

"Lopez, at your service, Captain Quinn," Jorge grinned, "How could I refuse?"

Jonathan called in Billy Wong. "Billy, I'm going to Cuba. I'll be back within three weeks. When I get back, I want you to have all my gear packed, everything but the furniture, it's not worth taking. Don't forget Captain Jones' mementos. They go where J & Q goes."

Billy's eyes opened wide. "Oh! We go Cuba live?"

"That's right, Billy. You don't want to go?"

"Billy go where Captain J go. Number one man." he replied.

Still he didn't look too happy.

"All right, Billy, suppose you tell me what the trouble is, as if I can't guess." Billy dropped his gaze to the ground and said nothing. "I know you spend a lot of time at the other end of town. How many women and how many children, Billy? You better tell me the truth."

"Billy always tell Captain J truth. Billy, he have only one womans but two childrens," the little man said, looking down at the floor.

"Is the woman your wife?" asked Jonathan.

"Oh, No! She concubine. Billy saving money to buy ploper bride from China one day," he said proudly.

"Billy, you little heathen, I tell you what you are going to do." Billy Wong looked up at Jonathan, a worried expression on his face.

"You get your woman and children ready to go to Havana with us."

A big smile appeared on Billy's face. "You velly good man, Captain J. Billy Wong t'ankee you takey Billy Wong's people. No trouble, you see."

Jonathan started to dismiss the little man when he had another thought. "Billy," he said.

"Yes, Captain J?"

"You take woman, children, clothes, furniture. No goats, no chickens, and especially no pigs. You sell. Then we'll buy new ones in Cuba. Understand?"

"No goats, no chickens, just two pigs, Captain J," Billy smiled. "No pigs, Billy. A cat or a dog, but no pigs."

As a matter of record, the last crates to be unloaded from *Tropic Bird* at Havana were foul smelling and emitted grunts and cackles.

The year 1881 brought much change and no small amount of sadness. Jonathan received word that Doctor Theodore Perkins had passed away. The letter from the doctor's attorney said that he was found by his elderly servants at his desk, his head resting on a patient's medical papers. The attorney explained further that the doctor's will stipulated that Luky and Arabella were to have use of his house and all the earnings of a small trust, his life's savings, for as long as they lived. Upon the death of the last survivor, the house and any remainder of the trust would go to Bethany.

The letter said the doctor's funeral was attended by several hundred people from the town and surrounding area. In the absence of living close friends healthy enough to carry his coffin, six Confederate veterans served as pallbearers with Tom Boatner and aging Jefferson Jay Little walking solemnly behind the coffin.

Jonathan arrived in Vicksburg as soon after as he could. He stayed at the house, mothered by the two grieving Negro women who had been so faithful through so much trial and sorrow and change. He commissioned a marble headstone for the doctor's grave which was located not far from that of the Quinns. The tombstone had a Confederate flag carved below a cross, and beneath the flag, the words:

Dr. Jacob Theodore Perkins 1810–1881 Never refused a call. Never failed a friend.

Captain Quinn made arrangements with attorney Jason Todd to manage the affairs of Shamrock and to ensure that the terms of Doctor Perkins' will, especially as to Luky and Arabella, be carried out. Before Jonathan left, he arranged for needed painting and repairs to the house, and firmly established the fact that the two women of color who would continue to live in the house were 'caretakers of his niece's inherited property', a cover story just in case anything was ever brought up about the two black women living in the uptown white neighborhood. He needn't have worried. Luky and Arabella were considered by the town's people an institution unto themselves.

In Paris, the doctor's beloved and bereaved godchild did not attend school the day after Jonathan's letter arrived.

I love you, Daddy Ted, she whispered. *You were the kindest man in the world. Tell Mama and Grandmama and Great Granddaddy I love them and that I'm all right.* Tears, which had seldom defeated a little girl's will, flowed silently down a young woman's cheeks. *The world I grew up in is gone.*

* * *

The headquarters for Jones & Quinn Shipping Company was moved to Havana, Cuba. The old office and marine supply store at New Providence would remain open. The *Barca Vela* and another shoal draft schooner would operate inter-island routes out of the Nassau office. The first mate of *Tropic Bird* became her captain while Jonathan and Jorge Lopez began a search for a new larger ship. Through Felipe de Alacon's contacts, J & Q was awarded a contract from the American Sugar Refining Company for shipping large quantities of sugar to the U.S. With Jonathan's financial support Felipe put their jointly owned plantation into full production of sugar and tobacco.

Only one thing was missing in the life of Jonathan Quinn. In Havana, he purchased a townhouse. When asked by the seller if he intended to remodel and refurbish the building, Jonathan answered, "Yes, of course," and promptly had the house boarded up. Earlier he had purchased two buildings on the waterfront of Havana Harbor. The larger of the two was a warehouse. The smaller two story one was remodeled to serve as a marine supply store and J & Q office on the first floor with living quarters above just as in Nassau.

For months Jonathan spent seven days a week attending to the demands of the growing business; fitting out the new ship, scheduling shipping consignments and monitoring operations at Havana Harbor, Nassau and the plantation. As busy as he was, no one had to remind him when it was time for his long-scheduled trip to France. He had promised to spend Christmas with his niece in Paris, at least that's the excuse he gave Captain Lopez and Felipe Alacon.

On a bright sunny December day, the modern passenger liner entered Cherbourg Harbor. It was colder than the day *Alabama* had sailed out to do battle with *Kearsarge* some seventeen years before, but the harbor was as Jonathan remembered it. He stood at the ship's rail looking into the crowd of families and friends of arriving passengers. *How nice to have someone welcome you ashore.* In all his sailing to foreign ports there had never been anyone to greet him but an occasional business associate. He tossed his cigar over the side, picked up his valise and joined the line of passengers walking down the gangway. *At least this time I'm walking ashore at Cherbourg instead of being carried like a corpse.*

"Uncle Jonathan! Over here!" Jonathan looked up surprised to see Bethany, Mannela Wombi, and a lovely dark haired French lady wearing a fashionable fur hat and shoulder wrap to match. He pushed his way through the crowd, swept past Bethany and grabbed Louisette up in his arms, "I have missed you Madame Buisson. How wonderful for you to be here."

"I hope you don't think I'm too brazen a woman for being here. Bethany insisted I come," Louisette said. She looked genuinely embarrassed, a blush on her cheeks. "Probably all Paris knows by now."

"I certainly hope so," Jonathan replied. "I want the men of France to know that Captain Quinn, the old one-eyed pirate, has stolen the most beautiful lady in France right out from under their snobbish noses."

"You are terrible, Captain, and I am a ruined woman."

Jonathan realized he had not spoken to his niece. "Bethany! Hello!" He nodded to Mannela.

"So you finally notice me, Uncle," she laughed.

On the way to the train station, the captain turned his attention to Mannela. "What have you to report on a certain day student in your care?"

"I have had no problems with her schooling, Captain, although it is tiring to keep up with her other activities."

"Other activities?"

"Now, Uncle, don't rip your jib. Louisette has introduced me to everyone in Paris. We go to concerts, museums, to the country to see the lovely chateaus of France and I go riding on nice Sundays."

"Here I leave for a few months only to find upon my return that you two have become a team. You're probably the most sought after pair in France, certainly the prettiest." With a mock frown he turned to Mannela. "I expect a full report on my niece including an accounting of her school marks."

"I thought I was your business partner, Uncle, not a simple school girl."

"Your business at the moment is education. After all, who wants an ignorant business partner?"

"You will see that her marks reflect excellence in all categories," Mannela assured him.

"There you have it, Uncle," smiled Bethany.

"My God, all three conspire against me."

"Ladies, do we detect fear in the mighty Captain Quinn?" his niece asked.

"You would detect fear in Zeus if he had to contend with the three of you."

"Should we take that as a compliment, ladies?" Louisette joined in the fun.

"You can take it as fact," Jonathan answered.

It was well past nine in the evening when their train arrived in Paris and they reached the house on Villa Said. Marie served dinner to the group. The food was delicious, conversation and laughter abundant.

On Christmas morning, Notre-Dame was so crowded they had to stand at the very back during the service. Jonathan whispered, "Will this be over sometime before New Year's?"

After the service, Louisette led them up 397 narrow steps to the top of Notre-Dame's north-west tower. With lungs panting, legs crying for relief, they emerged on the upper works of the tower some two-hundred feet above the city. They found a few other people there, mostly young lovers it seemed to Jonathan. It was clear, windy and cold, but the view of Paris was spectacular. Before them, blackened zinc, ceramic tile, dark slate, and green-stained copper roof tops, church spires, domes, grand boulevards, narrow ancient streets, broad parks and the graceful flowing curves of the river Seine blended into the patchwork quilt of Paris.

"Have you ever seen such a view?" Jonathan said. "It would never have occurred to the common sinner I am that one was allowed up here."

"The people of Paris have climbed up here for hundreds of years. Even when the city was hardly more than a village," Louisette said. "Look," she pointed, "You can see the boundaries of the old city and the haphazard patterns of growth further outward."

Bethany walked away to give the couple time to themselves.

Standing close to him, Louisette took Jonathan's hand in hers. "Even stained with the accumulated grime of centuries, it is beautiful to me . . . but also sad. It is a city of romantic love and violent civil revolt. A strange combination, don't you think?" She turned to face him, smiling sadly.

"Louisette," he said, "could you ever leave your beautiful city?" She did not reply. "Marry me, Louisette. Come with me to Cuba." She looked at him for a moment, then out over the city. "I'll bring you back to visit every year if you like, I promise," he said, "Come with me."

Desperate to tell him her sad secret, afraid she might never tell him if she didn't do it now, she confessed, "I can't give you children, Jonathan. My marriage was childless. I can't give that to you." She looked up with tears in her eyes. "I love you," she said, and put her cheek against his chest. "Can't we continue, just as we are?"

"It's you I want, Louisette. I never needed anyone before. Marry me now. Come to the islands with me."

"If you are sure, Jonathan."

"You will leave Paris?"

"Yes," she smiled through big tears, "This city has become as sad for me as Shamrock must be for you."

He wanted to hold her, to kiss her, but there were sightseers around them. He thought it would embarrass her. She took his arm and they walked over to join Bethany.

She looked at the pair and laughed. "What is it?" she asked. "You both have the look of children up to some mischief. Why do I continually get the feeling when I am around you two that I am the grownup?"

The wedding was a small, elegant and happy affair attended by old family friends glad to see their Louisette smiling and gay after so many years of self-imposed mourning.

Madame Marie was happy for Louisette, but sad. Her 'child' was leaving Paris, leaving the continent, leaving Marie. *But,* she consoled herself, *Madame will keep the house. I, Marie, will care for it, of course, and the Quinns will visit Paris while Mademoiselle Quinn is living in the city.* Standing on the La Havre docks with Bethany and Mannela, she waved a tearful good bye to Captain and Mrs. Quinn.

Sultry, lush Havana welcomed the lovers. The townhouse was opened and aired for Louisette's inspection. Though in disrepair, the architecture was grand: large rooms, tall windows, thick walls and high ceilings designed to provide cool comfort in the tropical heat of the island's capital. In back there was a walled courtyard with a gold-fish pool and luxuriant greenery.

Their voices echoed in the cool emptiness of the house.

"If you like it, it is yours to refurbish and furnish as you desire, at least until the money runs out."

"You bought this house and then went to Paris assuming I would come didn't you? Was I so predicable a conquest?" she asked.

"I was the conquered one, Madame Quinn. I would have begged on my knees for you to come back with me."

"And what if I had not? What would you have done with this lovely old house?"

"I would have left it boarded up as a memorial to my broken heart."

"You are a charming scoundrel, J. Hillary, but I love you just the same. I accept the challenge."

"What challenge?"

"Why the one to see if I can spend all of your money on this house, of course. I intend to be very good at it."

CHAPTER 16

The school for young women offered classes in language, art, history, music, and the skills of social etiquette expected of every lady of society. Bethany enjoyed some of them, considered language classes necessary but tedious and was bored a great deal of the time. She found nothing to interest her in the school's social activities, although she made friends with some of the girls like the Spanish ambassador's daughter with whom on occasion she attended functions at the Spanish Embassy.

After several months of observation, Bethany concluded that the school was designed to perpetuate the dependency of young women on their families and the husbands chosen for them while fostering an immature and silly attitude of snobbery. There was no conscious effort, as far as she could determine, to teach them any self-reliance. She was set apart from them by the freedom and experience of growing up in the company of her godfather in war-torn Mississippi, and by the world of commerce to which her uncle had introduced her.

On weekdays, Bethany dutifully attended classes as prim and proper as any other young lady, but on weekends, under Mannela's supervision, all Paris was open to her. Louisette had presented her to the *salons* of Paris society while Louisette's friend, Edouard Manet, took delight in introducing her to the *avant-garde* café crowd.

The salons were sponsored by wealthy grande dames *to encourage the exchange of new ideas and creativity in the arts,* and in no small part for their own entertainment and aggrandizement. Each jealously competed to fill their salons with persons *au courant,* the intelligentsia and those who had celebrity, notoriety, or recognized talent in the arts and sciences. Pretty young women and witty young men were courted to round out the gatherings which provided platforms for serious intellectual debate and irreverent wit. Art, theater, dance, politics, social mores and philosophy were open to discussion, challenge, praise, criticism, and sarcasm. Nonconformity was in vogue.

One of the favorite topics of discussion was the darling of non-conformists philosophy, Friedrich Nietzsche. He claimed the industrial era would flatten culture and proposed, as a remedy, the breeding of a new aristocracy of supermen. Bethany found Nietzsche's ideas disturbing, especially his pronouncement that women were dangerous playthings, and that in his world of the future, men would be trained for war while women procreated warriors ad infinitum. Bethany wanted to put the philosopher down as silly, but his words haunted her. In her lifetime there had already been too many warriors, too much war. *I wonder what Nietzsche would think if I told him I was literally born of war, that my father was a bullet?*

Bethany began to tire of the salons. She had become bored by the upper crust of Paris. She found many of their number spoiled, arrogant, narcissistic and insincere. The café society was much more fun. Forty-nine year old Edouard Manet took the position of mentor to and protector of Bethany Quinn. She easily garnered the attention of artists, writers, musicians, poets, dandies, university students and the wealthy bored aristocrats of Europe, all those who drifted through the endless party that was Paris.

The fact that Bethany Quinn appeared "worldly-wise beyond her age" made her all the more attractive, even a mystery. To many of the males she encountered, young or old, she represented the quintessential object of desire, or so her mentor, with great amusement, informed her. Manet noted that she could handle a compliment or jealous jab with equal grace, and to his surprise, she could easily foil lustful approaches without taking offense or offending the perpetrator.

The attention was both a surprise and a source of amusement to Bethany. At one party, while standing with her back to a couple, she found herself the topic of discussion.

The woman remarked, "They say she came from the defeated South, the States Confederate or something. You know, that terrible American war."

The man replied, "Yes. I understand her uncle was aboard the Confederate vessel that was sunk during a battle off Cherbourg."

"Have you seen her uncle? Someone said he is scarred, has only one eye."

"No, but did you know he married Madame Buisson and took her away to a Caribbean Island?"

"No! I do not believe it."

"Yes. It's true. And do you know the girl has an exotic, mulatto Creole woman from Haiti for a chaperone?"

"Haiti? Where they had that terrible Negro uprising?"

"The same. The woman's father was a Frenchman, her mother, a slave."

"Now I know you are joking."

"But it's all true. I swear it."

"And you are infatuated with that young woman?"

"Of course, and so is every man who sees her."

"You men are such children. You drool over the young and inexperienced for their shallow beauty and innocence while it is the more mature woman who can truly show you the pleasures of being a man."

"My dear Madame Brunetière, is that an invitation?"

"Discretion has opened the door to many a boudoir, Maurice, my dear."

"Tonight?"

"Not tonight! Tomorrow after lunch. My husband will be at his club, as usual."

Undetected, Bethany moved quietly away.

Mannela instructed Bethany in "the wily ways of the weaker sex: men." She determined her charge would neither fall victim to the weakness of her own flesh and emotions, nor become the slave of some skilled and devious libertine. On the other hand, she assured Bethany that when the time came, there was nothing wrong with enjoying sensual pleasures on her own terms.

"And just when will that time come for me?"

"Not before you can handle it, I pray."

"Handle it?"

"Yes. Handle it without the grand illusions of some silly, naive girl. Handle it with awareness of the consequences, with discretion, without the loss of your own self respect, and especially without the need to give up your independence."

"You have not said anything about love, Mannela."

"Love and passion are two different things, and wise is the woman who knows it. A marriage of passion and love is far more rare than common marriage of man and woman."

"That is not a happy thought, certainly not a romantic one."

"No, it is not," was Mannela's reply.

Mannela was satisfied that she had prepared her eighteen year old protégée as well as any white woman could be prepared to enter and survive the adult world on an equal footing with other women, and a vastly superior one to any man.

Bethany was not quite aware of all of this. She had the self-confidence she had developed as a child, a sense of honesty, a taste for adventure, a mischievous streak, but she did not consider herself a *femme fatale* by any means. On the other hand, Mannela knew that she was exactly that.

Bethany accepted invitations for dinner, riding in the park, for the ballet, the theater, and parties, always chaperoned by Mannela as was her uncle's strict rule. Many a whisper stirred whenever "that young American woman" appeared at the theater or ballet, she in evening dress, her escort in white tie and tails, the two accompanied by the exotic but dignified, French speaking mulatto island woman.

When Bethany asked if she could have a little more privacy occasionally in the company of friends, Mannela answered, "Only if I approve of the friends first." She would allow Bethany her amusements, but it was her intention not to allow her to be harmed.

Bethany tolerated her last year of school, but delighted in her lively café crowd . . . the picnics in the parks and weekend parties at this author's flat or that artist's loft, sometimes at a Chateau in the country. Through Manet she met such luminaries as Hilaire-Germain-Edgar Degas, Pierre-Auguste Renoir, Claude Monet, Émile Zola, Henri René Albert Guy de Maupassant, and once, even the venerable Victor Hugo.

At one gathering of notables at the home of Madame Guillaume, Bethany was amused rather than shocked when Guy de Maupassant took the floor to succinctly describe the libertinism flourishing in Paris. "During the last year, according to public records," he announced, "2,344 wives left their husbands and 4,427 husbands left their wives. I am told that here in Paris 5,000 prostitutes are registered and an estimated 30,000 freelancers are not. I am also aware that the term, *Grande Horizontale*, is not uncommonly applied to certain ladies of society." Applause and laughter followed.

One weekend, a group traveled out to Chatou for a boating party. They were driven to shelter by rain and settled down at the Restaurant Grenouilliere which, Bethany discovered, meant froggery. There was a charming and very pretty young woman in the group by the name of Aline Charigot. Bethany learned that she was Renoir's favorite model and lover. Renoir made many sketches of the group that afternoon and from them a painting he titled *The Boating Party.* In it he placed Aline Charigot in the forefront holding her little dog. He painted Bethany just on the right upper margin in the back of the crowd wearing hat and gloves with her hands covering her ears. He told her it was because she always pretended not to hear him whenever he asked permission to paint her in the nude. There were others, non painters, who just wanted her in the nude. She laughed, flirted, was kissed and adored by many, but gracefully retained her virginity in a Paris where such was a rare commodity.

Mannela made a mistake regarding Bethany's well-being, a mistake which sneaked ever so slowly past her calculated defenses. The mistake was Jeremy Wright.

He was, from the beginning, overly attentive to the needs of his partner's niece. Wright made it a point to call on Bethany during his frequent business trips to Paris, always taking her to lunch and always dutifully reporting Bethany's status to Jonathan by letter. Mannela attributed his actions as an attempt to favorably impress Jonathan and thereby improve their waning business relationship. Bethany thought it sweet of him, even gallant, to escort her to expensive restaurants. Mannela grew comfortable in allowing him to take Bethany to lunch unaccompanied. After all, he was Captain Quinn's business associate and certainly aware that only a fool would cross the captain, especially when it came to the welfare of his niece. Mannela was correct in her assumptions when dealing with a sober Jeremy Wright. However, Jeremy Wright was frequently not sober.

Bethany hardly noticed a subtle change in his conduct. He often held her hand while he talked to her. She was always interested in learning how he conducted his part of the business, and he was delighted to have her attention. He willingly told her trade secrets that he kept from Jonathan. In fact, he would tell her anything she wanted to know as long as she stayed in his company. Gradually, when they were together, he began to change the subject of their discussions from business to rather risqué anecdotes. She grew uncomfortable with him and began to find excuses not to see him. One Saturday, while Mannela was out shopping, Wright showed up at the apartment unannounced. Bethany allowed him in before she realized he had been drinking. He was different than she had ever seen him . . . serious, dark.

"Bethany, I can no longer conceal my longing for you," he blurted.

"Don't be silly, Jeremy. You've just had too much to drink." She tried to dismiss him.

"Don't trifle with me, Bethany. You are grown now. I see the way other men look at you, the way you respond. You are the most beautiful woman I have ever seen. Let me be the one to teach you, Bethany. I can teach you so much." He pulled her to him and kissed her hard on the mouth.

"Jeremy, stop it! You're drunk." She pushed at his chest with both arms. He tried to kiss her again. She twisted out of his grip and moved toward the bedroom. He was quickly at the door and pushed his way in before she could lock it.

"Jeremy! Mannela will be back any minute. You get out! Jonathan will kill you.

Now stop it!" She slapped him across the face, cutting his lip. He pushed her hard, shoving her across the room and onto the bed.

"I love you, Bethany. I must have you." He moved toward the bed where she had fallen on her back, her legs not quite touching the floor.

She looked straight at him. "Jeremy, would you like to see my legs? I'm told they are quite nice."

Jeremy stopped, was even shocked as she began to lift her skirt and petticoats revealing her legs sheathed in black silk stockings. "You cunning little whore! You do want me!" He moved toward her, his triumphant leer accented by the trickle of blood from his cut lip.

Bethany pulled her skirts higher and reached for the garter on her left leg. He stopped in excited anticipation of having her disrobe on the bed before him. She withdrew something small and shiny from the garter and pointed it at Wright.

Sitting up on the edge of the bed Bethany spoke calmly. "Jeremy, don't make me shoot you." She cocked the hammer. "You're drunk. You're making a stupid mistake. Leave now, Jeremy, and I'll forget this ever happened."

"Why you flaming little cunt! You won't shoot me, not with a toy like that." He took a step toward her, just one.

The pistol was pointing at his chest. Jonathan had taught her if she had to use the gun, to aim at the largest target, the torso, but she deliberately lowered the muzzle and fired.

"Bloody hell!" Jeremy screamed. He hopped around the room holding his right foot in both hands. "You little bitch!" He fell into a chair and stared at the blood oozing through a hole in the top of his expensive, polished boot.

Bethany stood by the bed. No longer frightened, she could hardly contain her anger. "Get up! Get up and get out of here! Now!" She cocked the hammer a second time.

Looking directly into the twin barrels of the tiny pistol pointing at his face, Jeremy's passion quickly cooled, his mind sobered by the intense pain in his foot. The gravity of what he had done finally registered as did the possible consequences should Captain Quinn find out about it. "For God's sake, Bethany, I couldn't help but desire you. Don't you see? I was willing to throw everything away for you, business, my life, anything. You have driven me mad, I see that now. Yes, you are the kind of woman who can do that to men. You must know that."

Bethany didn't know that. She had been frightened by him, and now her own anger frightened her.

"Out," she said in a low controlled voice, "or I'll kill you." Jeremy struggled up out of the chair. He was plainly afraid now, but not of the pistol. "You are going to tell your uncle, aren't you?"

"If I told him he would kill you," she answered, "which is why he will not learn of this from me. You are not worth risking him to the hangman."

"But what of the business, can you allow me to carry on our business? I depend on our business."

"You had best do that, Mr. Wright, or explain why to Jonathan." She waved the pistol toward the door. "Now get out!"

"You Quinns are a vicious, cold, bloody lot." Jeremy said as he limped painfully toward the door.

Bethany snatched a towel from the wash stand and tossed it at him. "Wrap that around your foot. I don't want you bleeding all over the house."

Mannela returned to find Bethany on her hands and knees scrubbing blood from the floor in her bedroom. Bethany looked up at her. "I suppose there is no use asking you not to ask?" Mannela was shocked and required immediate answers from her charge. "Bethany Quinn, what has happened here? Is that blood? Are you hurt?"

"I shot Jeremy Wright," Bethany said calmly, "not ten minutes ago."

It was the first time Bethany had ever seen Mannela's composure shaken. She grabbed Bethany off the floor, took the cleaning rag from her, and sat her in the chair. "I am listening."

After she had heard the whole story she was filled with disgust, disgust at Jeremy Wright, and disgust with herself for a lapse of judgment. That aside, her immediate concern was about the long term effect the incident might have on Bethany. It was just such trauma that had isolated her own feelings for so long.

"I don't want this to make you fear or hate men as happens to some women after such an attack. I don't want it to rob you of the future pleasure of lovemaking. I don't want this to make you not like it."

"Oh, Mannela," Bethany said, "I didn't shoot him because I don't like the attention of men. I shot him because he didn't have my permission."

Mannela at first was stunned. Bethany added, "I meant for that to be funny." Then she smiled and they both broke out laughing. It was a little less humorous a few minutes later when a Paris gendarme knocked on the door.

"Madame," he greeted Mannela at the front door, "Forgive the intrusion, but a gunshot was reported in this neighborhood. Have you heard anything?"

"No, nothing at all," Mannela answered.

"I see. Well, just the same, may I come in and look around. I am, of course, doing the same in all the apartments of this building."

"One moment, please, I will ask my mistress." Mannela disappeared. After checking once more to see that all traces of blood had been cleaned and the hole in the floor covered with a throw rug, she returned to invite the policeman into the apartment. He seemed embarrassed but carried out an inspection of every room including a peek under the beds and into the armoires. "Looking for the body, officer?"

He turned to see Bethany smiling at him. "Mademoiselle, I beg your pardon for the intrusion." At the front door, he politely touched his cap in salute and walked down the hall toward the next apartment.

"Am I to tell your uncle?" Mannela asked, already knowing the answer.

"You know better. He would call me home immediately, probably kill Jeremy, and dismiss you."

"And Mr. Wright?" Mannela questioned.

"Mr. Wright will be as good as gold, I think. He will certainly do as I say from now on. I might even find him useful. And certainly he can still make a profit for J & Q."

"You surprise even your teacher, Mademoiselle Quinn. Yes. You have graduated, I think," Mannela said with some pride.

Bethany found herself adrift at a grand party given by Madame Dagobert de Mudon. Her young escort was busily engaged in conversation with several friends. She restlessly moved from one small group to another, bored with gossip and shallow conversation.

He had a weathered, suntanned face with a scar on one cheek and wore the uniform of a French soldier. There was an air of quiet confidence about him instead of the arrogance she had detected among younger French officers. He had, she decided, eyes that gave a hint of boredom, or was it sadness? He stood against the wall alone. Several times Bethany glanced his way. The last time he returned her gaze with a smile. Embarrassed, she walked to the refreshment table, her champagne glass empty.

"Mademoiselle Quinn, may I fill your glass?" The soldier was at her side.

"You have me at a disadvantage, sir. You seem to know my name, but I do not know yours, Captain. You are a Captain are you not?"

"You are very observant, Mademoiselle. May I apologize at my rudeness and introduce myself. I am Henri Bourget, a poor soldier at your service."

Bethany found him refreshingly lacking in pretense in a room full of Paris peacocks and dandies.

"Well, Captain Bourget, how is it that you know my name?"

"I would say that every man in this room has asked the name of the lovely young lady with the interesting accent and emerald eyes, even this old soldier."

"I don't see an old soldier. Is there one here?"

"Perhaps not if a young lady is willing to grant him the pleasure of her conversation."

"And when did you ask someone my name? Was it when you caught me stealing a glance at you just now?"

"I asked your name three weeks ago."

"Three weeks!"

"Yes, the first time I saw you. It was at the Opera. You were wearing a white dress."

She looked up into his eyes. They were smiling. For an instant, Bethany had the uncomfortable feeling they were looking inside her and could see what she was feeling.

"Well, Captain, I must return to my escort, it is almost time to leave."

"Yes, of course. Is your chaperone with you tonight?"

"I see you know about that also. Does it seem silly to you in this modern age?"

"I think it is charming. If I were your uncle, I'm sure I would insist on such an arrangement for my young niece alone in Paris."

"My, you seem to know a lot about me, Captain. Is it just curiosity about a Southern American girl?"

"It is the foolishness of an older man about a beautiful younger woman. I hope I have not offended you."

"The younger woman finds offense only at the reference to an *older* man. I see only boys and men here, and I sometimes tire of the company of boys. For instance, take the tall one there," she indicated three young men standing in front of the marble fireplace. "He claims to be a count or something. He is with my boorish young escort, a banker's son who can talk only of money. The serious one with his back to us studies music. I believe his name is Debussy or something. As you can see, they seem uninterested in the company of this young lady."

"I have seen you one other time," he said, "You were riding in the Bois de Boulogne."

"I believe you have been spying on me," she laughed.

"In France, taking notice of a beautiful lady is not spying. It is the national pastime," he smiled. "But I would prefer the role of escort to that of spy. Would you consider riding with me next Sunday? I can provide your chaperone with proper references if you like."

"Why, Captain Bourget, I would love to go riding next Sunday."

"Do you know a stable called Le Cheval du Roi?"

"Yes, I know that stable."

"Would two o'clock be convenient?"

"Two o'clock, will be fine." Bethany hoped the excitement she felt was not obvious.

They rode that Sunday, and the next. They often dismounted and walked along the trail talking. Sometimes they picnicked in the shade of trees. The wit and laughter of their conversations veiled the desire that played between them like a butterfly in the wind.

"He is a soldier, and he's ten years older," argued Mannela. "He is no boy, this one, and that makes him dangerous for you. He could take your heart, child, but he knows he may not keep it. Your worlds are not the same. I don't want you hurt. I don't want you to betray your family, your duty. I don't want to see your uncle's heart and dreams broken when he finds you have run off with a French soldier."

"All you say is true. I know that. He is leaving for some French territory, Cochin China or something, half way round the world. It is his career, his duty, his life. I cannot change that. He understands as well as I do. He says all the things you do. I know there can be only the moment, but I will have it, Mannela."

"Why him? Why now?"

"Because for me it is time. Because I trust him. Because he is gentle. I can give you no rational answer, nothing that makes sense. I won't even try."

"Have you thought perhaps he reminds you of your uncle, that perhaps it is your uncle you wish to love? You never had a real father. It would not be unusual for someone like you to look for a father in older men."

"Don't complicate this more than it already is. I ask for your protection, not your blessing. I will find a way to see him alone even if he resists, which he will. If I walk away from this I will always wish and wonder and regret. Desire, lust, a silly girl's infatuation, love, what ever it is I will not let this special time, this special man simply pass without feeling, without touching, without experiencing his embrace even if I can have him for only a short time."

"You risk too much. An open indiscretion, an over-familiar gesture between you in public and you harm your uncle and Madame Quinn. You are asking me to risk the same. You are not talking here of petting with an innocent boy in a garden. And what of him? He will feel pain too. He will know the lonely end, knows it now, before it has begun."

Mannela paused, looked into Bethany's upturned face for a long moment. She knew the force of passion . . . and she knew Bethany. The strong willed Quinn would find a way no matter what she did to stop it. "If I can't stop you, if you must do this, we must plan a way."

Henri tried many arguments, but none was strong enough. "What you ask, dear Bethany, no man could refuse. In the end it will be painful for both of us. You must know this. It is a love neither of us can keep except in our hearts. This thing you insist upon, this invitation, this brief affair will haunt me all my life. I, of all people, should know."

Bethany listened quietly. Her answer to all his arguments was the same. A pleading look, a silent kiss.

Their discreet rendezvous was carefully chosen. Henri had moved from the bachelor officers' quarters to take up residence in a small apartment. Bethany knocked timidly and was trembling when Henri opened the door. It was a pleasant apartment, not fancy. A vase filled with roses stood on a small table before a window. There were three open doors off the parlor, one leading to a small kitchen, one to the latest in living quarters innovations, a newly installed water closet, the third to a bedroom. Books lined several shelves at one end of the main room and there was a small fireplace at the other.

"I feel a little strange, not embarrassed, just awkward," Bethany said. "Would you hold me just a moment?"

The soldier stepped forward and held her to him, gently, her head on his shoulder. "I am the one who feels awkward, worse, guilty. I know you should not be here."

Bethany spoke without lifting her head from his shoulder. "Don't speak of guilt. There will be enough of that later. I was afraid you would not be here. This little apartment, it is all we will ever have, our only time is now. I'm not ashamed, just a little afraid I will disappoint you. I want you. You knew that from the first time we kissed in the park. I have wanted you since I first saw you smile at a silly girl looking at you from across the room. I don't want to be a silly girl ever again. I want to be a woman. Teach me."

"I'm not sure I can do this," he said. "I have never wanted anything as much, nor been as afraid."

She looked up at him. "Afraid?"

"Afraid of hurting you, afraid of the haunting memories of you that will follow me the rest of my life. We should not do this thing." She put her hands behind his neck, stood on her tiptoes, and kissed him full on the mouth. He stiffened, hesitated, and then surrendered to a passion he no longer controlled.

Henri lifted her in his arms and carried her to the bedroom. The afternoon sun filtering through the window's shutters patterned the wall behind the empire bed with muted light. He slowly set Bethany down upon her feet.

She looked at him and at the bed and stepped back. She was afraid, afraid because she did not know how to do what she had come to do. She was afraid of disappointing the man who stood before her. *How many women?* she wondered, but forced the thought from her mind. Standing, she began to undress, deliberately but not teasingly, her eyes focused on the floor.

Henri dared not move as he watched her unfasten the buttons and lift the dress over her head. She dropped her petticoats to the floor, and balancing like a dancer on one leg at a time, removed her shoes and silk stockings. Something shiny dropped on the pile of petticoats. She removed the pins from her hair. It fell in raven cascades about her shoulders. Her well-formed breasts were clearly visible through a gossamer silk chemise that covered her torso and hips.

My God! Henri thought, *No man could walk away now. I have never seen anything so beautiful.*

She did not move and he realized she was waiting for him. He undressed where he stood, not as gracefully as she, he knew, but with dignity. Without embarrassment he removed the last of his garments.

She stood looking at him in the soft light. His body was beautiful, lean, trim, perfect except for two jagged scars, one at his upper shoulder, the other on the right side. She was sure her knees were shaking as she took three steps toward him. He embraced her beautiful young form. They kissed lightly, timidly, as if tasting some strange, exotic, forbidden fruit for the first time.

They moved to the edge of the bed and slipped between the clean linen sheets without a word. He kissed her forehead and stroked her body as she looked up at him with sparkling green eyes.

She could not control the pleasure and excitement she felt at his touch, his kiss, the warmth of him against her. Raised on one elbow, he looked down into her eyes, bent down and kissed her deeply. There came the sweet warm sounds only a woman can make. She pulled at him, "Please, Henri, please!"

Afterward, she rested her head on his shoulder listening to his breathing and heartbeat. He gentled her close and kissed her cheek. Gradually her breathing slowed and she fell asleep.

Adam's real tragedy was that he knew the consequences of eating the apple and still could not help himself. Henri, propped up on one elbow, looked down at the lovely girl next to him, her hair spilled over the pillow, her dark eyelashes accenting the lovely complexion radiating from a face serene in sleep. *She represents the essence of what men live and die for, whatever other excuses may be written.*

He was being gentlemanly by gathering her clothes from the floor and putting them on the bed when he noticed the small silver pistol.

"You are even a more dangerous woman than I imagined." He presented her with the weapon, true surprise showing on his face.

"Yes, I am," she smiled, "and don't you forget it."

Bethany pulled on her stockings and garters, picked up the deadly little jewel, folded its trigger, and slipped the pistol into its place with no explanation at all. She could not help but laugh out loud at the incredulous expression on his face.

On a bright day in April of 1883 the couple met at Le Cheval du Roi stable. He lifted her up to the side saddle on one of the horses they had reserved and mounted the other. They walked them side by side down the bridle path. Time now weighed heavily upon their thoughts. For a long while they rode in silence. The last of Bethany's schooling, her reason for being in Paris, would be finished at the end of May. Captain Bourget's staff assignment in Paris was over. His scheduled departure to the Orient was approaching.

"Tell me about this Cochin China that takes you away," Bethany broke silence.

"It is an exotic country which became a French protectorate by invitation."

"Invitation?"

"But of course. When troops sent on an expedition by Napoleon marched into it back in 1859, France invited herself to protect the poor defenseless country."

"Charming diplomacy. And they need you more than I do?"

"There is trouble there. I am a soldier," he answered.

The couple dismounted, tethered the horses in the shade, spread a tablecloth and opened a picnic hamper. It was a Sunday like the one on which they had first ridden together, only it was warmer now. Bethany laid out lunch on the cloth while Henri opened a bottle of wine and filled two crystal glasses from the basket.

"Tell me about the scars." she said, and passed a piece of bread to him. He was lying on his back, his jacket rolled into a pillow beneath his head.

"I thought you agreed not to ask again."

"I told a fib."

He was silent for awhile. "I try not to think about those days," he said. Bethany remained silent. "I have never told anyone about them, but I suppose you of all people have a right to know. You may not like what you hear." Bethany said nothing. After a moment, without looking at her, he began almost as if telling himself the story.

"The one on my shoulder came from a Prussian at Sedan. I was fresh from the Academy and convinced that France had the finest army in the world. We did have a better rifle. Our Chassepot had twice the range of their Dreyse, but our generals had forgotten what Napoleon taught the world about artillery. Worse, they had improved little on his weapon. The German artillery was far superior. Steel, breach-loading Krupp six pounders that could fire ten times faster than our guns. They cut our ranks to pieces." He absently moved a hand to touch the scar on his cheek. "I was lucky. I lost a small piece of flesh while many around me were blown apart. Carnage and confusion ruled. The Grand Army of France was routed like a ragged mob. Being a young fool, I tried to rally men streaming past me. They paid no attention even when I threatened to shoot them. I finally joined them in retreat only I made the mistake of stopping to look back. There on a little rise was the enemy, maybe a half dozen Germans. I fired my pistol twice, I think it was, before one of their riflemen found his mark on my shoulder. How silly I was then."

"How brave," Bethany replied.

"Not brave! Naïve, ignorant," he replied.

"Don't be so gloomy. You went home alive."

"Home?" He seemed to ponder that a moment. "I tried." He took a long sip of wine. "At the German hospital I was told that the Germans had captured Paris but stayed only a short time. We didn't believe it, but it was true. Bismarck didn't want Paris. He just wanted France to leave Germany alone and took Alsace-Lorraine as a buffer. Did you know that Napoleon III was also captured at Sedan? The Germans released him with all the other prisoners.

"Napoleon III fled to England and France formed the Third Republic. By the time I reached Paris a group that called themselves the Commune of Paris had started civil war." His expression grew dark and angry.

"Henri, you don't have to finish. You were right. I shouldn't have asked."

He looked through her as if she wasn't there. "When I couldn't cross the barricades of the Commune to reach my family, I heard the Republic was raising an army at Versailles to defend my country against Frenchmen, if I can use that term for those Communard bastards gone mad with class hatred instilled by the writings of Karl Marx. The scar on my side came from them. In the last days when they knew they were beaten, the Commune committed an orgy of savage slaughter. They killed defenseless civilians: teachers, doctors, shopkeepers, priests, nuns, anyone considered bourgeois, part of the establishment; men, women, children, those who refused to join their fight. They invented new barbarous ways of killing for their own entertainment . . ." He had to pause before the words would come. "They killed my mother, my father, my sister, and my young bride. We had been married just before the war with Germany. A neighbor who survived told of the unspeakable things they did to my sister and my . . ." he could not finish the sentence. "They burned their bodies, all of my family, in our house. That is what I found when I came home *alive*, as you put it."

"I'm so sorry, Henri," Bethany tried to put her hand on his shoulder.

"Let me finish!" he said in agony, "You should know all of it." *What more, for God's sake, could there be?*

"I went mad they say," he continued. "When we cornered communards in a house or building, I entered ahead of my soldiers. They thought the brave lieutenant was leading them. I was ignoring them. I wanted to do the killing myself, kill all of them, or perhaps, have them kill me. When they tried to hide, I found them. When they tried to surrender, I killed them. I remember the killing. I don't remember my commander having my own troops take me into custody. When I was rational again, I found myself in a place untouched by war, a sanatorium in Normandy. On clear days I could see the ocean far across green fields . . ." He paused, as if seeing the view once again. "I must have stayed there six months, maybe more, unaware of time. And then I became bored, restless . . . cured, I suppose. Anyway they let me return to what I know best. The army was . . . is all I have left, my only family, my only home. They offered me garrison duty here, but I could not bear to stay in Paris. I volunteered for the Legion. I've been in Algeria for the last eight years. There's been fighting and killing enough there, but I prefer the desert sands to the blood stained streets of Paris. I'm here now only to attend staff school and receive a briefing on my new assignment. Like me, Paris seems well on the outside, but when I walk her streets I am reminded of scars that do not show and will not heal."

He looked at her, his eyes no longer wild. "So now you know why I request-ed foreign service, this time trading desert sands for the jungles of Cochin China where, I am told, France has built a beautiful city at a place called Saigon. If you had not captured me with those green eyes, I would have already left for my new assignment. Instead I requested leave to be with you. It is, perhaps, the cruelest act I have ever committed. Now, I will carry the guilt of leaving you, memories to haunt me tempered only by the knowledge that you will be far better off free of me. You see, I am afraid of having a real family again. I could not survive losing another. It was insane of me to allow this to happen, to hurt you."

"Henri, we agreed. No regrets, remember?" Bethany wanted to change the mood. "Besides, my poor soldier, you could not help yourself. Madame Wombi and I cast a Voodoo spell on you. It was out of your control. Of course, you will miss me terribly." Bethany smiled.

The cloud passed from his face. "Oh, now you chide me," he laughed. "Well, they say the oriental girls in Saigon are very pretty—slim, with long dark hair. And they are taught French in school."

The shield of her smile fell. "I am slim with long dark hair and have been taught French in school."

"Now, it is you who break the agreement. Perhaps the gods have given us a moment's reprieve from separate courses we cannot alter. You could not bear the life of an army wife. You would hate it."

"But I want to try. I don't care about the differences of . . ."

"Bethany! We agreed not to spoil a single day. It could only end badly. You have a duty to your family. The army is my family. I accepted the duty of a Legionnaire. It is no place for you."

Bethany started to speak but he put a finger to her lips. She bit it, hard, and turned away for just a moment to dry her eyes.

"Pour me another glass of wine," she said, "and then take me to your apartment, our apartment, and make love to me as if the world will end today." She finished the wine, got up, and started across the field.

"But where are you going?"

"To get the horses. I told you, I want to make love to you better than any woman ever has or ever will."

"You are a scandalous lady," he laughed, "Come back here! I cannot be left to clean up the paraphernalia of a picnic while a woman captures the horses. It's unbe-coming an officer and gentleman. What if my troops find out?"

"They will say you are the luckiest man in Paris," she tossed over her shoulder as she headed toward a cluster of trees where the horses were grazing.

She rode back leading his horse. Looking down at him holding the picnic ham-per in his hand, she bantered, "For calling me a scandalous woman I should make you walk all the way back to the stable." He looked up at her, not sure she didn't mean it. "But a poor old soldier like you would be too worn out to make passionate love." She dropped the reins of his horse at his feet and galloped away.

"Dear God, what a glorious creation." He tossed the basket, mounted his horse and chased after her.

There was a deadline to their weekend lives together and because of it their passions were allowed unbridled reign within the confines of their private rendezvous. Sometimes they cooked dinner in the tiny kitchen. Sometimes Henri brought in dinner prepared at a small restaurant nearby. Once, when a planned picnic was rained out, they spread the picnic on the bed, opened the wine, got naked as the day they were born, and fed lunch to each other. They skipped dessert.

He continued to ask why she would not tell him about her family. She finally tired of making excuses and told him everything except the origin of her birth, told him the fact that J & Q Shipping sometimes dealt in arms.

He expressed both sorrow and amazement and much later humor. "My God," he said, "I thought I held an innocent angel only to discover she is a gunrunner, which I should have suspected when I found her beautiful thigh laced with a pistol. I shouldn't be surprised to discover that you are a spy and assassin."

"You have found me out, Captain. I am spying on a French officer and plotting to kill him with love."

"My dear, the French officer finds he is helpless and at your mercy. Why don't you begin?"

She truly did make love to him better than any woman ever had or ever would. In the beginning he had been the teacher. Somewhere along the way, she became the teacher. She learned to satisfy all his desires and those of her own. Bethany was nineteen.

Lying naked next to her, Henri said, "You have given me joy when I had forgotten even the word, much less the meaning. You have taught me to live again, to notice blue skies, the laughter of children, the fragrance of flowers, to believe there still is goodness in the world."

She kissed him. Too tired to make love again, they fell asleep in each other's arms.

They could not face a goodbye. Henri agreed not to tell her the date of his departure. There would simply come a weekend when he would not be at the rendezvous.

It had seemed a sensible plan at the time, very mature, very brave. He thought he had kept his departure a secret their last afternoon together and she let him think just that, though she knew, the way a woman always knows when a man is trying very hard to shield her from the truth. She smiled and he kissed her and said, "Perhaps tomorrow," the way he always did, but she knew.

That Sunday morning she thought, "But could I have been wrong? Do we have another day?" She dressed and hurried to the rendezvous only to drown in the silence of the empty apartment. In the bedroom she found a dozen roses and a note lying on the bed.

Forget your old soldier, and forgive him if you can, dear Bethany. A whole world awaits your youth and beauty and spirit, a world I could never give you. I will love you until the day I die.

Henri

His Legionnaire's insignia was pinned to the note. She lay on the bed, their bed, for a very long time. Finally she folded the note, pinned the insignia on her dress, gathered the flowers, closed the apartment door behind her and walked to a nearby café where Mannela waited as always.

On the way home they passed two young lovers on a park bench. With a teary smile she handed the roses to the surprised girl and walked away.

Back in her apartment she slipped Henri's note into the pages of her diary and pinned his Legionnaire's insignia on the back of the front cover.

Her schooling had ended.

CHAPTER 17

The wind was calm, the sea slick as oil when the island of Cuba began to emerge on the hazy horizon. Mannela and Bethany stood watching their new home slide shimmering toward them like some giant green salad spilled across a translucent aqua plain. Dolphins played under the bow of the vessel as it sliced through the calm water, its wake the only disturbance on the flat morning sea. It was still cool, but the rising tropic sun would change that, had changed that by the time the island was close enough to clearly distinguish its features. Lush greenery reflected the sun's brilliance as if polished. By contrast, shadows were so starkly defined as to appear to be shattered pieces of night left behind in the sudden explosion of a tropical dawn.

Cuba's beauty was tempered only by the foreboding walls of Morro Castle guarding the entrance to Havana Harbor. Rising darkly from rock cliffs, crowned by the flag of Spain, it served to remind all visitors that Cuba was still ruled by the 300-year-old hand of the Spanish Conquistador. The vessel slipped unmolested past the fortress into Havana Harbor only to be accosted by a fleet of bumboats hawking fruits and souvenirs to waving passengers.

Jonathan, waiting on the dock, was markedly impressed, not just by the beauty of the nineteen year old standing at the ship's rail, but by something more, a subtle change. He could see it in her face, the way she carried herself down the gangway , something that had not been there before; the aura of a woman. He instinctively knew Bethany was no longer his or anyone else's little girl.

He voiced his observation to Louisette.

"Well, Captain Quinn, that is the very reason you sent her to school on the continent, to become an adult, a woman," Louisette replied.

"So it's all my fault."

"I suppose along with the blame, you may also take pride and some credit for your niece being the most stunning young woman to come to Havana since the arrival of Mrs. Jonathan Quinn," Louisette answered with a smile.

"I hope her Spanish is better than that of the preceding Quinn beauty."

"Vayase, hombre! Por usted, no comida en mi casa este noche." she replied.

"I take it all back. I don't want to go away and not have dinner at your house. Why can you speak perfect Spanish only when you scold me?"

"Because, like all women, I think more clearly when I am angry," she replied with a mocking pout. "Besides, it is fun. You are such a coward when it comes to women."

"I am when it comes to you and Bethany, and don't let me forget Mannela. The three of you could make a coward of a bull elephant."

Bethany walked gracefully down the gangway and joined them while Mannela gave their papers to a Spanish official and saw that their trunks were loaded onto a cart for transport into town.

"Hello! I'm here at last." Bethany said in perfect Spanish. She hugged Louisette and then Jonathan. She turned around for inspection, and still speaking in Spanish said, "What do you think?"

"I don't think Cuba is ready for such a beautiful lady," Jonathan replied. He picked her up in his arms for a hug and a kiss on the cheek. "I am so glad to have you back."

"Put her down, Jonathan! That is no way to treat a lady," said Louisette laughing. "You are causing a dreadful scene. Bethany, what do you want to do first, Dear?"

"I would love to take a long bath and then eat half a cow. I'm starving."

They turned up narrow Obispo Street in the old quarter. Some of the buildings were over 200 years old. There were shops and homes in a mixture of architectural styles ranging from the old Moorish influence of low tiled roofs and wooden balconies transplanted from southern Spain, to the neoclassical design of the Quinn's house boasting a stained glass window above a beveled glass door with a second floor balcony surrounded by lacy, wrought-iron railings.

A familiar figure met the carriage at curb-side. "Oh! Missy Quinn! Billy Wong velly happy see you. All house miss you velly much. Anything want you, just call Billy Wong, Madame Quinn's number one man." He bowed and then smiled proudly.

"Billy, I thought you were Captain J's number one man?"

"Captain J, he number two in house now. Billy Wong always man to number one in house."

He giggled and ran toward the baggage wagon as Jonathan made a mock swing at him. "You heathen, I'm going to skin you alive one of these days."

"Come in Bethany," Louisette said, "I want to show you all we've done here."

The house was 'U' shaped with a stone paved courtyard enclosed by a high wall across the back and landscaped with lush greenery bordered by flowers. In the center there was a round pool filled with gold fish, water lilies and hyacinths in bloom. As was the custom in Havana, the large windows facing the street were protected by graceful iron grillwork curved outward to allow the windows to be swung open for ventilation. The central hallway leading from the street to the patio was lined in indigo tile. The floors were all mahogany except for the hallways and kitchen which were paved with unglazed Spanish tile waxed to a fine sheen. The rooms were painted in pastel colors and the furniture was of provincial French style accented by oriental rugs and Italian crystal chandeliers. The house and patio were equipped with gas lighting. Walls were hung with lovely impressionist paintings that Louisette and Jonathan had collected in Paris. Lace curtains veiled open windows admitting cooling breezes while louver shutters protected the interior from direct sunlight and tropical rain. Bethany was delighted with the apartment that had been prepared for her. It took up the entire second floor wing on the west side of the house opposite that of Jonathan and Louisette. Mannela was given an apartment on the ground floor at the end of the wing opposite the kitchen. Billy Wong had a small room off the kitchen. He also had a cottage on the outskirts of town for his concubine, children, pigs, chickens and goats which he would visit whenever the mood suited him. After Mannela's arrival, he began living full time at his cottage in an obvious effort to avoid her as much as possible. He did not want to risk being turned into a frog.

The next morning Jonathan looked up from the breakfast table surprised to see Bethany up so early. He turned toward the kitchen, "Billy, bring another breakfast for Miss Bethany," then smiled at his niece. "No Spanish lady would arise at this hour, hardly a gentleman for that matter. What brings you to breakfast so early?"

"I'm a partner in the Quinn business and I intend to earn my keep."

"You are ever a surprise. I was afraid the social whirl of Paris would have spoiled you. Most ladies your age are more inclined to find a rich husband than to learn the business of business."

"You aren't trying to tell me I would be an embarrassment, or that you do not want me to take an active part, are you, Uncle?"

"I'm saying I've treated you somewhat as the son I'll never have, and I'm feeling a little guilty about it. I don't want you obsessed with that old family dream of a new Shamrock. I've come to realize all of that was just a dream of a dream that ended before you were born. We're just absentee owners of a tenant farm in Mississippi with sad memories. You're too young and beautiful to waste your life in the business world. Hell, you already stupefy men with your beauty and scare 'em with your independent spirit. Now you want to intimidate 'em with business skills."

"Suppose you allow me to determine where to waste my life. I don't intend to be merely someone's pretty trinket. I had no *fashionable ladies* in my childhood to teach me how. What I had was a wonderful, loving godfather who took me in, gave me a love for life and learning, and allowed me the freedom as a child to pursue both. I had two black nannies who tried their best to make me into a lady even though they were never allowed to be *ladies* themselves. I've never been sheltered, not like other little girls who had mamas and daddies watching over them and dictating their every move. Can you picture me sitting around looking sweet, doing embroidery? I'm a grown woman, Uncle. I will not be forced by convention to dutifully subordinate my own zest for life to the first socially acceptable man to propose matrimony, especially if his intent is for me to stay at home, serve tea, and punctually have a child every twelve months 'till I am as worn out as so many poor women I have seen."

"Great God!" was all Jonathan could manage.

"Do I shock you, of all men?

"Damn right you do! Scare the hell out of me. Where did you get all that?"

"From being a Quinn, of course. Uncle Ted said I got my hardheadedness from my great grandfather, courage from my grandmother, and spunk from my mother. My formal education I owe to you, Captain, and my worldly education to Paris. Now let's go to the office."

Jonathan's mouth opened but he couldn't think of a reply. They walked down the street to the dockside office adjoining one of two large warehouses leased by J & Q Shipping.

"Uncle?" Bethany said as they walked, "Why did you say that you would never have a son?"

"Did I say that?"

"You mentioned it. Why do you think that?"

"Because Louisette cannot have children. She didn't want to marry me because of it. She told me that day we were on the roof of Notre-Dame. She is everything to me, worth all the dreams I ever had before I met her."

The early morning mist hanging over the harbor was rapidly disappearing in the warmth of a new tropic day.

A look at the books showed that business practice in Cuba was similar to what it had been in Nassau. The sugar boats had to be scheduled, the back-haul cargos booked, accumulated, and accounted for, the warehouses managed, the J & Q marine supply store managed, the Nassau office accounts of island trading reviewed, inventories taken, accounts collected, payments made. Bethany had forgotten none of the details of daily operations. Her business sense both pleased and confounded Jonathan.

A little before lunch he said, "Come on with me, Bee Bee," and led the way to a boat dock where a small steam launch was moored, her bright work and polished brass fittings shining smartly. A Cuban skipper waited aboard.

"I thought you might like a tour of one of the world's finest harbors," Jonathan said. "Come aboard."

Bethany stepped back to look over the fine little craft. A green shamrock outlined in gold leaf decorated the gracefully rounded stern.

"This is my toy," he said rather sheepishly.

"I want to blow the whistle," was her reply.

He helped Bethany aboard. A picnic hamper waited on a small table set in the curve of the stern. They settled into comfortable wicker chairs underneath a green and white striped canopy. The little launch moved quietly away from the dock to the rhythmic puff and hiss of its small steam engine to weave its way through harbor traffic. The cargos of ships at anchor were being transferred to shore by lighter while small coastal traders and fishing boats were moving to or from Havana's docks.

"Tell me about the island and the people."

"Where to begin?"

"With Columbus," she replied.

"We might be out here a week."

"As long as we don't run out of wine or steam."

"Well, Columbus thought he had found the back side of India. That's why we call Sitting Bull an Indian."

"Uncle, everyone knows that sort of thing. Get on with Cuba," Bethany chided him.

"The Muslims are right," Jonathan sighed in mock disgust, "women shouldn't be educated. Anyway, Queen Isabella, who had the imagination to launch Columbus toward a new world, was interested in a return on her investment."

"Sounds like some other ship owner I know."

"Yes. Well, ship owners are like that, and may I remind you, partner, that we won't be in business long if our ships don't bring a return."

"Back to Cuban history, Uncle."

"The gold hunters, conquistadores, followed Columbus and were quite successful in stealing gold from the Indians, ship loads of it from Mexico and South America, all in the name of the Spanish Crown and God. Queen Isabella and King Ferdinand V were quite religious, considered themselves the protectors of the Church and had wonderful ways of carrying out their self-appointed duty. They unleashed the inquisition in all of its unspeakable cruelty, all with the blessing of the Church. Ostensibly the inquisition was created as a way to rid Spain of Jews and Moors, or convert them to the Catholic religion, but it was also very useful as a means of political repression against anyone considered an enemy of the Crown. It gave a fearsome incentive for generous contributions to both the church's and the Crown's treasuries."

"That's all very interesting, Uncle, but what has it got to do with Cuba?"

"I'm coming to that. The inquisition spilled over into Spain's colonial polices. After all, if a member of the Spanish aristocracy or a rich merchant, with the approval of the Crown and Church, could have his flesh torn from his body by priests wielding red hot tongs in the name of God, then surely it mattered not what Conquistadors did to heathen savages in the new world. The first order of the church was to convert the poor devils to Christianity. They had lovely ways of doing that. They tortured those who resisted, killed those who refused, and rewarded those Indians who converted by working them to extinction. Legend says there was a chief named Hatuey who didn't much like what Velásquez and Cortés were doing to his people and his island and let them know it. The Spaniards sentenced him to be burned at the stake. At the last moment, a priest offered him spiritual comfort if he would become a convert. Hatuey refused, saying he could not accept a God that promoted such cruelty."

"My goodness," said Bethany. "What are they going to do to us when they find out we're Episcopalians?"

"They'll probably hang me, especially if they find I've got a warehouse full of rifles in the Bahamas. As for you, when they find out you have Mannela the witch in your employ, they'll burn you at the stake for sure."

"Back to your lecture, Uncle, and quit calling Mannela a witch."

"It will cost another glass of wine," he said. Bethany filled both their glasses.

"Where was I?"

"You were burning Indians at the stake."

"Right. The treasures from all over the New World were consolidated here at fortress Havana and shipped on to Spain to fill the royal coffers and, of course, those of the Church. I'm told you can see the very first Indian gold brought from the New World decorating the ceiling of a great cathedral in Spain.

"With such merciful Christian ways, the Spanish soon ran out of Indians. The answer to their labor shortage here on Cuba and other islands was to bring in African slaves, the first in the New World. Either the Africans were fed more than the Indians because the Spanish had an investment in them; island Indians had cost them nothing you see, or the Africans were hardier. They survived. It may interest you to know that slavery is legal here, though the practice is supposed to end completely three years from now in '86."

"My God! I hope we're not slave owners."

"You know me better than that! God knows we learned what dependency on slavery eventually did to the South."

"All right, Uncle. Let's stick to Cuba. Why did we move here?"

Jonathan motioned toward the picnic hamper. Bethany began to set the little table.

"During the Ten Years War, America's official policy was to support and supply the Spanish in return for Spain opening Cuba to American trade and capital investment. We're here because I was able to get a contract from the American Sugar Refining Company to transport sugar to America. The bastards have a monopoly. Planters, including the Quinns, don't have any choice but to sell their sugar to them at their price. Still, we're making money here, a good deal of it."

"The island and most of the people here look prosperous. I haven't seen any signs of doom."

"In spite of appearances," Jonathan continued, "the agony of this beautiful island will continue."

"Can you explain that to me? After all, we're making money, the island is beautiful, the people seem friendly."

"I think I am boring you," he said.

She poured another glass of wine. "Wet your whistle with this and tell me more."

He took a sip and continued. "Spain lost most of her North American territory to European wars and her South American colonies to rebellion. As a result, Cuba has taken on new meaning. It represents Spain's fierce pride, not to mention a very handsome yearly income. Still, Spain governs Cuba in the same old way that cost her so many other colonies. All the government offices, from governor to clerk, go to friends of the Crown born in Spain. The lowliest Spanish bureaucrat is ranked socially higher than the most successful Creole. As a result, many Spaniards send their pregnant wives home to have their babies born in Spain. Spaniards born here are considered island Creoles and looked down upon as second class citizens. Out of resentment, they think of themselves as Cubans not Spaniards. You know the rest. For more than half a century Cuban nationalists have failed in one rebellion after another. As we speak, the embers of rebellion still seethe beneath the truce from the Ten Years War. When the Cubans have recovered sufficiently, they will try again." Jonathan paused to take a sip of wine. "Not soon, but one day. In any case, I'll have advance notice from old friends in time to get you and Louisette out before that happens. Until then, we have a very profitable and legitimate shipping business."

"And when fighting resumes, bigger profits from 'special cargo,'" Bethany commented.

"Is that a cynical or optimistic statement, Bee Bee?"

"It's simple truth. Truth can neither be cynical nor optimistic. It can only be the truth. That's what Mannela taught me."

"It's sometimes a little eerie what that woman comes up with," Jonathan said. "She's a handsome woman. I've never seen a person carry themselves with more dignity. She's educated, speaks French, English in a beautiful island accent and now Spanish. She has a sort of sixth sense I don't pretend to understand. Do you know Billy Wong is scared to death of her?"

"Yes, I know that."

"And I suppose you know something about it you're not going to tell me."

"Oh, I will tell you that he thinks she can turn him into a frog," Bethany answered.

"And can she?" Jonathan asked with a smile.

"I really don't think Billy Wong wants to find out."

"I don't think I do either," replied Jonathan. "Now pass the chicken and tell me how Paris was when you left."

"I was ready to leave. It was, like me, a little older, and maybe a little sad."

"Ah, and what was his name?"

The quick question caught Bethany off guard. "Does it show? I thought I had done well to hide it."

"If some boy wronged you, tell me and I will teach him some manners."

"And if he wasn't a boy, and he didn't wrong me?"

"Then we should change the subject for at least three reasons," Jonathan said.

"Such as?"

"First, I don't think I want to hear any more. Second, I doubt if you will tell me anyway, and," Jonathan hesitated.

"And?"

"And, you're not my little girl anymore, are you? You're all grown up, a woman in every sense of the word. I could see it when you came off the ship yesterday."

"Yes, Uncle, I'm all grown up."

Jonathan refilled their glasses. "I love you, Bee Bee. It's going to be very hard for me to let go of my ragamuffin. I kept pushing you, telling you that together we had to somehow build everything back. Now I worry that I've been selfish. What have I done to you, Bee Bee?"

"Nothing, Uncle. I am a Quinn, just like you,"

"Perhaps that's what worries me the most," he smiled.

They grew quiet and viewed the inland bay, Bahía de la Habana, that was Havana harbor.

Bethany broke the silence. "It's a sad history for such a beautiful place."

"Some would say the same of Shamrock," Jonathan replied. The wine was running low when the launch returned them to the dock. They walked down narrow streets past shops and homes, some in pastel colors to offset the monotony of white-washed walls.

"Havana is a lovely city, but where is everyone?" Bethany asked. "I don't see a human stirring. I don't even see a dog stirring. All the shops are closed."

"An old Spanish custom," Jonathan explained. "After a leisurely midday meal, everyone takes a nap in the shade during the hottest part of the day. Then things stir again late afternoon when it's cooler."

"What a lovely custom. See, the Spanish aren't all bad. I'll race you to the hammock. Buenos tardes, mi tio," Bethany disappeared up the stairs, a little tipsy from the wine. She joined the citizens of Havana as they retired in the heat of the day to quiet, thick walled, high ceilinged rooms where soft light filtered through louver shutters and connubial and domestic delights could be shared in peace.

Bethany, eager to see more of Havana, rousted Mannela out to stroll through the streets after shops reopened for the second half of the business day. Except for morning shopping hours when women crowded the street stalls, shops and dim, cavernous stores, Havana seemed largely a male city. Bethany noticed female faces peering down from ancient balconies or from behind ornate, wrought iron grills that protected opened windows facing the street. She saw young eyes wearing virginity's expectancy and matronly faces seemingly resigned to daily monotony. There were exceptions. Bethany noticed that some of the young women exhibited delicate skill in the ancient art of flirtation. With their eyes alone they seemed able to convey a hint of the delightful exotic whenever young men walked past.

"Have you noticed, Mannela, how some of those ladies flash their eyes at passing men. I bet it has taken generations to accumulate such skill. However protected, isolated, treated like property, females find a way, don't they?"

"Those who are women do," Mannela answered.

They followed the sound of Spanish music to a café that opened onto a small plaza. Most tables were occupied by men. There were a few couples and one or two families scattered among them.

"Let's sit for a while and have something cool to drink."

"Only American women or whores would sit alone unescorted by a man in public places in Cuba," Mannela replied.

"Well, then, which shall we be this afternoon?"

"I think you should keep walking. You don't want to embarrass your Uncle on your first day out in Havana."

Bethany laughed, "Oh, all right, I'll wait 'til tomorrow."

It was Thursday, and on Thursday nights it was customary for the Cuban to bring out his entire family; portly wife, beautiful slim daughters and bright eyed children of all ages, to walk the streets, listen to café orchestras, sip sweet orange drinks, and chat with friends. It was through such a crowd that the two women finally threaded their way back to the Quinn house for dinner.

"Uncle, do you think Cuba is ready for a ragamuffin with unladylike business sense; a scandalous sportswoman who plays tennis, sails boats, and rides horseback wearing pants like a man?"

"You see, Louisette, I told you my niece is more trouble than she's worth."

Louisette ignored him, "I want to hear about Paris."

It was late when Bethany finally called time. "Sleep is calling this child."

"Night, Bee Bee." Jonathan helped with her chair.

As Bethany climbed the stairs, servants turned down the gas lights and began to clear the table. Jonathan moved behind Louisette and eased her chair back. As she rose from the table, he pulled her close to him in a playful embrace.

"Jonathan, not in front of the servants!"

"Louisette, my sweet, if you don't hurry up those stairs, I just may lose complete control and really give them something to talk about."

"You are a wicked man, J. Hillary."

"Yes, ma Petite, and it's all your fault."

The following week Jonathan arranged an appointment with the Spanish governor so Bethany could present her letter of introduction from the Spanish Ambassador in Paris, the father of her school friend, Maria.

"Well, that was all proper and formal, but I wouldn't say it was overly friendly."

"Protocol, by definition, is formal, and the Spanish are very formal. However, you not only came with a letter of praise from Spain's Ambassador to France, you took the Governor's breath away. You will get an invitation to every official social function at the Governor's house, I guarantee. I won't be surprised if even Captain and Señora Quinn receive invitations as a courtesy to Señorita Quinn."

"Those things are boring, but I suppose the Quinn ladies can be persuaded to attend provided they get new dresses."

"I should have seen that coming." Bethany smiled, "Poor Captain Quinn."

After the meeting, they stopped for lunch at a café overlooking the harbor. The "Yankee" captain with the eye patch and torn ear was a familiar sight in Havana, but his beautiful niece was something new.

Bethany looked around the café. The crowd was mostly male. There was not a single unescorted woman. Just as her uncle took a sip of wine she asked, "Is it true that only whores and American women would come sit at a place like this alone?"

Jonathan choked on his wine, "Where in thunder did you hear that?"

"From Mannela. She wouldn't stop with me at a café when we walked around town last week."

"Good for her."

"So it is true?"

"You are in Havana, not Paris. The Spaniard is very protective of women. Reputation is everything."

"The Spaniard is very repressive toward women. They all look like stuffy, vain, dandies to me. I don't intend to cast my eyes down or hide behind a fluttering fan to cater to their egos."

"Their what?" asked Jonathan, a little shocked.

"Ego. It's a term used by a new kind of doctor. In Paris they are all the rage. They study the emotional workings of the human mind. Ego means, well, where self pride resides, or self importance, or something like that. They would say that you, Captain Quinn, have an enormous ego."

"Who the hell would go to a doctor like that? Sounds loony to me."

"Yes, you might be right. The only one I met pulled on his little goatee, fidgeted with his pince-nez spectacles and tried to look down my dress. He chased me all evening asking questions about what kind of dreams I had and what I thought of my parents."

"What the devil did you tell him?"

"I said that my father was a bullet that went around emasculating men in uniform."

Jonathan spit another mouthful of wine. "My God! You didn't say that? What did he do?"

"He asked me to have a private session with him."

"A private what?"

"I told him I couldn't possibly do such a thing because my guardian was a jealous sea captain who would probably find out and have his inscrutable Chinese crew shanghai him and sell him to the Turks."

"You're teasing me, I hope," Jonathan said without conviction. "My plan didn't work. At the next party, the vile little man was back and brought three of his colleagues from the French Academy to meet me."

"Bee Bee, please don't talk like that here. Havana is not libertine Paris, and the Spanish are not known for their sense of humor, and especially not from jokes in public from a woman."

"Well, I will try for your sake, Uncle, but I am used to going where I want and saying what I please. Perhaps someone should warn these brave, noble Spanish men that if they confuse me with a whore, they are going to suffer more than crushed pride."

"You are going to turn me gray just as Arabella said."

"Yes, I am," she said with a frown, becoming very serious, "I think I can now guarantee it."

He did not know what to say. He had seen her mood suddenly change as if she had been reminded of some weighty problem.

"Bee Bee, tell me what it is. If you don't like it here, we'll work it out. If you don't like Spanish men, there are more Americans arriving here every week. You haven't had a chance to meet them. There's a fun social community here. You'll see."

The frown disappeared and her old smile was back.

"You're right, Uncle. You have to realize that a woman has the privilege of her moods."

A month later there was no longer any doubt in her mind as to what was wrong. She asked Mannela to walk with her. All the way down to the foot of Obispo Street, on past the Plaza de Armas and the palatial Santovenia mansion, Bethany didn't say a word.

"Why don't you just tell me?" Mannela asked at last.

"I have a plan, but it depends on how skillful I can be."

As they walked home Mannela carried a worried look on her face for the first time since Bethany had known her. "You are risking everything. You know that don't you?"

"Just be patient with me a little while longer."

Bethany picked her time carefully. Jonathan and Louisette invited her to join them for dinner at La Zaragozana on Calle Monserrate, a very fine old Havana restaurant established in 1830. She wanted a public place. In public Jonathan would not cause a scene.

Louisette wore a stylish black, watered-silk dress with Arabian pearls. Bethany's dress was made of deep green satin with black lace trim. In her hair she wore a pair of silver Spanish combs trimmed with delicate gold filigree. As Jonathan escorted them to their table, the two slim, dark haired ladies drew the attention of everyone in the room. One young Spaniard turned to another, "I would gladly give an eye and both ears for a pair of women like that."

A string orchestra filled the room with soft music. The food was beautifully presented. Bethany ate little and didn't touch her glass of wine. She hardly spoke a word until coffee and dessert were served. Then without prelude she asked, "What are we going to do for a Quinn heir?"

Louisette dropped her fork. It made a loud clatter on her plate. "Why on earth would you bring that up, especially here?" Jonathan asked. "You know our situation," he said taking Louisette's hand. "I don't understand you tonight. First you pick at your food, say not a word during dinner, and now, out of the blue, you hurt Louisette."

"If I marry, any heirs of mine won't have the Quinn name," Bethany continued.

"They'll still be Quinn heirs," Jonathan said, his patience wearing thin.

"Please hear me out. I am not doing this to hurt either of you. This is very hard for me."

"Then why bring it up here in public? Why not wait until we are home?"

"Because at home you would intimidate me. Here, in a room full of people, many of whom know you, you have to remain rational, listen to what I have to say. I have a plan, but it's entirely up to the two of you. Hear what I have to say and then you may do what you will when we reach home."

"For God sakes, Bee Bee, what on earth has gotten in to you? I've never seen you like this."

"That's because I've never been like this. I'm pregnant."

"By God! I'm going to kill Mannela. And you're going to marry the father."

"Oh, dear Bethany." Louisette held out her hand to her husband's niece.

Bethany's voice trembled with emotion, "It's not Mannela's fault. I alone am to blame." She paused a minute to look at Jonathan and Louisette. "I will not tell you about the father except to say he is a man of honor who does not know. I didn't know until after I arrived here. He is so much like you, Uncle. I love him, but he must never know. He is a soldier. It is his life, all he has. He has been through so much. He could not give it up anymore than I could abandon my heritage to go with him. I would never ask it of him nor he of me."

"Soldier, hell! His duty is here. Where can I find him?"

"He boarded a ship in Marseilles for Suez and the Orient beyond. He is a man you would like and respect, Jonathan, that's all I will ever tell you. Now do you want to hear what I have to say or not?"

Jonathan started to speak, but Louisette squeezed his hand, hard.

He fell silent, waiting.

Bethany took a deep breath. "I have . . . no, the three of us together have two choices. One, Mannela is knowledgeable in the ways one can choose not to have a baby. There are risks, but I trust her skill."

Now Louisette was the one who started to speak. It was Jonathan who squeezed her hand for silence. She looked at Bethany, and Bethany knew what the pleading look meant from a woman who could not have children.

"I was so careful. I had no intention to become pregnant, but now that I am, I want to have this child, this baby from a man I love, a man I knew from the beginning I could never keep." She fought off tears as she spoke. "We need a Quinn heir," she continued, "Why else have you worked so hard, Jonathan? We can have this baby, all of us, if you are willing. Be it boy or girl, there can be at least one more Quinn generation. Should it be a boy, he can carry the Quinn name."

"A Quinn with no father?"

"Do you think I haven't thought of that, Uncle? Have you forgotten I was a Quinn with no father? Do you think I would want that for a child of mine—people in school and town whispering and sneering behind its back the way they did when I was a child? Damnit! Hear me out!"

"I'm sorry, Bee Bee. I shouldn't have said that. What do you want of us?"

"Louisette will say she is pregnant. You, Jonathan, will send her to America to have her child. Spaniards send their wives home so their children will be born Spanish and not Creole don't they? Why should Americans be any different? You will, of course, send your niece and Mannela along to look after her. Once we are there I will become Louisette Quinn. The official papers will record the birth of a child to Jonathan and Louisette Quinn. Louisette, the real Louisette and the baby will return, mother and child. I will be 'aunt' Bee Bee, nothing more." Bethany looked at the couple across the table from her. "I can do this. I can give you this child to raise as your own. No one will know except for the three of us, and Mannela. The secret will be safe as long as we live. We must all swear to that."

Jonathan started to speak, but Bethany stopped him. "You, both of you, must decide. I don't want an answer now, but you must not take long to decide. I can't hide my condition much longer." There was total silence at the table. Everyone was absorbed by their own thoughts when Bethany noticed the waiter patiently standing beside the table, a small tray in his hand. "I believe the waiter is trying to give you the check, Uncle."

"What? Oh yes, the check."

CHAPTER 18

Bethany wanted her baby born in Mississippi, but the Quinn tragedy of Shamrock had made the family name too well known. News of a new Quinn baby in Jackson or Natchez and certainly in Vicksburg might bring unwanted interest under the circumstances. It was decided that New Orleans with a population of nearly 200,000 and modern hospitals would be safe.

Jonathan was told he absolutely could not go with them. "In the first place you just couldn't act like a husband when it is your niece who is having the baby. Bethany is convinced that you would say something in front of a nurse or doctor that would give the whole thing away," Louisette told him. "One slip and you would ruin Bethany and make a bastard of your heir." Still he complained, and when that failed, he whined a little.

"Even a Spaniard would go home to check on his wife. It will kill me to sit around here worrying for months."

"Go on a trip with Jorge Lopez. It will be good for you. Take your mind off of us," Louisette offered.

"Captain Lopez doesn't go on trips. He looks after the ships from the office in Havana and the one in Nassau."

"In that case, Uncle, go to England and check on Jeremy Wright. I bet there has been no audit of your joint business for years."

"And you can go on to Paris to check on the house and Marie. While you are over there you can take Marie shopping for baby things," Louisette added.

Captain Quinn had never been as anxious, lonely and irritable in his life as during the long months of waiting. Billy Wong, on the other hand, was delighted. "Just like old times, Captain J," he beamed, "Just you and your number one man." He could not hide his pleasure at being rid of Mannela for an extended period of time. "Maybe get one, two ladies up back stairs same like old days hanky panky."

Jonathan threw a shoe at him.

Everyone tried to stay clear of Captain Quinn. The clerks couldn't get away, but his captains and crews tried hard to stay at sea or hide ashore when home port could not be avoided. Quinn spent the time running back and forth between the Havana office and the one in Nassau, generally driving everyone ragged. Finally Jorge Lopez told Jonathan that if he did not go somewhere and leave the business and the personnel alone, including himself, he, Lopez, would personally put him in irons and send him on a long cruise until his wife came back. "If you are so worried," he said, "why don't you go check up on how she is doing, anything, but please, I can't get any work done."

"Are you threatening me with mutiny?"

"Si, Senior!"

Informing his staff that he was going to see his wife in New Orleans, Jonathan left for Charleston and from there took passage to England. He had decided that he would follow Bethany's advice and check on Wright in London, then go to Louisette's house in Paris and buy "baby things." After all, he had to play some part in the great event. He had already converted the small study next to his and Louisette's bedroom into a nursery with hand painted flowers, birds, ponies, fish, and sailboats brightly decorating the walls. In Paris, Marie would help him pick out whatever one picks out for babies, he told himself, rather proud of the whole idea.

A bloated, rummy-looking Jeremy Wright was not happy to have Captain Quinn barge into his London office unannounced. "Let's go to lunch, Jeremy. The treat is on me," Jonathan said in a perfectly friendly manner.

"Jonathan! What a surprise! Lunch? Well of course, old man. I know just the place." Jeremy was not too convincing in his attempt to look pleased at Jonathan's visit.

"Expensive, I'll bet."

"Well, yes, of course, since you are buying."

Jonathan noticed that Jeremy carried an ebony, gold handled cane and walked with a slight limp.

"Looks like whiskey and overeating has gotten to you, Jeremy," Quinn remarked, pointing to the cane. "You have the gout."

"I bloody well do not have gout." Jeremy flagged a cab.

"Well, what the hell is the matter then, shoot yourself in the foot?" Jonathan joked.

Jeremy turned a little pale. "I had an accident that's all. Just a bloody accident. Bones didn't knit properly. I don't appreciate your making a joke of it. It's a serious matter."

"The only things I have ever seen you serious about are money and women, and frankly you do better with money."

"Damn poor thing to say, damn poor," Wright complained, obviously not happy with the conversation.

"That's it isn't it? Women. What did you do? Break your foot jumping out a window to escape some irate husband?" Jonathan couldn't help but laugh at the expression on Jeremy's face. "Did some wench slam her door on your foot?"

Jeremy was furious, and relieved; furious at being teased about a matter he did not consider funny in the least, relieved that Bethany obviously had not told her uncle or Jonathan would already have shot him. Still, he could not resist the temptation Jonathan had presented him. He said, much to Jonathan's surprise, "All right! If you must know, a little bitch shot me in the foot." Jonathan wouldn't have believed it if Jeremy hadn't appeared so serious. "Damn a woman with a pistol! Ought to be a law. They have no sense about such things. She could bloody well have killed me."

"I know one who would have," Jonathan said smiling.

"Now that your accusation of gout has proven false, could we drop the subject?" Jeremy protested.

"Fine," Jonathan said. "Let's get down to business. After a great deal of thought, I've reached the conclusion that it's time for us to call it quits, Jeremy. I'll take North and South America and the Caribbean. You take the rest, Europe, Arabia, Asia, Africa. That way I won't wind up killing you for shorting me the way you have done for years."

Jonathan expected Jeremy to loudly protest, but he said nothing, just rode along in the cab weighing the situation. He dealt with a lot of shady characters, but it was Jonathan Quinn who made him feel uneasy. He always felt uneasy with honest men. "An honest arms dealer is dangerous," he used to say in certain circles because it sounded funny and tended to excuse his own terms and conditions of doing business. In Jonathan's case, however, it was not funny. He had seen Jonathan's temper flare once when someone not only tried to cheat him, but threatened to kill him. Once was enough. Jonathan Quinn was not the sort of man one should cheat or threaten.

They arrived at the restaurant, went inside, and were met by a waiter who fawned, "Your usual table Mr. Wright?" Jeremy nodded.

Once they were seated Jeremy said, "Times are changing. You have a successful legitimate business these days. You no longer depend on arms deals, don't need them to survive like I do. I'm starting to sell to governments now, some in North Africa. You might say I'm more legitimate now myself, a respectable merchant."

"I wonder how legitimate your British government would consider you if they knew just who you were selling arms to in India and Egypt, or if the Turks found out where certain Arab tribes are getting their arms," Jonathan said. "You're selling to bandits and potentates. I was approached on some of those deals."

"You weren't so critical when you needed my contacts, my knowledge, my sources for the arms you sold to the Cubans. You weren't so pious when I fetched you out from behind the arse end of a mule in a weed patch in Mississippi."

Jonathan struggled to hold his temper. He wanted to finish it without a scene. "Suppose we settle the goods consigned to the London warehouse as of today? After we take inventory, either of us can make a buy-sell offer. The one who makes the offer gives the other the choice of buying or selling at the stated price. I know what we are carrying on the books, Jeremy. You can make an offer here and now, or we can go take an inventory."

Jeremy needed time to think, and the waiter gave it to him. "Bring the beef cart and a bottle of claret, your best," he said, "My associate here is paying."

The waiter plied their plates with thick slabs of roast beef and boiled potatoes while the sommelier fussed over a bottle 'of our finest', making much ado over its dusty French label.

Finally Jeremy made his move. "I'll give you twenty thousand for your half."

"And we are through, clean, you'll give me all J & Q records at the office?" Jonathan asked. "I don't want a trace of our former business records left, not a ledger, not a scrap of paper with mention of J & Q or my name on it."

"Agreed," Jeremy said with great relief. Without reporting the fact, he had already sold almost half the inventory for thirty five thousand. He had cleverly put the money in an investment that would make him a little on the side and therefore hadn't yet reported the sale, nor split the proceeds with his partner. He never anticipated an accounting so soon. His little side investment still had some months to go before maturity. *The point is moot now,* Wright smugly thought.

Once at Jeremy's office, Jonathan, without asking permission, started going through files, correspondence, invoices and Jeremy's desk drawers.

"Open the safe, Wright, and then sit in that chair over there," Jonathan ordered. Jeremy did as he was told until Jonathan lit off the fireplace and began to burn papers.

"Christ, Quinn! Go easy now! You can burn papers that have your name and J & Q on them, but don't burn my papers!" Jonathan, paying no attention, picked up a stack off Wright's desk and walked toward the fire.

"Look here! I need those records. Money's owed me on some of those."

Jonathan looked as though he were going to throw the whole lot in the fire.

"For God sake, Jonathan!" Jeremy protested.

Jonathan, papers in hand, turned to face him. "More than half the warehouse consignment is gone. I took inventory of everything in it before I came to see you. I know what we were carrying on the books. There is no record of sales or receipts entered on the ledger, Wright. I can assume you have been making a little arbitrage, a little private interest, a little special profit for Jeremy on your partner's money all along, haven't you? You did the same thing to Captain Jones. You always gave us our money sooner or later just not any of the profits you made by risking our capital. I should have stopped you, but damn my soul I needed you then. Well, as you said, I don't need you any longer. Cutting free now won't clear my conscience, but it will clean you out of my craw." Jeremy was truly scared now. Jonathan's eye cut into him like a torch. "If you want any scrap of paper in this room," Jonathan continued, "any name, any address, any figure, any purchase order, any account records, then I suggest you get down to your banker and get a draft for forty thousand dollars for J & Q's real fair share with back interest. You have an hour before I destroy every piece of paper in the place."

Jeremy was white as a sheet. "God damn your soul!" he said as he left.

"He very likely will," Jonathan said to an empty room as he began to search the office more thoroughly. He took all the drawers from the furniture and looked behind and under them, looked for secret drawers, looked behind pictures and under the carpet. He burned every document, invoice, letter and note that held any reference to J & Q. He continued his search until he found, under a false bottom of a large, burled walnut cigar humidor on Wright's desk, two small notebooks. One was the object of the search. It contained the names and addresses of arms sellers and buyers all over the world. The second book was a surprise. It contained a list of

Jeremy's debtors and the amount each owed him. Jeremy Wright, Jonathan discovered, was, among other things, a high class book maker. The names on the list were right out of the London social registry, obviously those with a taste for gambling. Jonathan put the first book in his pocket and the second one back in the box. He replaced the false bottom and all but one of the cigars, sat down for a smoke and waited for Wright.

"Here's your damn money, Quinn. Now leave me alone." Jeremy handed Jonathan a bank draft, British pounds sterling equivalent to the agreed dollar amount. Jonathan examined the document, put the draft in his coat pocket and left the office without a word. Wright collapsed into his chair.

Captain Quinn went directly to Jeremy's bank where he arranged to credit the full amount of the note to the J & Q account at Barclay's Bank in Nassau. From the bank, he went to his hotel room and spent the afternoon copying every name, address and comment that was in Jeremy's little book. When he had finished, he carefully enclosed the book in wrapping paper, addressed the package, took it to the hotel concierge and arranged for a courier to deliver it to its owner.

I would love to see the expression on his face when he opens the package. The cheating bastard should be damn grateful I didn't burn both his little books, especially the records of gambling debts and loans owed him.

Two days later Jonathan was sitting in Louisette's house in Paris enjoying Marie's French cooking. She was beside herself when he told her that the doctors had been wrong about Louisette and that she was expecting a baby.

Marie had one complaint. "Madame Quinn should be having the baby in Paris where I, Marie, could look after her." Captain Quinn assured her Louisette would have the finest medical care available and tried to explain that since the child would be American, it should be born there. "Yes," she pronounced at last. "Perhaps it will be acceptable because having a baby in New Orleans is almost like having a baby in France. However, you must promise to bring the baby here for a visit with me in Paris. I am too old to cross an ocean. Louisette and the baby must come so I can show them off to Paris." She was delighted when Jonathan asked if she would accompany him the following day to shop for *baby things*. "You have come to the right person. I, Marie, am an expert in such matters."

Jonathan left for Havana after seeing all the *baby things* properly crated, labeled and shipped prior to his own departure.

"Mrs. Quinn? Mrs. Quinn?"

Bethany had thought at times she was dying, and for a while she was right.

"There's a stubbornness in that young woman that just wouldn't let her go . . . wouldn't let her go . . . let her go . . ."

There was a voice, far away at first. Bethany heard the voice again. "Mrs. Quinn?" She could not see the voice and struggled to open her eyes. A haze slowly cleared revealing the painted blue ceiling of a room that smelled of antiseptics. She was floating, yes that's it, floating in a cloud. There was no pain any longer. She turned her head and could see the voice. It wore a white apron that had a red cross on its bib. The voice sounded sweet, but its face was blurred.

"Welcome back," the voice said, "you have a fine baby." Bethany tried to speak, to let the voice know she understood.

Her mouth felt so dry. There was a lingering odor of ether on her breath. She could not quite get a response from her vocal cords, so she tried to smile instead.

The voice said, "I see that smile. You understand don't you? Well, you just rest a little longer and then we will bring him in and introduce you."

The white haze began to close in again, but not before the voice said, "I am going to let your maid come in and see you now, Mrs. Quinn. She has been here all the time, would not leave even for a minute."

The voice moved to the foot of the bed. "Captain Quinn certainly must love you very much. He wanted you to have the best of care. It's too bad he had to be so far away, but I don't blame him in the least for not wanting his son born in some foreign country. Your maid has sent a telegram to him in Havana. Your husband will know that he has a son, and that you and the baby are fine."

Jonathan has a son! Henri's son! My son! With that thought she allowed sleep to roll heavily down upon her. She recognized sleep. It was not death. Death was different. Death had come very close, had reached gently out to her, Bethany knew that, had felt that, but Death had changed her mind and gone away.

On February twenty-fourth, 1884, a telegram from New Orleans addressed to Captain J. H. Quinn, J & Q Shipping, Havana, Cuba was delivered. Jonathan signed for the message and ripped it open before the delivery boy was out his office door. He read it twice to be sure the news was real.

"Jorge! Jorge!" Jonathan shouted.

Lopez, startled by an urgency in Jonathan's voice he had never heard before, ran into the office to find him walking up and down waving a telegram in the air. He did not know what to expect. Maybe one of J & Q's ships had been lost.

"Jorge!" Jonathan shouted, "We have a son!"

Greatly relieved, Captain Lopez offered his enthusiastic congratulations.

"Jorge, don't look for me for a couple of months. I want mother and child fully recovered and in strong health before they travel. You will have to handle all company affairs." Jonathan walked to a cabinet, took out a bottle of brandy and two crystal snifters, handed one to Jorge and poured a healthy measure into each. "To the newest Quinn!"

They drank the toast just as Billy Wong came in bringing the Captain's lunch.

"Billy Wong, you little heathen, have a cigar," Jonathan grabbed a fist full and emptied them into the startled little man's cupped hands. "You are now Uncle Billy Wong. We have a son!"

Billy dropped several of the cigars. "Oh, fortune smiles on house of Quinn, Captain J. Most auspicious occasion! Velly big in China."

"I have some work to do here before I can leave. You go home and pack for me."

"Uncle Billy pack, chop chop, Captain J!" Pigtail flying, he ran out of the building toward the Quinn house.

"I have never seen him move so fast," Jorge laughed. "Now what can Uncle Lopez do?"

"I'll need some cash, Jorge, and would you see if you can get me on Plants new ferry to Tampa and wire for Pullman tickets for me from Tampa through to New Orleans." Jonathan took pen and paper, wrote out an address and handed it to Jorge. "Here's the address of the Pontalba apartment on St. Peter Street." Jonathan handed Jorge the note. "Telegraph me there if you need me."

Jorge started to leave when he turned and asked, "Captain Quinn, what will you name your son?"

Jonathan looked perplexed. "I don't know. Whatever his mother decides."

"Of course, Captain. I am sure Senora Louisette will choose a proper name."

"Louisette?" The letter had said 'Mother weak but out of danger'. "Oh yes, Louisette. I am sure she will choose a name that pleases me."

Jonathan had insisted the baby be born in a hospital, an expensive practice uncommon at the time. After traveling from Havana by ferry, railroad and finally the St. Charles Avenue street car, he arrived at Touro Infirmary, recently relocated from the warehouse district near the river to the new and sparsely-settled uptown district of New Orleans.

"Meet Jonathan Ansel Quinn," Bethany smiled up at him, "He's named for you and your father. We call him Ansel."

Jonathan stood in the room by the bed looking first at the baby and Bethany, then across the room at Louisette dressed in a starched maid's uniform.

"Well, pick him up, Jonathan! He won't break. He's quite healthy the doctor says." Bethany smiled up at him.

Jonathan looked lost as to how to go about lifting the pink, wiggling bundle.

"Here, Captain Quinn, I will show you," said Louisette crossing the room. She lifted the baby and placed it in his arms. "There, just hold his head steady. That's it, Captain. You will get used to it in no time."

Jonathan looked down at the baby. "Well, Master Quinn, I am very pleased to make your acquaintance. Isn't he a little small?"

"Just how big do you think a baby should be?" Bethany laughed. "I think a seven pound, fourteen ounce boy is about all I could have survived."

"He's a big strong boy," Louisette said, taking the baby from him. "Good-bye Captain Quinn," she moved him toward the door.

"But I just arrived," Jonathan protested.

"It is time to feed the baby, and after that, mother and child need their rest."

"What am I supposed to do?" Jonathan looked dejected.

"Why don't you go to the apartment, Captain," Louisette answered with a coy grin. "Mannela will help here. Mother and the baby will be dismissed from the hospital tomorrow. Madame Quinn has asked that I go to the apartment later today and take care of all of the Captain's needs."

As the three ladies broke out laughing, Jonathan actually blushed and retreated down the hallway.

By the time Louisette arrived at the Pontalba apartment, Jonathan was happily waiting in an upstairs bedroom where he had found Louisette's belongings. Later, when she lay contented in his arms, he said, "I shall have to compliment Mrs. Quinn on how well her maid took care of the Captain's needs this afternoon." Louisette snuggled her lovely naked body closer to his and playfully bit his good ear.

Captain and Mrs. Quinn, the real Mrs. Quinn, departed for Cuba with a fine two-month old baby boy and a hired French Creole wet nurse for young Ansel.

Bethany refused to go with them. "Just look what having a baby has done to me. I don't intend to return to Cuba until I have regained my figure even if I have to starve."

Both Mannela and Louisette knew that was not the reason. Bethany was ever sweet, seemingly happy and satisfied with the arrangements for the baby, but Louisette had caught her holding her baby and crying. Bethany hardly spoke to Mannela on the long walks they took to help her regain her strength. "She is a little melancholy," the doctor had said. "It is not uncommon among women after giving birth. She will be fine in time." After three months of long walks and picking at her food, Bethany did lose weight, but not her deep feeling of sadness.

"Let's pack, Mannela, I've got to get out of New Orleans."

"Are we bound for Cuba?" Mannela asked.

"I'm not ready for that . . . and the part I must play for the rest of my life. I need a little more time Mannela. We are going to Vicksburg, to Doctor Ted's house where I grew up. There are two dear old people there I want to see again. I may never have another chance."

When she arrived with Mannela, the two gray-headed women who 'looked after de place' made a fuss over her. Their baby had come home. They were a little cool to Mannela, but civil enough. At seventy-one, Arabella's eyesight was failing, but she wouldn't let on to it. Luky was thin and stooped, but her mind and memory were clear.

On the first night, Bethany called the hotel and had supper, complete with wine, delivered to the house.

"What you doing all dis here fo', Miss Bethany? We ain't too old to fix fo' you like we always done."

"I'm giving a party for two very special guests, and guests are not supposed to have to do any fixin's," Bethany smiled. "So quit fussin' at me. It's y'all's party."

They were thrilled. In all their lives, no one had ever given them a party, even a little one, and certainly no one had ever sat them down and served up a wonderful dinner sto'-bought from a hotel.

The occasion was a little teary at first, but pretty soon Bethany found she had no choice but to suffer all the old stories about the trials and misadventures of her childhood. The telling of them was a great production with Arabella and Luky taking turns. "Our baby is home," they kept saying. Mannela was amused by all the stories and encouraged their telling. In turn she told about Bethany's stay in Paris and Jonathan's marriage and the wonderful news that a new Quinn baby boy had been born.

Bethany did her best to join in the fun, but it was an effort for her. She excused herself and went to bed in her old room leaving the three women so deep in conversation they hardly noticed she had gone.

Those two wonderful old women know me better than anyone else in the world, and yet they know only the girl in the stories, not the woman I am now. That thought somehow seemed very sad to Bethany as she drifted off to sleep. She tossed and turned while dreaming of a lonely little girl and a baby that had been given away.

The next morning Arabella told Bethany, "You eat'en like a bird, and you ain't laughed once since you been home. I believe you has a case of da' old fashion blues, Honey. Dey comes and dey goes. Now you too pretty, too smart, too rich and too young to be worrying yo' self wit' nothin'."

"She right, Miss Bethany. Time you got yo' self a man. How come she don't have a man, Mannela?" Luky asked.

"Now hush up 'bout dat man stuff, Luky," answered Arabella before Mannela could speak, "men de cause of de blues for most ladies."

"All right, you three. I was discussed enough last night," Bethany said. "I am fine. I have had very nice men friends. I just haven't had any I wanted to keep."

"Ain't dat de truth!" laughed Luky, "Neither has I."

Bethany continued, "I don't want to hear any more talk about me. I'm just a little tired from traveling so much lately. Can't a girl come home for a little peace and quiet?"

"Course you can, honey. Us two old crows jes having ourselves a fit of happiness we so glad you here," said Arabella, "No mo' teasing our baby, y'all hear?"

"I don't see any old crows here," Bethany smiled. "I just see two wonderful people I love."

"We is old all right. Done quit countin' at seventy," Lucky volunteered. "Dis house and de money Doctor Ted and you done left us is all we need 'cept gittin' news 'bout Massa Jonathan and you. We 'jes look forward to yo' letters, honey. A lady from de 'Piscopal church stop by twice a month to read 'em fo' us. We gittin' along 'jes fine. Ain't we Arabella?" Arabella nodded confirmation.

"You certainly seem to be," Bethany managed a cheerful smile. "Now I have heard enough about me. That's all you two have been talking about. I want to hear about you, and all about Vicksburg,"

"Well, ain't much to tell." said Arabella.

Luky agreed, "'bout everybody po', black or white. Farmers scratchin' for a livin', store folks in town ain't sellin' a whole lot dey tells me."

"Things mo' better for the whites ever since de Yankee soldiers left some years back, but ain't so fo' de black folks," Arabella said, squinting to see in the dim light of the parlor.

"Now 'jes hush up 'bout dat kind'a stuff. She don't want to hear all dat," Luky interrupted.

"Yes I would like to hear about the way things are, the way you all see them," Bethany said.

"Well, all I know is what I been told down to de church. We goes when we can," Arabella continued. "After de soldiers left, the white folks done run out what de called de carpet bagger government; the blacks and the scallywags and such. Some of dem niggas got to acting pretty high and mighty with de soldiers behind 'em. Some of 'em force a white woman right off de sidewalk, get to drinkin', talking smart. Weren't no call fo' dat kind a thing. 'Jes make things worse fo' honest black folk. Now some of de bad stuff was going on when you was a girl, but Doctor Ted, he don't let on 'round you, but me and Luky knowed 'bout it. You tell 'em Luky, you get's 'round mo en me."

"She talking 'bout vigilantes. Dey terrible frightening, does terrible things."

"What things, Luky? What are you talking about?" Bethany asked.

"Hangin's and beatin's and shootin's some blacks get too uppity, or talks 'bout votin' again like de done during reconstruction, or dey don't gets off de sidewalk when a white passes 'em."

"You're talking about the Knights of the Camellia, the Ku Klux Klan and such," Bethany said, "I knew about all of that, but I thought that was over, that things were settled down after the state was re-admitted to the Union. Jonathan said General Forest disbanded the Klan and it was outlawed after that. I must have been only about six then."

"You didn't hear nothing Doctor Ted didn't want you to hear, child," Luky continued. "Seems like de mo' time goes by de worse it gits. Got black folks scared to death all out in de country. Most of dem Yankees what come down here and took over things after de war done pump black folks all full'a notions 'bout doin' as dey please, but dey done left cause dey scared too. Whites ain't been left out by de Klan, neither, and not jes Yankee whites. Tell'em 'bout dat white man right here in town, Arabella."

"We seen em one night," she said. "Come right down past de corner dere. 'bout twenty of 'em all dressed in sheets, had hoods over dey heads, some carrying torches. Mighty scary looking. And some of 'em carrying crosses like dey devil's preachers or somethin'. Luky thought dey might be coming after us cause we livin' here among the town whites, but I tells her ain't nothing of the kind. Folks 'round here knows 'bout us. Treats us kindly. Why, white ladies look in on us every week to see we all right."

"Git back to de story, Woman," Luky said.

"Well, come to find out a man what clerked down to de Bateman General sto' had took to drinkin' and beatin' his wife and cherren. Dem Klan devils drag him out on his front yard and whupped him with a leather strap till he be crawling on his knees beggin' 'em to stop. De told him he better not drink no mo' and to leave his wife and cherren be, or dey be back."

Bethany met that afternoon with lawyer Todd, a veteran who had read law after the war. He had managed the Quinn's affairs in Mississippi since the death of Doctor Perkins.

"How's Jonathan, Miss Bethany?" Todd asked.

"He is the proud father of a son."

"Ole' Jonathan's starting kind'a late. I got three children, one grown and two almost through school."

"My, you have been busy since the war, Mr. Todd."

Todd looked embarrassed and changed the subject. "I don't git much courtroom work, but lots of deeds been changing hands on account of tax sales. I do legal processing and recording of those." Upon reflection, he thought it best to change the subject again. "I knew your mama, Miss Bethany. She was a pretty thing just like you, only her hair was strawberry blonde. You have her eyes kinda, but hers weren't so green. She was only about fifteen the last time I saw her. I hope you don't mind my saying so."

"I love to hear things about her. I was too young to remember her very much, you see."

"Of course you were," he said. "Now I have the books laid out on the table there in the study for your review, the ones on Shamrock, and the ones on the trust for the old nigger women. Just take your time and call me if you have any questions."

"I'm sure everything will be in order, Mr. Todd, but I wish you wouldn't refer to Arabella and Luky as 'niggers'. They are like family to me. They helped raise me and took care of Doctor Perkins."

"You are right, Miss Bethany. Used to be just white trash used that word. Guess we've all gotten a little common round here since the war."

He was surprised that she spent so much time going over the books, matching up receipts, going through bank records. Finally she returned to Todd's office. He rose from his desk until she was seated.

"What's all this I hear about Klan activity? I thought things were better now. The war has been over for twenty years."

"That's a poor subject. You sure you want to talk about that." Bethany nodded, "You'll find it very hard to shock me, Mr. Todd."

"I'm sure I would never try, Miss Bethany." He paused a moment. "When the war ended things just got worse. 'Course, you was a town child. Things were a little better in town. Grant sent food into the city after the surrender, but that didn't last. The army fed the blacks around here, but not the ex-Rebs or their families out in the country. What they ate had to come out of their own land. There was no money, paying jobs were scarce; share croppin' and maybe a little loggin' and sawmill work. Lot of folks were struggling to hold on to a little piece of their land. State Government was run by carpetbaggers, nigg . . . I mean blacks, and scallywags, backed by soldiers under martial law year after year. Got to where whites sometimes got treated poorly by blacks and got arrested by soldiers if they acted up about it. Somethin' had to be done and the Klan did it. Put the fear in 'em. But it got out of hand, got too violent, went too far like any mob, only worse 'cause it was all secret. Nobody had to answer, nobody would tell, nobody would speak out against 'em. It got so the people who the Klan was supposed to protect got afraid of 'em too. It was outlawed in '71, but it just went more secret. I think most men, if asked, would be afraid not to join. It's the way the Klan gets protection and support. You speak out against them, you get a yard full of hooded riders. Like I said, there maybe was a need when it started, but now it's mostly just bullies venting frustration and hatred. Why, before the war, nobody paid attention to where blacks went, I mean around town. I remember sitting in a saloon with my daddy and some men. A freed black came in, they all knew him, had a barber shop where white gentlemen went. He just walked up and put his money down and got a drink like everybody else. We always had a nigg . . . a black nanny sit at the table with us children when daddy took us traveling before the war. I mean sit right in the hotel dining room with us children. Stayed in the room with us at night. Nobody paid any mind. Now if a black tried to get a drink in a white saloon he'd be hung by sundown. People down here gonna hurt for a long time . . . lost their sons, brothers, husbands, fathers, lost their homes, their land. Guess the people got no one to lay blame on but the poor blacks. It sure weren't their fault things turned out so bad, but in hard times seems like folks always look for someone to put the blame on. The Klan runs around with a Bible and a whip claiming some sort of twisted righteous justice. I work with the law, Miss Bethany, and I can tell you there ain't much of it in Mississippi."

"Well Mr. Todd, in Cuba things are not so different. Spanish law enriches the Spanish and represses the Cubans, black and white and all in between, and there's a lot in between. Spain treats Cubans worse than the Yankees treat Southerners. Seems to me as long as the whites and blacks here at home keep stirred up against one another, the Yankees are gonna have everything their way. As uncle Ted used to say, the Yankees sure as hell outnumber us and out vote us in the Congress."

Todd couldn't think of a thing to say. He had never heard a woman, especially one as pretty and young as Bethany Quinn, so outspoken. And it was obvious to him that she knew her way around a set of books. *It's gonna take one hell of a man to take on that little lady, but what man wouldn't want to try?* "What else can I do for you while you are here, Miss Bethany?"

"Mr. Todd, the books are in perfect order as my uncle said they would be. He thinks very highly of you."

"Thank you, Ma'am. He is respected around these parts. He managed to keep hold of all ya'lls land. Not too many been able to do that."

"I would like to see that land, Mr. Todd," Bethany said. "I see we have sixteen white families and twenty seven that are black sharecropping the place."

He looked at her in a peculiar way. "Are you sure, Miss Bethany? I mean, after all that happened there?"

"I'm sure, Mr. Todd. We'll leave before first light with a team of good horses hitched to a light buggy so we'll make good time. I'm sure we can arrange with some family along the way for us to sleep over if necessary. A pallet of quilts on the floor will do me just fine."

He was reluctant, and tried his best to find an excuse not to go, but as he explained to his wife for the third time why he had to take an overnight trip with a young and beautiful woman, "The Quinn account is our bread and butter, honey."

* * *

The sunrise revealed the dusty Natchez road before them, some stretches of it clay-gravel, some sandy loam, all of it long neglected with pot holes, ruts, and in places where it dipped down through shady hollows, muddy crossings. Bethany and Mr. Todd passed formerly cultivated land that had been given over to brush, weeds and loblolly pine. Staggered along the way where sharecroppers struggled with small plots cut from former grand plantations, Bethany could see men and boys, and often women and children, toiling in the fields. Every family they passed, whether black or white, seemed to have the same range of offspring: lap child, porch child, and yard child. They all had a menagerie of dogs, chickens, a mule, a few a pigs, and maybe a cow out back in a muddy pen near an unpainted house. Some had laundry flying on a line out back near a wash pot. Often the travelers would see a thin, bedraggled woman with a new baby on her hip pausing to look toward the road at the buggy and the dressed-up lady riding in it.

Bethany had Lawyer Todd stop at a cabin situated near the road. A barefooted woman with stringy hair wearing a faded, homemade dress came out on the porch. She lifted her hand to shade her eyes from the sun.

Pretending to need a drink of water, Bethany stepped from the buggy before lawyer Todd could help her down, and walked up to a crude gate in the split-rail fence separating the cabin from the road. A cur dog barked from under the cabin, but the woman shushed it quiet.

"It's been a long journey, ma'am," Bethany called. "Might I get a drink of water if it's not too much trouble?"

Shy of any stranger, but still wanting to see a lady dressed in such fine, store-bought clothes, the woman nodded and stepped into the shadow of the cabin's dog-trot. The roof was sagging. The yard was dirt, not a blade of grass growing. A few chickens were scratching for bugs. On the corner of the porch, the sunny end, a small pot stood with yellow flowers peeping over its rim, the only splash of color to be seen.

Directly the woman returned, walked out to the gate and handed Bethany a jar of well water dipped from a bucket drawn fresh that morning. It was still cool. Tasting slightly of minerals, it had a good earthy flavor. The woman wouldn't take money for it, so Bethany offered her linen handkerchief. "Please take it for your kindness as a favor to me," she said.

The woman, carefully touching the lace around its edges, folded it with care. She smiled shyly, revealing a missing tooth. Her skin was suntanned and weathered. Bethany guessed she must be in her mid forties.

"How many children do you have, may I ask?"

"I got two livin'. Lost three to fever. My two boys is out thar helping Jasper. She motioned to the field where the father and young sons were working. My oldest, he's thirteen, and his brother's twelve. I was sixteen when the oldest came," she said proudly.

My God! Bethany thought. *This poor woman is only twenty-nine.*

Lawyer Todd helped Bethany back into the carriage and they continued on in silence, Bethany thinking of the hard field work her own mother and grandmother must have done at Shamrock.

Late in the day they turned up the Quinn plantation road. What had once been an uninterrupted sea of endless cotton was now a patchwork of small plots sharing the same image in common with the tenant farm where Bethany had stopped for water. The plots were sometimes separated by crude fences, sometimes bordered by vacant fields covered in scrub pine, brush and wild grass. Bethany knew the back breaking labor made the tenant families a bare living, while the shares they paid for the privilege, in a good year, rarely met the taxes and expenses for Shamrock. The land hadn't shown the Quinns a profit since the war. Good year or bad, the only one certain to make a profit off of Shamrock was lawyer Todd, but as far as Bethany and Jonathan had been able to determine, he was honest to both Shamrock and the tenants. Bethany had heard that was far from the norm if truth be known. That wasn't to say that most land owners were dishonest. It's just that times were hard, she reasoned, even desperate for those trying to hold on and rebuild. For those who had money, land could be had cheap by trading a few pennies an acre for a poor widow's signature on a deed, or at tax and foreclosure sales, but making the venture profitable was another matter for Southern farmer or Northern investor alike. For a desperate farmer or dishonest investor there was always the temptation to cheat the tenants, and cheating was so easy. For the less than honest manager there was an opportunity to charge the tenants a little more and pay the owner a little less. Then there was the easy path of overcharging for staples and supplies at a company store and charging high rates of interest on credit accounts. If the tenants didn't like it, they could get off the place and start over somewhere else. Of course, it was harder for them to leave if they were in debt, and they were usually in debt, even on places that were run fair and honest.

Men working fields and women hoeing vegetable gardens, washing clothes or drawing water from wells paused to watch apprehensively as the carriage came into view. It wasn't time for Lawyer Todd to "tally 'em down" in his book. When he passed on by, they became more curious than concerned. They had never seen him bring a lady out to the place before. The carriage crossed the big level and then went out of sight following a sunken road down and across a shaded hollow before rising once again to cross fields standing fallow. Presently they ran onto a section of the road overgrown from disuse. Knee-high weeds were growing up between the bare, hard-packed wagon ruts. The road climbed a gentle rise to what the locals referred to as the *Old Place*. No one visited the site any longer. Some didn't because Lawyer Todd had told them the owners didn't want anyone disturbing the place. Most stayed away because of rumors about terrible happenings that had occurred there. The few men and boys who had hunted and camped around the site said they had seen and heard strange things in the night, said the place was haunted for sure.

The carriage turned onto the remnants of what had been a circular drive and stopped at the foot of the brick steps that once led up to Shamrock's wide veranda. Bethany surveyed the panoramic view from the carriage. Tall weeds covered most of the ground except in places where ivy and Virginia creeper had somehow survived in scattered patches and climbed three of the four blackened chimneys that stood as sentinels over the ashen ruins. Behind the chimneys the old brick kitchen lay in ruins. Bethany climbed down from the carriage and walked to the kitchen. The door lay on the ground, the windows were broken, and the roof sagged like a swayback mule. All she found was a crude homemade table, a broken chair, and the odor of molding dampness. Nothing was familiar. The anxiety Bethany had harbored in coming to this place faded.

Satisfied, she returned to the carriage and paused beside it to brush away the beggar's lice that had accumulated on her skirt. Her purse dropped from her hand and landed near the foot of the old steps. Bethany knelt down to pick it up. There, close to the ground, she looked up at the curving stairway with its rusting ironwork railings and was suddenly filled with the strange sensation that she had been exactly at that spot before, had seen the same view of the steps with the tall chimneys silhouetted against the sky. She stood up quickly, her purse still on the ground. Her breath came in shallow quick spurts. She felt slightly faint.

"Are you all right, Miss Bethany?" Todd asked.

"What? Oh, yes. Just stayed bent over too long. Almost made me dizzy," she lied.

It had not been frightening, just startling, she decided. And she realized why. From an adult's eye level, nothing looked familiar to her at all, but when she had stooped to her knees to pick up her purse, her eyes were no longer on the level of an adult. They were near the level of a small child. Bethany knew she had stood in that exact spot as a little two-and-a-half-year-old child and looked up past the steps to the mighty chimneys standing against the sky. She must have done it often, for somehow it was still in the primal reaches of her memory. It was that revelation that startled her. She bent down again, only this time she put her hands on the moss covered steps. Slowly she moved her eye level higher, one step at a time, the way a child's vision would have taken in the scene as the child climbed step by step toward the landing that would have seemed so high and daring. She had been that child. No one had told her about the stairs. This was her own memory unlocking the door to the dungeon where slept a child's terror. Now she was frightened. All her life she had occasionally had strange and disturbing dreams that made no sense, but now . . . she wished she had not come. She knew it was too late to run. She would have to finish it now, whatever *IT* was, or never return.

"Are you sure you are all right, Miss Bethany? You look a little pallid."

Bethany walked past the carriage without answering. She moved through the tall grass, drawn toward a brick cottage surrounded by oak trees and scrub brush. She stumbled on something in the weeds, something that gave way softly at her step. She looked down at what was left of a wooden frame of some sort, the wood rotted to a damp pulp that crumbled at her touch. She stooped to look closer and saw tiny traces of green paint. Nearby a steel rim lay on the ground enclosing the remains of wooden spokes. *It's great grandfather's goat cart!* At that realization, terror assaulted Bethany. *I remember it! My God! He died here!* The muffled sound of shots echoed in her ears. Barely able to stop the scream in her mind from escaping her lips, she backed and raised her eyes to a dark, shadowed doorway.

Against her will, Bethany was drawn the remaining distance to the brick cottage. It too was in decay, its roof partly fallen in, its floor rotting away under a bed of leaves. At the doorway she was compelled to look inside, to step inside. It was unfamiliar, almost empty. She took a few timid steps into the cottage. Cold tentacles of fear slithered around her in the dim light. It was not the remnants of a loom against a wall or the chair on its side near the fireplace that made her fight for breath. In the deep shadow of a corner, something not quite distinguishable caught her attention. A child's dim memory told her what it was before she walked to it. Yes! Her memory! No one had told her, no other living human on earth knew her mama had put her in it. A shiver raced up her spine. She now knew from where her terrible childhood nightmares had come. *Oh God! It was all real!*

The wicker trunk had collapsed, bits of it lying in little piles on the floor. The lid lay in pieces across the bottom. In the horrible dreams her vision was always partially blocked by some sort of curtain. Standing there she knew it hadn't been a curtain at all. It had been the side of the wicker trunk through which she saw the dirty black boots walk past. She knew now that in the nightmare the baby's feet that she always saw standing in blood were hers. A two and a half year old baby had watched something too horrible for her to understand. *Why was there never any sound in the dream?* The answer came to her. *My mama didn't scream. Dear God! She was protecting me so I wouldn't cry out and betray my hiding place.* For a moment, Bethany couldn't breathe. She knew she had climbed out of the wicker trunk after the boots had gone, had stood in her mother's blood. Bethany could hear her own baby voice echoing. *Mama. Wake up, Mama.*

She had to lean back against the wall to keep from falling. Her gorge rose up her throat in spasmodic waves and drove her to her knees. What little had been in her stomach was long on the floor by the time she was able to stop the insistent, dry heaves. With dirt and leaves sticking to her hands and knees, she struggled to her feet and walked trembling to the doorway. She wiped the spittle from her lips and chin with the back of her hand. For a long time she stood there with beads of perspiration on her forehead and the taste of bile in her mouth.

Finally Bethany brushed the leaves and dirt from her skirt and stepped from the shadows into bright, warm, welcoming sunlight. Standing there, no longer trembling, she lifted her eyes to the ruins of Shamrock. At that moment, Bethany knew the impalpable terror of her childhood nightmare would never again drag her into dark places. That was over. Shamrock would no longer be a place to fear. This was Quinn land, her land. She would banish its sadness and return the Quinns to it, at least the youngest Quinn.

Bethany waved to Lawyer Todd to let him know she was all right, and began to walk along a worn dirt path so hard packed it would not support growth even after lying fallow for more than twenty years. It led down a gentle slope and through several hundred yards of brush and trees to a row of cabins. She found the small front porch of one of them still strong enough to support her weight and sat down. The cabin had been whitewashed at one time for she could see traces of the lime mixture in the cracks between the board and batten siding. Some of the cypress planks were badly warped by sun and rain; some had fallen away where the handmade nails that once held them in place had rusted to powder. Bethany had no memory of the slave cabins.

Mama's diary said they all lived here: Arabella, Grandmother Nannie, Great Granddaddy Daniel, ole Nicodemus, and Mama until she had me and they moved her and Arabella up to the brick weaving cottage.

She pulled the gold chain and locket Jonathan had given her out of the high collar of her dress and opened it. The faces of a lovely lady and pretty young girl smiled up at her, her mother and grandmother. She had tried over and over to remember them, the sound of their voices, but she could not.

"Miss Bethany," Lawyer Todd broke the stillness. "Miss Bethany, we best be getting a start. We'll have to find a place to spend the night on the road before dark."

Bethany looked up at Todd with a blank expression and he repeated himself.

"That won't be necessary Mr. Todd, we'll sleep in the carriage."

"Why Miss Bethany! We can't sleep in the carriage! With no one to see that we don't, I mean that we, I mean, what will I tell Mrs. Todd?"

"I know what you mean, Mr. Todd. You won't have to tell Mrs. Todd anything. I can drive a team as well as you. We'll travel all night, take turns driving and sleeping. The horses will be homeward bound. I doubt if they need anyone to drive really. They will probably head straight for home once we are on the main road. They've made this trip many times with you haven't they?"

"Now I don't know, Miss Bethany. Being on the road at night might not be safe."

She gave him the kind of look women use when they have made up their minds. Being a married man, Todd understood.

A short time later they were on their way. Todd had been silent on the Shamrock lane, but as he turned the team onto the main road, he laughed. "Dang if you ain't yo' uncle's niece, Miss Bethany."

"What does that mean?" she asked, and then laughed. "Never mind, I know what you mean."

She had forced herself to come to Shamrock with suppressed fear, more than fear, with a deep, dark, haunting dread. She had found all of it waiting for her, but she had faced it, the horror, the loss, the waste of a family, her family. Now it was over—the dread and the fear. She had stood on the land once more, Quinn land. She could never forget the horrible tragedy, nor fill the empty hole in her life or Jonathan's, nor erase the scars, but she could live with all of it now, could walk the land and never look back. The manor was no more, but the land was. Jonathan had been right to hold onto it.

"Mr. Todd?"

"Yes, Miss Bethany?"

"Hand me the reins and get out your pencil and pad. I want to give you instructions for Shamrock." She took the double reins of the team and waited for Todd to get a writing tablet and pencil from his worn leather satchel. "Mr. Todd, I want that brick cottage torn down and every brick and timber of it hauled clear off the place. I want the ground where it stands plowed so grass will grow there. I don't want a trace of it left. Pay a fair price for the labor, and see it's done right. Next, I want a livable house built at Shamrock. Pick a nice site with lots of shade-trees somewhere distant from the ruins of the big house so that you can't see them, and so you don't have to pass them to get there. A simple farm house will do; three big bedrooms on one side of a wide dog trot, a big living room and kitchen on the other. I want the house built facing south with fourteen foot ceilings. I want wide verandas all the way across the front and the back connected by the dog trot for cooling in the summer. You ought to be able to cut all the timber needed right on Shamrock land. Sink a well on the site. Plan to situate the kitchen next to the well with a hand pump over a sink so no one will have to carry water from the well. Put a fireplace in every room but the kitchen. I want a big cook stove in the kitchen. Give the roof lots of overhang to cover the verandas and put wire screen on every window. Don't skimp on the windows. I want full length French windows. And screen in the dog trot, no, close it in with screen doors over French doors at both ends so they can stand open in the summer and draw in the breeze. And Mr. Todd, I want you to build a smaller cabin not too far back from the house for servants. It will need two bedrooms on one side and a kitchen and sitting room on the other with a dog trot in between like the big house. I guess they will both need outdoor sanitary facilities for the time being. Get the best craftsmen you can. I guess we'll need a barn as well. Put gutters around the house to collect water in a big cistern elevated off the ground so water can flow from it by gravity. Do the same with the barn. When the house is finished, I want it furnished with comfortable furniture and everything needed to make it a home right down to bedding, pots, china, glassware, window curtains, everything. You can get your wife to help pick out things. I want you to include a big toy box filled to make a young boy happy. Lastly, make sure there's a library of good books, novels, new American writers, and some children's books. In a few years young Ansel Quinn will be spending summers here. We don't want him turning into a Cuban or a Spaniard do we? He's a Mississippian by birthright, and he ought to know his roots are here.

"Mr. Todd, are you getting all this down?"

"Yes, ma'am."

"Good. Now after all of it's built, I want you to hire the most trustworthy, hard-working family on the place, black or white, to look after it, keep it clean and in repair. Give them double the land they work now at free rent and a mule and wagon and plow to work it."

Lawyer Todd looked over his notes. "Even with usein' the timber off the place, all this is still gonna cost a goodly amount. Have to bring the carpenters from Vicksburg, and the hardware and windows and that screen up from New Orleans, or more likely all the way down from St. Louis. It will likely take a timber cruiser and crew with an ox team months to mark the best trees, cut 'em and bring 'em up out of the woods. Then we have to get a sawmill put up on the place. The sawed lumber ought to cure at least a year. I figure it might take three or four years to get the place all finished. Ordering and getting all the furnishings and such up here could take a while too. The kind of house you talkin' about . . . well it's all gonna cost a pretty penny, Miss Bethany. Jonathan is gonna holler."

"Jonathan isn't to know, Mr. Todd. You get me estimates for everything. You'll have plenty of time to do that before I leave. I'll check them and make sure everything is included, and add twenty percent to the total for good measure. I'll make arrangements with the bank for a working account, and I'll pay you five percent of the total to see it's all done right. And, Mr. Todd, anything saved under the total estimate I'll split with you fifty-fifty, but don't let me catch you or the carpenters cutting materials or quality or shorting the laborers to show a savings. That would cost you the Quinn management account."

"Just as you say, Miss Bethany."

"Write me of the progress and bring a photographer out to take pictures during construction and when it's finished. Send all correspondence concerning this matter in plain envelopes addressed to me personally, not to J & Q Shipping. I don't want a word mentioned about this in the regular Shamrock reports you send to Jonathan. I don't want rumors about it in town either. This is my business and my money. It's not to be mixed with the Shamrock accounts. Have you got all this down?"

"Yes, ma'am."

All four of them, Bethany, Lawyer Todd, and the two horses were bone tired when they reached Vicksburg early in the afternoon.

Arabella and Luky were at the door full of questions about Shamrock, but were afraid of the answers.

Bethany waved them off. "Later. I'll tell you everything later. First, I want a hot bath and about two days' sleep." She walked toward the kitchen undressing as she went. The copper bath tub had been placed in the kitchen next to the stove several years ago because the old women were too frail to carry buckets of hot water to other rooms, much less up the stairs.

"I had running water put in for y'all and a gas water heater installed too. Now why don't you use it?"

"We like de running water fine, but 'dem heaters is dangerous. We heard tell one blowed de side out some lady's house in Jackson," Luky said.

"Like to kilt' her." Arabella added, "Them things is a menace, sho' 'nuff."

"'Sides, we too old to change over to all them new-fangled-thing-a-ma-jigs," Luky said with finality. "When yo' wants hot water, yo' got to turn 'dis nob, light de whatchamacallit with a match, turn de knob some mo' to light off de big burner. 'Den, WHOOF! Dat thing whomp out at you like it gonna set fire to ya. Scare me ever time I tried it." Arabella nodded in agreement. "This here big pot a' hot water we keep on da' stove will do jes' fine."

And so it did. Fresh and clean, Bethany slipped nude between soft cotton sheets in her old bedroom upstairs. With cool zephyrs flowing through an open window shaded by a huge oak, she slept soundly, waking only to eat the light supper Luky brought up to her.

"Laud! Look at you! Ladies ain't s'posed to sleep in de natural like dat. Ain't you got no shame?"

Bethany smiled.

"If you ain't acting like some of 'dem hussies Doctor Ted done snuck in here once't in a while."

It was Bethany's turn to raise an eyebrow. Then both women burst out laughing.

"Bless that man's sweet and fiery heart, Luky. I'm glad to hear it. He deserved a little diversion now and then."

"Diversion! Is dat what white folks calls it?"

"Luky," Bethany said laughing, "Go fuss at Arabella. I'm sleepy."

Bethany ate everything on the tray, drank a glass of milk and fell back onto the feather pillows for a full night's rest. She had freed the ghosts of Shamrock.

CHAPTER 19

Bethany swept down the gangway at Havana with a half dozen young men in trail carrying her packages, hand luggage and Mannela's valise.

"My partner is an extravagant woman," Jonathan said just as Bethany joined them. "How could you possibly have so much luggage?" He waved his hand toward a gaggle of young men falling over each other for the privilege of carrying her baggage.

"They're only being gentlemanly," Bethany said as she thanked them and waved good bye. "They're all too young to keep anyway. As for the baggage, half of it contains the latest fashions from New Orleans for Louisette. You haven't bought her any new dresses in ages. The rest are my same old clothes except for one or two things." She turned to Louisette, "In New Orleans I bought this new thing from Paris that you wear instead of a whole corset. It holds you in place," she indicated her bosom, "without being tied up from stem to stern in some torture device. It's called a brasieré."

Jonathan laughed, "For Pete's sake, Bee Bee."

"Anyway, I'm through traveling for awhile. I'm broke, so I hope business is good."

"Broke?"

"Yes. I have assumed a rather sizeable obligation."

"Obligation? What have you done now, Bee Bee?" Jonathan's frown was real this time. "Mannela, what has she done?"

"The lady did not confide in me, Captain. This is the first I have heard of it."

They left Jonathan grumbling to himself and settling things with the Spanish customs agent in the accepted way . . . with a bribe.

Bethany rarely did things in the accepted way. She disdained domesticity. "I don't abide the *busy fingers, empty mind* theory for women." She didn't like to cook, hated ladies socials and claimed she was not interested in marriage. She spent most of her time working, taking care of the kind of business details Jonathan tended to neglect. She could convince even the most reluctant shipping agents in Havana to transport their products on J & Q ships even where official Spanish policy forbade it. It was her idea to form a separate American company to operate between Havana, Puerto Rico, and America while keeping the original British J & Q Ltd. to trade between Nassau and the British, French, and Dutch islands of the Caribbean.

She was the only woman in Havana to have a sailboat of her own. Most Sundays she sailed it from Havana Yacht Club. At first, only a few Havana ladies were brave enough to flout male disapproval and go sailing with a female skipper. The Latin men were reluctant to subordinate their male superiority by accepting an invitation to sail with her, she never let them take the helm, but the young American men in Havana jumped at the chance. The Latins soon modified their code of chauvinism to allow a sail with the beautiful and daring young American *marinerita*, although the governing board of the Yacht Club refused to let her race in their regattas. The Spanish male ego would not risk defeat at the hands of a woman.

Properly attired in a long white dress, she played lawn tennis with a few American girls and a handful of Cuban ladies brave enough to throw aside Spanish custom that frowned on the participation of ladies in public sports. A short time later the daring game of mixed doubles was introduced at the club and caused a furor.

At bodegas it was customary for ladies to wait in their carriages under silk parasols while iced drinks of honey water, sherbets or fruit juices, sometimes laced with gin or rum, were brought out to them at curbside. Bethany raised eyebrows by preferring to have her whiskey inside with the men. She rarely went to such places alone, but she would if the mood suited her. Bethany's favorite watering hole was *La Piña de Plata*, The Silver Pineapple on Obispo. (Years later the name was changed to Floridita in an attempt to attract American Tourists. It would one day become Hemingway's favorite haunt.)

Last but not least, Bethany loved to spend free time with toddler Ansel. She had promised Louisette and herself that she would never be more than a loving 'aunt' to her baby. Only rarely did she drop her guard and allow a peek behind the curtain that hid a mother's heart. One day she looked up at Jonathan from the floor of the nursery where she was playing with Ansel and confessed, "These are my sweetest, happy sad times," handed the little boy to him and left the room with teary eyes.

Bethany sought diversions and quickly found them in the social life of Havana, accepting invitations to the theater, dinner, the opera, picnics, regattas, balls and parties. Some of Bethany's escorts were Latin, some American. The young Americans seemed immature to her, while the arrogant, formal bearing of the handsome young Latins bored her.

She found the functions at the Spanish governor's palace terribly dull, but she attended them to promote good relations between the Spanish authorities and J & Q Shipping. She often heard Spanish aristocrats talk of their self-assumed superiority over the Creoles. "All this talk of Cuban independence is futile," they would argue. "Cuba is the plum of the Caribbean, Spain's plum, and it shall remain so."

Restless, she refused proposals of marriage and refused less noble invitations from the more adventurous of her suitors . . . with rare and discreet exception.

She discovered Cuba's most popular sport, *pelea de gallos*. It was, of course, another of those places where *nice ladies* didn't go. Bethany asked a friend to take her. She would see for herself.

The crowd was at a fever pitch when they arrived. Skinny little men with beards, fat sweaty men smoking big cigars, handsome dons in expensive suits, a sea of straw hats and an assortment of perfumed, painted ladies packed the stands surrounding a low-walled, dirt-floored circular pit brightly illuminated under a low overcast of cigar smoke.

"My, what a charming crowd, Luis." Bethany had to shout for her escort to hear over the din of the mob. It was obvious to her that Luis Herrero was a well known patron of the sport. Late as they were, they were shown to a box seat, its tenants having been evicted by the management the moment Herrero arrived.

"Why are they all waving and shouting at one another across the ring? Look some are waving at me."

"They are placing bets on the birds of their choice."

"How much do they bet?"

"There's no limit, but one *monedas*, that's five dollars, is the minimum. A person can bet as many monedas as he wants, but he better have the money to pay his debts. These people are serious gamblers."

"I want to bet," she shouted.

"Of course," he answered and offered her a wad of bills. "No," Bethany answered. "I'll bet my own money."

"I insist," he said. "You are with me." She ignored him.

Down in the pit two trainers held their birds apart, encouraging them to peck at each other. One combatant was brown with iridescent green tail feathers. The other, slightly larger bird was as black as Chinese-lacquered ebony except for his fine, blood-red tail plumage.

"I like that chicken," Bethany said, indicating the brown one. "His green tail feathers match my dress."

Everywhere across the ring men were vying for Bethany's attention, yelling and signaling with combinations of upheld fingers and fists full of notes.

She picked out a fat one in a sweat stained linen suit, waved back at him, and pointed to her green tailed combatant. "Mi guerrero!" she shouted. He tipped his hat and gave her a wide grin without removing the stump of his cigar.

She was getting into the excitement of things now and accepted another bet from a man standing at the pit rail. He held up ten fingers. Bethany nodded agreement just as the trainers let the birds go.

They flew off the dirt floor at each other. At first, when blood began to fleck the ring, Bethany thought she might get sick. Then Luis leaned over and explained to her that by waving back at the two insistent little men across the ring, she had bet them fifty dollars apiece on the brown cock against their black one.

"Get up and fight, you chicken!" she screamed when her bird went down on its back, feet kicking, wings dusting the cockpit floor. He must have heard her. He got up, ran sideways into the cockpit wall, shook himself, coughed a little blood, and as if suddenly remembering what he was about, flew at the black bird with a vengeance, puncturing a neck vein with his razor sharp steel spur and putting him down for good.

During the course of the evening, Bethany bet like a veteran. She was ahead over four hundred dollars before she lost most of it on a richly feathered dandy which she later described as "a hell of a racing chicken."

Luis was impressed. "Three of the gamecocks you picked belonged to me," he said proudly. "You are a fine judge."

"And how many of yours made me money?" she asked.

"One," he smiled sheepishly.

"Are you coming down with something, Bee Bee?" Jonathan asked her the next morning, "You sound a little hoarse."

"No. I'm fine. I just yelled a lot last night at the cock fights," she said.

"Cock fights! Bethany, ladies don't go to cock fights."

"One did last night," she answered and kissed him on the cheek. "Bye! I have a tennis game this morning."

"My niece is the topic of all the loose tongues in Havana," Jonathan said to Louisette in bed one evening, "and I don't know what to do about it."

"What you say is true," Louisette said without allowing Jonathan to see her smile. "We Quinns must bear the burden of having a one-eyed, wild captain on the one hand and a green-eyed wild beauty on the other."

"Well?" said Jonathan, ignoring the part about the 'wild captain'.

"Well what?" Louisette replied uninterested.

"Well what am I to do?" he asked. "When she gets bored here she goes off alone to Vicksburg and won't tell me what she does there."

"Would you say that your niece is intelligent, willful, spirited, fascinating, exhilarating and sometimes outrageous?"

"Exactly."

"Can you tell me what you would change, anything which would not detract from all that you love about her?"

He thought about that a moment. "Only one thing. I wish she would find a man bold enough to be her husband."

"Well then, why worry about it? Let the town gossip. I happen to know that quite a few of the ladies admire her for her independence. True, the weak, petty majority despise her for that same reason as well as for the fact that men adore her. Now go to sleep."

The eighties had brought a time of relative peace, but as Cuba marched toward the twentieth century, nationalism regained strength. There was a flowing undercurrent of unrest that occasionally rippled the surface. One would see *CUBA LIBRE!* slashed in crude, bold letters across a village wall, and now and then in Havana itself. They were reminders that the old independence movement was still alive, a movement impatient for one more chance, a movement with a history of savage violence.

With theaters, graceful plazas, fine restaurants, an opera house, a race track, electric lights, streetcars and booming commerce, Havana was the most beautiful city in the Caribbean, and the wealthiest. J & Q prospered. It had enlarged its office staff to match its growth, but with the larger staff Bethany had less to do. She began to tire of Havana, the Yacht Club set, the dull aristocratic parties and the mostly supervisory work she found herself performing. Then there was her love life, or rather the lack of it. It was 1890. Bethany was twenty-six years old.

"Are you telling me I am an old maid, Uncle?"

"Yes! Why don't you do something about it? More than half the eligible men on this island as well as those in Vicksburg would ask to marry you if they thought they had half a chance; even though nine out of ten of 'em are probably scared to death of you."

"What a pity. So many boys, so few men."

They had the same conversation at least once a month. Bethany received the expected letter and packet of photographs from lawyer Todd. Things had not been the same in Vicksburg since Arabella and Luky had passed away, but the new house, cottage and barn at Shamrock had been finished. It had taken much longer than she had expected, and more money, but she could now reveal her Vicksburg surprise. Everything was finally ready, Ansel was six. It was time.

"Do you mean to tell me that all this time you have been visiting Shamrock instead of staying in Vicksburg?" Jonathan was looking at photographs of the house for the first time.

"Every stick of it is paid for. There's a room there waiting for Ansel with a toy box that would please any little boy. He can't just grow up here speaking Spanish and French and English with a strange, mixed accent, and then go away to some boarding school without at least a touch of his heritage, without knowing who he is—a Quinn, a Mississippi Quinn. I have planned this for a long time. He can spend summers at Shamrock, swim in the creek, climb trees, ride his own pony, get dirty as a little ragamuffin. It's what your grandfather and father would have wanted. You know that's true. How can he be the only Quinn heir and not know where he comes from, not know his home? He will be the fourth generation to grow up at Shamrock, at least during summers. The ghosts of Shamrock are all waiting to be freed by the return of Quinns to the land."

Jonathan had put Shamrock out of his mind. Now Bethany caused a conflict of memories. His boyhood came flooding back, the musty smell of the deep woods, the earthy odor of freshly plowed fields, the scent of summer rain. He remembered his first hunt in the chill of fall and the trips into Vicksburg, the candy store, watching the river boats from high atop the bluffs.

"Jonathan?" Louisette said. "JONATHAN!"

Jonathan returned to the present from his brief reverie of childhood. "Bee Bee, I don't know if my guilt and the ghosts will ever let me go back there."

"You can go home, Jonathan." Bethany answered. "In the ruins I faced the horror of my childhood nightmare. I know now that it was real, but it's over. All of it is over. Shamrock is begging us to accept that. It's time Quinns walked the land again to free it from the darkness of that terrible day. Take the Shamrock bowl out of the attic, Jonathan. Take the bowl and Ansel home."

Jonathan stood silently for a moment, Louisette looking up at him anxiously, Bethany holding her breath.

"All right, Bee Bee," he said. "I'll try for the boy." He swept Ansel up off the floor where he had been playing. "You want to go see Shamrock, son?"

"Can we go on a boat, Daddy, and ride a train, and see cowboys?"

"Sure we can. You can be a cowboy if you want." Jonathan noticed the worried look on his wife's face. He put his arm around her. "You will like the country there in the spring, Louisette. It's beautiful. The dogwood will be in bloom." He turned to Bethany, "How many bedrooms did you say, Bee Bee?"

"Three!" she cried, "When can we leave?"

Ansel Quinn would grow up spending his summers at Shamrock with "Aunt Bee Bee." Bethany would judge the passage of summers more by Ansel's age than by the calendar.

His would be an interesting generation. In his second summer at Shamrock, 1891, Ansel turned seven. So did Mussolini and Yamamoto. Eddie Rickenbacker, Dwight Eisenhower, Adolf Hitler, and Erwin Rommel were all one year of age. George Patton was five, Hideki Tojo, six. Franklin Roosevelt was eight, Stalin and Douglas MacArthur, eleven, Albert Einstein, twelve, Winston Churchill, sixteen.

Once she was satisfied that Ansel would be safe at Shamrock with Bethany, Louisette was happy to have Jonathan all to herself for most of the summer every year. The couple would sometimes sneak away to Paris. They never stopped being lovers.

On a November day in Havana, a gentleman walked into J & Q Marine Hardware and placed a large order: coils of rope, kegs of nails, a dozen machetes, bolts of canvas, rolls of wire fencing, hand tools and various other supplies. Bethany noticed him through her open office door. While a clerk totaled his purchases, she walked over and introduced herself, and as a pretense for her boldness, explained to him that her family appreciated his business.

He bowed graciously. Speaking English as fluently as Bethany spoke Spanish, he said, "You must be the Señorita Quinn of whom I have heard so much. Even in the countryside there is talk of your beauty."

Before she could respond, or even blush, he continued, "May I introduce myself. Antonio Alverez, your humble servant."

He was, she judged, maybe thirty-five. He had dark hair, but light, gray-blue eyes, unusual for a Spaniard. She remembered reading somewhere that the ancient Visigoths of Spain were blond and blue eyed. He was tall, about five eleven. His fair skin was sun tanned.

Damnit! Look at those eyes; confident, but with a trace of sadness. Why am I a sucker for that look? Henri had it. Once burned I should know better.

Alverez signed the bill, nodded politely, and turned to leave. He stopped, as if he had forgotten something, walked back to Bethany and asked, "Would it be too forward of me, that is, would it offend the Señorita if I asked her to consider having dinner with a stranger? I shall of course ask your uncle for his permission."

"You do not have to ask my uncle's permission. I make my own decisions about such matters. Would that offend the Señor?"

"I have heard that American women are sometimes independent minded and that Captain Quinn's niece is independent as a rule."

She looked up sharply, only to see a warm smile on his face. "You may call at nine o'clock, Señor, at Captain Quinn's home on Obispo," Bethany replied, more to answer a challenge than to accept an invitation.

"I shall be there, Señorita," he replied.

"Do you mean you just accepted an invitation from a stranger, someone to whom you had not even been introduced?" Jonathan asked incredulously. "What's wrong with all the men you've properly met? What is this man's name?"

"He's a good customer of ours, a Señor Antonio Alverez."

"Tony Alverez?" he responded. "Well, yes, I know him, met with him this morning. He, ah . . . He doesn't get to Havana often." With a perplexed look on his face, Jonathan started to speak, thought better of it, and walked out of the room.

Now what was that all about? Bethany wondered.

Señor Alverez arrived promptly at nine. He had no carriage. They walked. Alverez was plainly dressed like a man of modest means. She noticed with amusement that he wore his wide brimmed hat rather low on his forehead, shading his face.

"Would you mind dining at a little neighborhood café here in old Havana? It's not far. I promise the food will be excellent."

Bethany, deducing the man may not be able to afford the more expensive dining establishments, thought it refreshing to find a Latin willing to be honest about his circumstances.

"I'm sure that will be charming, Señor," she replied.

She had never noticed the neighborhood café with its plain facade and small sign over the door. The proprietor smiled when Antonio entered, and came toward him clearly indicating recognition. Alverez nodded his head almost imperceptibly and the man stopped. He formally welcomed them as he would any other customer and asked the name.

"Alverez." Antonio responded.

The proprietor replied, "Ah yes, Senior. Your reserved table is upstairs." He motioned to a waiter standing at the foot of the staircase.

Bethany hadn't missed the act of non-recognition between the two men, but said nothing as they were led to a private dining room on the second floor. All was very proper. Bethany was seated at one end of a small dining table, Señor Alverez at the other. The waiter stood discretely in the corner of the room when his services were not required. The food was marvelous, the wine, Spanish and very good, the conversation, witty and warm. As the evening drew to a close, Bethany realized that Alverez had somehow managed to coax her into telling a great deal about herself without revealing a morsel of information about himself other than that he lived over a hundred miles down the island on his family's plantation.

"Perhaps the Señorita might consider visiting the country, with your chaperone, of course. I can offer you beautiful mountain scenery, and if you enjoy riding, your choice of the finest horses in Cuba."

"I do not have a chaperon, Señor. I am too old for that, but I do have a companion that has been with me for many years," she said. "Do you always issue so many invitations to ladies you have just met?"

"I rarely issue invitations at all," he replied.

"I just might accept, Señor. Yes," she answered, "I've grown bored with Havana. We Quinns have an interest in a farm somewhere in your area. It will give me a chance to see it. Are you sure my companion and I will not distract you from work."

"There is not a man alive you would not distract, Señorita," he smiled. "I will write down directions, what train to catch, where to get off. Simply telegraph my billing address giving your expected day of arrival." He asked the waiter to bring him pen, ink and paper.

"You are a mysterious man, Señor Alverez. The proprietor obviously knows you, but you wanted to keep that a secret. My uncle looked very strange when I told him your name."

"Really?"

"Yes, but he said nothing, absolutely nothing. He allowed me to go out with you without an argument, so he must consider you a gentleman. I'm independent, but I rarely defy my adorable, one-eyed, half-eared uncle."

Alverez laughed out loud. "I will remember that charming description. Many men I have known might agree with the one-eyed, half-eared part, but few would think him adorable, although everyone would apply the word in describing his niece."

"You and my uncle know each other, that is clear," she said, ignoring his compliment, "and obviously there is a great deal neither of you is telling me."

"To you, Señorita," he raised his glass. "You have turned this humble dinner into a most memorable feast."

"And you are changing the subject again," she said.

He smiled and motioned the waiter for the check.

As they walked from the restaurant, he again pulled his wide-brimmed hat low over his eyes. He said very little until he was at her door step.

"I hope to see you in the country, Señorita. I can not," he stopped and corrected himself, "I do not get to Havana very often, I'm afraid, but tonight . . . well, it has been one of the most pleasant and enjoyable evenings I have had in a long, long time." He bowed, kissed her hand and having done so, held it in his for a long moment while he looked silently into her receptive eyes. "Buenos Noches, Señorita, hasta la proxima vez."

He waited on the steps until she was safely inside. No carriage, no fancy clothes, he blended into the foot traffic along the street and disappeared into the night.

"All right, uncle, I want you to tell me about the mysterious Tony Alverez."

"What did he tell you?"

"Absolutely nothing. It was easy to see that you two know one another."

"So?"

"So quit being so obstinate! It is infuriating. You allow me to go out with someone quite mysterious, someone you know all about, and neither of you will tell me a thing. He didn't even want to be recognized. He kept his hat over his face. Who is he hiding from, or was he ashamed to be seen with me?"

"He has reasons, believe me. And as for you, there's not a man alive who would be ashamed to be seen in your company. He's a gentleman I'd trust with my life. Beyond that, if you want to know more, you will have to ask him."

"That's exactly what I intend to do."

"Bee Bee, Darling, you may not like all you find."

"Then why don't you tell me."

"Because I trust him to tell you in his own time. It won't be easy for him. Very little has been easy in his life. God knows you both need something in your lives besides work . . . but the two of you? I don't know."

Bethany had rarely seen Jonathan so tender and concerned. That in itself was a warning.

The train puffed and jerked its way east southeastward across the plains toward the Sierra de Escambray mountains. It was hot and sticky in the first-class coach, an old American rail car hitched behind another car crowded with farm laborers, itinerant merchants, a scattering of wives and children, chickens and goats. The two passenger cars were coupled at the end of a string of freight wagons. Soot and the acrid odor of smoke from the locomotive filtered in through the open windows. The view was of flat land planted to the horizon with sugarcane. They stopped at villages, remote sidings and occasionally in the middle of nowhere to let off passengers or pick up little groups of field workers for passage to the next village down the line. The trip seemed endless.

What am I doing? I meet a man for dinner a month ago, a perfect stranger, and now I am traveling on this miserable train to God knows where to see him again. Maybe what Louisette says in jest is true . . . all Quinns are crazy.

The sun was low on the horizon when they reached the station at Cienfuegos, a town beside a bay of the same name on the southern coast of Cuba.

He was dressed in khaki riding britches, white open-collared shirt, polished boots and a wide-brimmed white Panama hat. Tony Alverez helped Bethany and Mannela down from the high iron steps of the rail car.

"Señorita Quinn, let me guess. The trip was impossibly long, hot, and generally miserable."

"Why Señor Alverez, you took the words right out of my mouth, but here we are at last."

"You are here, but you are not quite there," he answered. "We still have a way to go, but I hope you will find the trials and tribulations of your journey sufficiently rewarded."

His driver carried Bethany's and Mannela's trunks to the rear of the carriage and secured them on the boot.

"The breeze from the bay is a reward, Señor."

"You will find our little compound at the foot of the mountains more pleasant still, Señorita." Alverez helped the women into the carriage. "I hope you will excuse the worn upholstery and aging finish. This carriage is about all of the finery left from the old days before the soldiers of the Crown burned our hacienda. We do not get much opportunity to use it, but Alonzo cleaned and polished it as well as he could in anticipation of your arrival."

The carriage, Bethany noticed, was hitched to a perfectly matched pair of chestnut geldings. "Were there any plantations that weren't burned?"

"Very few," Alverez answered.

"It was the same back home in Mississippi," she said and grew silent.

They arrived well after dark at a large house with wide galleries all around. It was plain, but well built with large rooms, high ceilings, and comfortable furniture. Two servants met them at the door.

"I know how tired you both must be," their host said. "Señora Wombi, Anita here will show you to your room. You will find a hot bath all ready, and I will have supper sent to you if that arrangement is satisfactory."

"That will be most kind of you, Señor Alverez," Mannela answered.

"Señorita Quinn," he turned to Bethany, "Maria here will take you to your room to the right at the top of the stairs where a hot bath is also waiting. I think you will find everything you need. Your supper can be sent up to your room, or if you prefer, you may take it in the dining room where I would be honored to join you."

"Señor Alverez, I'm absolutely bone tired. I'll be much better company tomorrow."

"In that case, perhaps you will join me for a late breakfast in the morning, say nine o'clock."

"That would be wonderful," Bethany replied.

"Until tomorrow, then."

Bethany soaked in a huge copper bathtub filled to the brim with steaming water scented with perfume. It was welcomed luxury. The room was plain, clean and neat. The furniture was masculine, made from dark polished wood. The large bed had a canopy from which mosquito netting was draped. The walls were bare except for an oval framed mirror hung on the wall over a wash stand. It was, she happily concluded, a totally masculine room. No woman's influence was evident.

She stepped out of the bath feeling clean and cool, put on a light cotton nightgown and sat down to a delightful meal brought up to her by Maria.

A full tummy and a soft bed—Heaven. Bethany parted the mosquito netting and slipped between the clean sheets. The window curtains swayed lightly in a gentle evening breeze. Compared to the noise of Havana, the night-chirping of crickets and katydids was a soothing serenade. *It sounds like Shamrock*, Bethany mused before falling asleep.

Breakfast was served on a small, shaded patio surrounded by flowering plants, Begonias, Jacarandas and Mariposas, which Bethany knew as Butterfly Jasmine, and flowering trees the names of which she had no idea. It was a beautiful setting, but her host proved as evasive of her questions as ever.

"Would you care to ride in the foot hills?" he suggested. "We could carry a picnic lunch, and," he smiled, "perhaps there I will have gathered enough courage to make a confession, or at least satisfy some of your curiosity."

"Confession?" Bethany asked. "That sounds serious."

"I owe you that. And later, if you don't decide to shoot me," he smiled, "there is much here I would like to show you."

"So far," she said, looking straight at him, "I have shot only one man."

It was his turn to look surprised. The way she had said it left little doubt that she had, in fact, done it.

"That was a delightful breakfast, Señor Alverez," Bethany said, "but if we are going riding I had better dress for it. Oh," she added, "please, no sidesaddle for me."

When she reappeared on the patio she was dressed in black twill riding pants, a white, long sleeve silk blouse, black English leather boots and gloves, and a black, low crowned, wide-brimmed hat with chin strap. Her long raven hair was combed back and tied with a ribbon. A black leather riding crop hung by its strap from her wrist.

"Bravo!" he said.

Bethany laughed. She could see that he was both surprised at her attire, and sincere in his compliment.

"Alonzo!" he called. "Bring the horses."

Alonzo and a stable boy returned leading four Spanish Barbs, the beautiful and coveted Spanish-Arabian breed. One, a stallion, was solid black. He pranced nervously, tugging at his lead and tossing his head. The second was a chestnut filly with white stockings. The third was a beautiful dappled-gray mare, and the fourth, a snow white gelding.

"They are the most beautiful horses I have ever seen," Bethany said, speaking Spanish. "I'll take the black one."

"Ayeee! Aye! Aye!" Alonzo cried.

Her host stepped forward. "I should have said you may choose any but the black. He is my horse. I would, of course, let you ride him only he is a little spirited. In order for me to get on him, Alonzo has to hold him tight, pull his head down and bite his ear. Once I am on him, he is a noble beast, but unless you have someone bite his ear very hard, he will not stand still and allow anyone to get on him."

Bethany walked to the stallion. He flared his nostrils and lowered his ears. She spoke to the animal in low tones, took off a glove, and stroked his muzzle with her hand. The stallion sniffed her scent, then moved his nose against her hand.

Bethany looked at Alverez and smiled. "Alonzo, bite his ear if you must. I intend to ride him," she said.

Alonzo looked at his jefe. Alverez shrugged his shoulders. Alonzo tugged on the bridle with both hands. The horse was not cooperative. He tramped in a circle around Alonzo. The stocky little groomsman was tenacious. With great difficulty he pulled the horse's tossing head down to where he could get hold of an ear and bit down on it hard. The horse stood perfectly still. Bethany laughed at the ridiculous scene. Without waiting for assistance, she quickly lifted her leg to put her foot in the stirrup, grabbed a hand full of the horse's mane, and pulled herself up into the saddle.

Alonzo relaxed his bite on the horse's ear and quickly stepped back. The animal pranced skittishly, hopped a time or two, kicked out in Alverez's direction, and tried to bite Alonzo.

"What is his name, Alonzo?" Bethany asked.

"Diablo Negro," was the reply. "He is a black devil, Señorita. Please be careful."

"Diablo," she said, "Easy boy. Easy."

Perhaps it was the novelty of a woman's voice, or the small amount of weight he felt in the saddle, or the light, but firm touch on the reins, or perhaps his stallion instinct told him of the presence of the feminine gender. For whatever reason, and to the amazement of the men standing by with anxious expressions on their faces, Diablo settled down and behaved himself.

"Madre de Dios!" said Alonzo, "She has made a saint of him." Alverez laughed out loud, saluted Bethany, and climbed onto the dappled gray barb. They rode side by side down a road that led past row upon row of flashing, silver-green, young cane stalks stretching to the horizon. Every field hand they passed took off his hat as the owner and the lady rode by. They were not only surprised to see a lady with their Don, but to see one riding *that crazy, damn, black horse of his.*

Diablo tried several times to take the bit, gain his head and charge off in a run. Each time, his fleet-footed, head-tossing shenanigans were rewarded by a sharp whack from the lead-weighted handle of Bethany's riding crop applied firmly between his ears. With such lessons in manners, he settled down and gave no further trouble.

"I think you have ruined my horse," Alverez observed, smiling. "He has never allowed anyone but me to ride him, and he has never acted so docile in his life."

"Perhaps that's because you have always made riding him a contest between yourself and Diablo. I think it is probably a game enjoyed by both of you. I've simply showed him it's not polite to play games with a Southern lady."

"That is precisely why we are having this picnic."

"Oh," Bethany replied, "I thought we were having a picnic because I am a beautiful and desirable woman and you wanted the pleasure of my company all to yourself."

"No wonder you frighten the young men away as your uncle has told me."

"My uncle has discussed his niece with you? I think Diablo is not the only one who has tried to play games with this lady. You did notice how I put a stop to such attempts did you not, Señor Alverez?"

"Oh, yes, Señorita Quinn. I can only hope you realize my poor skull is not as thick as Diablo's."

"My uncle is also in trouble. The idea of discussing me with his friends. Speaking of that, he has a plantation somewhere near here with a partner, Don Felipe de Alacon. He has tried for years to get me to make that miserable train trip to see it, but it was your invitation that persuaded me to travel all the way here. Do you know the place and Don Felipe? I suppose I should try to actually meet him and see the place while I'm in the area."

"Yes. I do know of this man, Alacon," he replied, "but we can talk of him later. For the moment just look around you."

They were on top of a bald hill covered with wild flowers. The blue sky was hung with fluffy clouds as if painted by an artist's brush. To the east, the terrain stepped upward toward the 3,000 foot peaks of the Escambray Mountains. Southward, Bethany could see the cultivated land of the valley, and in the distance, the Bahia de Cienfuegos. "It is a lovely place, Señor Alverez. The vista from here is breathtaking."

Alverez dismounted, placed hobbles on both horses and helped Bethany down. "Please call me Antonio."

"All right, Antonio, if you will call me Bethany." After a moment she asked, "Aren't you hungry, Antonio? If you will spread the picnic cloth, I'll set out the food."

Antonio took the picnic paraphernalia from the saddlebags. He handed three wrapped packages to Bethany, spread the picnic cloth on the grass and opened a bottle of wine. They sat down facing one another.

"It's so much cooler here in the hills," Bethany remarked while unwrapping the fresh fruit, cheese, and bread that had been prepared for the picnic.

"It's cooler because we are almost a thousand feet high," Antonio replied. "Still, it is sunny out here in the field. Perhaps you would rather we ate over in the trees where there is shade."

"Oh no! I want to sit right here in the middle of all these wild flowers. It's the kind of place I loved as a little girl. I used to ride my pony up on the bluffs of Vicksburg, stand in a field of wild flowers like this, and look out across the river to Louisiana."

"You mean as a little girl you were allowed to go riding alone?"

"Riding, hiking, anything I wanted. I was quite a tomboy I guess, but there was really no danger. No one in Vicksburg would hurt a child, and I really didn't go far. I thought I was very daring, but my guardian and my nanny always had a pretty good idea of where I was."

"Wonderful," he said.

"What is wonderful?"

"Americans, children, and you. You are wonderful. I just hope you are also forgiving."

"There you go again, being mysterious. Now pass that loaf of bread, pour the wine, and tell me whatever in the world is this big secret of yours."

"We eat first," Antonio said. When they had finished eating, Bethany held out her empty glass. Antonio refilled it.

"Antonio," she said, "tell me about Señor Alacon and the plantation he has with my uncle."

"It is a long story."

"I'm in no hurry," Bethany answered, and took a sip of wine. "Since you and your uncle are partners with this Alacon, I suppose we should start at the beginning."

"As long as the wine holds out," Bethany smiled.

Tony began the story. "Felipe Alacon's father was from an old aristocratic family in Spain. As the youngest son, he chose to seek his fortune in the new world, Cuba to be exact. Through his family's connections to the Crown, he obtained a minor bureaucratic position in Havana. At first he held the typical Spanish attitude that Spanish Creoles, peasants and slaves were here merely to serve and enrich Spain. Out of boredom, perhaps curiosity, he began to travel the length and breadth of Cuba. What he saw was a wonderful land full of hard-working people. He also saw the frustration of the Spanish Creoles brought about by tariffs, taxes and the corruption of many Spanish bureaucrats. The senior Alacon began to change his attitude. He was Spanish, an aristocrat, and part of the ruling bureaucracy, but he was not corrupt. He found he did not like, nor agree with the way Spain and her minions governed Cuba.

"With his savings, money borrowed from his family and the blessing of the Crown, he obtained a thousand or so acres of land. In spite of his aristocratic origins he did not sit around watching others work. He learned about sugar, processing and markets. Early on, this proud Spaniard learned first-hand the frustration of the Creole landowners. America wanted sugar and was willing to pay for it, but Spain held a monopoly on trade. One sold only to Spain or not at all. Spain, of course, profited by reselling Cuban sugar to the world. Tariffs, taxes and payoffs to bureaucrats narrowed his profits. Even so, he began to prosper. With hard work the estate grew to over five thousand acres.

"A marriage to a young lady in Spain was arranged by his family. The couple had a son, Felipe, the Alacon who is your uncle's partner. Because he was born in Cuba instead of Spain, he was labeled a Creole. Felipe was sent to school in Spain where he learned from Spanish boys that being a Creole meant being second class. Unhappy and longing for his home in Cuba, Felipe was allowed to return at age fifteen to spend a year at home before going on to university in Madrid. At least that was the plan, but The Ten Years War interfered. Céspedes, Maceo, Gómez and Garcia became the leaders of an army raised from the countryside. It was made up of men proud to be called Cubans, not Spaniards. At first the Spanish garrisons made fun of the rag-tag, Creole army, but the Cubans gradually took control of the eastern half of the island."

"Yes," said Bethany, "my uncle has told me all about it. I suspect I know more than you would guess."

"No," Antonio said. "I know you are privy to your uncle's role in that conflict, and I would not say a word now except you are his niece and partner."

"Since you obviously know so much" she added, "then you know J & Q made no small amount of profit from its, well, shall we say, 'special cargo' business."

"He and Captain Jones earned it. They supplied the revolution when few would take the risk. The American government supported Spain. Your uncle was very courageous and often risked his life. Had he been caught by Spain, he would have died a very unpleasant death. Had he been caught by his own country, he would have been imprisoned. Had any Cuban nationalist betrayed him to Spain or America, he would not be allowed in Cuba today to operate his ships or conduct any business here. Yet he lives in the middle of Royalist Havana, a brave and clever man."

"But I have taken you away from the story of the Alacons," Bethany said.

"Ah, yes, the Alacons. The war turned more than nasty. After five years the senior Alacon, to remove his young son from the conflict, sent him to Madrid to conclude a marriage arranged with the daughter of a wealthy family with strong ties to the Crown. Felipe obeyed his family's wishes. It is the way with Spain. The girl was pleasant enough at first. Then, against the protests of both families, he brought his bride back to Cuba. Those were difficult times. The revolutionaries burned plantations and destroyed mills to deny profits to the Royalists and to Spain. The Royalists burned the plantations of those they suspected of helping revolutionaries and often imprisoned or killed the owners. The Alacons were already suspect. Don Alacon had freed his slaves. As a result, his workers were fiercely loyal to him. Worker loyalty was something Royalist planters no longer enjoyed. When Felipe and his bride landed in Santiago, he found that his father and mother were dead. The plantation lay in ruins."

"What did he do? What of his poor bride?"

"The governor gravely told Felipe that it was the revolutionaries who killed his father and mother. Felipe was not persuaded by such lies, but he loudly professed his outrage at the rebels and his loyalty to the Crown. He fought liars with lies. He was afraid to confide in his wife for her family in Spain was close to the Crown. He put her in an apartment in Havana and told her he must try to rebuild the plantation. He supplied food to Maceo and hid arms and ammunition on his land. When he traveled to Havana to see his wife, he complained to the Royalists about the lack of protection in the countryside for loyal planters like himself, all the while obtaining information of value to the Cuban revolutionaries. He quickly became more useful to the revolution in Havana than in the countryside. That is where he became friends with your uncle who, in those days, was recklessly bold, some said crazy. He would sail into Havana Harbor to trade ordinary goods, set sail for some other Caribbean island, double back under darkness, sneak inshore to some beach and deliver arms to the Cubans. Felipe became your uncle's contact in Havana responsible for coordinating every arms rendezvous. When the rebels began to run out of money, Felipe offered to trade half his land in return for a set value in arms. Your uncle was the only one who would accept the offer. He had already done much more for the cause than he had been paid to do. He sent a small schooner to Tampa many times at his own expense to pick up medicine, food and money raised for the rebels. I bet you did not know about that."

"No. I never knew a J & Q ship to sail without a profit," she laughed.

He laughed too. "Yes, that is your uncle. Makes it all the more remarkable, but that was not the end of his generosity," Alverez continued. "After the truce, after the Crown had been fought to a draw, nothing changed. Spain ruled as it always had done. The people in the countryside were desperate after ten years of war. Your uncle transported food and seed and Alacon distributed it to many Cubans. Felipe, with your uncle as a silent partner, had a 5,000-acre plantation to rebuild, but no money with which to rebuild it. Your Uncle helped."

"But why did Felipe need my uncle's aid? His wife's family in Spain was wealthy. She could have helped him."

"His wife? She was young and spoiled, but she had given him children, two daughters. Alacon worshiped the little girls. He knew the years in Cuba had been hard on his wife, but he was sure when things got better that she would learn to love it as he did."

"And?" Bethany asked.

"He was wrong. Felipe made the mistake of telling her of his dreams for a free Cuba and of his role in the Ten Years War. Why not? She was his wife. It was safe to tell her after the Pact of Zanjon ended the fighting. Surely she would understand, even be proud of him."

"What happened?"

"As it turned out," Antonio continued, "Felipe did not know his wife at all. She was outraged to learn of what she called her husband's 'deceitful and traitorous acts against the Royalists'. She told him she was finished with Cuba, that she would no longer allow a revolucionario into her bed. He had deceived her. He had deceived Spain, and by doing so, had deceived the Church. She was going home. She said she would tell their families how he had betrayed their trust, their honor, and Spain. 'You have disgraced us all,' she screamed at him."

"Did she do all that?"

Her host focused on the horizon. "Oh, yes. Before her departure for Spain she told the Governor of her husband's activities and placed herself under his protection while arranging transport to Spain for her daughters, herself and her household goods. As a result, in spite of the Pact of Zanjon, an attempt was made to imprison Felipe on a charge of treason. They claimed he did not qualify for amnesty under the Pact because his signature was not among those of former rebels who agreed to lay down their arms. He didn't deserve to be treated as a soldier. He was a spy and a traitor. He would have been quietly hanged in Castillo del Morro had he not fled Havana."

"But that was over ten years ago. Surely all that is behind him now," said Bethany.

"Several attempts have been made on his life, and to this day he is definitely a *persona non grata* to the Royalists in Havana. He was no peasant revolutionary. He was one of them and therefore is reserved for special hatred. They consider him a threat. They know it is not over."

"What of his little daughters?"

"His wife said he would never be allowed to see them. She convinced both families that her husband had betrayed them, had betrayed the Crown, had followed a Black man named Maceo against the Royalists, had disgraced them all. Both families immediately disinherited the wayward Felipe lest the Crown think they, in some way, might have supported him in his treason. They also made one other act of attrition lest the considerable power of the Spanish Catholic Church be used against them. At the request of both families, the Crown called upon the Pope to excommunicate him."

"My God! Does association with Alacon endanger Jonathan?" Bethany asked, suddenly concerned for her uncle.

"Felipe is safe in the countryside. His enemies in Havana will not venture into this part of Cuba to find him. The people here are loyal to him and to Cuba. As for your uncle, he is not officially associated with Alacon. The books you keep refer to the plantation as a J & Q enterprise does it not? It is legal for Americans to invest here since the Pact of Zanjon. It was a reward to your United States for its support of Spain against the rebels. The Alacon land, all 5,000 acres of it, was recorded as having been sold to your uncle in '84. It was considered a common business transaction. It was widely rumored that Alacon took the money and went into exile. Incidentally, there was no money, at least for the sale. After the war, Alacon had no money to rebuild. Your uncle invested considerable funds to rebuild and put the land back into production. In Havana, your distinguished uncle is a respected Yankee trader who by his commerce in sugar adds to the coffers of Havana and therefore of Spain. Not only that, but he enriches the pockets of more than a few bureaucrats in order to make his business less complicated as is the custom. Your uncle and Alacon are partners by private agreement."

"But how do you know all of this?" Bethany asked.

"It is all part of the confession of a selfish and unforgivable deception caused by a man's fascination with a spirited and beautiful lady who may shoot a second man."

"Now, Antonio, why don't you just tell me what you're trying to say."

He took a deep breath, a long swallow of wine and looked directly into Bethany's eyes. "There is no Antonio Alverez. I am Felipe Alacon."

Bethany could not speak. She stood up and turned her back to him. Then she turned around and faced Felipe who was also on his feet. "You're right, I may shoot a second man."

"The man would not blame you. In fact, from the look on your face, I think he is fortunate the lady is not armed."

"There you are wrong, Señor Alacon. This lady is always armed. Before I shoot you, why don't you tell me why, when we were in Havana, I could not be trusted to keep your secret."

"It was not a matter of trust."

"Then why?"

"Because you would not have come. You knew from your uncle that Alacon was married. After seeing you for the first time, after our dinner together, I was afraid to tell you, afraid you would not see me again. Here I could muster the courage to tell you everything. I foolishly hoped that you . . ."

"You were right. I would not have come. You are married."

"Yes. Divorce is unheard of among the old families in Spain. It is not allowed, either by the church or by Spanish law, which in this case, is the same."

"You could have appealed for an annulment. After all your wife is married to an excommunicate, isn't she? I would think she would want an annulment."

"Never. In the eyes of the Church and Spain it would make bastards of my children."

"And you are telling me that you are the poor, lonely, noble Don Alacon who has had no one in his bed for what, ten years? And now I suddenly awaken him the minute he sees me?" Bethany was furious.

"There have been women in my bed. It is true. But—"

"But what? A man must have his fun? Am I any different from the others?"

"I knew I was in trouble the first minute I laid eyes on you, that no matter what I did, it would be wrong. But you share some blame as well," Felipe said.

"I share blame?"

"You spoke to me with those eyes of yours. Tell me it is not true . . . if you can."

In spite of her anger, Bethany could not look him in the eye and deny it. "So, to satisfy your own, what? Lust? You used a false name, took me to dinner, invited me here all because you could see that I was indeed intrigued by the mysterious and gallant Señor Antonio Alverez? You have made a fool of me." She threw her glass of wine in his face, turned, and started for the horses.

"Wait! Please! Where are you going?" he pleaded.

"To race the wind. Diablo might try to kill me, but he is too noble an animal to make a fool of me."

Felipe caught her arm, spun her around, and kissed her until her tight resisting lips softened and her arms stopped pushing him away.

"You said you are armed," he said, "then shoot me if you like." He released her and stepped back. "I was wrong to bring you here. I have no right to your company. I have no right to even ask you to forgive me, but I beg you to do so." Bethany would not look at him, did not speak. "I will take you back and arrange for your return to Havana." He started to turn, but paused and added, "I am not sorry I kissed you."

She looked at him. Felipe lowered his sad, blue-gray eyes and walked back to gather up the picnic basket and the hat he had carelessly tossed onto the grass when they arrived. It was, she knew, a scene she had lived before with a man named Henri. *Damn lonely, sad-eyed men.*

He was on his knees gathering the silver and china into the basket when Bethany walked up from behind and sat down beside him. "To be honest, Felipe Alacon, I, not you, made a fool of me. You angered me because I didn't want to know the truth. You walked into the store and spoke to me with those blue-gray eyes of yours. And, yes, damnit, I answered back with mine. That's why I'm here, isn't it? I wanted to spend a week with Antonio Alverez."

She put her arms around his neck, kissed him, and stood up. "No more talk. I want to go."

They stood up and walked to the horses. Felipe held Diablo's reins at the bit with both hands while Bethany patted his neck and spoke to him before attempting to mount.

Surprisingly, the stallion stood perfectly still and let her swing up into the saddle.

"I was right," Felipe said, "you have ruined my horse."

"For you he will be the same old Diablo," she answered. "It's just that, like another scoundrel I know, he prefers to be charming when in the company of ladies."

"Perhaps he knows you are armed," he said. "By the way, where do you hide the weapon, if I may ask?"

"You may not," she responded. "If you are very lucky, you may find out for yourself. On the other hand," she continued, "if you are unlucky, you may find out from me. I suppose it depends on how naughty you are."

"I shall be good as gold," Felipe replied.

Bethany laughed, "In that case, you may never find out at all." Once they reached the road, Bethany cried out, "Race you to the house." She gave Diablo the free rein he had been fighting for and beat Felipe by six lengths.

After a bath and late siesta, Bethany dressed for dinner. She wore a delicate black lace dress over flesh tone silk. Her hair was held high on her head with silver combs. Raven ringlets fell about her ears. The dress had a 'V' neckline covered by sheer black netting that ended at her throat in a black lace collar. She sat at one end of the table, he at the other. They ate quietly with little conversation. He did not speak for fear of offending her. She did not speak for fear of being too bold. She caught him looking at her.

"Your eyes could capture the devil himself," he confessed. Bethany ignored the comment. "Since this is my last night in the country, what does one do for evening entertainment? I don't think we should be alone under the circumstances, especially since Mannela retired early this evening."

"Ah! You will be surprised to learn that I had planned entertainment for your stay here. Tonight, if you like, we can *go native*, as you Americans say. A little unsophisticated for an American lady, but you might find it amusing."

"Go on. Let's hear the rest."

"There is a little building about a mile down the road. I could say it was a meeting hall, but it is really the local bodega."

"What a charming idea," Bethany answered.

At Bethany's suggestion, they walked. As they neared, they could hear voices and laughter drifting on the still night air. A single oil lantern leaked little ladders of light through louver-shuttered windows while from the open door, a broad, yellow beam spilled out across the porch to the dirt road.

"Buenos Noches, Don Alacon. Welcome Señorita," said a plump, gray-headed woman from behind a bar crudely made of wooden planks. There were almost a dozen people in the room, some sitting at tables, others standing along the bar. Some were white, some black, some in between. They all grew quiet and turned to look at the jefe and the lady.

"Come, sit here, Don Alacon," a cocoa skinned Cuban said as he got up from a table at a window near the door. "You will get a little breeze here." The man moved to the bar.

"Muchas Gracias, Jésus," Felipe said, "Hello, Ortiz, Rivera, Josefina, Julio, Maria."

It was obvious to Bethany that he knew the names of nearly everyone there and that they were not uncomfortable to have the master of the plantation among them.

The heavy set woman shuffled from behind the bar. She wore a simple calico dress that draped like a tent down to her woven-grass sandals. Her bosom and rump swayed and jiggled in turn as her weight rolled from one foot to the other. There were beads of sweat across her forehead and upper lip. She had a jolly face and a smile that revealed two missing teeth.

"Y por la Señorita?" she asked Don Alacon.

Bethany turned to Felipe.

"Well you can have ocoro mimba, a homemade rum," he said in English so as not to offend the proprietress. "It goes down your throat like fire and will make your toes curl. If you drink too much of it, your head will detach itself from your body and roll around on the floor all night. You will spend tomorrow morning running around your room trying to catch the naughty, aching thing so you can put it back on your shoulders where it belongs."

"Lovely," Bethany replied.

"Or," he continued, "You can choose homemade wine, not very good, a bottle of warm Cuban beer, not bad, a glass of real brandy, my own stock kept here for me, or a sweet orange drink like the ones you can get in Havana only without ice, I'm afraid."

Bethany looked around the room and saw a woman drinking beer from a bottle. "If it would not embarrass you to have a lady drink from a bottle, I will have a beer."

"Dos cervezas, Rosalita, por favor," he said.

Rosalita nodded and returned to the bar to fill the order.

"That is some 'little rose,'" Bethany remarked.

As they talked, more people drifted in. Bethany was taken by the beauty of two women who sat down with a man of light color at a table toward the back of the room. One, the younger of the two, was tall, slim, and jet black with the delicate chiseled facial features of the Nubian women depicted in ancient Egyptian wall paintings. Her hair was close cropped and accented by gold earrings.

The other woman was older, maybe thirty, Bethany guessed. She was exotic looking: slim waist, firm, rounded breasts and clear, taut skin the golden color of champagne.

"Felipe," Bethany said, "who is that remarkable looking, light skinned woman over there?"

He turned slightly and looked toward the back of the room. "Her name is Lola Teurbé. She is quite something don't you think?"

Bethany had to admit that she was. "But what is she doing here? Surely a woman as pretty as that does not work in the fields." She looked at Felipe. "Or should I ask you such a question."

"She lives in Havana, owns a small club there. She comes to the plantation sometimes to see her daughter who lives here with her mother. She does not want the child growing up in the streets of Havana."

"Where is the father?"

"There is no father."

"I see," said Bethany.

"Does my frankness shock you?" he asked.

"No. Does that shock you?"

He ignored the statement. "You have not asked the real question that is on your mind, I think."

"All right," she said. "Have you?" Felipe smiled. "Would it matter to you?"

Bethany took a swallow of beer and looked over the two women. "What about the other one while we are at it."

"The answer is the same for both," he said. Bethany looked up at him. "Neither one has been in my bed. I don't think I would answer a question like that from anyone else."

"Perhaps in regard to any other man, it would not matter to me." Their eyes met, and they fell silent.

The crowd grew as the night wore on; the noise in proportion to their consumption of rum. The added bodies raised the temperature inside while a light rain increased the sticky humidity. The room smelled of cheap perfume, vanilla bean talcum, spilled rum, stale beer, cigar smoke, and sweating bodies.

"It is getting a little crowded," Alacon said, "Would you prefer to leave?"

"Not yet," She answered, "I'm enjoying myself. This crowd is a little different from the people of the Bahamas. And you are different," she added.

"And how am I different," he questioned.

"British owners would hardly sit in a bar with their workers," she answered.

"Neither would the Spanish, but you forget, I am Cuban. Rosalita!" he called. "Otra vez, dos cervezas."

In a dim, back corner of the room, someone started beating the top of a table with finger tips and palms. Across the way, another took up the cadence. The beat was joined by the sound of spoons rapping on a tin plate. A man seated across the room took up a guitar and strummed a rich timbre into a rhythm that seemed to blend an Africa beat with the Gypsy music of Spain. It was different from the native music of the Bahamas, wilder, more complex.

"Lola!" someone shouted. "Lola!" cried another. "LO-LA! LO-LA!" the room began to chant.

"I am not sure we should stay," Felipe said. "Things get a little out of hand on Saturday nights. They want Lola to dance for them. I would venture it would not be considered proper entertainment for ladies from Mississippi."

"I wouldn't think of leaving, unless of course, my staying might embarrass you. These are your workers."

Felipe shrugged his shoulders. "Don't say I didn't warn you. How is your beer?"

"Actually," she said with a seraphic grin, "I think I would like to try a little of that rum."

"I think I am in trouble," Felipe said, "Rosalita! Por favor." The room was alive with primitive rhythm from the impromptu percussion orchestra. Other women wore plain cotton dresses and sandals. Lola wore a thin, linen dress with lace trim. The neckline was cut in a low revealing curve. Long earrings dangled from her pierced lobes. Her shoes, visible from under the hem of her gown, were high heels, worn, but fashionable. The way she sat with her legs crossed revealed her slim hips and thighs.

Lola stood up, her dark eyes flashing in the lantern's light.

"Bravo! Olé!" There was applause all around.

The beat dropped to a low smoldering rhythm. With the graceful glide of a cat Lola moved to the center of the room. Light from the lantern on the bar filtered through the thin linen of her dress, revealing the absence of petticoats; revealing every curve and line of her body.

Lola slowly began to sway back and forth, arms at her sides, palms open, fingers extended, legs apart. Every pair of eyes in the room was fixed upon her. Slowly she coupled her steps to the underlying rhythm. Her body and hands transformed the energy of the beat into motion and form as if every muscle and sinew were somehow directly connected and controlled by the fingers, palms, sticks, and spoons that beat the throbbing rhythm. As she danced, the music slowly increased in tempo, intensity, and passion. Her body swayed, her shoulders and breasts followed the quick, surface tempo of the guitar, her hips and thighs rolled to the steady base beat. She gathered her floor length skirt up almost to her thighs flashing the golden skin of her shapely legs in shameless tribute to a perfect body. As the beat had guided her movements in the beginning, her movements now took control of the rhythm. The hands of each musician synchronized to the movement of her body. The beat became soft, subdued, intensely sensual as she moved her hips in harmony with the pulsating sounds. Everyone in the room could feel her energy and passion.

Lola gradually brought the tempo down, dancing slowly around the room until she stood in front of Bethany, swaying to the beat. Perspiration made her smooth skin glow like bronze in the flickering lamp light. Swaying there, she held out both hands and with rotating fingers she gave Bethany a silent challenge.

All eyes were suddenly fixed upon Bethany. For a moment she did not move, did not blink. Lola smiled the smile of a victor, a smile that Bethany knew was intended to be one of superiority.

She returned the smile and did not break eye contact with Lola. Without looking at Felipe, without any hint of questioning hesitation, Bethany slowly rose from her chair.

Felipe was too surprised to move.

"Olé! Ayeeee! Aye! Aye!" the cries rose from around the room. The tempo picked up. As Bethany moved to the center of the room, Lola smiled again, this time with approval, and moved away to stand at the bar.

Bethany had always wanted to abandon herself to the primitive beat of drums since the first time she had witnessed the firelight dances among the islanders of the Bahamas. She had danced in her mind and often in front of her mirror in the privacy of her room.

She began by following the command of the rhythm, but soon commanded the rhythm to follow her. Her arms, hands and fingers kept the beat of the sticks and spoons while her body moved to the base beat of the guitar. Her shoulders rolled to the rhythm, revealing the lovely shape of her breasts. Her legs were covered to her ankles by lace and silk, but no dress could cover the sensuous movement and passionate grace of her dance as she moved around the small circle, her eyes sometimes closed, sometimes flashing emerald fire.

This was no clumsy effort by some lady to mock the passion of the Cuban people, nor was it an inept attempt to copy an artist. No one in the room could take their eyes off the jefe's lady who danced with such genuine primal fervor. Her lips wet, her mouth slightly open, she danced across the temperatures of passion; warm, and the beat quickened; hot, and the intensity soared; molten, and the rhythm slowed to the subtle undulating flow of lava.

Her face flushed and glowing with perspiration, she moved before Felipe and raised her hands high over her head. The beat raised to a peak and stopped suddenly as she dropped them to her sides.

There was total silence. No one spoke, no one moved. Then, as if by signal, the room exploded in applause and cries of "Bravo! Excelente! Olé! Viva la Señorita!" Bethany turned and looked across the room at Lola. The fiery Cuban queen laughed, walked across the room with two bottles of beer and handed one to Bethany. "You and this night will become legend," she said. "There is no other aristocratic lady in Cuba who could do what you just did, who would have the courage to try, who feels such passion in her soul. I salute you Señorita Quinn." She held up her beer. "Yes, I know your name. I have heard of you in Havana, the beautiful green-eyed Yankee, desired by all men, and among the women, admired by the strong, despised by the weak. Now I know why." Lola lifted her chin, "And, of course, you know about me." She nodded slightly to Felipe who was standing behind Bethany. There was a sadness in her voice as she spoke, but no hint of apology. She did not lower her eyes. "Don Felipe, Señorita Quinn." She lifted her beer once more in salute and walked gracefully across the room to join the handsome olive skinned man still sitting at her table with the Nubian.

"I think it is time, don't you," Bethany said. She was breathing hard, her dress streaked with perspiration. Felipe gave her his handkerchief. She took a sip from the bottle Lola had given her, patted the handkerchief over her face, throat and the back of her neck, and walked out of the building followed by Felipe. As she left, the room once again burst into applause led by Lola Teurbé.

The pair walked halfway to the hacienda without speaking. "I must assume by your silence that I have both embarrassed and offended my host tonight. I apologize. I did warn you that I was an impulsive lady."

Felipe stopped. With his hand he gently touched her chin and turned her face to his. "I think you are the most wonderful woman I have ever had the privilege of meeting."

He kissed her on the forehead. She did not move. He took her face in his hands and kissed each closed eyelid and then pulled her to him, pressing her warm damp body against his own, kissing her lips.

The moon occasionally peeked from behind the clouds as they continued walking, hand in hand.

They entered the house. At the foot of the stairs he said, "I don't want you to leave tomorrow."

"I know," Bethany answered. "But, please, I need time to think." She looked down at the wetness of her dress and brushed damp curls from her forehead. Then she laughed. "Look at me, I'm terrible mess. I'm exhausted and emotionally drained."

"Of course," he said, with a hint of disappointment.

He stood at the foot of the stairs and watched as she climbed the steps.

Almost at the top, she turned and looked down at him. "I can't be so dishonest as to let you think I don't want you, nor so foolish either." She held out her arms to him.

The first time there was no subtlety, no teasing, no casual touch, no light playing of the senses. Their clothes lay entwined on the floor while their moist bodies met writhing upon the bed. Raw animal energy uncontrollably coalesced into sensuous pleasure.

They lay in each other's arms, their bodies slick with perspiration, each silently fathoming the deep wanton excitement of the flesh, the calenture, the shameless satisfaction that washed over their exhausted bodies. The curtains rustled lightly as a night breeze wafted the scent of gardenias into the room.

Back in Havana, Bethany joined the Quinns at dinner. While waiting for dessert to be served, Jonathan took a news clipping from his coat pocket. "A friend in Nassau clipped this obituary notice from *The London Times* and mailed it to me. I thought you all might find it of interest." Jonathan read the article aloud.

Whilst attending a banquet at his club, the honorable Jeremy W. Wright, Esq, M.P., collapsed and died of heart failure after proposing a toast in honor of the Queen's birthday. The honorable Wright was noted for his service on the Royal Committee of Arms and Munitions. He is survived by a maiden aunt in Cornwall, Miss Nettie Jane Wright.

"How sad for a man to be survived only by an old maiden aunt," Louisette said.

"I'll tell you one thing," Bethany said, "There will be no survivors around here if anyone starts referring to me as Ansel's old maiden aunt."

"I don't think beautiful ladies are ever referred to in such terms," Jonathan said. "Certainly neither Ansel nor I would ever do such a thing, would we, Son?"

"No, sir," replied Ansel, "I don't even know what old maid means."

"Good," said Bethany, "It will be a lot safer for you never to learn. It is a term no doubt coined by a reprehensible cad. No lady, regardless of her age, would appreciate the use of such an outdated expression."

"Who was Jeremy Wright," Ansel asked, thinking it best to change the subject.

"As far as I am concerned, he was the quintessence of rascality," commented Bethany.

"What is rascality, Aunt Bee Bee?" Ansel asked.

"It's characteristic of a person that is not respectable or trustworthy," she answered.

"And in no way worthy of ceremony," Jonathan remarked. "I have never been very proud of my association with him. No telling how much money he got cheating Deuteronomy, me, and everyone else who dealt with him." Then Jonathan laughed.

"What's so funny about that," Bethany asked.

"I was just thinking about the one person who probably gave him his just rewards."

"Who would that have been, dear?" asked Louisette.

"I don't really know. I found old Jeremy hobbling about London on a cane some years ago and accused him of having the gout, said it was a sure sign that he was over the hill. He took offense. You know what a vain dandy he was. The more I teased him the more upset he got until, in anger, he blurted out the cause for his limping. I suppose he thought it more manly than the gout. He said a woman shot him in the foot."

Bethany dropped her glass of wine. Jonathan, Louisette and Ansel looked at her in surprise.

"He deserved it," she responded, composing herself and dabbing at the spilled wine with her napkin.

"No! He couldn't have been referring to you," Jonathan said. "I'm afraid he could, Uncle," she replied, "and close your mouth, you look like a dimwit."

"You shot Monsieur Wright?" Louisette asked.

"Yep," Bethany admitted, "Won't hurt to tell you now."

"With your garter pistol?" Ansel asked.

"How do you know about that, young man?" Jonathan questioned.

Before he could answer Bethany said, "That's right, Ansel, with my pretty little pistol your daddy gave me."

"Why, for Pete's sake?" Jonathan asked.

"He got a little pushy."

"Pushy? You shot a man for being a little pushy?"

"Yep. He pushed me into my bedroom in Paris and onto my bed."

Jonathan turned purple. "I would have killed the son of a bitch."

"Jonathan!" Louisette said, "Don't you use language like that in front of this child."

"Yes dear," he answered, and then to Bethany. "Why didn't you tell me?"

"That is exactly why I didn't tell you." Bethany laughed.

"I don't see anything funny about a bastard pushing my niece, onto a bed intending to . . ."

"Jonathan!" Louisette admonished.

"Well, with dishonorable intentions," he said.

"What are dishonorable intentions?" Ansel questioned.

"Ask your mother after supper," Jonathan replied.

"Captain Quinn, you are the most noble, protective, adorable uncle a girl could have."

Jonathan turned to his wife, "Have I missed something?" Louisette shrugged, "I married into this insane family so why ask me for a sensible answer?"

"Looking back, I can laugh about it now," Bethany said. "First he couldn't believe his eyes as I lifted my skirt to my thighs. Then he saw I had done so, not to encourage him, but to get my little pistol. He jumped back stuttering and jabbering that I didn't have the nerve to shoot him and came at me again. I didn't want to kill him."

She noticed Ansel was staring at her. "Actually, Ansel, I meant just to shoot into the floor and scare him, but I missed the floor and hit his foot, don't you see."

"Oh, Aunt Bee Bee, you should learn to shoot better than that." Jonathan tried to hide his smile. Louisette gave Ansel the 'you-better-sit-there-and-be-quiet look'. Bethany continued, "Well anyway, he left squealing like a stuck pig. I almost felt sorry for the lecherous scoundrel."

"He was damn lucky I didn't find out," Jonathan replied.

"Have you noticed, Louisette?" Bethany asked. "Men have no sense of humor."

Bethany spent ever more time in the country, leaving Mannela in Havana with the excuse that Louisette needed her company. "Louisette has so few real friends, and none of them speak French. Besides I've noticed that Jorge Lopez spends a great deal of time with you Mannela." *And why not? You are strikingly attractive.*

The very wise and knowing Mannela smiled. "I'll come to the plantation once in a while to tell you the gossip . . . which, you realize, will be mostly about you."

The only one suspicious of the arrangement was Billy Wong. He was still scared to death of Mannela.

Havana began to notice the frequent absences of Miss Quinn. "Parties just aren't the same without her."

To justify her frequent trips to the country, Bethany told friends her uncle wanted her to learn the workings of the J & Q plantation. In fact, she did just that, reviewing the books and acquiring managerial skills necessary to run the large enterprise. Of course it wasn't necessary that she move in with Felipe, but she happily did, settling into a routine of traveling to Havana every other month to dampen gossip, stay current with the shipping business and see Ansel.

The relationship between Bethany and Felipe was discretely kept within the family. "Señorita Quinn," they said, "simply preferred to live in the country away from the hot, increasingly noisy and crowded city." Whenever in the capital, she went to parties, the yacht club, taught Ansel and friends sailing, and even accepted some of the many invitations from gentlemen in order to keep up appearances.

At the plantation, Bethany and Felipe worked and played together, shared laughter and quiet moments, read books aloud, had heated intellectual discussions on all manner of subjects, and engaged in unrestrained molten sex when the mood struck them.

For Bethany, it was an intensely happy time, perhaps as good as mere mortals are ever allowed. For Cuba, it was a respite, a mercurial stillness rippled by rumor of a new rebellion roiling just below the surface.

Fifteen years after the Ten Years War had ended, the Cuban people saw little change with the exception of the abolition of slavery in 1886, and legalized trade and investment with and by the United States. Spain carried on as usual. There was excessive taxation; Cuba was being made to pay Spain's debts from the Ten Years War. Government positions remained closed to Cubans. The law continued to be by royal absolutism; no freedom of the press or the right of assembly without the approval of the Crown-appointed governor.

Several Cuban leaders had chosen exile after the Ten Years War rather than trust their safety to a Spanish treaty. José Julian Martí y Pérez was one of them. He fled to New York where he became a journalist, a poet, and an organizer and fund raiser throughout the United States and Caribbean in support of a free Cuba. Martí was not a military man and knew it. He turned to fellow exiles, Máximo Gómez, Antonio Maceo, and Calixco Garcia. They had become experts in guerrilla warfare during the Ten Years War.

As 1894 moved toward the new year, Jonathan and Felipe began to go on extended business trips. Bethany feared what that might mean. Her fear was soon confirmed by a whisper on the wind, *This time we will win!*

On one of the rare occasions when Jonathan came to the plantation, Bethany confronted both men. "Why lie to me?" she asked them, her eyes on fire, her nostrils flaring in anger. "I know who Gómez, Maceo and Garcia are. I know they're coming back. The whole countryside knows it. I don't even have to ask if the rumors are true. I see it in your expressions. Oh, yes, I know about this man Martí, too. I know there will be war, but why, for God's sake, do you two have to be involved? We have money. We have other places we can go. You have Louisette and Ansel, Jonathan, and you, Felipe, you have me. Are you both insane? Either of you could have been killed the last time. What makes you do it? It can't be money."

The men remained uncomfortably silent as Bethany vented her fear and frustration. "They say it is not cruelty or revenge or treasure that lead men to love war. It is the same thing that leads men to love women—excitement. Is that what draws you to this stupid madness? That's where y'all have been on all these sudden business trips isn't it? Getting more and more involved. Don't be fools! Give them money, the plantation. Give them anything but yourselves." She stood up, tears welling in the corners of her eyes. "I'm terrified! God! How can I lose either one of you? Felipe, tell me why? And you, Jonathan, what will you tell Louisette and Ansel?"

She cried angry tears and left the room trying to fight off a creeping feeling of helpless panic. Jonathan and Felipe followed her to her room and said all the things she expected them to say.

"Bee Bee," Jonathan began, "We have investments in Cuba. The Cuban people depend upon both of us. Felipe knows the countryside. The people will follow him. I know the Cuban shoreline. I know better than anyone how to get through a blockade. The Cuban people provided me a new start when we had nothing. They are the source of our fortune. How can I abandon them now? How can I take their money and run?"

With Felipe the answer was even easier. "I am Cuban. These Spaniard Royalists, they killed my mother and my father. You should know better than anyone what that means. You were there when a man murdered your mother. How could you love me if I had so little honor as to run away now when my country needs me?"

Bethany sat on the edge of the bed, the bed she shared with Felipe. She wiped tears from her face with the backs of her hands as she had done as a child. "So, Jonathan," she said, "when will you tell your beautiful, loving wife that her worst nightmare is waiting in the wings. She already knows what it is to lose a husband to war, and now she risks another. What sort of example will you set for Ansel? That war is the glorious destiny of manhood? The example my granddaddy and great-granddaddy and the whole stupid, arrogant South set for you? When will you tell her?"

"When I have to," he said lamely.

Unable to look her in the eye, he left the room.

That night while Felipe slept beside her, she resolved to prepare herself as best she could to lose the man she loved and somehow to survive if that happened. The boy, Ansel, was the reason. She would live to see her son become a man.

By February of 1895 Cienfuegos had grown to a respectable size. It had a busy port, a new electric company like Havana, and would soon have telephones. The grand opening of a new theater for the performing arts promised to be the social event of the year.

Felipe and Bethany arrived at the event in the fine old carriage with Alonzo driving.

"I am proud to have the privilege of escorting the most beautiful Cuban lady in Cienfuegos this evening," Felipe said as he helped Bethany from the carriage.

"I am not Cuban, Señor," Bethany countered.

"Sooner or later this island makes a Cuban of everyone who lives here," he replied.

"Well, it hasn't made a Cuban of me, yet."

"True. But it is a generally known fact that ladies from the Southern United States, especially those from Mississippi, are among the most difficult to convert."

"Is that a fact? And what qualifies them as difficult converts?"

"Well, they are said to be beautiful, but stubborn, and some, it is rumored, wear firearms in their skirts to enforce their headstrong ways."

"I see," Bethany replied. "For a minute there I thought you were trying to insult Southern womanhood, but I see you were just admitting their superiority when it comes to maintaining civilized manners in the company of foreign devils."

A sign proclaimed, *THE THOMAS TERRY THEATER.* "That's a strange name for a Cuban theater."

"Thomas Terry is one of the richest members of the new Cuban-American sugar oligarchy. If the gentleman wants to spill a little of his sugar to build a theater in our city as a token of good will . . ." Felipe began.

"And a monument to himself," Bethany interrupted.

"Of course," Felipe continued, "and with Spain's blessing. So why shouldn't the Cuban people accept the gift?"

"Cuban people, indeed," said Bethany. "All I see here are the wealthy who, may I remind you, are for the most part against Cuba Libre."

"Yes, of course," Felipe said, looking around the crowded lobby. "The wealthy are always the last to welcome change. And why not? Another nationalist rebellion will mean a halt to production of sugar, no profits, no return on the millions of Yankee dollars being invested in Cuba, no taxes for Spain, no graft for bureaucrats. The planters, the bankers, the businessmen and America will side with Spain just like last time. They will risk their money to prevent change. The Cuban people will risk their lives to bring it about."

"Damnit! You and Jonathan are wealthy planters and businessmen."

"Cuba should belong to Cubans, but you said we were not to discuss such things."

"That's right," Bethany flashed, and walked into the auditorium ahead of him.

Spanish Bureaucrats, land owners, bankers, American investors, and wealthy merchants escorted wives, mistresses and lovers into the auditorium.

Bethany took Felipe's arm. They made a striking couple as they walked down the aisle toward their seats. She wore a new Battenburg dress, he, white tie and tails. A touch of gray was beginning to show at his temples.

Many had come down from Havana or up from Santiago de Cuba for the occasion. A woman from Havana recognized Bethany. "Good evening, Señorita Quinn," she smiled, "We don't see you at the Yacht Club as often as we would like, but then Captain Quinn says you are spending all your time looking after your plantation these days." She leaned close and hid her face with an ivory fan, "Now, I see why. Your escort is quite handsome."

Once seated, Bethany turned her attention to the new theater. The proscenium was decorated with lyres, trumpets, laurel wreaths, and in the center, a cast relief of a bearded man. *A Greek player, or the theater's namesake?* Bethany mused. The ceiling was painted with naked nymphs cavorting among clouds tossed on a pale blue sky.

Bethany motioned to Felipe, "That is a naughty ceiling."

"You are naughty for noticing."

"Back home someone would have to go right up there and paint clothes on those nymphs. Otherwise, Bible-thumping preachers would storm the podium calling on God to strike blind any sinner with the shameful audacity to stare upon such shocking nakedness."

"Since you brought it to this sinner's attention, it is a pleasant ceiling," Felipe said looking up. "Now if that plump one over near the corner just had green eyes." Bethany hit him with her folded ivory fan.

Startling news arrived just after intermission. A messenger delivered a telegram to the district governor who was sitting in the front row. He climbed onto the stage to interrupt the performance. "Ladies and Gentlemen, please give me your attention. I have just received word that there have been simultaneous uprisings near Santiago and Havana." The shocked crowd grew noisy with chatter. The governor asked for quiet to allow him to finish. "Our Spanish troops have defeated the insurgents near Havana and taken their leader, Julio Sangüily, prisoner." There were cheers from the audience. The Governor again asked for quiet. "I must tell you that nearer Cienfuegos, in the vicinity of Baire, the rebel forces under Guillermo Moncada are still engaged in revolt. Havana has full confidence that this situation will shortly be brought to a conclusion and the spark of rebellion quickly extinguished."

The news alarmed everyone in the theater, but especially Felipe. The revolution had begun badly before all the players were in place. He knew Gómez and Martí were still in Santo Domingo, and Maceo had not yet left Costa Rica. He was afraid to think what information would be forced from the captured Sangüily. The Spanish were very good at torture as the history of the Inquisition would attest.

Alonzo did something he would ordinarily never do. He entered the theater and searched among the *aristocracia opulento* to find his Don Felipe.

"Forgive me, Jefe, but you must leave," he said, twisting his hat nervously in his hands. "I have brought the carriage around. Please, Señor," he added, and looked pleadingly at Bethany for support.

"My God, Felipe, do as he says. We must leave. Alonzo is right."

Once the bright lights of Cienfuegos were behind them, Bethany lost the control she had exhibited in the confused, excited and frightened crowd milling about the theater. She buried her head against Felipe's shoulder.

"I'm afraid for us, Felipe. Oh, please, let's leave Cuba. We can go to Shamrock, to Paris, anywhere but here."

"You know I cannot. We have discussed all this before. Now listen to me." He took her by the shoulders and held her firmly facing him. "You must leave for Havana in the morning. You will be safe there, at least for a while, long enough for you and Louisette and the boy to make an orderly departure from Cuba."

"Oh, Felipe! God! It's all come so fast. We've been so happy, and now . . ."

"Listen to me!" Felipe said. "You must get to safety in Havana. You must not be associated with the rebels or their cause. You will say that you returned to Havana because Captain Quinn is concerned for your safety, that he wants Spain's protection for his family and business. You will say nothing, nothing about the revolution. Do you understand?"

Bethany nodded her head weakly.

"A whisper could get you and Jonathan arrested. You must not try to contact me. I will get word to you from time to time. You must not mention my name, not even in your house. Remember," he warned, "a servant seeking a reward from the authorities, a friend who's loyalty you judge incorrectly, a person in the street, anyone might turn you in as a sympathizer and bring Spanish authorities down on you, on your uncle and his family. You must understand."

"I understand, Felipe. I will not go to pieces like this again. But if I cannot get you and Jonathan to avoid this madness, I will not leave Cuba. I am stronger than you think."

Felipe held her close as the carriage moved through the darkness. They made love that night, but it was not impassioned, though each pretended their part for the other.

Rain was falling the next day when Alonzo put her on the train. Bethany, looking through the soot-dirtied, rain-streaked window, saw the little man standing beside the tracks, water pouring off the brim of his hat. He waved shyly as the train pulled away.

BOOK FIVE

CUBA LIBRE

CHAPTER 20

The Cuban leadership considered Jonathan too valuable an asset to risk by open participation in the revolution. They needed Captain Quinn in Havana where he could secretly direct supply operations and gather information. His first assignment was to secure the means to return the exiled revolutionary leaders to Cuba. It would be no easy task. Spain knew they were coming.

Arrangements were made for Marti, Gómez and their respective parties to board freighters scheduled to pass close by Cuba en route to the United States. The incognito passengers would be dropped off in small boats from their respective freighters to land at night on Cuba's shore. Transporting Maceo from Costa Rica would prove to be the more difficult task. Maceo was being watched. He could not simply board a passing island trader. He would have to be picked up off a Costa Rican beach at night.

After some weeks of searching, Jonathan located a small, fast, shallow-draft schooner operating out of Tampa, Florida that was suited to the task. The vessel, paid for out of Cuban revolutionary funds Marti had raised in New York, was appropriately named *Honor*. Its registration papers were falsified to make the transaction and ownership untraceable. The vessel was quickly provisioned and made ready. The task of finding a qualified and trustworthy captain was extremely sensitive. Time and secrecy were of the essence. The revolution had begun prematurely and was going badly. Captain Lopez volunteered, but Jonathan would not allow it.

"We have a business to run, Jorge," he told him.

Late at night a fishing boat approached the schooner *Honor* lying offshore from a deserted stretch of Costa Rican beach a few miles from the village of Puerto Limon. Maceo laughed when he boarded the schooner and saw its captain. "Who hired this one eyed sailor?" he howled, "He is almost as old as I am and twice as ugly."

"I'm the only fool I could find, General," Jonathan replied holding out his hand. "And I should have had better sense."

Quinn and one carefully picked crewman had sailed *Honor* to Costa Rica. There simply wouldn't be room aboard for a larger crew and the 22 revolutionaries they were to take aboard. Splitting the watch between only two men, four hours on, four hours off, plus any sail changes that had to be made, was exhausting, but Jonathan had loved every minute of the voyage. The seventy foot schooner was fast and responsive. It had been too long since he had experienced the joy of sailing a small vessel. He also had to admit there was the excitement of the venture fueled by memories of his youthful blockade-running days.

Maceo, a huge man, the *Bronze Titan* as he was sometimes called, took Jonathan's outstretched hand into his thick, crushing fingers. Turning to the 22 companions he had brought aboard, he explained, "I know this man. Now listen to me! This man is too valuable to our cause to be lost. If need be, protect him with your life. Through him come guns and medicine."

Skirting Jamaica to the east and the Caymans to the west, they crossed the Caribbean Sea without incident. Upon reaching Cuban waters, *Honor* turned north westward leaving Cape Cruz and the Sierra Maestra Mountains astern. Jonathan took them inshore, skillfully running between Cuba's southern coastline and the many cays of Jardines da la Reina. It was shortly later that trouble came swimming up their wake.

Just before nightfall, a lookout aloft saw a smudge of smoke on the horizon behind them. Dawn revealed a Spanish gun boat steaming some eight miles astern and steadily closing the distance. Maceo looked questioningly at Jonathan.

Quinn shook his head. "Even in this fresh breeze we can't outrun them. They may fetch our range before the sun goes down."

"What do we do, my friend?" the general asked.

"If they haven't our range by dark, we'll run south for international waters."

"And if they close before dark?"

"Then we beach her and run for it on shore. But remember, it could be that our friends back there were expecting us. If that's true, you can anticipate trouble onshore as well. In any case, we're a long way from our planned rendezvous. Your Cuban friends won't meet you. And . . ." Jonathan paused, looking back at the smudge of smoke on the horizon.

"And what, my friend?"

Jonathan smiled, "Old sailors are a burden ashore. Some don't run as fast as they used to."

"Neither do old generals," Maceo growled.

For eight hours Maceo noted the progress of the gunboat steaming up their wake. They could now see the hull clearly, a black trail of oily smoke billowing from its stack. "You were right, Captain. They will be on us before dark. Better to beach her now," he said.

Jonathan nodded. "Have your men gather their weapons, and what ammunition, food and water they can carry." He lifted the boat's compass from the binnacle, put it in a canvas bag and handed it to Maceo. "We will need this once we move inland from the coast."

Jonathan ordered the centerboard raised and slipped the shoal-draft vessel in close along the breaker line just beyond the outer bar. He picked a large wave and rode its back across the shoal, driving *Honor* toward the lee shore. "Brace yourselves!" he shouted.

Honor's bow fell hard onto the shallow bottom just off the sandy beach. The stern swung round and she rolled on her port side, throwing men into the surf. The relentless, wind-driven waves repeatedly lifted and pounded the vessel shoreward, breaking her as the crew struggled against the foaming undertow to make their way ashore. Some lost their supplies. None lost their rifles.

Within hours a small mounted Spanish patrol found them in the bush inshore.

A pattern of engagement and disengagement followed. There were short skirmishes during which the small band would fire a volley or two, forcing the Spaniards to dismount and seek cover. The little band would then melt into foliage often so thick it was hard for men to penetrate, impossible for horses. If caught in sparse brush, one or two volunteers would fight a rear guard action to slow the pursuers while the majority fled.

The Spanish were tenacious. They mercilessly pursued Maceo across rugged foothills, down valleys choked with palm and banana groves, through thickets and uneven terrain interspersed with swamp and marshland. Some of the Cubans were killed, some captured, some found themselves separated to endure terrible hardship eluding the Spanish on their own without aid of compass, map or food.

Maceo told Jonathan to stick close by him. It was a dangerous place to be. The Spanish knew their quarry and could easily distinguish the huge man from the rest of his followers. All their fire seemed directed at him.

Jonathan often heard the distinct whack of bullets hitting foliage around him, but with his family in Havana, his real worry was being identified among Maceo's followers whether alive or dead. He stripped his pockets of all identification papers, darkened his hair with berry juice, smeared mud on his face and took a wide brimmed hat from one of their dead and pulled it down over his forehead. He threw away his eye patch. The scar tissue clinging to the hollow contours of his empty eye socket was no pretty sight, but he hoped it would make him appear to be just another old revolutionary carrying his scars from the last war if the enemy should get close enough to notice, or found his body if it came to that. It was the best he could do.

Maceo seemed not to have lost his legendary luck against death. Four times bullets passed through the brim and peak of Maceo's hat without harm. The fourth time it happened, Jonathan laughed.

"What is so damn funny, Amigo?" Maceo said, retrieving his hat and poking a finger through a new hole in the brim.

"You keep bending over to pick up that sombrero and they are going to shoot you in the ass. After four shots to the head with no effect, they'll figure that's where your brains are."

The General was not amused.

By day they moved anytime they could without drawing fire. They moved all night, every night, because the Spanish did not. One night they stumbled across Spanish pickets and exchanged confused fire in the darkness. During the engagement the general's brother, José Maceo, disappeared.

When their food ran out, they lived on wild, sour, lemons and limes and green bananas. Resting in a thick grove late one afternoon, Maceo looked at Jonathan and shook his head.

"What's the matter?" Jonathan asked.

"You are one ugly, white Yankee sailor, amigo," Maceo answered with a laugh.

"True, and here I am with a general who is lost in the middle of nowhere with a handful of exhausted troops while Spanish soldiers are combing every bush for him."

"For us, Amigo, for us."

"I'll be damned if that's so. They're looking for you. I'm not here. Everyone in Havana knows I'm on a business trip to New Orleans," Jonathan replied.

"True," the almond-skinned man said. "I somehow forgot Capitán Quinn is not here. What a load off my mind. I can't think of a more useless burden in the middle of thick, verdant surroundings crawling with enemy troops than a worn out, one-eyed sailor missing half an ear. He probably couldn't see to shoot them even if he could hear them coming."

"He can't hear them coming because his general talks too much," Jonathan answered.

"Ah yes, thanks for reminding him," Maceo said and paused to look and listen as he often did. Then he leaned back against a tree, began to peel a green banana and said in a more serious tone, "I think it is true that they knew we were coming."

"I'll tell you what is true," Jonathan said. "I'm too damn old for this. I keep thinking I can't go any further, that my heart is gonna bust, my lungs split. By the end of the day my legs are shaking so I have to kneel to pee. When it comes time to move on after we stop to rest, I'm so stiff and cramped I want to cry. Sometimes I find myself actually wanting to get shot just so I can stop running. How many of us are left, and how much ammunition?"

"Ten besides you and me; maybe not enough ammunition."

"Twelve of yours have been lost already?"

"It's time to go again, my friend, before we find ourselves among them."

"Maybe your brother is hiding or captured. I didn't see him go down," Jonathan offered.

"Perhaps," Maceo answered.

The two dirty, tired, hungry, middle aged, mosquito-bitten warriors helped each other up and began again.

After two weeks, the last two days of which they were without food and sick from bad water, Maceo, Jonathan, and the last four of the original twenty two of Maceo's men stumbled onto a band of revolutionaries nearly a hundred strong. Maceo was greeted with wild acclaim.

The exhausted general did two things before falling into a hammock for much needed rest. He saw to it that the four surviving men were fed and their wounds cleaned and bandaged. His second act was to order a squad of cavalry to immediately deliver Jonathan to the coast and, with utmost secrecy, get him aboard any friendly fishing vessel they could find.

"Officially," he said loudly, so Jonathan could hear his explanation to the hand-picked men assigned the task, "that scarred old Yankee capitán over there in the bushes dancing with diarrhea is not here. He is on a business trip to New Orleans. Instruct the fishermen to get him on a boat to the Bahamas, Jamaica, the Caymans, anywhere, but get him out of Cuba. Now that should be simple enough."

"Simple?" Jonathan asked as he weakly emerged from his latest bout with swamp quick-step. "How come everything is always so simple to you?"

"Because I follow orders without wasting time talking like a complaining old woman. How far behind us do you think the Spaniards are?"

"All right, General, I'm going," Jonathan said.

"Good," replied Maceo taking a bottle of thick brown liquid from one of the rescue party. "Take a swig of this." He handed the bottle to Jonathan. "It is claimed that this concoction will either kill the bugs in a man's belly or the man himself. I'm giving you the honor of having the first bottle. If you live, I'll give some to my troops."

The troops thought that was funny.

Jonathan uncorked the bottle and swigged down a measure. "Hot damn! That's awful." He corked the bottle, put it in his pocket, and held out his hand to Maceo.

Maceo gripped it firmly. "Adios, Capitán."

"Give 'em hell, General." Jonathan climbed onto the back of a wiry little horse and fell in with the squad of rebel cavalry that would lead him to the coast. He turned in the saddle and looked back at Maceo. The big, strapping mulatto smiled. They exchanged salutes the way men do when they part knowing it could be for the last time.

Weeks later, Marti and Gomez were each dropped off in lifeboats from separate passing freighters and made their way to shore. Marti was nearly drowned when his boat capsized in the surf. He was pulled choking to the beach and revived. Word soon flashed among the people. "Martí, Gómez, Maceo, Garcia they are here!" Men from all over the island flocked join them in the shadow of the Sierra de Escambray Mountains. Most of them, unlike Martí, were neither poets, politicians or idealists. They were citizen soldiers. For them, the time for words had passed. *Cuba Libre!*

In the Ten Years War, Spain had expended three hundred million dollars and suffered more than a hundred thousand casualties while the Cuban revolutionaries lost some fifty thousand killed. The new *War of Independence* would be much worse in ways neither side could imagine.

"Louisette," Bethany begged, "you must take Ansel and go to Shamrock while you can. When Jonathan gets back he will tell you the same thing. We have to make plans for your trip without delay."

"But, Bethany, I don't know a soul in Vicksburg," Louisette protested. "I know you are thinking of my welfare and Ansel's, but I don't want to leave Jonathan. How can I? Will you leave? If I agree will you come with me?" Louisette knew what Bethany's answer would be.

"I can't go," Bethany said. "You know I can't, but you must take Ansel away from this madness. They say soon there'll be open warfare all around Havana, maybe in the city itself. Food will grow scarce, disease may run wild. Other American families are leaving. Ansel's American school will close any day," Bethany pleaded. "You must get Ansel away from here!"

Frowning, Louisette was silent for a long moment. Then she offered, "I know a compromise we can agree upon. I know you are right. You love Ansel as much as Jonathan and I do. What if we send Ansel to Jonathan's old school in the South, this Marion Military Institute? He will be safe there."

Bethany answered without hesitation. "I agree, and the sooner the better."

"Jonathan will be angry with me for not going myself, but I will not. My place is with my husband," Louisette said, "for as long as I have a husband." She looked up with tears in her eyes. "God! Have I come so far only to face another war that could take another husband from me? It is too much for one family, your Civil War, our Franco-Prussian War, the horrible Commune revolt in Paris, the Ten Years War on this very island and now another nightmare. And the guns! God forgive us, we sell the guns."

"We sell them to the Cubans," Bethany said defensively. "They fight for freedom."

"Without guns they wouldn't be able to fight."

"Oh, they would fight," Bethany replied. "They just couldn't win. Maybe they can't anyway, but they will try."

A thin, exhausted Jonathan returned to Havana aboard *Olivette*, the ferry that ran from Key West. The next morning, after dismissing questions about his sun-burned face, loss of weight, and run-down condition, Jonathan listened as his wife and Bethany stated in no uncertain terms that they would not leave Cuba, but presented a plan for sending Ansel away to school. He was not pleased with the women, but knew arguing with them was futile. He agreed that Ansel should go and the sooner the better. That day at lunch they all gathered to explain to eleven year old Ansel what had been decided.

"But why can't I stay here with you and Mama and Aunt Bee Bee? I'm not afraid," Ansel pleaded. He was afraid, but not of staying in Havana. "The boys at school say those old revolutionaries will never come into Havana. The Spanish call them mambises. Mannela said that in African that means 'children of the vultures', but in Spanish it means 'the dregs'. What are 'dregs'?" he asked, but before anyone could answer he continued, "I don't want to go to school so far away." That's what he was afraid of, going far away all alone.

"Son," Jonathan said, "in bad times like these we all must do our duty as best we can. Your duty is to go to school."

"You ran away from Marion," Ansel replied. "Who told you that?" Jonathan flared. "Aunt Bee Bee."

Jonathan looked at Bethany. She shrugged her shoulders, "How was I to know?" she said lamely.

"That was different," Jonathan said to Ansel, "There was a war on."

"There's a war on now, Daddy," the boy replied.

Jonathan was being painted into a corner. "Yes, and now I have to look after your stubborn mother and your obstinate aunt, and that is a full-time job. What I have to ask you to do is to go to Marion and look out for yourself. That's a lot to ask of an eleven-year-old boy, I know, but you can do it." The boy stood a little taller now that his father had placed such responsibility and faith in him. "I'll make a deal with you. I'll buy you a fine horse and a new baseball glove. With your own horse at Marion, you can join the cadet cavalry. You'll like it, you'll see."

"Will I have to go all the way there by myself," the boy looked worried again.

"I'll tell you what, son," Jonathan answered. "There's a steamship scheduled to leave next week for Mobile. I know the captain. I think I can get him to take us along. If that works out, you and I will sail with him to Mobile, and then I will take you to Marion myself. I've been wanting to go back and take a look after all these years."

"All right," the boy said quite seriously, "but y'all are gonna miss me around here."

Jonathan smiled, but the words nearly tore the hearts out of the women, though they too smiled in front of their brave little boy. Ansel left to pack.

"You don't mean to tell us you're taking that boy on one of the gun running boats," Bethany said, "because if you are the deal is off. The whole Spanish navy is out there stopping boats for inspection. How do you know some informant hasn't identified the boat? I don't care if it's empty, they'll hang everybody onboard."

"Calm down, Bee Bee. You know I wouldn't risk that boy. It's an American freighter that brings canned tins of food to Havana for the damn Spanish army. I'll get the boy safely there."

"This war could last for years," Bethany said bitterly, "If it does, he won't be a boy when he comes home, he'll be all grown up." She looked at Jonathan, "And damn it, it just had to be your old military school. They'll turn him into a soldier. It just goes on and on doesn't it?" She stormed out of the room.

Louisette walked to her husband and put her arms around him, her head against his chest.

"Please go with the boy, Louisette darling. I worry so with you here. I can't do anything about Bethany, but I should order you to go."

"Whatever the future holds I will be near you, J. Hillary. After all I have been through, don't deny me that."

He reached down and kissed her. "You are the most delicate, beautiful and mule-stubborn wife in the world."

She looked up at him and smiled. "Yes," she said, "and much more than you deserve."

CHAPTER 21

The news was always bad, sometimes worse than bad. Gómez engaged a Spanish force under the command of General Sandavol in an open and successful battle at Jarajueca near Bayamo, but victory came at a heavy price. José Martí, father of the revolution, fell in his first engagement with the Spanish army. Against all advice, he had insisted on riding a fine white horse. He said he should be seen by his people on the battlefield. The Spanish did not know who was in the saddle, but they knew such a fine animal must belong to a leader. They cut him and his horse down.

For the Cuban people, the cost of revolution escalated. Spanish authorities combed through 15-year-old records and intelligence reports from the Ten Years War and began arresting everyone they could find who had been connected with the insurgents of that conflict. Old men were dragged away and imprisoned. Others were accused of treason, hauled into Havana and shot against the walls of Cabaña Fortress. On more than one occasion, Bethany and Louisette heard the sharp reports of the firing squads.

In spite of such measures, the ranks of the revolutionary movement continued to grow. By July, Maceo had 7,000 men, a month later, 16,000. His cavalry, including himself and Felipe, were mounted on small scrawny horses that were hardy and could live off scrub land. Felipe had offered his beautiful barbs, but Maceo wisely declined. He and his officers would not make the same mistake as Martí.

The revolutionaries carried a variety of weapons: military rifles supplied by blockade runners, captured Spanish rifles, sporting rifles, shotguns, anything they could find. Many had only machetes. Even so, there were two things the rag-tag Cubans could do well: move fast and fight. The Spanish forces quickly tired of the constant ambush attacks they suffered in the field and withdrew to the towns. As a result, much of the eastern countryside belonged to the *revolucionarios*. Small cavalry units of no more than 200 men each made lightning raids deep into the western half of the island, burning cane fields, destroying mills, wrecking rail lines, anything to hurt Spain's pocketbook and, hopefully, to make the United States demand that Spain give in to save American investments.

Spain's reaction was swift and brutal. Havana's press printed the words of Spain's prime minister, *"Cuba shall remain Spanish though it takes the last man and the last peseta."* More than 200,000 Spanish army troops were ordered to Cuba to join the 50,000 regular troops and the Royalist militia already there.

As 1896 approached, smoke from burning fields could be seen from Havana by day, and at night the horizon glowed orange from the flames. In the east, the towns belonged to Spanish troops, the countryside to Cuban nationalists. None-the-less, the revolutionaries were losing to an inescapable enemy—*TIME*. They had to defeat Spain before irreplaceable men, money and supplies were expended or once more face stalemate in a broken, ruined Cuba.

Felipe's troops finally obtained uniforms of a sort: khaki cotton pants and shirts. Some had boots, most wore sandals. Armed with repeating rifles, razor-sharp machetes and riding wiry, tough little horses, Felipe's men were ever on the move. They lived off the land, attacked where they were least expected, captured supplies from the enemy and took no prisoners.

Shortly after the New Year arrived, Felipe led an attack at Mal-Tiempo. His troops, desperate for ammunition, charged the Spanish outpost using only the cutting edges of their machetes. They totally surprised the garrison and hacked their way in to capture 30,000 rounds of ammunition.

In the beginning, the killing had come hard to Felipe. It got easier. At Mal-Tiempo he cleaved a man through collarbone and rib until the blade of his machete stopped against the man's spine. Felipe saw the body gape open in a spray of crimson spume, the startled eyes staring, dying, the pistol falling from the hand, its owner collapsing to earth. For Alacon it was but another horror dumped into his soldier's unwilling memory.

In the bewildering stillness that seems always to follow battle, Felipe sat wiping the blood from his machete. Combat with cold steel leaves a particularly gruesome scene. He watched as his troops plundered the hacked remains of the enemy. They were practiced in the art. First they took arms and ammunition, then they tried shoes for a fit, and then, if there was time, personal effects: money, watches, rings.

They fight without pay, he thought to himself, *yet they rob the dead of ammunition first. When they start taking rings, watches and money first I will know that the war is turning us from the cause of freedom into common bandits and murderers.*

As he surveyed the vulture's feast before him, he knew his worst nightmare was that he might grow to like it—the killing, confusing the smell of blood with that of victory. *It has happened to men around me. They begin by killing for the cause until, in the dungeons of their minds where madness holds court, killing becomes the cause.*

Desperation brought about a new, novel innovation in military logistics. A strikingly-handsome woman traveled from town to town organizing a unique ammunition supply source for the Cubans. Her job was to convince prostitutes to accept pay in cartridges from Spanish soldiers. The 'ladies' thus recruited gave their handfuls of bullets to the insurgent army, sometimes in exchange for money, sometimes for the promise of it, often as not, simply for the cause. The woman's name was Lola Teurbé, and her *cantina soldiers* supplied thousands of cartridges to the revolutionaries.

Lola continued to run her own cantina in Havana. Often, when returning from a trip recruiting *cantina soldiers*, she delivered field reports to her assigned contact in the capital. When she first told her Havana contact about the special program, the contact asked, "How could the Spanish soldiers be so stupid?" Lola threw back her head and laughed. "Spanish soldiers are not stupid," she said. "They are just horny."

Lola's contact in Havana was a little shocked, but couldn't help but laugh.

Tucking Lola's field report away, Bethany carefully checked the alley before she stepped from the doorway into the street and calmly walked away. To make sure she wasn't being followed, Bethany would wander about, stopping at different shops before delivering the report.

Along with the field reports there was occasionally a letter from Felipe. Rare, cherished, often weeks old, the words written by his hand on wrinkled scraps of paper. She read them and then burned them. His words were all she had of him.

Re-supplying the Cubans became increasingly difficult. Besides the Spanish patrol boats, United States Navy ships were trying to intercept blockade runners. By enforcing America's neutrality they protected the U.S. trade agreements with Spain and investments in Cuba. When the American Navy caught blockade runners, the ships, crews and the expensive, desperately needed cargos were impounded. The Spanish Navy was more pragmatic. They confiscated the ships, supplies and hanged the crews. Exceptions were sometimes made for those who could prove they were American citizens. They were sent to languish in Spanish prisons. Some of them would decide hanging might have been better.

Jonathan knew the waters around Cuba and had more experience in the tricks and skills of blockade running than any man in Cuba. He passed his knowledge to the captains running supplies to the insurgents and risked late night clandestine meetings to coordinate landing rendezvous.

Bethany knew the risks he was taking. One day at the office she confronted him. "Damn it, Jonathan! I know what you are doing. You told me the rule of this business was to never get personally involved. You're not Cuban. You never will be. What the hell are you doing? Don't you know every time there's a knock on the door Louisette's heart stops? When you're home its fear they've come to hang you, when you're away, that they've come to tell her you're dead. We both know, don't we? You're still looking for that victory that was lost so long ago?"

"Maybe," he said, and then losing control added, "Because I'll be damned if I'll be on the losing side again. I don't know how to make it happen, yet, but I damn well know the way to victory."

"How?" she asked angrily.

"By getting the United States into this war."

"That's crazy. Why should they? Why should American boys come over here and get killed?" she was screaming back at him now.

"Because these people need help, goddamn it. Because it's the right thing to do."

"When has that ever worked? Even if the Cubans win their freedom they'll have no money to rebuild what the war is destroying. Cuban scallywags and Spanish and American carpetbaggers will come in here and take over just like what happened in the South. The people won't be any better off. The only difference this time is that the carpetbaggers will be big companies that will drive us out of business along with the Cubans. Tell me Jonathan, when was the last time you saw a government, any government, do something because their conscience was bothering them?"

"They will do it to protect a hundred million dollars of American investments."

"Maybe, but that hasn't happened yet."

Jonathan replied angrily. "By God, there's no other way to save those men in the field. An excuse to get America in this thing has to be found."

"How does one create an excuse to involve one's own country in a war?" she asked.

"I don't know. But damnit, what do you want me to do, quit? You want me to leave Felipe and the rest out there like our Southern boys were left thirty years ago—out of food, out of ammunition, out of blood? Is that what you want?"

Not waiting for an answer, Jonathan continued. "Do you know what Garcia is begging for? Do you think ammunition is first on his list? God knows he needs it, but what he's begging for is quinine. That's right, pills before bullets. It's the same with Gómez and Maceo. Every man in the field ought to have one quinine pill a day. A hundred days supply for fifty thousand men is five million pills. We can't even get them a hundred thousand. They're watching nine men die from malaria for every one that dies from bullets.

"And you," he said, his frustration and anger spilling onto Bethany, "you ask *ME* why I stay. Why can't I get *YOU* to leave? You say I'm in danger, that you worry about me when there's a knock on the door. It's you I'm frightened for. For God's sake, you're a spy! You get information right from the Governor's palace. You charm information from his aides, from officers at parties, from the Governor himself. You exchange messages with field contacts. You think I don't know about that? Hell, you're probably supplying the information I get on the movements of Spanish patrol boats." Bethany looked mildly surprised. "They could hang you, Bethany. I have begged you to leave. You don't risk yourself for a cause, or for Cuba, or for family fortune. You condemn me for taking risks to try to help people who are fighting for freedom while you risk everything for one man. Tell me. If I said, all right, all of us are getting out of Cuba, would you leave without Felipe?"

Bethany didn't answer.

"I see," he said, calming down a little, "And you stand here tormenting me with guilt for not leaving, for not betraying principles I was raised to believe in, for not abandoning an obligation I accepted from those who trust and depend upon me. You curse me for not agreeing with those who say that honor is nothing but a silly word. Honor is real! It touches a man's soul. Without it, a man is lost in a swamp of self-loathing. Do you think I don't know the fear in your heart, in Louisette's heart? Do you really think that I am not afraid?"

Bethany' anger deflated into fatigue and guilt and the pinpricks of her own inner fear. She put her arms around Jonathan and laid her head on his shoulder. "I just want you and Felipe out of this. I want to call him in and all of us to leave. I want you both to live. Is that so wrong and selfish?"

"Oh, Bee Bee, Darling, don't you know that I wish I could call him in? Do you think he would come? Don't you know I'm sick and tired of it all?" Jonathan held her and looked out the window across Havana Bay. "You're right about one thing, baby. I'm not Cuban. When this is over I'm going home to Shamrock, I mean for good. I'm tired, Bee Bee, but I just can't leave while they're dying."

General Martinez Campos was regarded a gentleman and a soldier of honor, even by his enemies. He was a warrior of compassion as regards the treatment of civilian populations. Spain, however, took into consideration only one fact. He was not winning, at least not fast enough. Campos was relieved of command. Spain wanted someone who would deal firmly with the 'peasant rabble', someone without so much concern for colonials, someone who would crush the rebellion once and for all. General Valeriano Weyler y Nicolau, Marquis de Tenerife, a Spaniard of German decent, was the man for such a job. Although Cubans were aware of his reputation, none were prepared for what followed his arrival.

Jorge Lopez had long been concerned about J & Q Shipping and the risks Captain Quinn was taking. He traveled from Nassau to personally urge Jonathan to get back to business and away from the dangerous course he was following. Jonathan brushed aside Jorge's concern and used the occasion to rage about Weyler.

"Do you know what the bastard Weyler is doing? He's removing every man, woman, and child from the countryside and laying waste to it; burning their farms, fields, houses, confiscating their cattle and food. He's crowding all the country people into great barb-wire pens like animals. Weyler calls it *Reconcentrado*. His intent is to deny food, support, and any hiding place to the rebels. Once an area is cleared, anyone seen there will be considered an enemy of the crown and fair game to be shot. People in these, these . . ." Jonathan struggled for a new term, "these *concentration camps* are dying from malaria, cholera, dysentery, typhoid and plain starvation. Weyler is going to wipe out half the population."

"Capitán Quinn," Jorge argued, "you have risked enough, given enough. It's time to get out, to get Señora Quinn out, to try and persuade Señorita Bethany to go with you. Even Cubans are leaving. They are fleeing on anything that will float."

Jonathan ignored him. "Do you know the bastard is going through the prisons, dragging out anyone thought to have been a leader and having them shot? It just gets worse, Jorge. How can I leave while I can still help?"

"What can you do here for your Cuban friends that you cannot do from Nassau?"

"Coordinate supply landings," Jonathan answered. "Things here change too fast for me to do that from the Bahamas. I can't leave, Jorge, not yet. Quit worrying about me and get back to Nassau. I appreciate your concern, but that's where I need you. We're shipping damn little sugar, most of the cane has been destroyed, and what 'special cargo' we had left in the warehouses I sold on credit, which I doubt we'll ever collect. Your operation is the only one making any money. You have to keep things going."

Lopez turned to leave.

"Jorge," Jonathan said, "thank you for making the effort. If anything should happen to me, Louisette, Bethany and the boy will need you."

Captain Lopez hesitated at the office doorway.

"Well, what is it?" Jonathan asked.

"Nothing that can't wait," Lopez answered.

That evening, Jonathan found Louisette and Bethany in a gay mood for the first time since the revolution began. Billy Wong seemed the happiest of all.

"All right," Jonathan eyed the smiling ladies, "what's going on here?"

Mannela came into the dining room dressed in a lovely flowered silk print.

"What is going on?" he asked again.

A knock came at the front door. Billy Wong rushed to answer it.

Smiling like a Cheshire cat, he ushered in Captain Lopez.

"Jorge," Jonathan said, "I thought you were leaving."

"I sail at midnight, Capitán."

"Well, here, sit down with us. You are just in time for supper and some sort of celebration these silly women won't reveal to me. Louisette, have another plate set out for Jorge."

Everyone laughed. Jonathan looked from one face to another. *Laughter is so rare these days*, he thought. For the first time he noticed an extra place was already set at the table. Before he could make sense of that discovery, everyone was seated.

Bethany tapped her water goblet with a spoon. "This is both a happy and a sad occasion. Sad because our dear Mannela is leaving us. Happy because Captain Jorge Lopez has come to claim his fiancée."

Jonathan sat speechless with his mouth open.

"I was going to tell you this afternoon, Capitán, but at the time you were too busy boiling my Spanish ancestors in oil."

"By God man! After all these years of avoiding the bonds of holy matrimony, here you snatch from within my own household, with stealth and secrecy I might add, one of the most attractive, intelligent, and formidable women I have ever known. I congratulate you, sir, and wish every happiness to the bride. But as for certain conspirators . . ." he looked at his wife and niece.

"If it makes you feel any better," Bethany answered, "I knew nothing of this until Mannela discussed the matter with me last week. We were going to have the wedding here next month, but since Jorge arrived without warning this morning, I urged them just to get on with it. They'll be married in Nassau."

Jonathan looked around the room, and then at a stoic Mannela. "Just how long have you two been courting?"

Mannela looked at Jorge, "I believe it would be fair to say some seven years, off and on of course, you know how these sailors appear and disappear with the tides."

"She used Voodoo on me, Capitán."

"I may one day if you keep joking about it," Mannela smiled, and took his hand. It was the first time she had ever shown open affection in front of those she had served so loyally over the years.

The party went on until almost midnight. At dockside there were tearful good-byes and promises of visits. Bethany hugged Mannela and stepped back to see for the first time in all their years together, tears in her eyes.

At age forty-one, Mannela would have a real marriage and home of her own.

For the first time in her life, Bethany would be without a personal servant, companion, and confidante. It was a custom she had inherited as a child from the fading ruins of an antebellum Southern culture.

After losing their Civil War, more than a few Southerners, bitter in defeat and financially ruined, sought new opportunity further south in Mexico, South and Central America, and like the Quinns, the islands of the Caribbean. There were others, mostly educated professionals, who turned toward a re-united America for opportunity. The United States consul-general in Havana was one of the latter. Fitzhugh Lee was a short, plump, 61-year-old, cigar chewing ex-Confederate major-general and nephew of Robert E. Lee. That he had been appointed United States consul-general to Cuba was a mark of political acumen on his part.

If Lee's appointment was controversial in Washington, it was considered catastrophic in Madrid. Spain quickly determined that he was not the ideal representative they had hoped America would send to Cuba. They tried several times to have him recalled. The Spaniards recognized an adversary when they saw one, and in a Cuba erupting in revolution, they saw Fitzhugh Lee often. He spent a great deal of time at the Spanish Governor's office presenting papers to obtain the release of imprisoned Americans. The Spanish were convinced the official Washington petitions he presented were in behalf of Cubans Fitzhugh only claimed were naturalized American citizens.

Jonathan and Bethany would sometimes visit Lee's office to hand him a slip of paper with a name on it. "Fitzhugh," they asked, "would you check and see if this fellow isn't an American citizen?" Lee knew that Spain needed the continued support of the American government and that American businesses had large investments in Cuba. He used those facts to get what he wanted. If there was the slightest chance of success, Fitzhugh would make a show of contacting Washington to claim a naturalized American citizen had been wrongly mistaken for a Cuban and imprisoned. Through means Fitzhugh never explained, copies of naturalization papers proving the subject party to be an American citizen would arrive some weeks later in the consulate's sealed, diplomatic mail pouch. The political prisoner was usually released and ordered deported from Cuba.

Shortly after General Weyler's *reconcentrado* was implemented, he arrogantly marched his men into the Pinar del Río area declaring he would "put an end to this rebel, Maceo." Maceo's troops, using hit and run tactics, wrought such havoc on the Spanish army that they were forced to retire.

Weyler was furious. Faring no better than his predecessor, he decided on a new tactic. Where Spanish arms had failed, perhaps Spanish gold would succeed.

On December seventh, Maceo called a meeting of his lieutenants at a ruined farm within 20 miles of Havana. Only a small force was present. A larger group might attract attention. Twilight was sliding toward darkness at the abandoned, burned-out farm by the time the small party arrived. The first order of business was to feed the officers and men, many of whom had traveled most of the day without eating. General Maceo, Colonel Felipe Alacon, Francisco Gómez (son of General Máximo Gómez) and several other officers sat together eating near an old rock wall where their horses were conveniently tied within easy reach.

"How is your malaria, Felipe?" Francisco asked.

"As long as I have quinine I can keep it under control. How's your arm?"

"Another few weeks and it will . . ." Francisco stopped talking and held up his hand for silence. "Did you hear something?" The others listened.

"It's only the horses," an officer called Maldonado said. He was charged with security for the meeting site. Felipe got up and started toward the wall. "I'll have a look just the same."

Maldonado also got up, but instead of following Felipe, he moved away from the group.

"Maldonado!" Francisco called, "Where are you going?" Maldonado began to run.

A fusillade of rifle fire erupted from the top of the wall. Felipe dove among the horses at the base of the structure. Over the sound of rifle fire a shout came from the opposite side of the wall. "He falls! Viva España!"

Felipe turned to see Maceo and several men around him lying on the ground. He cut loose a horse and ran with it to where Maceo lay. In spite of a hail of fire, Felipe and another officer were able to get Maceo's two-hundred seventy pound frame over the saddle. The horse was shot down before it could move half a length. The man who had helped get Maceo on the animal fell against Felipe, knocking him to the ground. Francisco Gómez ran to the wall and with his good arm led a second horse to Maceo. Cuban rebels were returning fire now, trying to provide cover. Felipe got to his feet and attempted to lift Maceo's limp body across the horse's saddle. He could not do it even with the help of Francisco's one good arm. Desperate, they knotted one of Maceo's wrists to the horse's tail and began to drag him away. The second horse made ten yards before it too was shot down. Felipe turned to free Maceo's body and felt a searing impact against his thigh. He was knocked to the ground beside the dying horse. Francisco lay on his side holding the animal's lead in his good hand, his lifeless eyes fixed on those of Maceo. Two men rushed in to get Felipe. He saw both fall. His last conscious thought was of the traitor, Maldonado, running for safety.

Bethany knew the minute she saw Jonathan enter the room. "It's Felipe, isn't it?" She stood up, the color gone from her cheeks, her body trembling.

"He's alive, Bethany, he's alive."

She had not heard from Felipe since word of Maceo's death had been splashed across the Havana newspaper almost a month before. "Thank God," she cried, "Where is he?"

"Here in Havana. They have him at Morro prison."

"I'm going to him."

Jonathan put his arms around her. "That's the one thing you must not do, Bee Bee."

"I must go! Without help he will die in there."

"Listen to me, Bethany!" Jonathan grabbed her by the shoulders and shook her. "If you go to see a rebel colonel, how long do you think it will take your dear friend, the Spanish governor, to come for us?"

"Fitzhugh!" she said suddenly, and started for the door.

"Bethany!" Jonathan grabbed her arm and stopped her, "I'll bring him here. It'll be safer that way. Please, Bee Bee."

Bethany stopped struggling and seemed to shrink in his arms. "You can let go of me now." She walked to the sideboard, poured a stiff shot of bourbon and threw it down. After a long moment she turned, wiped her mouth with the back of her hand, and admitted, "You're right. I would have run out of here and placed us all in danger. Please ask Fitzhugh if he can come right away."

"There's not a great deal I can do," Fitzhugh Lee said gravely, "He was with Maceo."

"You have to get him out. You have to!" Bethany pleaded.

"I'd eat nails and walk on fire for you, Miss Bethany, if I thought it would free your man, but the truth is it won't. What I can do is storm the castle and convince the ogre that the American government is interested in this man, that they insist he and all such officers of the rebel army be treated as prisoners of war and not traitors or criminals. I've already convinced the Spaniards that my government intends to monitor such treatment to determine that it is in accordance with accepted rules concerning prisoners of war. Normally, Spain wouldn't give a damn, but the last thing they want right now is for America to get even more stirred up. Back home, Hearst, Dana and Pulitzer have found a way to triple sales of their newspapers. They are daily pumping out journalistic sensationalism about Cuba. Papers across the country are following suit for the same reason—increased sales. Napoleon said 'One hostile newspaper is more to be feared than the points of a thousand bayonets', and the Spanish are beginning to agree. The front pages of American newspapers depict Weyler as a butcher who's turning this island red with Cuban blood, and it's not just U.S. readers who are taking notice. A number of influential citizens of Madrid are asking questions. Now, that's good for your Felipe. With both Madrid and America watching Havana, Weyler won't likely shoot your friend, but they are not going to let him go either."

"What if he's wounded, sick? They won't feed him. They'll let him die."

"We won't let that happen, Miss Bethany, but you can't be involved. You can't even speak his name in this house. I insist on that. Not a word. I know more than I want to know about certain activities of certain American citizens here in Havana. I have enough trouble as is, and you are in enough danger without running around announcing yo' concern over a colonel in the rebel Cuban army. Now surely you can see my point." Lee held up his hand to keep Bethany from interrupting. "Now what we're going to do is this. Arrangements can be made, are made all the time, where the guards allow family to bring food to prisoners. Costs a little money and everything that goes in gets inspected, but it's done. What we've got to find is a trustworthy woman willing to take food and medicine to the Colonel. It has to be someone outside this household with absolutely no connection to the Quinns. You furnish me the name of someone like that you can trust and I'll have someone approach her. That way, no one can trace her to you. It's the best I can do for now, Miss Bethany."

Lola feared prison more than death, but she crossed the bay and climbed to Morro's gates with food, clean clothes, bandages, antiseptic, quinine tablets, a gallon tin of water and what would be most precious to Felipe, a bar of soap. She also carried two bottles of wine, one for the gate keeper and one for the sergeant of the guards.

Although it was hard to disguise her sultry beauty, she did everything she could to make herself unattractive. Still, she had made up her mind she would grant favors to the guards if she was forced to do so in order to accomplish her mission. As it turned out, the dirt she smeared on her face, arms and ankles, her ragged black dress and wildly unkempt hair were enough to discourage them.

Lola gagged as she was led down into the bowels of the fortress to Felipe's cell. The smell was unbearable. The dimly lit passage was lined with ancient, heavy-timbered, ironclad doors. Like prayers from the damned, muffled moans and cries echoed along the hallway.

Felipe's cell was a six by eight foot tomb. Except when the small observation window in the cell door was opened, there was no light. The cell was putrid. Felipe's filth overflowed from a bucket seldom emptied. Shortly after he was taken prisoner, a Spanish army doctor removed the bullet from his upper thigh and treated the wound, but once he was turned over to prison authorities he received no further medical attention. The wound was infected, but it had not become gangrenous, perhaps because of the uric acid in his urine, some of which he daily collected in the palm of his hand and poured on the wound. He had no other means with which to irrigate the running sore. He was given barely enough water to drink. Then again, perhaps there was no gangrene because maggots hatched on the wound and fed on dead tissue. He left the wound exposed to the air and flies. He slept on a lice infected straw mattress under a single blanket and wore the same torn, blood-stained, filthy uniform he was wearing when he was captured. Twice a day he was dazzled by the dim lamp light of the hallway when the little window in the cell door was opened and his meager rations passed through. The two daily meals were always the same, weak soup, a cup of water and sometimes a hard crust of bread. He had suffered only one bout of malaria, not a particularly bad one. Still, it had nearly killed him. He wasn't sure how long the attack had lasted; he had no way of keeping track of time even when his mind was lucid. The worst times came when he was fully aware of his situation. In the darkness, he had begun to dream that death was freedom.

"Don Alacon," Lola whispered through the small window in the heavy door. She strained to see into the dark void. "Don Alacon," she said again, "I have been sent by a friend."

CHAPTER 22

It was agony for Bethany to continue attending social affairs after Felipe's incarceration at Morro Castle but she had little choice for two reasons. Her attendance at such gatherings, especially official government functions, provided invaluable intelligence for the Cubans, and the act of suddenly dropping out of Havana's social functions would attract attention, or worse, suspicion, something the Quinns could ill afford. It took considerable self-control and concentration for her to put on a cheerful face while circulating among Spanish officials knowing at any time she could receive word of Felipe's execution. More than once on the cusp of fitful sleep, the morbid question of whether or not it would be easier had Felipe been killed pricked her conscience. One learns to live with such a loss after time, but to know that just across the bay, Felipe was struggling to survive unspeakable conditions while she danced and dined with his enemies was to suffer atrocious guilt.

One evening at a garden party at the governor's palace, Bethany was approached by a young man with the milk-white skin and the rosy cheeks of a cherub.

"Habla usted inglés?" he asked in halting Spanish. He couldn't have been more than eighteen or twenty, she guessed, but he was not shy about the fact that he found her attractive. Bethany answered with a nod.

"Wonderful," he said relieved, "My Spanish is a bit lacking, I'm afraid, but I simply couldn't come all this way and see a Spanish beauty like yourself without at least knowing your name. I do hope you don't think it too rude of me to introduce myself. Winston Churchill, at your service."

"You're British!" Bethany replied, genuinely surprised. "What on earth are you doing in Havana? By the way, I am Bethany Quinn." She offered her hand.

Young Churchill lightly kissed her gloved hand. "And I believe you're American."

"Southern American," she replied.

"My mother is American," he volunteered.

"That practically makes us cousins," Bethany smiled.

"Then may I ask what brings my charming cousin to Cuba?" he asked.

"I live here. My family has a shipping business headquartered out of Havana."

At that moment they were joined by the Governor. "I see you have met our distinguished visitor," the Governor said in Spanish as he joined them, "Perhaps, Señorita Quinn, you would be kind enough to introduce him to some of my other guests. Señor Churchill's father was Lord Randolph, a member of Parliament, but you might find it more interesting to know that his mother is American."

"Why, yes, Your Excellency, he was just telling me about his mother."

"Well then, Señorita Quinn, Señor Churchill, enjoy yourselves." The Governor nodded politely and moved off to speak with other guests.

"I missed most of that I'm afraid," Churchill said.

"He said your father was a lord. Does that mean I should have curtsied when meeting his son?"

"Certainly not. I'm just plain 'ole Winny, if you like, of Her Majesty's Fourth Hussars."

"So you're a soldier. Seems I recall that Spain was once your greatest enemy: the Armada, Sir Francis Drake, all that ruckus. I'm told Drake tried to take Havana in his day." In mock seriousness, Bethany continued, "Why I declare, Winny, have you come to spy? Seems you English never give up."

"Actually, I'm on leave from the army," he said somewhat defensively, leading Bethany to conclude he really was spying. "I'm here as a reporter for the *London Daily Graphic*. Fetched myself a trip to Cuba to see the little war these Latins have cooked up. Must be amusing to you Americans, it being in such close proximity to your shore. I'm going out on a foray toward Mantanzas on Monday with a cavalry unit commanded by a Colonel Salas Cañizares. Do you know him, by chance? I should like to know a little about the fellow."

Bethany shook her head, "I've never met him."

"No matter." He continued, "Just hope he's the aggressive type. With a bit of luck, I might get to report firsthand on a little action." Bethany had to bite her tongue to keep from jumping down his throat. Instead she forced a smile, "I doubt you'll see any action. We're told these rebels don't really fight very often. They're said to run around burning sugarcane mostly. But do be careful, you hear? I wouldn't want my newly found American cousin to get his fool head shot off. Wouldn't look good in the *Graphic*."

She meant the last part. As soon as she could corner Fitzhugh Lee, who was at the party, she led him to a quiet spot in the garden and told him about the plans of the young British visitor, and asked, "Is he of any real importance?"

"You mean if he got himself killed over here?" he asked.

Bethany nodded.

"It would not do the situation any good, that's for sure," Lee responded. "According to the advance information I received from Washington, the whipper-snapper's ancestor was the first Duke of Marlborough and his father was a powerful member of Parliament. He died just a couple of years ago. I'd say the last thing the rebels would want is blame for killing a member of one of the best known families of the British Empire. The English might raise a ruckus, even support their old rival Spain against the rebels to uphold England's honor and all that sort of thing."

Bethany left the party with deep anger and concern. Anger at the foolish plans of the rosy-cheeked English boy. Concern because she was aware, from information she had transmitted only the day before, that Gómez knew of Cañizares' patrol and had ordered Pedro Betancourt to ambush the Spaniard. It took until Sunday afternoon for her message to reach Gómez. It took all Sunday night and well into Monday before Gómez's messengers located Betancourt in the field. The rebel commander planned to ambush Cañizares at twilight when the Spanish were worn out from their march and not likely to pursue their attackers into falling darkness. It was an excellent plan, and Cañizares was a prize Betancourt had maneuvered long to trap. He was furious at the order to cancel his attack.

"I have waited months for this opportunity," he complained to his lieutenant. "Now, when I have the son of a dog, I am ordered to let him go!"

Though he vented his temper at all those around him, at General Gómez, at the devil himself, he followed the order. From a concealed position he slowly scanned the Spanish column through his binoculars until he found the object of his anger, a short, fair skinned young man in khaki suit, pith helmet and polished brown boots, riding beside a Spanish lieutenant. "You will never know what a lucky Englishman you are," Betancourt seethed through clenched teeth.

America was bored and tired of a lingering economic depression. Newspaper sales had been lagging throughout the country when 35-year-old publisher William Randolph Hearst stumbled onto a way of boosting the circulation of his newspapers beyond all expectations. He began to put stories of the Cuban rebellion on the front page under banner headlines. The articles presented the conflict as if it were some adventure serial complete with shocking daily installments dripping with blood and atrocities. How exciting! Readers could have war with their coffee and toast at the breakfast table. Other publishers were quick to follow Hearst's lead. The American press unwittingly became the Cuban rebels' most powerful ally.

Jonathan learned that fact at La Piña de Plata where he often stopped for a drink after work. It had become the favorite watering hole of American correspondents covering the rebellion.

"What are you looking so glum about, Freddy?" Jonathan sat down next to a rotund gentleman. "Here you are in Havana, not much to do, plenty of good rum, ice to pour it over, pretty women to look at . . ."

"The bastard expects me to go to the front, as if there was one, and get my ass shot off."

Jonathan leaned back and made an exaggerated observation of the man's considerable backside. "Looks to me like that might take a lot 'a shootin', but it'd be hard to miss."

"That insult will cost you a drink, my Rebel friend." The big sandy-haired, ruddy-faced man from Canton, New York, motioned the cantinero to refill their glasses. With some degree of celebrity from his illustrations of the American West, Frederic Remington had landed a job with Hearst's *New York Journal* and was sent to Cuba to cover the war as an illustrator and correspondent.

"I told that bastard Hearst there is no front. Hell, I told him there is no real war, not like the public imagines; great armies clashing on the plains of Cuba." Remington took a sip of iced whiskey. "If the damn Spanish knew where the front was they'd go there, engage the Rebels in a set piece battle and finish the thing now wouldn't they? If Spain can't find a front, how the hell am I supposed to find one?" Remington took another swig. "You know what the bastard wired back? He said, 'You furnish the illustrations, I'll furnish the war.'"

"Can he do that?" Jonathan asked.

Remington shrugged, "Hearst with the *Journal*, Dana's *Sun*, and Pulitzer with the *World* have driven their respective circulations to record highs pumping Cuban blood and guts all over their front pages. Papers all over the country have picked up on the ploy."

"But the U.S. government and big business are doing everything they can to keep America out of this Cuban mess," Jonathan suggested.

"It doesn't matter a tinker's damn what the government and big money want. The public has war fever because of what's on the pages of their newspapers. Hell, if there's no new Spanish atrocity to report, the papers just make one up."

"Is that a fact?" Jonathan said with, what seemed to Remington, a peculiar grin on his face. "Cantinero!" Quinn called. "Give this damn Yankee another drink."

If the wealth and might of a nation is assumed to be reflected by the trappings of their diplomats' offices, one would, upon entering Fitzhugh Lee's office, have the impression that the United States was a backwater nation with little wealth and almost no international standing; which was, in fact, the general opinion held by the nations of Europe in 1897.

Lee's office was a large room with plain white walls yellowing with age and a tile floor. The few chairs scattered about had cane bottoms without cushions. Bookcases crammed with neglected volumes lined the walls. A dusty world globe sat on the top of a roll-top desk crowded with stacks of papers. A large map of Cuba hung in one corner opposite an American flag. An odd four-inch-high platform the size of a card table lay on the floor under Fitzhugh's chair so the short man could sit high enough to comfortably reach his desk. A rather worn, black, leather chaise lounge with a soiled bed pillow was shoved against one wall. Lee apparently took his daily siesta at the office.

The Consul General rose from a cloud of cigar smoke to greet his visitors. "Miss. Bethany, what a pleasure. As for you, Captain Quinn," he said with mock grumpiness, "what kind of trouble are you going to drop in my lap this time?" He drew up two chairs and invited his guests to sit.

"Are the newspapers back home really whipping up war fever?" Jonathan asked.

"If you mean the likes of Hearst and Pulitzer the answer is yes. They're driving the President crazy. Congress is gettin' mail by the car load, all of it pro-Cuba. Seems the people have forgotten what the war was like, at least up North where they never saw any of it. And don't forget we're in the worst economic depression this century. The whole country is looking for something to take their minds off their troubles. News of Cuba's *War of Independence* reads like a serialized dime novel, but I think it will take more than sensational journalism to force the Congress to vote for American intervention."

"What do you suggest by *more*, Mr. Lee?" Bethany asked.

"Now both of you know I don't intend to suggest a darn thing. And I don't want to know what's in your pretty mind Miss Bethany, or yours Captain," he said turning to Jonathan. "My job is to take orders from the Department of State, protect the lives and property of American citizens, and stay out of Cuban internal affairs."

"Lives and property of Americans," Jonathan repeated. "How would you go about protecting them?"

"Any means I can persuade the government to provide if there was a clear and present danger," he answered.

"Does that mean the U.S. Army?"

"It does not," Fitzhugh answered. "At least not right off."

"All right. What might be done *right off* if American lives and property were threatened by Spain? Hell, they already burned American property all over the country."

Fitzhugh scoffed, "Now, we all know who burned what, don't we? You asked a question and I'll answer it, but I'm not going to play games with you and get myself in trouble." He took a drag off his cigar. "If riots or fighting threatened Havana, endangered American lives here in the city, I would request a U.S. Navy ship to ensure the peace, or use it to evacuate Americans if that failed. That's the best I can expect from Washington as things stand. Now, you two get out of here and let me do my work."

As they rose to leave, Lee said, "I almost forgot, Miss Bethany, I have some news. The Spanish have agreed to move your friend from Morro Castle's dungeons to the Cabañas Castle prison. Now, I know that doesn't sound like much, but believe me, conditions are better there."

"Cabañas! That's where they've shot so many Cubans. We've heard the shots."

"Believe me, Spain is painfully aware of what is being printed by the American press. Even Weyler knows it would be a mistake to shoot legitimate military prisoners, especially officers like your friend. I'm doing the best I can for him, Miss Bethany."

Bethany left, not certain what Lee told her was true. She didn't think Lola told her the truth either.

Lola had never described to Bethany the abhorrent conditions in which she found the tortured, sick, almost dead, Don Alacon. All she told Bethany was that he was alive.

Desperate action often makes a bad situation worse. In the summer of '97, an Italian anarchist by the name of Miguel Angiolillo was recruited by a Cuban agent in Paris and paid 500 francs to go to Spain and assassinate the arch-conservative Spanish premier, Antonio Cánovas del Castillo. Angiolillo promptly earned his pay by killing Cánovas in the spa town of Santa Áqueda. (Miguel Angiolillo was promptly caught by Spanish authorities and garroted to death in the town of Vergara, Spain.) Prospects for peace did appear to improve. A moderate, Práxedes Mateo Sagasta, became premier and was able to form a liberal government opposed to the war in Cuba. He recalled

General Weyler, appointed General Ramón Blanco y Erenas in his place, and instructed him to *Fight the Cubans in a Christian and humane manner.*

Premier Sagasta immediately took steps he felt would lead to peace. He proposed granting Cuba autonomy under Spain. The American Congress applauded the move as a way to end the war. Unfortunately, Sagasta's plan created a strange consensus against autonomy. The Cubans suspected autonomy would result in Spain ruling Cuba in the same old way under a different name. Spain had promised reforms after the Ten Years War and delivered nothing. On the other side of the fence, the Spanish residing on the island feared Cuban retribution if autonomy was granted. The result was continued Cuban resistance in the field and Spanish dissension in the cities.

Lee advised President McKinley that although prospects for peace might have improved with a new government in Spain, there was trouble brewing in the island's capital. He suggested U.S. naval ships show the flag in Havana Harbor to calm the very real fears of the many Americans there.

The President wasn't ready to go that far, but he allowed his Secretary of the Navy, John Davis Long, to move the battleship *Maine*, America's newest and best, from Chesapeake Bay to Port Royal, South Carolina. There, he figured, the ship would be close enough to reach Cuba in an emergency, but far enough away not to alarm Spain. Her captain, Charles Sigsbee, was ordered to keep her bunkers filled with coal and standby.

Deteriorating conditions in the Cuban capital gave Lee reason for worry. Food was getting scarce in Havana, American citizens of Cuban descent were being mistreated, and American businesses were facing difficulties because of the war. The Consul General, as well as other Americans on the island, voiced real concerns to Washington.

At Port Royal, Sigsbee received a message originating from the assistant secretary of the navy, Theodore Roosevelt. It read, *Be prepared to sail. Orders to follow.* Orders did follow. On the 10th of December 1897, *Maine* departed North Carolina for Key West. As an excuse for the battleship's presence in the area, several smaller vessels of the Atlantic Squadron were sent to join her for "naval exercises" off Dry Tortugas.

On the 12th of January 1898, Bethany and Louisette were returning from Jonathan's office when an angry mob swept past them toward the offices of the government controlled Havana newspaper. The two ladies were roughly shoved into a doorway. Louisette was upset more by Bethany than the crowd. Since the revolution began, Bethany had begun to once again decorate her lovely thigh with Jonathan's gift from years before. She quickly retrieved the little pistol.

"Mon Dieu!" Louisette scolded Bethany, partly for showing her leg in public, but mainly because she thought it unladylike for women to handle firearms, "I thought you put away that terrible toy years ago. Surely, you would not shoot anyone here in the street."

"I'll shoot the first son of a bitch who lays a hand on us," Bethany said, stepping back into the street and leading Louisette away from the disturbance.

"What language! All the Quinns are crazy," she said in French. Louisette always reverted to her native language when she was aggravated.

"Yes, we are, and if I have to shoot someone it is your crazy husband's fault."

"My Jonathan? No, how could that be?"

"Because no man or beast, and certainly not his niece, would dare face J. Hillary if they allowed anything to happen to the woman he loves more than anything in the world." Bethany smiled at the petite, still lovely French lady.

"Never mind about me. Here you are, guns, spying. Yes! I know about that. And I know your revolutionary lover is in prison. You should be married to some nice young man in Mississippi."

"Walk faster, Louisette."

"It's this narrow skirt. French women are not in the habit of choosing fashions designed for running."

The sound of breaking glass and shouting swept up the street behind them. Narrow skirt or not, Louisette beat Bethany to the corner. A moment later the two ladies flattened against a wall to avoid another group of rioters running down the street. Bethany was surprised to see several armed Spanish soldiers among them.

Angered by the newspaper's support of Madrid's autonomy plan, the mob, composed entirely of Spanish protesters, smashed windows and attacked the newspaper's workers.

The occurrence of a riot was enough to alarm Fitzhugh Lee, but as he ventured out to observe the scene himself, he saw a situation that was more threatening than he expected. General Weyler had been sent home, but leading the riot were some of his former officers and militiamen, all of whom were armed. What was even more alarming was that Havana did nothing to quell the violence. Lee was convinced that Spanish authorities were losing control in the capital. He wired Washington.

The battleship *Maine* was anchored off Dry Tortugas on the night of January 24 when a lookout spotted navigation lights fast approaching. Alerted, Sigsbee ordered his engineer to get up full steam even before the vessel reached them.

The torpedo boat *Dupont* came alongside and delivered the following message: *Maine to proceed to Havana, Cuba and make a friendly call. Stop. Pay respects to the authorities there. Stop. Particular attention must be paid to usual interchange of civility. Stop. Torpedo boat must not accompany Maine. Stop. The squadron must not return to Key West on this account. END.*

An agreement had been reached with Spain. *USS Maine* would be allowed to visit Havana. In exchange, the Spanish battleship *Viscaya* would visit New York.

Maine got quickly underway for Havana. Her crew spent the night passing ammunition from the magazines up to the seven fifty-seven millimeter Drigs-Schroeder and the four thirty-seven millimeter Hotchkiss guns on deck.

On the twenty-fifth of January, 1898, Jonathan, Louisette, Bethany and Fitzhugh Lee stood among several thousand Cuban citizens lining the shore to watch the American battleship enter Havana Harbor. The vessel looked splendid with her white hull, straw-colored superstructure, stacks, and masts, and her four big, black, ten-inch guns glistening in the sun. She was flying bunting in salute, adding a holiday flare to her entrance. The ship was impressive. Everyone knew she was there to protect American citizens and property, but neither the Cuban people nor Spanish authorities felt threatened. Madrid had gained general approval by the U.S. Congress for her plan of autonomy for the island and been assured that peace would bring new American investments. War with America was the last thing Spain wanted.

As *Maine* passed beneath Morro Castle, master harbor pilot Lopez, taken aboard at the sea buoy, pointed out a group of numbered dots representing mooring buoys on the harbor chart. "Would this location be satisfactory?" His finger moved to a dot marked #4. Sigsbee nodded. A short time later, Lopez left *Maine* tranquilly moored to buoy number four in Havana Bay.

Captain Sigsbee, in the company of American Consul-General Fitzhugh Lee, presented himself and his officers to the Spanish authorities. Madrid had ordered the Spanish governor to avoid any trouble regarding *Maine* or her crew. Friendly reception or not, Sigsbee was determined to take every precaution to safeguard his ship. Marine Sentries were armed and posted about the deck, ammunition was piled near all the light guns. Any boat approaching the ship, however small, was to be challenged and turned away. To preclude any incidents in the capital, the enlisted crew would not be given liberty ashore. Only officers would be allowed on Cuban soil. Within a few days, all tension of the situation faded.

In January the temperature in Havana averaged eighty-five to ninety degrees Fahrenheit. Seasonal rain showers only added to the sticky humidity and did nothing to improve the sultry heat for the 354 enlisted men crowded aboard *Maine*. The poorly ventilated iron ship quickly became uncomfortable. To make the ship a little more livable, the main boiler fires were banked and only the two small auxiliary boilers were kept active to drive generators to provide electric power for lights and pumps. Bored with little to do day after day, the crew could only look longingly at the beautiful city of Havana and talk of the delights they were missing ashore. Happily, news arrived that the Navy planned to send the battleship to New Orleans by February seventeenth for the annual Mardi Gras celebration. The scuttlebutt about liberty in New Orleans greatly improved morale.

The Navy was satisfied that America had shown its might and its ability to quickly respond if Madrid did not protect American citizens. Consul General Lee was not so convinced. He argued that in order to maintain the status of protection they had gained, the *Maine* not only should not be moved, but an additional ship should join her. What if real trouble flared up? *Maine* would have to stay on station to protect Americans in Havana. Spain would surely cut the underwater telegraph line. Only a second ship, even a torpedo boat, he argued, would guarantee a message got through in case of trouble. Washington was not persuaded. Sending *Maine* to New Orleans during Mardi Gras would boost public relations and Navy recruiting.

Venting his frustration to Jonathan over a glass of bourbon one afternoon, Lee let slip the proposed departure date of the American battleship. That information was relayed through Bethany to the insurgent command as a matter of routine intelligence.

Within days Jonathan received an urgent request to attend a clandestine meeting in the city. The message addressed the obvious danger such a meeting posed to all concerned, but stated circumstances of the first order made attendance imperative. On the appointed night, a closed carriage slowed but did not stop on a darkened street in the deserted wholesale district of Havana.

Jonathan stepped quickly from the moving carriage and hid in a doorway for several minutes. He then walked several blocks, turned a corner, and doubled back twice to be sure he wasn't being followed. Satisfied, he turned down an alley and knocked on a door marked Almacén Ferretería de Aviles (Aviles Hardware Warehouse). A peep hole in the large warehouse door opened. Jonathan could see only a partial face, wrinkled brow and dark eyes, peering out at him. He heard the movement of a bolt and a Judas gate in the large door opened. Jonathan stepped warily into the building. Without a word, the doorkeeper, an old woman, closed and bolted the door, picked up a candle and led him up two flights of stairs. She pointed to a ladder fixed vertically to the wall at the end of the hall, and left.

The ladder ended at a hatch in the ceiling. Jonathan scaled the ladder, pushed open the hatch and climbed through into a windowless attic illuminated by a single oil lantern. When his eyes adjusted to the dim light, he saw a handful of men waiting silently. He nodded to the one man in the room he recognized and took a seat on a crude bench. The heat was stifling.

"So," the man said standing, "We begin." He surveyed the shadowy faces in the room. "I don't have to tell you how bad things are. Nor do I have to explain that our only hope for victory is to get the Yankees to intercede against Spain." He looked at Jonathan. "Without that help, the best we can expect is another stalemate in which event all will have been for nothing. Cuba will lie crippled under Spanish rule to suffer Madrid's retribution. On the other hand, if an aggressive act against American interests can be carried out in such a way as to place the blame upon Spain, we can be assured of two things according to our sources in the Estados Unidos. The Americano press will demand América's honor be defended, and the people of América will support retaliation against Spain. It must be something the Americano Congress cannot ignore. Providence has handed us such an opportunity. Before its scheduled departure, an act of aggression must be staged against the Yankee battleship and blamed on Spain."

The statement stunned Jonathan. The speaker turned his attention to the grave faces around him. His next words left Jonathan aghast.

"We began exploring the possibilities shortly after the Americano ship arrived. We don't dream of doing great damage, of sinking the grand ship. We don't want to harm her Americano crew. All we need do is create the impression that Spanish conservatives, Weyler's supporters, carried out an attack against the ship. Its very presence offends their Spanish honor. Our agents in América have assured us that the Americano press will blame such an act on Madrid. However, Capitán Quinn, we need your help in solving two problems which Señor Castallano will explain."

A voice from the shadows of the smoke-filled room spoke up. "One problem is to determine the right amount of explosives required to create the impression of a serious hostile act. We don't want it to appear to be the work of amateurs. The attempt must be convincing, something on the order of a naval mine. The world will know we Cubans do not have access to such a weapon. The second problem is to determine some way to deliver the explosives."

There was a period of silence. Dimly lit faces turned toward Jonathan. Castallano invited, "Your thoughts, Capitán Quinn."

In the tiny overheated room, Jonathan broke out in a cold sweat and remained silent for nearly a minute trying to fathom some way to discourage plans he thought insane.

"Seems to me you have more problems than that," Jonathan finally responded. "You can't get aboard the vessel. It will do no good to float a device against her sides because of the thick armor plate that I'm sure extends several feet below the waterline. Such an attempt would look amateurish. That leaves the unarmored bottom hull plate. Where *Maine* is moored, the harbor is about six fathoms deep. You will have to have a waterproof device that can withstand the pressure down at least thirty-six feet if you are going to set it on the bottom below her. Even if you succeed in making a device that is waterproof, how will you detonate it? It would take over a mile of wire if you wanted to use electricity even if you can get your hands on an electric waterproof detonator, not that they have proven reliable as yet." Jonathan hoped he had discouraged the whole idea.

A little man with thick glasses stood up, "As Señor Castallano said, we only have two problems, Capitán, selecting the proper amount of explosives and getting the device under the ship. We have solved the problem of detonating the device. I am a chemist and have spent three weeks, since the ship arrived, perfecting a reliable explosive device. We have had three consecutive successes at a depth of six fathoms."

"How," Jonathan responded weakly.

"We use a barrel weighed down with explosives and pig iron, enough to give it a slight negative buoyancy; that is, it sinks, but barely. It will sit lightly on the bottom. If anchored on a tether, we expect it will swing with the tide. If we could tie it off the mooring buoy, for instance, it would stay approximately beneath or close to the ship however it swung with the tide. In any case, the explosion would be close enough to be taken as a serious attempt against the Americano ship. How to deliver it is the second problem. We know how to detonate the device." The little man dabbed the sweat off his brow with a handkerchief. "Are you familiar with gun cotton?"

"Yes," Jonathan answered, "It's touchy stuff, used in making explosives, artillery shells and such."

"Si," agreed the chemist, "There are two kinds."

Everything had been said in Spanish up to that point, but Jonathan now interrupted. "Just a minute. My Spanish is fair when it comes to everyday conversation, but if you're going to explain all this in scientific terms, I need someone to interpret for me."

"I will speak in English," replied the chemist proudly, "I was educated in New York. Now, as I was saying, there are two kinds of gun cotton. One is made from pine fiber and is called tri-nitro cellulose. It is non-hygroscopic, that is, it does not react with water. Therefore it is not of interest here."

"But I thought you wanted something waterproof," Jonathan replied.

"Let me finish, please," the little man said somewhat impatiently. "The second type of gun cotton is made from cotton fiber saturated with pyroxylin. It is hydroscopic. If sea water comes in contact with pyroxylin, the free sulfuric acid in the gun cotton is chemically attacked by the bromine, iodine, and common salt contained in seawater. This causes a rapid rise in temperature resulting in a sudden explosion. That is how we will trigger the bomb. A jug will be placed into a water tight, weighted, barrel containing dynamite. The neck of the jug will extend outside the barrel through a tightly sealed bung hole. The jug will be packed full of pyroxylin gun cotton. The neck of the jug will be plugged with a water-soluble paste and the jug corked to keep out water. Inside the dry barrel, wrapped around the jug, will be a fuse train consisting of a small amount of lead azide and gun powder. When lead azide is lightly packed, not too confined, it will flash like powder, only much faster. Used as a fuse, the initial amount of azide will ensure the detonator ignites before any water can reach it. Azide is a sensitive substance. When densely packed and tightly confined, it will detonate like dynamite. The fuse will lead to a large tightly wrapped ball of lead azide positioned in the middle of the dynamite package. This mass of azide will detonate with enough force to set off the dynamite. When the barrel is released, the cork will be pulled from the jug allowing water to slowly dissolve the soluble paste plug. Within an hour or so, salt water will reach the gun cotton, react with pyroxylin and boom." The chemist smiled proudly.

Smart little bastard, Jonathan said to himself.

"What we need to know, Capitán," said a man from the shadows, "is how much dynamite, in your estimation, will it take to blow a hole in the bottom of an iron ship . . . not big enough to sink it, you understand, but enough to make it look as if the Spanish tried to do so."

I don't even want to know about this, and they are asking me. "You are hesitating, Capitán, and we understand. The ship is manned by your countrymen. But, Capitán Quinn, even if a handful of them are killed, what measure is that when compared with 200,000 Cubans who have already died? Hundreds are dying in the camps each day. Some are dying this moment as we speak. It must end. I regret that after doing so much to help us, we now need your knowledge to aid in this effort, but we have no choice but to ask you. However, we assure you your confidence here will never be violated, nor ours. Everyone here has taken an oath. No one in this room will ever speak a word under penalty of death for themselves and their families. I am sorry, but it is unavoidable that you are one of us now."

Jesus Christ! Jonathan struggled to resolve the terrible dilemma of his own conscience. He had tried to envision some means of securing American involvement in the war himself, but he was appalled at the thought of taking violent, clandestine action against an American ship to accomplish that goal. True, he had fought against ships of that flag once, but that was a different time, a different America, a different cause. On the other hand, not only was a hopeless war tearing an island and its people apart, but his own future and fortune was now at risk unless peace could be obtained.

Damn me! Bethany was right. I've violated my own rule; been personally involved for years; too goddamned deeply involved. He could feel sweat under his arms running down his sides, sweat beginning to drip off the end of his nose. It wasn't all due to the heat in the room. He looked at the dimly lit faces around him. *This is a dark way to gain the light of freedom.* Jonathan slowly rose to his feet.

"It's not a simple matter, gentlemen. I can't get aboard, and the navy does not give out drawings of its war ships. I can only speak in general terms and guesses with no guarantee of accuracy."

"We understand, Capitán."

The hell you do. Now my whole damn family's in this thing.

John paused again. *No way out now.*

"From what I've seen of her, I estimate *Maine* to be over 300 feet long, maybe 60 feet wide, displacing five or six thousand tons. I know from the harbor pilot who brought her in that she's drawing about four fathoms. She is, gentlemen, a formidable chunk of iron. To float a device against her would do nothing as I told you. We can assume that her sides are heavily armor plated well below the water line. Dragging a mine under her would be clumsy at best and the attempt would probably be seen by lookouts. We must remember that there are other ships moored out there. A loose mine won't choose sides. The greatest risk is that your Cuban rebels could get caught. That would ensure the end of any popular support by the American people. Make no mistake about it. You risk turning the American people against you, against all you have worked to achieve."

"Capitán. We have no other choice. We know of nothing else that will rouse the Americans to take action. We have little left with which to fight."

"All right," Jonathan took a deep breath, tried to gather the strength to continue. "You must consider that a new iron ship of war may have double bottoms. However, ships' bottoms aren't armor plated. If you get enough explosives under her you will punch a hole in her."

"What do you mean by enough?" the man asked.

"Well, at her current draft you can figure she has 12 or 15 feet of water under her keel. The way you have explained your device to me, that means you have got to have enough bang to come off the bottom through ten or 15 feet of water and blow in her hull plates. I'm no expert on mines or hydraulic pressures. My guess is that it will take maybe 50 pounds of dynamite directly underneath the ship to hole her. Like you said, you don't want to sink her or kill her crew. Besides, git'en the device under or near the ship will be the trick. No boat is allowed near her, not even a skiff."

"We were hoping you could suggest a way," said a voice from the dark.

"You mean besides asking swimmers to commit suicide?" Jonathan said jokingly.

"We have thought of that," the voice replied. "We're running out of time, ammunition, men, and all the while our women and children and old people are dying in the camps. If there is no other way we have young swimmers who have volunteered."

Another voice reminded, "If the ship leaves for New Orleans as planned, we have less than a week left, gentlemen."

"The explosive will be ready," the chemist promised, "but someone must find a way to deliver it under the ship."

Bethany was waiting in the dark when Jonathan returned to the house. "I know you have been to a meeting. Orders for six men were sent out and your name was one of them. I tried to get here in time to stop you. You were crazy to risk a meeting in Havana. Go ahead and tell me. It has to be grave or they wouldn't have risked exposing you."

Jonathan checked the hallway to be sure no one else of the household could be listening.

"If I tell you, you will be at risk. So will Louisette."

"That's funny, Jonathan. Do you think I'm at any less risk as it is? What do you think would happen if my activities were discovered, if I let slip one word of what I know? Don't you think I know the Cubans would try to kill me before the Spanish could make me talk? If I were arrested, you would have about ten minutes to escape before they came for you and Louisette. Now tell me damnit. Or would you rather I ask them myself?"

Jonathan had little choice. If Bethany carried out her threat, the very act of asking would get them all killed. He told her as little as he could about the meeting, but emphasized the threat to the family should he be blamed for leaking information about the plan.

"My God, Jonathan, have you gone mad? That's an American ship! Those are American sailors, a lot of them Southern boys. At the governor's reception I met one officer from Virginia and another from Georgia."

"They're right about one thing, Bee Bee. That ship is the only chance to get the American Congress to act. If you want this thing to end, *Maine* is the key. Otherwise the rebellion will fizzle out just like before. All will be lost and Felipe will rot in prison. Why should they let him go? They made that mistake last time with Gómez, Garcia and the others, and they know it. They aren't likely this time to turn loose experienced guerilla leaders only to have them come back and start another war."

"But an American ship! Oh, God! If American boys are killed, even to save Felipe, could I live with that on my conscience? Could you?"

"Hell, Bethany, fifty or so pounds of dynamite won't sink a battleship. If they do find a way to get it under her, it might punch a hole in her bottom. The crew will seal off the damaged compartment and Congress will raise hell about the attempt to sink her. I'm not saying that no one will get hurt. When you fool with explosives that's a risk, but the idea is to make a convincing strike against the ship, not sink it or kill its crew. With a little luck there shouldn't be serious injuries, especially if it goes off at night. No crewmen are likely to be working down in the storerooms and bilges at that time of day. I've learned they're only running a small boiler to provide lights. There won't be more than two men in the engine room, and I'd judge that will be well aft of any mine."

"Something could go wrong."

"Yes it could, Bee Bee. A warship has ammunition magazines and we don't know where they are, but it's likely they're under the big guns and well protected. It's a risk, but it's the only chance to get America in this thing. Besides, if someone during the next day or two doesn't figure out a way to get the device out to the ship, all this will be academic. *Maine* is scheduled to depart any day. The Cubans are so desperate they told me if no one comes up with an acceptable plan, young Cuban boys will try to swim the mine out at night."

"Surely, they wouldn't allow that. It'd be suicide."

"They're already training a dozen volunteers."

It was Lola who actually gave Bethany the idea. The two met in the market place to exchange messages.

Bethany told Lola, "I have nothing official today, but I was hoping you would have word of Felipe."

"I will see him tomorrow," Lola replied, "He has gained a few pounds I think. His spirits are better. He gets a little sunlight in his new cell and sometimes they let him into the courtyard."

"How will I ever thank you for what you are doing, the risk you're taking."

"You owe me nothing. I've always loved him, but from a distance. That is the safest kind of love they say, the one you cannot have."

Bethany changed the subject, "How are things with you?"

"My cantína is making a little money, but my girls are complaining about the American ship."

"Complaining? What has *Maine* done to them?"

Lola laughed. "Nothing! That's the trouble. All those horny American sailors out there and not one of them allowed to come ashore. My girls say it is very uncivilized of the Yankee navy."

The idea slipped into Bethany's mind like quicksilver.

He watched her enter the office and walk across the room to the window. She stood there a moment looking out at the battleship floating tranquilly at her mooring.

"I think I have a way to deliver the mine if your Cubans can figure out the mechanics of how to conceal it and tie it to the buoy," she said without turning around.

"You have a way?" Jonathan asked skeptically.

"Don't laugh," she said. "The plan involves cantina girls and horny sailors."

CHAPTER 23

The many small boats moving about the bay steered well clear of *Maine*. When she first anchored in the harbor, bumboats loaded with souvenirs and fruit went out to greet her but were driven away by armed Marine guards posted on deck. Discouraged, the bumboats turned their attention to the newly arrived American passenger ship *City of Washington* moored to the south of *Maine* and two Spanish navy ships, *Legazpi* and *Alfonso XII*, moored just northwest of her.

The sun was low on the horizon when the young Marine guard on the bow noticed a particular whaleboat among the small craft plying the harbor. It attracted his attention for two reasons. It was loaded with a very colorful cargo and it was making directly for him. Lola's girls, waving and shouting, had already passed close aboard the Spanish naval vessels in the harbor.

In the case of an ordinary bumboat, the young Marine would have immediately called the sergeant of the guards, but he decided to hold off a few minutes, at least until the boat was close enough for him to look over the ladies crowding every seat except those occupied by the four oarsmen and the coxswain manning the rudder. The guard posted amidships on the port side as well as a dozen or so sailors lounging on deck also noticed the boatload of lovelies waving gaily as their craft made directly for the bow of their ship.

The oarsmen pulled hard with every stroke. It was not the load of sweet painted ladies that made such work of rowing. It was the drag beneath the keel. Fastened to the bottom of the whaleboat, a hinged round frame of iron straps held a barrel locked in place by a single pin. Two heavy fishing lines, one attached to the locking-pin of the hinged frame and one attached to a cork sealing the neck of a glass jug protruding from the center of the barrel, ran aft where they were fastened to the gunwale within reach of the coxswain. A third, slightly heavier line was anchored to the barrel itself and led from under the boat up the side and over the gunwale where it ended in a coil affixed with a hook at an oarsman's feet.

Without a hint as to its real purpose, Bethany suggested to Lola that because there had been no problems since *Maine*'s arrival, no hint of trouble in Havana, that maybe the crew, prompted by an invitation from her girls, could persuade the captain to let the sailors have one day of liberty ashore. Lola was told a local fisherman could furnish a boat. She accepted the offer and instructed her young ladies to ride out to the battleship and tease and taunt its Yankee crew, show the pleasures awaiting them in Havana. The ladies could use the business.

A group of sailors gathered on the forward deck at *Maine's* bow as the whale-boat approached.

"Hey, Yankee sailor boys! You come Havana have good time, no?" a young girl hailed as the boat glided just under the bow. "Si! Si!" said another standing up on the seat, "You come Havana, we have party." She wiggled her hips and blew a kiss to a chorus of hoots and cat calls from the men on deck.

The girls wore brightly colored clothes. Some had blouses that hung low off their shoulders revealing a generous amount of cleavage, while others sat with their skirts above their knees, all playing to an eager audience.

"Come on guys, move it. You're gonna git me in trouble," protested the young Marine. "You there in the boat, move away. Vaya! Vaya!" He turned to a sailor next to him. "That means go, don't it?"

The girls giggled and called up to them in broken English, some making unmistakable gestures. The sailors hollered and whistled their enthusiasm. The young guard knew things were out of hand. "Sergeant of the guards!" the baby faced Marine called at the top of his lungs. The command was dutifully repeated by the guard amidships.

"Now what the hell did you go and do that for?" complained a gunner's mate standing next to him. "We ain't seen snatch since Port Royal and here a whole friggin' boatload comes out to remind us what we been missing, and you start balling for your friggin' sergeant."

"Yeah, shithead. What you think them sweet pussies gonna do, attack a battleship?"

A pimply faced kid grinning from ear to ear asked, "Hey Chief, how many days in the brig would I git for accidentally falling off into that lovely pile of tits down there?"

"You're too young to know what to do with pussy if you fell in it," the chief replied. "Any man thinking of dropping into that boat should know he'll be cleaning bilges 'til he's so old he'll forget what it's for. Now take a good look and back off so the Marine here can do his duty."

"I like you, Yankee sailor," yelled a plump girl in a low cut blouse that did little to conceal her voluptuous bosom. She pointed at the chief, "I got what you want, muchacho."

"You just wait for me, Darling," he said. "They can't keep us locked on board forever."

The girl took her ample breasts in her hands and lifted them out of her blouse for all to see. A great cheer went up as every eye focused on the sublime display.

The whaleboat was directly under the bow where the ship's heavy mooring chain hung vertically from the hawsepipe to the shackle on the mooring buoy. One of the oarsman on the starboard side held to the buoy to keep the boat from drifting. With such a remarkable pair of breasts to hold the attention of the men hanging over the bow, it was a simple matter for him to snap the hook attached to the end of the line to the buoy ring and ease the weighted line coiled at his feet into the water. He nodded to the helmsman. The barrel was tethered to the buoy.

"All right, break it up! I want every swinging dick off this bow right fucking now!"

"Aw, come on Sergeant, what the hell harm is a boat load of sweet young pussy gonna do?"

"Yeah, Sarge. Look for yourself. Ain't they beau-tee-ful?"

"You're what's beautiful, chief. Out here egging your crew on when you should have cleared the deck yourself. I ought to write you up. What the hell you trying to do, get my boy court-martialed? Shit! I ought to write all of ya' up. Now clear the bow you worthless, horny bastards!"

"Fucking jarhead," someone said as the sailors reluctantly moved away.

"I heard that!" the sergeant spat. "Any more remarks like that and I'll show you a fucking jarhead all right. Now move!" He leaned over the bow, "You down there. Get that fucking boat moving, you comprende? Vayase!" He turned to the private. "I ought to kick your butt, you little monkey fucker. Allowing that boat to approach like that and then letting half the fucking crew gather up here. What the hell were your orders? You think you're posted on the bow to look at pussy?"

"No, Sarge, but I couldn't a' kept them fellows off the bow if I was to shoot at 'em. An how was I to keep that boat load of women off. Nobody told me I was to shoot a boatload of girls, Sarge. I called you. I done followed procedure and called for help. What was I to do?"

"You're to act like a fucking Marine, handle the situation! That's what the hell you're to do! Christ! What do you think they assign Marines to Navy ships for? Fucking sailors ain't supposed to have no brains. But you're a Marine posted to this ship to keep order. Don't you ever fucking forget it! You hear me, boy?"

"Yes, Sergeant!" the boy shouted.

"You screw up just one more time on this cruise and your ass is in the brig."

"Yes, Sergeant!"

While the sailors cleared the bow and the sergeant chewed out the young guard, the helmsman of the whaleboat reached casually behind him and pulled hard on the line attached to the pin beneath the boat. The holding cage dropped open and the barrel was free. As the heavily tarred, weighted barrel slowly settled toward the bottom, the helmsman jerked hard on the second line. The cork pulled free from the neck of the jug exposing the water-soluble plug. With the ladies waving and blowing kisses the boat pulled away toward the city docks.

Across the bay, the sun rolled toward the west drawing a dusky veil behind it. Below the dimming, glassy surface, the strong tidal flow of Havana Bay eased the barrel slowly to the end of its tether. It settled lightly on the bottom twelve feet beneath *Maine*.

Darkness floated down on the anchored ships as the gay lights of Havana welcomed the ladies back to shore. "Come on girls," Lola said, walking out on the dock to meet them. "The pleasure cruise is over. Time to go to work." The whaleboat pulled away to disappear forever. It would be chopped up and burned far up the bay.

Laughter spilled from the open portholes of *Maine's* forward crew quarters and drifted merrily across the still water. The sailors who had been privileged to see the boatload of beauties were describing them, in anatomical detail, to those who had not.

The ship's officers were not informed of the incident. The sergeant who had handled the situation didn't see any reason to embarrass the Corps or the young lieutenant in charge of the Marine detail. Captain Sigsbee was in his quarters writing letters while many of the officers relaxed in the ward room toward the stern. It would be another hot, boring night aboard *Maine*.

Quivering ribbons of reflected light streamed across the placid black water from the four brightly illuminated ships at anchor in Havana Harbor. Standing behind the windows in the darkened office of J & Q Shipping, Jonathan and Bethany looked out across the serene setting.

"I met her captain Sigsbee at the Governor's reception. Fitzhugh Lee introduced us," Bethany said. "You might be interested to learn that as a young officer he had blockade duty at Mobile Bay."

"I wonder if he ever tried to catch the old *Virgin*?" Jonathan mused.

"Perhaps, but there is an even greater coincidence," Bethany continued. "When Lee mentioned that my uncle served on *Alabama*, Captain Sigsbee remarked that long after the war he commanded, in his words, 'the aging veteran *Kearsarge*'."

"Well, that is poetic. Wait 'til he sees what an aging veteran from *Alabama* has helped devise for his dandy new command."

"I thought you were over all that."

"I did too 'til you mentioned *Kearsarge*. To hell with anyone who ever sailed aboard her."

"You said the explosives would do little damage and not kill her men. Now damn it, Jonathan, did you lie to me?"

"I hope not with all my soul. I only meant that a hole in the bottom of his new ship will embarrass the hell out of him. Anyway, it looks like nothing's going to happen. It should have gone off an hour ago. If it ever goes off, and it's under the ship, which it may not be, it shouldn't do more than punch a hole in the damn thing, just enough to make Congress raise hell with the Spanish to end this war. The Rebels have had it, Bee Bee. Without American intervention it's all over. Even Fitzhugh, the little feist, is spoiling for a fight."

"I don't want more fighting, damnit," Bethany said. "I want it over, all of it. I want Felipe out of that horrible prison and the dying to stop."

"That leaves *Maine*, doesn't it?" Jonathan stated. The silence in the room grew heavy. "Damn thing isn't going to work," he said. "There's a lot of pressure down at thirty-five feet. The barrel probably leaked full of water. That's what happened to the mines at Mobile Bay. Let's go home, Bee Bee, the thing's a dud. I told Louisette we would be home for dinner by nine and it's five after now."

Louisette, Bethany, and Jonathan were sitting at the dinner table when the lights went out all over Havana.

At 9:40 p.m., Tuesday, February 15, 1898, an explosion ripped a small hole through the hull of the battleship *Maine* slightly to the port side of the keel near frame number 20, bending a steel bottom plate inward. Had the explosion occurred a few feet forward, it would have done little more than flood a small stores compartment. Instead, the charge blew searing hot gases up into a small reserve magazine containing ammunition for the six-inch forward guns. The ammunition in the compartment ignited. The resulting explosion breached the adjacent bulkhead of the main forward magazine, detonating the five tons of high explosives stored there. The force of the explosion was so powerful that it momentarily lifted the forward section of the battleship out of the water.

Ashore, electricity was knocked out throughout the city as the shock wave from the blast roared across Havana. At the Quinn house on Obispo, dishes crashed down from shelves, windows shattered, and the lights flickered and went out. For a moment everyone at the table was stunned silent.

"Oh God! Jonathan!" Bethany started, "What have we . . ."

"Hush, Bethany!" he ordered, "You stay here with Louisette. I'm going to find out what in heaven has happened."

"But my God! It wasn't . . ."

"Bethany!" Jonathan said again.

Billy Wong and the serving staff entered the room carrying candles. The little Chinese man exclaimed wide-eyed, "What happen, Captain J?"

"Take care of the ladies, Billy," Jonathan ordered, "I'm going out to see what has happened. Everyone remain in the house. Do you understand Bethany?"

Bethany was silent, her expression twisted with an agony that Louisette mistook for fear.

Jonathan ran all the way. Breathless, heart pounding, he found the harbor in the throes of pandemonium. The sharp shrieks of ships' whistles and the frantic shouting of men giving orders in Spanish echoed across the water. Search lights aboard the *Legazpi* and *Alfonso XII* gave an eerie, supernatural aura to the scene. At dockside, an army of excited correspondents were commandeering small boats. They had a story at last. Jonathan brushed several aside and jumped into the first boat he saw. Two reporters already aboard protested, "Just a minute here! We've hired this boat." Jonathan grabbed one by the collar and belt and threw him up on the dock. The second one volunteered to leave.

"Let's go," he said to the Cuban skipper and his crewman. "See if we can save some of the poor devils."

"Si, Si, Capitàn Quinn!" Like nearly everyone on the waterfront, the helmsman knew the captain.

The small boat headed out into the harbor to join launches from the Spanish war ships and a flotilla of small Cuban boats converging at the center of the appalling scene. The twisted, entangled remains of *Maine* appeared ghostly stark in the sweeping beams of search lights. Adding to the frenzy was a chaotic chorus of shrieking whistles, and human cries.

Maine was sitting on the bottom. Her bow was gone. What was left of her above water was a burning hulk. Shells, previously piled on deck near *Maine's* light guns, began to cook off from the heat of the fires. Spaniards and Cubans alike were risking their lives to haul bleeding American seaman from the water while the exploding shells sent deadly shrapnel whizzing across the harbor.

A magazine! It must have set off a magazine! Jonathan was appalled, but too busy to dwell on his complicity and guilt. He and his little crew joined in a night's work that would forever be remembered for the horror of it. Several times Jonathan reached down to grasp what he thought to be a sailor, only to discover that it was but half a sailor torn apart by the explosion. It was a common occurrence for rescue personnel that night. As fate would have it, Jonathan's party picked Sigsbee and an officer named Wainwright from the water off *Maine's* stern. They joined a steward, four badly injured sailors and several mutilated bodies aboard the small craft. Blood sloshed in the little boat's bilge. Sigsbee requested they be taken to the anchored American Ward Line ship, *City of Washington*.

Hours after the explosion, Jonathan returned home. His clothes were wet, bloody and smeared with oil. Almost whispering the words, he told the frightened women, "*Maine* is gone, her forward powder magazine exploded."

"Are there many casualties," Bethany asked with trembling lips. "Yes," he said gravely, "Very many." It was the first time either of the women had ever seen Jonathan openly shaken.

In the shadows and flickering candlelight, Bethany's face was marred by a terrible expression of despondence. Louisette put her arms around her and thought of all the times she had leaned upon Bethany's strength. Now, Bethany's usual courage in the face of adversity appeared shaken to its foundations. Jonathan tried to console his niece, but she would have none of it. She broke away from Louisette and ran up the stairs to her room.

Jonathan followed her but she locked her door and would not speak to him. He pleaded, but her door remained locked. Heart sickened, fighting his own devils, he walked to his room where he lay sleepless long into the night listening to muffled sobs coming from Bethany's quarters. Later he heard her moving around the house, but decided it better to let her alone. He was too troubled himself to handle a confrontation with Bethany this night.

Driven to confront the horror she was sure she alone had wrought, Bethany dressed in the early morning hours and dragged her tortured soul unwillingly to the harbor. In the dim grayness before dawn she looked across the water. *Oh God! Look what I have done.*

Only *Maine's* mast and her aft superstructure protruded from the surface to mark the grave of the once proud ship. *Jonathan said this wouldn't happen. Without me it couldn't have happened.* A few small boats circled about, occasionally retrieving items from the littered surface of Havana Harbor made surreal by the stark beams of searchlights still sweeping the water. Bethany bowed her head and tried to pray. *Words! There are no words to overcome such guilt. God, I don't deserve forgiveness. I helped kill American boys.* She stood there, trembling, staring down at black water covered with floating debris. Absently she began identifying familiar objects: pieces of wooden crates, mattresses, clothing, half a life ring. She noticed a strange milky-white object bobbing sluggishly. It was ragged and stringy at the edges and there appeared to be movement around it. Bethany suddenly became violently ill. With tentacles of sinew and shredded entrails dangling from it, a headless, armless, legless human torso floated before her like an obscene giant jellyfish. It crawled with feasting crabs.

Remington bulled his way to the head of the line of journalists waiting to file their stories via telegraph to Key West for relay to the mainland. When Remington's wire reached New York, William Randolph Hearst shouted, "That's it! This means war!" The next morning, February sixteenth, the front page of his *New York Journal* blared:

CRISIS AT HAND! Cabinet in Session; Growing Belief In SPANISH TREACHERY!

Pulitzer wasn't about to be left behind. *The New York World* claimed:

EXPLOSION THAT SANK THE MAINE OCCURRED UNDER THE SHIP!

Over the next few days Newspapers printed the official death toll. Two hundred sixty-six Americans aboard *Maine* had died in the explosion. Congress called for an inquiry.

While the United States Congress debated going to war, Bethany Quinn descended darkly to the edge of madness. Against Jonathan's orders and without his knowledge, she slipped out of the house and attended the funeral service when the recovered remains of the Americans were buried with ceremony in a mass grave at Havana's Colon Cemetery. Veiled in black, she stood at the back of the crowd, but not so far away that she couldn't hear the speaker describe those laid to rest as "these brave victims of the *Maine*." The words tore into her heart. She knew they were her victims, every one. She fought the urge to run to the forefront, confess that she had killed them, and beg for someone to kill her and bury her agony with theirs. By the time she reached the house on Obispo she shook with uncontrollable tremors.

Bethany remained in her room and refused to speak even to Jonathan, the one person who knew the true cause of her agony. He went to her. She would not let him touch her. She would not look at him.

"Please Bethany, it was not your fault. They would have found a way without you. Don't imprison yourself, Bee Bee. I am the one to blame. I got you into all this. Forgive me, Bethany. You must stop punishing yourself. Please!"

As he was about to leave she looked up at him through streaming tears and confessed, "My selfish love for one man has cost 266 boys their lives." She shivered violently, her hands clenched into fists, "They'll never love, never feel a warm embrace, never smell the clean open sea, never be seen by their families again." She stood in her bare feet wearing a soiled robe and looked up at Jonathan, her face like a mask from a Greek tragedy. "That's what I've done, Jonathan."

He tried to hold her, to comfort her. She beat her fist against his chest and sank sobbing to the floor. "That's what I've done," she moaned.

He reached down and gently lifted her in his arms and carried her to her bed. He tried again to reassure her it was not so, that she was not the cause, that she must not blame herself. She lapsed into silence once more and ignored his presence.

Jonathan was fighting his own battle with guilt over *Maine* and more. He could not banish the image of an adorable little tomboy in ragamuffin clothes playing all alone in the backyard of the house in Vicksburg. He could still see her running toward his open arms calling, "Uncle Jonathan, Uncle Jonathan, you're back!"

A child born of a bullet, raised by an old doctor and a gun-running uncle, he cried in his mind. *And in spite of us she became a beautiful, giving, unselfishly brave woman. God forgive me! Look what I have done to her.* He walked from Bethany's room and wept as he had never done in his life.

There was more to torture his troubled mind. He feared that Bethany might say things that would incriminate them, incriminate the Cuban rebels. In that there was great danger. There was no doubt that if certain members of the Cuban junta thought Bethany unstable, thought she might compromise the revolution now when it appeared America would come to their aid, they would not hesitate to remove the threat. They would kill her, and they would know they would have to kill him to do it. *And Louisette?* he agonized. *Would they believe that she knew nothing? Damn those powder magazines! And damn me! But please not Louisette and Bethany. Thank God Ansel is safe.*

He tried desperately to convince Bethany to leave Cuba and go home to Vicksburg, but she would not. Worse, she screamed at him and said she would fight him if he tried to make her go. Her screams were loud enough to be heard on the street and brought Louisette running.

Bethany would not leave her room and kept the shutters closed. Little Billy Wong took food up to her every meal. "Please, must eatee Missy. Billy Wong bling velly good food today. You see," the little man would plead, but she ate almost nothing.

She was afraid to sleep. In her dreams she heard the terrible explosion over and over again and saw young sailors floating in pieces on the water, their dead eyes looking up at her. Terrified, she knew she was going insane. She finally agreed to let Jonathan bring a doctor.

His name was Enrique Murillo de Perez. Jonathan escorted him to Bethany's room and insisted on staying during the examination. He was afraid of what Bethany might say. The doctor was Spanish.

What Doctor Murillo found was a woman with hollow cheeks, deep circles under teary green eyes, hair unkempt in tangles about her shoulders, a patient malnourished and exhausted. She trembled continuously and wept for no apparent reason.

"Can you tell me what is wrong?"

"I don't want to live anymore."

"Oh, señorita, you must not think such thoughts. You must not lose the will to live. Think of those who love you."

"Yes," she said weakly. "Perhaps." She paused. Thinking was a difficult task. "My child," she said as if suddenly remembering, "I will try for him."

"She has a child?" the physician asked.

"She is speaking of her nephew, my son," Jonathan quickly answered.

"Yes," Bethany responded in a listless voice. "That child." After the examination, Doctor Murillo followed Jonathan downstairs where they joined Louisette in the parlor.

The old doctor was gentle and experienced. "Your niece has had a nervous breakdown and is very near exhaustion. If she doesn't get sleep and nourishment, she will lose her mind completely, and if not that, she will simply waste away. Do you know what has caused her condition? Sometimes if we know we can more easily help a patient recover."

"She saw some of the bodies of the men from the *Maine*, some of the pieces that washed ashore," Jonathan said, and it was the truth. "She knew some of them and is afraid there might be a war resulting from the deaths of all those American boys. She is very sensitive and frightened by war and wants the fighting in Cuba to stop, as we all do."

"We Spanish all hope America doesn't blame such a tragedy on Spain," the doctor replied, "but I can see why the señorita would be upset. The scene in the harbor was horrible. I was called to tend the wounded."

"What can you do for her, Doctor," Louisette asked, "We are so worried."

"Someone must sit with her at every meal and insist she eat, feed her by hand if necessary. And she must have sleep." He took out a pad, wrote out a prescription and handed the note to Louisette. "Señora Quinn, have this filled at the farmacéutico. The medicine is very strong, but it will calm her and make her sleep. See that she takes it four times a day, once after every meal and at bedtime. Do not let her have the bottle. Give her the prescribed doses yourself and keep the medicine locked away. The medicine will make her very passive, very peaceful. This medicine may save her from the terrible state she is in," he told Jonathan and Louisette, "but she will grow dependent upon it. You will have to take her off it gradually when the time comes." He shrugged his shoulders. "I truly know of nothing else to prescribe for such a case. I know the good Señorita has worked to help the people in the camps. I have heard her name. The camps are enough to depress anyone, and now this tragedy in our harbor. Believe me, she is not the only woman in Havana to suffer such melancholia in these times, but her case is the worst that I have seen."

He walked toward the door, "Perhaps if you could get her away from Cuba for a while, away from the troubles here."

Jonathan and Louisette saw the Doctor to the door.

"Remember, Señora Quinn, the señorita must have absolute rest and she must eat. I will return in a few days to see her."

The doctor had prescribed laudanum, a powerful and dangerous medicine. It was tincture of opium, in common use at the time. The medicine put Bethany heavily to sleep for the better part of two days. When she wasn't asleep, the laudanum kept her listless. One day dreamily dissolved into another. As days drifted past, she sometimes left her room to sit for hours on the patio looking at the flowers or watching the goldfish in the pool. Most of the time she simply sat in her room and stared blankly into space. She would occasionally acknowledge questions, but often chose not to respond. She didn't regain an appetite, would only eat if someone spoon fed her. Once, when Jonathan brought her a meal, she called him Doctor Ted and asked why Arabella wasn't feeding her.

Jonathan suggested to Bethany that she and Louisette might go to Shamrock for a little while. He said that when summer came she should be there for Ansel when he got out of school. "He can't come here." Bethany didn't respond.

"Take Bethany home to Mississippi, Louisette. Please," he begged. "Ease my burden here in Havana. If America comes into this mess, the Spanish will arrest Americans. Fitzhugh is already advising all Americans to leave. Please Louisette."

Bethany attempted a languid protest. "But Felipe," she said slowly, "He will need me, won't he?" Her voice trailed away.

Louisette did not want to leave, but she knew there was little choice. Someone had to be at Shamrock to take care of Ansel when his school closed for the summer. He couldn't be allowed to return to Cuba.

Bethany took no interest in packing. The servants packed for her. She was concerned about one item only. "Louisette, my laudanum, make sure we have enough for the whole summer."

That night Jonathan lay on his back talking to Louisette. "There's something you must do at Shamrock. You must get Bethany off that drug. It will destroy her, is destroying her now."

"Yes, but what else could we have done?"

"Nothing," he replied, "but she will do better at Shamrock, and with Ansel there, she will try very hard to get well. Doctor Murillo says you must not take it away all at once. You must wean her from it. He says it won't be pleasant for you, Darling. I'm sorry."

"I will bring her back all healthy and her old self, but you must tell me, what caused her to collapse? She has always been so strong."

Jonathan sat straight up in bed. "Look at me, Louisette," he said. "You must never ask her, and you must never listen if she wants to tell you. Please promise me you will not probe."

"But, Jonathan," Louisette protested, "dear Bethany couldn't possibly have done anything so terrible as too . . ."

"Of course she didn't," Jonathan interrupted. "But, Bethany knows things, secrets of the highest order, information that could endanger you and the entire movement for a free Cuba. Believe me, Darling, you must do as I say. Only a handful of people know what Bethany knows. It is very dangerous knowledge."

Jonathan turned out the light. Louisette snuggled very close to him and put her head on his chest. "How terrible that she must bear such a dark burden alone. I will do as you ask, my darling, only I wish you were coming too."

The two women left Havana aboard the ferry to Key West.

* * *

"Well, Captain J," Billy Wong said when he brought Jonathan's lunch to the office, "just like old times." He placed the food on Quinn's desk. "Oh yes," he said with some pride, "just you and me again, Captain J and his number one man."

"Just you and me, Billy," Quinn said, absently gazing out his office window at an American flag flying defiantly from the lone, bent mast protruding above *Maine*'s wreckage.

On March 28, the official report of the U.S. Navy Board of Investigation held at Key West, Florida verified that an explosion occurred outside the vessel and was caused by a naval mine. The media ignored the fact that the Board had not yet determined responsibility for the act. Headlines and editorials implied that Spain was to blame and called loudly for action.

Seven weeks later, Jonathan sat facing Fitzhugh Lee at the Quinn residence on Obispo Street.

"Tell me, Fitzhugh, what the hell are they waiting for? It's been almost two months since *Maine* settled on the bottom."

"Freshen these a bit, Captain," Fitzhugh motioned to the brandy snifters sitting before them, "and I will tell you what I know, and what I'm not supposed to know."

Fitzhugh sat at Jonathan's mahogany dining table wearing a white linen Panama suit turned beige with age. He pulled a silver cigar case from his coat pocket, selected one and offered the case to Quinn who declined.

"I'm listening," Quinn said while liberally refilling both glasses. Fitzhugh carefully clipped the end of his cigar with a tool designed for the task, put it between his teeth, struck a lucifer match with his thumbnail and lit it. He took a long drag and exhaled the smoke slowly with obvious satisfaction, leaned back in his chair and began.

"Part of the problem is that men with holdings over here who think they have a good deal with the Spanish, and long winded, self-righteous asses at home like William Jennings Bryan, Andrew Carnegie, ex-president Cleveland, Samuel Langhorne Clemens, and an assortment of artistic types have all been carrying anti-war, anti-expansionist banners. They are driving President McKinley up the wall. Now he doesn't want war himself, said he was a major in the Civil War and has seen the bodies, but Congress just voted 50 million dollars for defense. Fifty million dollars! The President knows which way the wind is blowing. Senator Henry Cabot Lodge told him that if he doesn't take action in this matter, the Republicans won't stand a chance in the coming election. Lodge pointed out the fact that newspapers, politicians, contractors, businessmen, and preachers are all carrying on about righteous causes and hollering for war. A lot of 'em are fired up enough to volunteer."

"Does your order for all Americans to be out of here by tomorrow night still hold?" Jonathan asked.

"Damn right, and that includes you. You've had plenty of time to tie up loose ends and close down. Don't give me any trouble on this."

"I've got things under control, can operate out of Nassau, but I don't like running," Jonathan said. "I had to do that in our war."

"Well come on with me. I'm not running. I'm just going home to get some help and come back here and win one. What do you say? Besides, the alternative is to maybe spend the duration in prison with your friend Alacon because no matter what I tell the President, there's gonna be a war. The streets may be quiet now, but when it starts, the Spaniards are not gonna look kindly on Americans walking around Havana." Lee took a healthy sip of brandy. "Tell you what. You come with me and I'll get you a commission as a Navy commander or a colonel in the Army, take your pick."

"I'll think about it," Jonathan replied. "Now tell me what you're going to tell the President."

"I'm gonna tell him I'm certain of two things: One is that *Maine* was destroyed by a mine. The second is that the Spanish government is innocent of any complicity in the sinking."

Jonathan choked on his brandy.

"I say something to upset you, Jonathan?"

"I just swallowed crooked," he answered. "Why don't you elaborate on why the board thinks it was a mine and who you think did it. Could have been an accident, maybe a spontaneous fire in a coal bunker cooked off an adjoining magazine."

"Bunker fire, hell. It was a mine! Now Jonathan, you know that it was hot as Hades out there on that ship. There were over two hundred men locked aboard an iron vessel with poor ventilation. I heard it was near a hundred degrees in that ship. Do you really think a smoldering coal bunker fire could burn long enough to 'cook off' ammunition without those sailors feeling the additional heat themselves? It would have taken days. Do you know how hot a compartment would have to get to cook off a six inch shell? I'm told over four hundred degrees! Some of those sailors sleep adjacent to the coal bunkers, right up against 'em. You think they wouldn't have noticed heat from a bunker fire? I'll tell you there's a lot of speculation back home. After all, a Spanish pilot brought the ship in and moored it at a buoy in a Spanish harbor. It could have been prearranged. Hearst is yelling 'Remember the *Maine*, to hell with Spain!' all over his paper, but the truth is that Spain had nothing to gain from such an act. They dispatched their battleship *Vizcaya* to New York as a gesture of friendly reciprocity to *Maine*'s visit here for God's sake. Her captain didn't know about *Maine* blowing up until a bunch of news people met his ship anchored in the fog off Sandy Hook. Now I don't think Spain would send their best ship to New York if they were planning to sink ours in Havana Harbor and start a war."

Jonathan took a large sip of brandy.

"It was a mine of some sort," continued Lee. "I'm sure of that. The Navy investigative board won't talk and they shouldn't, but I spoke with the one of the hard hat salvage divers who went down into the wreck to investigate. He said they found a couple of her bottom plates blown inward. That's a fact. He also said the wreck is full of bodies floating up against the overheads of passageways and compartments. Said he had to push 'em aside to get through the passages, said they were floating with their eyes open, jaws hanging, arms stretched out to him like they was asking him what happened. He said it was the most awful dive he's ever had to make and I believe him."

Jonathan felt sick, cold all over. *Dear God, forgive me if you can. I know it won't help, but I never meant for any of those men to be hurt. Damn me if you must for my part, but bless those men's souls.*

"Jonathan! You still with me? You look a little pallid."

"Sorry Fitzhugh. I was thinking about those sailors trapped in the wreck."

"Damn shame, all right. Anyway, to get back to what I know about the investigation. I talked with several survivors from the crew. There's no doubt in their minds that there were two explosions, one under the vessel and a bigger one, the magazines set off by the first one. Now I don't think it was a regular naval mine. That would have to have been supplied by the Spanish Navy, and you know what I think about that. But someone could have taken a container loaded it with explosives, somehow or other gotten it under the ship and set it off with a wired electric cap or something."

"Now who would have the wherewithal to do that, and what would be their reason if it wasn't Spain?" Jonathan asked, and held his breath.

"Army officers!" Lee said. "Weyler's bunch! Spanish honor and all that. I saw them armed in the streets leadin' Spanish voluntarios. They're backed by the old conservative party in Spain and they don't intend to have Cuba negotiated away through the proposed autonomy agreement. They probably plan to blame the whole thing on the Cubans, but either way they figure they can regain control, especially if Spain is thrown into a crisis with America."

Jonathan let out a sigh of relief and poured a fresh shot into Lee's glass, "Think the President will buy that, Fitzhugh?"

"I don't think it matters what McKinley thinks, what the Spanish government says or what Spain's conservatives do. The American people are fightin' the bit to go to war." Lee tossed down his brandy and stood up. "I'm going back to my place to pack and I expect you to do the same."

"All right, Consul General, but you better lead me back to a free Cuba and my business holdings here."

"You can count on that, Captain. I have a few business interests here myself."

Billy Wong worried about his pigs and goats, not to mention his concubine and illegitimate children. He didn't want to go with Captain Quinn. The fact was that he couldn't go. The U.S. Congress had passed Chinese immigration exclusion acts that forbade immigration by Chinese laborers.

Jonathan didn't think the little Chinese man was in any danger. "Billy," he told him, "I've locked up the warehouses and closed the business. Until I return, you are number one man. You watch after my office and Miss Louisette's home 'til I get back."

"Oh! Captain J, me do like same all time. Be number one man." On April 10th, 1898, Fitzhugh Lee and Captain Quinn were among the last Americans to leave Havana aboard the little ferry *Olivette* bound for Key West.

As soon as *Olivette* left the dock, Billy Wong ran down the street and up the stairs to the J & Q office. Once there, he walked around the desk and ever so gingerly sat down in Captain J's big chair. As he was lighting one of Quinn's cigars, he noticed through the new window glass that someone had hauled down the American flag from the bent mast of the sunken *Maine.*

Spain had been tried and convicted on the front pages of America's newspapers. Neither the Republican administration nor the Democrats could ignore the popular ground swell of support favoring war. On April 11th, President McKinley reluctantly asked Congress for . . . *authority to use American military and naval forces to end warfare on the island of Cuba and secure for it a stable government.* On April 19, 1898, Congress passed a joint resolution recognizing the independence of Cuba and authorizing the President to force Spain to relinquish the island. For the first time in 52 years, not since the Mexican War, America faced a foreign enemy.

It was after the fact that some bright bureaucrat in the War Department thought to take inventory of America's army. The figures tallied up were startling, both to the president and congress. While Spain already had 250,000 soldiers and militiamen in Cuba, Washington learned that the entire United States Army, including cooks and clerks, totaled just 26,000 troops. There had not been a regimental size formation, much less a combat training exercise, for 30 years, *not since reconstruction began following the end of the Civil War.*

On the other hand, raising 200,000 volunteers for the Army was easy. The citizens of the United States approached war over Cuba with flags flying from every front porch in every town across the country. Bands played as young men lined up to volunteer for a glorious war in the romantic tropics where they would slay the cruel Spaniard. Older men stepped up to pat them on the back and buy them drinks while young ladies made much of their bravery. The hard, if not impossible, task would be providing clothing, arms, housing, and food for the volunteers, not to mention training them for war. An equally challenging task was that of transporting an American invasion force to Cuba and Puerto Rico and maybe to the Philippines half-way round the world. The United States had no troop transport ships. In addition, no one seemed to know where Spain's Atlantic fleet was located. The Military wasn't happy with the prospect of launching an invasion only to have an entire Spanish battle fleet appear on the horizon.

In the middle of all the madness and confusion, Jonathan arrived in the States and traveled with Fitzhugh Lee to Washington. He could have gone home to join his family at Shamrock, but then again he couldn't. He had been involved one way or another in Cuba's struggle for freedom for over 30 years. "I ought to be there to see the finish, by God," he told Fitzhugh. Jonathan wasn't much on taking orders, so he declined Fitzhugh's offer for a commission. Fitzhugh himself became a general in charge of the Seventh Corps of Volunteers. General Fitzhugh Lee lined Captain Quinn up with a more independent opportunity.

Jonathan sent the following wire to Vicksburg in care of Mrs. J.H. Quinn, Shamrock Plantation:

Returning to Cuba with invasion fleet. Stop.
Have been made Maritime Adviser to Commander, U.S. Invasion Forces
Cuba. Stop.
Don't worry. Stop.

Love Jonathan. End.

It took two days for the telegram to be delivered to Shamrock. Louisette would have shot Jonathan herself if she could have gotten to him the day she received his wire. She cursed him, then prayed for him, then cried, then prayed for him again, asking God to take care of the stubborn, brave, one-eyed fool she had married.

The cable had a more profound effect on Bethany. Somehow it pricked a hole in the opiate veil that isolated her from reality. The first rational thought to disturb her narcotic-induced ethereal existence slowly awoke within her a fear for the future. She had comprehended Louisette's words, "Jonathan is going to war again." The thought ricocheted around her brain like a shot in a cave. A small switch was tripped in a brain broken by unbearable guilt and numbed by drugs. Somewhere a dimmed circuit began to glow and awaken a new fear. *Jonathan could be killed. Who would take care of Ansel and Louisette? Of Shamrock? Who would run J & Q Shipping?*

Louisette, out of desperation, had already begun to reduce Bethany's daily doses of laudanum. "Ansel will be coming home from school one of these days," she reasoned with Bethany. "We must get his Aunt Bee Bee all well for him. Isn't that what you want dear Bethany? Come on now, just a half teaspoon. No more."

It had been a one sided fight, but Bethany now willingly joined the struggle. It was not easy. Withdrawal brought on pain, cramps, sweating, unbearable anxiety. There were screams in the night when the terrible dreams returned. Louisette held Bethany in her arms through the bad times, but held back the opium even when Bethany crawled on her knees begging for it. Only once did Louisette fail, giving her a little of the medicine when Bethany's agony appeared too dreadful for anyone to bear.

There came a day when Bethany snatched the bottle from Louisette's hands. She grasped it to her as if it were life itself. By chance in front of her dressing mirror, Bethany uncorked the bottle and lifted it to her lips. That's when she saw the pitiful trembling, unkempt, soiled creature looking back at her from the silvered glass.

"Damn this vile drug!" she screamed. "I will not let Ansel see me like this!" She held out the bottle in a trembling hand. "Take it! Take it from me, Louisette! I can't do it by myself. Please." Her body shook violently. It took both hands for Louisette to pry the bottle away even with Bethany begging her to do so. Bethany's barely rational mind had determined to give it up, but her body fought to hold onto it.

She could handle some days without it. On others she would tear up the house looking for it, begging Louisette to give it back, cursing her, crying that she didn't want to give it up. Louisette lived the hell with Bethany, doing everything she could for her except giving her the one thing she craved.

Gradually the afflictions began to subside. Little things told wonders. Bethany began to brush her own hair. One day she put rouge on her lips. She noticed when her dress was soiled. She began to take long walks in the sun and pick handfuls of wild flowers. She gained a pound, then another and the hollowness of her cheeks and the dark semicircles under her eyes began to fade.

Bethany began a desperate struggle for redemption. *By accident of birth I was born a child of war. Could I have somehow been chosen to be the terrible means of ending the bloody war in Cuba? If so, who chose me, God or the Devil? Am I evil, God, or just Fortune's whore?* Those were not pretty thoughts, but they were the first rational attempts to face the guilt that had nearly destroyed her.

She fought day by day to rejoin the living. It was a struggle to force herself out of bed in the mornings. She had lived for months dressed in night clothes and a worn old bathrobe. She found it difficult just to get dressed, fix her hair, find interest in her surroundings, walk in sunlight.

There came a day when Bethany laughed at something Louisette said. Louisette laughed too, and cried, and hugged Bethany. A few weeks later Bethany passed a true milestone. "Louisette, can we go into Vicksburg? I need new clothes."

Color returned to her cheeks. The dullness that had veiled her lovely eyes began to lift. On the day 14-year-old cadet lieutenant Ansel Quinn arrived from Marion, there was a genuine sparkle in them. Her mind was clear, free of drugs.

With recovery came the burdens of a conscious world. Her joy was Ansel, her heartache, Felipe, her worry, Jonathan.

Immediately after Jonathan's appointment, he left Washington for Tampa, the chosen port of embarkation. He needn't have hurried. Never intended to serve more than a few small ships engaged in Caribbean trade, the Army now expected the Port of Tampa to accommodate thousands of troops from various staging camps around the country, their equipment, six months worth of supplies, and a vast hodge-podge of vessels given the task of transporting the invasion force to Cuba.

In all his shipping experience, Jonathan had never seen such confusion. Railcar loads of government supplies arrived with no bills of lading. Army officers went up and down the track breaking into boxcars searching for their units' supplies and equipment. There were no cotton tropical-weight uniforms for the regulars, but plenty of wool ones in various shades of blue. In the frequent rain showers of Tampa, the cheap uniform dye bled through to the skin of every man wearing them. For the first time, Southern as well as Northern boys could be called 'blue bellies' without prejudice. Viewing the assembled invasion fleet, a naval officer remarked to Jonathan, "The criteria for selection of transport vessels have obviously been narrowed down to a single requirement, that they float."

The bizarre Tampa Bay Hotel quickly filled to capacity with army and navy officers, government officials and journalists. Jonathan had arrived early enough to obtain a room there. Built to resemble a Moorish castle complete with minaret towers, it was the unofficial headquarters of the invasion force. If the architecture was a little exotic, its well-stocked bar and excellent dining room made it a dandy officer's club. Jonathan ran into Fitzhugh Lee there who introduced him to another ex-Confederate general, 'Fighting Joe Wheeler', now a Major General in the U.S. Army.

It would seem incongruous for a war to have a healing effect, but for the first time since the Civil War, men from the North and the South, black and white, volunteered to serve together against a common foe. Jonathan noticed it, heard men talking about it. After 33 years it was perhaps the first real evidence that the deeply scarred country had finally begun to heal.

After a long day of going over charts, pointing out features of Cuba's shoreline and making recommendations to the invasion planning staff, Jonathan retired to the hotel bar.

"My fine Rebel Captain," someone said as Jonathan entered the bar. Quinn recognized Frederick Remington. "Come meet my distinguished colleagues."

Remington introduced Jonathan to a group of hard-drinking, heavy-smoking, impatient correspondents: Stephen Crane, who had written *The Red Badge of Courage* and knew first hand the emotions of men under fire, Richard Harding Davis, already a famous war correspondent, Malcom McDowell of the *Chicago Record*, John Fox, Jr. of *Harper's Weekly*, and a reporter with his arm in a sling named James F. J. Archibald. He had been the only casualty on the first official U.S. Government attempt to re-supply the Cuban rebels. The mission was aborted after a day of being fired upon by Spanish cavalry who followed the supply boat's progress up the Cuban coast and repelled its every attempt to land.

"I hear you fellows are responsible for this war," Jonathan said. "Fred here tells us you know everything about Cuba and then some, that you are an advisor to general Shaftner and the Navy about Cuba's coastal waters," probed Stephen Crane.

"Says you served on *Alabama*," Davis added.

"Fred is a gossipy old woman who draws pretty good cartoons and writes his stories from a bar stool," Quinn replied, much to the amusement of everyone except Remington.

"He who insults the genius of my work can only redeem his show of ignorance by paying for the next round," Frederick responded.

"Is that a threat to slander me in that yellow dog rag you work for?"

"Absolutely," replied Remington, "What are America's newspapers for if not to get its journalists free drinks? Why do you think they call us members of a free press?"

"Barkeep," Jonathan called, "Pour an apology in the big man's glass and a round for these distinguished gentlemen."

Jonathan was in the bar with the usual crowd on the night of June 7, 1898, when someone rushed in and yelled, "They've found the Spanish fleet! It's at Santiago harbor. The show's on! Troops are loading." The young men present rushed out. The old hands didn't move. They knew there was plenty of time for one last drink, maybe two.

Jonathan joined Remington and his friends assembling their gear on the lawn of the hotel. He observed a marvelous variety of journalistic fashions of war. There were white linen suits with stiff shirt fronts, ties and patent leather shoes, canvas hunting suits and boots, white ducks and blue blazers, surplus army fatigues and safari outfits. The choice of headgear went from none at all to white Panama straw hats, old campaign hats, hunting caps, cowboy hats, and in the case of Richard Harding Davis, a British army pith helmet. The journalists were variously equipped with canteens, blanket rolls, haversacks, binoculars, Kodak cameras, whiskey flasks, boxes of cigars, bundles of writing tablets, pencils, sketch pads, six-shooters, belts of ammunition, hunting knives, and a machete or two.

"Hell, you boys don't need the army. Y'all could take the island yourselves."

Davis replied with a grin, "Captain Quinn, you steal us a boat and we'll give it a try."

Jonathan was assigned to sail aboard the transport *Seguranca* with General Shaftner, Commander of V Corps. They were joined by 33 officers, 477 enlisted men and five foreign military observers.

After weeks of waiting, the invasion fleet finally steamed for Cuba towing wooden water barges at the breakneck speed of four knots. The fleet approached Cuba at night, a good tactical maneuver unless one does it with all lights blazing. One newspaper wag reported, "The fleet sneaked up on Cuba looking like the city of Brooklyn floating on water."

"Hostilities have certainly begun in style," Jonathan remarked to a colonel standing at the rail beside him. *Seguranca* was cruising along with a band on deck loudly playing ragtime.

Politicians and rear echelon types safe at home agreed with Secretary of State, John Hay, when he dubbed the conflict a "Splendid Little War." The planning and preparation *had* somewhat resembled a comic opera, but the reality of the Spanish American War was anything but a lark to the men on both sides who fought it. They bled buckets. If the Spanish Government was not aggressive in its execution of a war it did not want to fight, such reluctance was not shown by the Spanish troops in Cuba. On the other side, the mixed batch of American regulars, volunteers, Rough Riders, and Colored troops proved as tough and aggressive as any ever gathered under the American flag.

There was a third party to the event—the press corps. It was later said in print that *The war from the beginning was a stimulus to the imagination of America driven by a press fully aware of its power to not only report, but make history happen, to create it by stimulating the 'hearts and minds' of a nation's people.* Hearst not only agreed, he referred to the conflict as *The New York Journal's* war.

Jonathan watched the Army land at two villages with romantic sounding names, Daiquirí and Siboney, then steamed with the fleet westward toward Santiago where the Spanish Atlantic fleet lay trapped. While Jonathan had not forgotten that his personal objective was to get to Felipe, he was stuck at sea off Santiago de Cuba nearly 500 miles from Havana. Restless and bored, Quinn transferred from *Seguranca* to *Iowa* for a visit with a friend, Captain Evans, *Iowa's* commander. He and Evans had finished breakfast and were relaxing in the ward room when the bugler sounded general quarters. Both men rushed to the bridge.

Captain Evans saw smoke toward the entrance of Santiago Harbor. "Damn! We were nervous that the Spaniards might try to slip away during the frequent rain squalls at night, but never expected them to try it in broad daylight."

The Spanish ships came out of the harbor in line and turned down the coastline to gain a head start on an American fleet struggling to get under way. Totally surprised, few American ships had full steam available. Several vessels had to fire up boilers that had been shut down to conserve coal. Had Spain's sleek ships been in top condition with clean bottoms, they may have escaped that day, but like *Alabama* years before at Cherbourg, they were sea-worn, their bottoms fouled, their advantage in speed lost.

Captain Evans rushed all hands to get *Iowa* under way. There was no time to transfer Jonathan back to *Seguranca*. To most men aboard that day, men who had never been in battle, it was a proud and glorious moment. Not so for Jonathan. He knew the hazard and hell of fighting big gunned ships at sea. His mouth was dry as cotton. The modern guns and ammunition on both sides were designed to tear iron giants to pieces. What a heavy naval gun can do to steel plate is awesome, to human flesh, ghastly beyond the mind's ability to comprehend.

It was neither glory nor victory that fixed that day in Jonathan's memory. The awesome gunfire, greater than anything he had ever seen, marked the first great battle between heavy gunned, fast, modern ships of steel. Even so, what Jonathan would remember most vividly occurred after the guns grew silent.

Captain Evans eased *Iowa* toward the grounded hulk of the *Vizcaya*, the grand ship that had visited New York barely two months before. Her mangled hull was aground and burning 400 yards offshore. Her crewmen were leaping into the water and making for a sandbar that lay between the ship and the beach. Jonathan saw her men, whole and wounded, crowded on the bar in chest-deep water. They could go no further. Onshore, a mounted band of Cuban rebels was making sport of shooting at them. Stray bullets plumed fountains of water, those on their mark, streams of blood. Among the stranded sailors, many struggled to hold the heads of wounded shipmates above water.

Jonathan wanted to look away but could not as the red streaked surface of the water began to churn with the dorsal fins of sharks. Through binoculars he watched the ocean predators make repeated runs at the men on the outside of the crowded bar. The sharks came at them open jawed. When they bit into men, they thrashed from side to side ripping away chunks of flesh while fellow sailors fought to hold onto what was left of their shipmates. Jonathan could see the victims' open mouths screaming, but was too far away to hear their cries. All the while the insurgents on shore continued firing.

Pointing, Jonathan shouted, "For God's sake, Captain, do something!" Evans ordered a warning salvo fired over the Cubans. They got the message and ceased their sport.

Jonathan turned his binoculars to the burning *Vizcaya*. As fire moved slowly, relentlessly aft through the ship, he could see the teak deck burning and bare steel plate turn ashen gray and then cherry red.

"My God, there are men still aboard!"

Wounded sailors, unable to climb the ship's rails and drop into the sea, were dragging themselves aft as the heat from the inferno amidships spread steadily toward them. Evans signaled the nearby torpedo boat *Ericsson* to try for the men still on the Spanish wreck while the auxiliary, *Hist*, and *Iowa's* own boats went in to rescue as many men as they could from the sandbar.

Jonathan watched as *Ericsson* turned toward the burning Spanish ship where desperate men awaited rescue. As if to remind Jonathan of the hell he had helped deliver to *Maine*, fire reached *Vizcaya's* aft magazine and she exploded.

Captain Evans was startled by the scream that issued from Jonathan's mouth. It was as grievous and forlorn a human sound as he had ever heard.

On the morning of July 3, 1898, Spain was considered a powerful nation among world leaders. By sundown her position in world affairs was irretrievably lost. The next day, July 4, 1898, the United States, a nation formerly unrecognized as having any real influence on global matters, became, in the eyes of Europe and Asia, a power with which to be reckoned. America was suddenly a nation of empire having taken from Spain by force of arms not only Cuba, but Puerto Rico and the Philippines.

It was over. On its birthday, the 4th of July, 1898, all America wildly celebrated victory. At Havana, the flag of Spain was lowered after four centuries of Spanish rule. Cuba Libre!

CHAPTER 24

Shamrock Plantation, 1915

Bethany finished the last page of the last diary. *Someday, Ansel Hillary Quinn my boy, these little books will shock you, tell you who you really are, things about your family you never knew, but not until after I am gone. It was a promise we all made a long time ago.* She carefully wrapped the two diaries in the original brown paper and string, placed it back in the desk and locked the drawer.

In the morning, Bethany awoke early after a restless sleep. By the time she was dressed she could hear stirring in the kitchen.

"Lizzy!"

The housekeeper shuffled down the hall wearing bedroom slippers, bathrobe and a white bib apron. She rounded the corner into the bedroom carrying a cup of coffee.

"You sho' up early this morning. I ain't even had time to fix breakfast yet, but this here cup of coffee ought to hold you whilst I rustle up bacon and eggs, or would you be wantin' pancakes?"

"Bacon and eggs will be fine, Lizzy. Then if you could help me pack I'd appreciate it. The steamer trunk is still in the attic. It will take both of us to get it down."

"Steamer trunk? Jes' where you going dis time? I know you ain't due back in Cuba 'til fall. It's that telephone bidnis ain't it. You ain't been the same since you got that phone call. You sho' you all right Miss Bethany?"

"Lizzy, I've got to wire Cuba, then be in New York by the last week of April. Then on to England, and when that business is done I'm going to Paris to see the boy. Now go fix us breakfast. We got lots to do."

"I ain't seen no lady does all you do. Don't know no man do such gallivantin' neither."

Lizzy left the room shaking her head and commiserating like she always did when Bethany planned a trip. "I s'pose you 'speck me to drive that Model T all the way back here from the train station. I hardly knows how to work that thing. It be more trouble than a horse and buggy. Crankin' it up and working all them nobs and petals. I be lucky I don't clumb up a tree in that thing. Telephones, 'lectricity, automobiles, guess we be lucky you don't fancy one of them flying machines. Lordy, Miss Bethany! And what I do if it break down foe I gets home?"

"Lizzy, I've got to make this trip so quit fussin' and help me pack."

"Yes 'um."

* * *

316

New York City, May 1, 1915

Bethany Quinn, the reluctant, regretful owner of a large forgotten cache of modern Mauser rifles, had accepted the British government's first offer without dickering. The British agent thought it a bargain. Bethany would have paid him to be rid of the crates marked with the faded lettering, '*MACHINERY PARTS, CHICAGO IRON WORKS*,' a few with deteriorating paper shipping labels marked *Alacon Sugar Mill* still attached. His Majesty's agent readily agreed to the old J & Q Shipping terms for such covert transactions: cash; half up front, the balance upon delivery on the dock at Liverpool, ostensibly untraceable payment to an untraceable source.

Sitting at the dressing table in a suite at the Algonquin Hotel in New York, Bethany asked herself, *Am I personally delivering this last dreadful shipment for penance or profit, or to say good-bye to the ghosts?* She looked at her reflection in the mirror. *That's all rubbish and you know it. You're using it as an excuse to see the boy.*

In the hotel lobby, the representative from a shipping agency that used to represent J & Q took her gloved hand. "Miss Quinn, you are as beautiful as ever."

"You haven't changed yourself, Georgie. You still lie just as sweetly."

The agent had told the truth—the lady was still beautiful. She was the one who lied sweetly. George had grown bald and portly since the old days.

He launched anew into the argument he had previously made to Bethany by letter, expensive long distance phone calls to Mississippi and telegrams to Cuba.

"Now Georgie, I'm not listening to all that propaganda. We've been through it a hundred times. I'm going. It's the last consignment, and I'm the last partner, the last of the ghosts."

"Some ghost. You turned the head of every man in the lobby just now."

She ignored the remark as she had always ignored compliments. The hotel doorman hailed a cab for the couple. As they neared Pier 54, Bethany asked, "Are you sure my trunk is aboard? I didn't spend all that money at Lord and Taylor's, Macy's and Bloomingdale's to have my new outfits left ashore."

"My business is shipping, remember?" he smiled. "I've seen luggage left on the dock."

George absently gazed at the traffic arriving ahead of them at the Cunard Company Pier 54. He noted a number of horse drawn hansom cabs interspersed in a long line of motor taxicabs, all disgorging passengers into a growing crowd teeming with excitement.

"It's you I'd like to see left dockside."

"We have arrived, my silly George."

Their taxi stopped at the terminal entrance where a crew was set up capturing the event with a handcranked motion picture camera. It would be the only moving picture footage taken from the terminal that day.

George helped Bethany from the cab and escorted her through the street entrance into the crowded passenger terminal.

"I appreciate you handling the cargo from Cuba to shipboard here." She kissed his cheek. "And don't worry. My God, that ship won the Blue Riband award for speed. Just look at her. She's a beautiful lady."

"Beautiful ladies can be dangerous, but then you know that." Her eyes fell and he immediately regretted the remark. "I'll worry you know? Please wire me as soon as you dock in Liverpool."

"George, darling, you're turning into a nagging old nanny," she smiled, "and I had my share of those a long time ago."

He was happy to see the sparkle return to her eyes. And such eyes! If there was no perceptible fire in them, there was certainly the hint of embers. George marveled at the woman he had not seen for what, more than 15 years? Except for tiny crow's feet at the corners of her eyes, her lovely face was smooth and free of wrinkles. *She must be almost fifty but could pass for a lady ten years younger.*

"Give me the copies of the bill of lading and I'll be off." she said.

It was his turn to smile. "I knew you would go in spite of all my arguments. You'll find the documents with a basket of fruit and iced champagne waiting in your suite."

"Champagne! Why, Georgie, you old romantic."

At the foot of the gangway they said good-bye. When she reached the ship's deck Bethany turned and waved before disappearing behind the rows of passengers crowding the rail.

On board there was an unusual number of journalists pestering the first-class passengers in the main salon. They all asked the same question as regards the well-publicized sailing. "What do you think of the war in Europe? Do you have any concerns because of the warnings from the Germans?"

They got little response from Alfred Vanderbilt, other prominent passengers and even less from the attractive lady in silk. Bethany would have nothing to do with them, considered them vultures preying on the fears, speculation, and rumors from yet another war. *I could tell them more about war than they could print,* she thought as she stood listening to the reporters badger passengers.

Half an hour later, the deep resonance of the ship's whistle signaled her imminent departure. Stewards moved through the saloon calling, "All ashore that's going ashore."

Just past noon, the first of May, 1915, mooring lines were hauled in and the great ship eased from her berth with the help of tugs. Once free, she steamed majestically from New York Harbor past the Statue of Liberty. It would be her 201st crossing of the Atlantic.

After dinner the first night out, Bethany retired to her stateroom with a bottle of wine for company. She took a sip from her glass, turned out the light and stood watching through the open porthole at the moonlight dancing on the waves.

Dwelling upon the past is a sure sign of age, she chided herself, but could not get her mind off the old days when J & Q Shipping was clandestinely engaged in supplying 'special cargo'.

Now, there is no J & Q Shipping Company, but here I am once again involved in the clandestine trade if only for one last transaction. Well Jonathan, for the first time I'm making a delivery. Not much to it this time. No dangerous, clandestine rendezvous in the middle of the night—just a legitimate meeting in a dockside office with a British official. And then on to Paris to see our boy.

She slipped into bed in the darkened cabin. Sleep was a long time coming.

Standing on deck in the brightness of a clear morning, she could feel the vibration of the powerful engines driving the great modern ship through the sea at 22 knots. *Jonathan would have been impressed,* she mused, *and I would have to tour the whole vessel from bridge to engine room with him like we did on Britannic when I was little more than what . . . 18?*

Aboard the great liner nearing mid-Atlantic, her fellow passengers sipped champagne, talked of the war and speculated when it might end. *They never end,* she could have told them, *in the memories of the survivors.* Bored with the naiveté of those discussing politics and war, she took a turn about the promenade deck where she watched a little girl, trying very hard to act grown up, lose all pretense when a little boy yanked her pigtail. She chased down the deck after him with determined vengeance. Bethany smiled remembering another little girl who could take up for herself. At dinner, a young woman traveling with her parents complained to Bethany, "Daddy won't take us on to Paris. He says it's because of the war, but I think it's because of all those handsome Frenchmen in uniform."

"Your daddy is a wise man," Bethany smiled, and excused herself from the table. Alone in her cabin, sleep brought visitors, old ghosts disturbed by her trip. Some were friendly, some were not, as the ship drove on through restless, dark seas.

The next day, first class passengers received instructions to close the blackout curtains over all windows and portholes at sundown. Most lower portholes had previously been blacked out with paint. Heavy black curtains were drawn over windows of public areas. Cabin stewards checked to see that the orders were carried out. "Merely routine for ships entering the war zone," the passengers were assured.

The air grew chilly as they crossed the 45th parallel. A steward brought a lap robe to Bethany where she sat in her deck chair taking in the fresh air while browsing through a book titled *French, Self-taught* to brush up a language she had not used for years. *The boy uses French daily,* she thought to herself. *I shouldn't think of him as a boy any longer. Ansel is a soldier, an officer, another damn Quinn involved in war.*

Satisfied that she hadn't forgotten all she had learned during the time she lived in Paris, she put the book aside to relax and enjoy the beautiful day. She noticed an elderly couple strolling arm in arm in the bright sunshine. They were chatting and obviously enjoying each other's company. *It must be nice to share your golden years with someone you love.*

At lunch, an English couple that shared her table engaged her in conversation.

"I overheard you talking about Cuba, that you spend part of your time there," the gentleman remarked. "We vacationed in America this year. It is so vast, isn't it? We are thinking we might try the Caribbean next season. What can you tell us about your little island?"

"My little island?" Bethany smiled. "Why, you will find Cuba the jewel of the Caribbean if you don't delve into its history or dig into its soil. Of course if you do, you will find mostly violence and blood."

She excused herself, stepped out on the promenade deck and walked all the way to the stern. Standing there alone she looked out at the ship's wake trailing far into the distance. *A majestic ship flying across silvered waves, but is she sailing into harm's way as some have warned? Does the enemy know her secrets?* Those thoughts returned that evening when the steward politely entered her suite to make sure the blackout curtains were drawn to cover the portholes. *Here is the most elegant ship afloat, sailing through the night with no light showing. Not the actions of an innocent ship, I would think. But then, like me, she is not an innocent lady. I know what she is carrying deep in her cargo holds.*

Whether walking the decks or sitting at dinner, she frequently overheard talk about the war, about whether Germany or England possessed the best and fastest dreadnaughts, how France needed the British Army to keep the Germans at bay. "Our English lads will bring us quick victory on land and sea," more than one gentleman had smugly said.

How naive these people are. They have no idea what modern weapons can do. I wish to God I was as ignorant.

Steaming through the night, the fastest ocean liner afloat was nearing home port. Her first-class passengers celebrated their last night at sea with a grand ball. In honor of the Americans aboard, the ship's orchestra introduced the novelty of a few new tunes by young American composers: Irving Berlin, Cole Porter, Jerome Kern, and something called *Blues* written by a Negro named Handy. The music was splendid, the ladies stylish, the gentlemen charming. Most men were attired in white tie and tails, but there were some in formal military dress. Among them was a British naval officer who startled Bethany.

"I must confess I have admired you from a distance since we embarked from New York. I hope you will forgive my boldness, but with the voyage almost over I had to at least ask you for a dance." She stared at him without saying a word. It was not his remark that got her attention.

"By the look on your face, I'm afraid I have offended you," he said.

"Not offended. Surprised. It's because you remind me of someone else who had an eye-patch like that and a smile much like yours."

"Really," he replied. "This silly thing?" He touched the black, silk patch covering his right eye.

They studied one another a moment. "Well," she asked, "are you going to just stand there, or are we going to dance? By the way, my name is Bethany Quinn. What's yours?"

He smiled and led her onto the dance floor. "I'm Peter Hampton, Madame Quinn, and I apologize for not arranging a proper introduction."

"It's Miss Quinn," she said as he took her in his arms, "But tell me, Commander Hampton, what was a British sailor doing in America, or do you refer to us as the colonies?"

"Quite the contrary," he replied. "You Americans suddenly represent a sizeable power in the world; proved that with your war with Spain. But it seems you are still not very interested in world affairs."

"Ah! So that's what y'all were doing; trying to convince us to get into the mess in Europe. It won't work Commander. We're neutral. At least I hope we still are. You Red Coats haven't changed President Wilson's mind I hope."

"You are a very clever lady. I'm not supposed to say a word about such things, but you'll be happy to know that my mission was a failure, that is, up to the moment you agreed to dance with me. Now, tell me about yourself and that fellow with an eye patch like mine."

They retired to a small table away from the orchestra where conversation was easier. He ordered a bottle of champagne.

It must be the wine making me carry on like a school girl. Here I sit telling a charming stranger the story of my life. If it's not the wine, I'm in trouble.

They danced and talked until nearly midnight.

"Officer Hampton, it's been a lovely evening, but it's far past my bedtime."

Hampton rose from the table and walked around to slide Bethany's chair back as she stood.

"Thank you, Peter."

The couple was almost at the exit when Hampton stopped. "Excuse me a moment," he said. "I seem to have forgotten something. I'll be right back."

She laughed when he returned to their table, picked up the half full bottle of champagne, their second, put two glasses in his jacket pockets, and followed her from the grand salon.

"Scandalous!" she said when they reached her door, "But come on in, anyway." He took her key, unlocked the door and held it open for her. "I haven't enjoyed unburdening myself to someone in . . ." she paused a moment thinking. "I don't believe I have ever told anyone the things I have told you tonight. It must be the champagne." Turning to look at him she added, "And that damn eye patch." He closed the door behind them. "I've talked enough. The rest, as they say, is history."

They sat down across from one another in the small sitting room of her first class suite. Peter Hampton retrieved the glasses from his jacket, filled them from the chilled bottle, and handed one to Bethany. "The rest may be history to you, but for the listener there are a few loose ends you have not quite tied together," he replied.

"My lord, Peter boy! Surely you must be worn out from listening to me all evening. I feel silly having bored you with too much talk already."

"Oh, no! You can't quit until you tell me what has become of all the players . . . Captain Jonathan Quinn, one-eyed like myself, and Louisette, Ansel, and Don Felipe?"

A faint curtain of sadness fell across her face. She took a sip of wine and looked at the man sitting across from her, the man with graying hair who no longer seemed a stranger.

"I don't know if you are taking advantage of a lonely lady," she held up her hand to stop his protest, "or the lady is taking advantage of you." She smiled a sad smile and fell silent for a moment. "I suppose I could finish the tale. Maybe then I can put it all away for good. It's time I did that, part of the reason for this trip."

Sitting on the small divan, Bethany took another sip of champagne. Her black taffeta dress rustled as she settled back on the pillows. Looking down into her champagne glass, she spoke in a soft, almost wistful voice.

"Has it really been seventeen years since Cuba was set free? America was jubilant. She had fought a righteous war to free an enslaved people she told herself, and perhaps it was true. The bit of empire that came with victory, Puerto Rico and the Philippines, was as big a surprise to America as it was to the rest of the world. We kept them, of course; hadn't promised them independence like Cuba you see.

"Then a wire came from Jonathan saying he had found Felipe. I remember being so happy. I was alive again. When the boat arrived in Havana, Jonathan met me looking older than I remembered, and very tired. But then, I'm sure I didn't look the same, either. I had been ill when I left Cuba. I didn't tell you that, did I? Jonathan seemed so happy to see me, lifted me up and spun me around as he had done the first time I arrived on the island when I was what . . . nineteen or so?

"'You fool', I said.

"'Yes', he said, 'we're all fools.'

"Jonathan took my hand and we started walking. 'Tell me about him, Uncle, tell me the truth,' I ask him.

"Jonathan said, 'He was there a long time, Bee Bee, alone in that little cell. His hair has turned white. He's not quite used to being free, I think. He won't talk about it except to say that without you and the aid you sent through Lola he would have lost his will to live. He doesn't complain. I haven't seen him shed a tear, but I haven't seen him smile either. He'll get better when he goes back to the country. I'm sure of it. They burned everything, but I hired workers to build a new cottage and new stables. Did you know Alonzo hid Felipe's horses in the mountains all this time? Felipe doesn't know. It will be your and Alonzo's surprise for him when the time is right. He'll gain strength and be his old self with your help.'

"When Felipe saw me, he cried. That brave and wonderful man cried, and then apologized, said he was ashamed. It broke my heart. We are so foolish. We raise little boys up tellin' 'em, don't cry now, be a brave little boy, and so y'all grow up holdin' everything inside, afraid to cry.

"When the house was ready we rode the train to Cienfuegos. Ever faithful, Alonzo was waiting for us with a one-horse buggy. The fine old carriage had burned along with the Alacon house and outbuildings. Many of the people had returned to the plantation. Many had not: the young who had fallen in battle, the old who had died in the camps. Felipe was afraid the families of those who had died would hold their terrible loss against him. People were gathered all along the road when I brought him home. He got out of the buggy and walked along speaking to them, calling their names. They seemed embarrassed by his tears and politely looked down so as not to see them. But they were happy tears, you see.

"He was limping when we reached the house, would always limp when he got tired. The wound to his thigh had healed, but you could almost fit a fist in the hollow where infection had eaten away the tissue.

"One day Alonzo told me the new stable was finished and that he had brought the horses out of hiding. I told Felipe I wanted to see the new barn. When we opened the door, Alonzo was standing there with that crazy damn stallion, Diablo Negro, and the dappled mare. He led them out into the sunlight. They were brushed and groomed and resplendent, and the mare was carrying a foal.

"We all stood there like fools, tears drowning our smiles while that fleet-footed black devil pranced and hopped around just as he had always done.

"'I will bite his ear when you are ready, Don Felipe,' Alonzo said. I laughed, and so did Felipe. He laughed!

"'Oh, I think not,' Felipe answered with his arms around the horse's neck. 'Diablo, like me, survived the war because he had a loyal friend.' He nodded to Alonzo and then smiled at me. 'I will not put a bit in his mouth ever again. He will spend his days free, breeding a new herd, and half of them will be yours, Alonzo. Partners, you, and I and Diablo here, how is that?'

"Alonzo was speechless. He tried to kiss Felipe's hand, but Felipe would have none of it. Instead he reached out and shook Alonzo's hand. It had never happened between them before, not in all the years and loyalty and love between them. Latin honor and tradition had not allowed it. 'Partners,' Felipe said again.

"We were truly happy. Felipe never went to Havana again. He devoted himself to replanting the fields, building a new sugar mill and raising Spanish barbs while I tended the books and business of putting the plantation back on a paying basis."

Bethany took a sip of wine. "For a while, people came from Havana to seek Felipe's advice in organizing a new Cuba. Estrada Palma, the first president of Cuba, asked Felipe to serve on his cabinet. Felipe refused, graciously of course, but he would not return to Havana. He told Palma, 'My time belongs to the land and the lady,' and smiled at me. I argued that he should be part of the first free Cuban government of his island, that he had fought so hard and long for it, had given so much of himself and his wealth. He said a strange and terrible thing. He said that he had learned too well how to fight, to kill, to destroy. He said that would be a problem for Cuba, that there were too many like him, men who would be impatient, frustrated by politics, men who were used to giving orders and using force to get things done, men who knew how to use the power of arms but would be corrupted by the power of politics. Felipe advised Palma, 'Study the countries Simon Bolivar liberated from Spain. See what has happened to them.' He warned Palmer, 'Keep revolutionaries out of your government.' Then he asked him, 'Do you know what Bolivar said in the end when he was dying, lonely and poor?' Felipe answered the question himself. 'Bolivar said, *He who serves revolution plows the ocean.*'"

Bethany brightened. "But don't think we were sad in those days, or that we sat around heavy-hearted, because we didn't. Those were happy times for us. Once in a while Felipe would come in and tell me to put on a beautiful dress, that there was a new play or opera or concert in town. We made every opening night at the theater in Cienfuegos. The people always stood and applauded their Don Felipe Alacon when we walked down the aisle to our seats. He said it embarrassed him, but I know it made him very proud. He would nod to show his appreciation. He was so dignified and still a handsome man, white hair and all.

"Our love didn't have quite the fire it had before the war, but it was a good love." Bethany paused. "We had seven good years after the war, but then his health began to decline. He still had occasional bouts of malaria and had never recovered fully from the terrible, debilitating years in prison. He simply went to sleep one night, and in the morning . . ."

Peter wanted to reach out and touch her, but he was afraid it would break the spell. He was truly fascinated by the beautiful woman and her story.

"Jonathan did go home to Shamrock," she said, changing the subject. "He made a lot of money after the war transporting sugar to America, and on the return trips, the goods and machinery needed to rebuild Cuba. Then one day he sent a message to me at the plantation. 'Going home to Shamrock' was all it said. He meant he was going for good, but no one believed it. He sold the sugar boats to the American sugar consortium, said they would buy their own and cancel our contracts sooner or later anyway. He set Billy Wong up with a restaurant on the waterfront and sold the Bahamas shipping company to Captain Lopez and Mannela on terms they could afford. I forgot to tell you that they would come to visit Felipe and me at the plantation once in a while. So did Jonathan and Louisette, and Ansel when he had vacation from school. Those were grand times.

"Jonathan insisted on giving me half the proceeds from everything. He set up a trust in New York with most of it, let me do what I wanted with the rest. He gave his half of the Alacon plantation to Felipe and me. He was appointed to some sort of maritime advisory commission by President Theodore Roosevelt and spent part of his time in Washington. He and Louisette split their time between Shamrock, Washington, and running away to Paris. They had a fine time.

"Olé Jonathan always said he would go out fightin'. I think he wanted to meet the Angel of Death with sword in hand like a warrior in a Wagner opera. He always had a boyish sense of drama. Death just tiptoed up behind that old sailor. He was sittin' on the porch at Shamrock with his dog and a glass of bourbon watchin' the sunset. The glass just slipped from his hand. He was 68 years old.

"Louisette seemed to waste away after that. She stayed at Shamrock for a while. Then she decided to go to Paris. She seemed cheerful enough packing for the trip. Not quite a year later she died in her house there. The doctor said it was pneumonia, but I think she died from a broken heart. People do, you know. Jonathan had been her whole life, even though she loved Ansel dearly."

Bethany brightened. "Now there is a Quinn right out of the mold. He's as handsome as his father, and as mule stubborn, steely-eyed steady, quick tempered, and in his own way just as sweet as Jonathan was."

Peter Hampton saw her mood change entirely when she mentioned Ansel. "And where is this chip off the old block?" Peter asked, glad that to see the sparkle back in her eyes.

"Ansel did exactly what Louisette and I didn't want him to do. Unlike Jonathan, he actually finished at Marion Military Institute. He liked military school of all things! He went on to graduate from West Point. Then, as a fresh lieutenant, he was sent off to the Philippines. Seems there were Muslim Filipinos, the Moro, that disliked America as much as they did Spain. You know where Ansel is now? In France, for God's sake. I'm on my way to see him. He's assigned to the French headquarters staff in Paris as a neutral observer for the U.S. Army. Turns out he hates the duty. He said he thought he would get to take a look at modern warfare but complains that he's not allowed to go to the front to see what's really happening, says that he has to hang around French Army Headquarters in Paris with a bunch of old French generals and staff. Only a fool of a Quinn would want to do something like that. He reminds me of that young English idiot who came to Cuba during the revolution as a neutral observer for your British army. He was a spy claiming to be a journalist. Churchill I think his name was."

"Winston Churchill?" Hampton asked.

"I suppose. He insisted I call him Winnie. Don't tell me you know him."

Peter looked incredulous, "I'm afraid that young idiot, as you call him, has grown up to be First Lord of the Admiralty. For this poor commander in His Majesty's Navy, your Winnie is second only to the King."

"Well in that case," she said, "maybe saving his life was a good thing."

"Saving his life?"

"Yes, but back to my Ansel in Paris," Bethany said, totally uninterested in Churchill. "He got the assignment by going to some of Jonathan's old friends in Washington, don't you see. Of course, the fact that he speaks fluent French and inherited a house in Paris from Louisette didn't hurt either. I've seen some of the bills for the parties he's thrown there. He may claim to live on his army pay, but I know better. I've been told he's not a bad officer. He's a first lieutenant now. Promotions come slow in the peacetime American Army. I wish to God he hated the military and would settle down in Mississippi."

"He should be safe enough over there." Hampton said, "You Yanks are sitting this one out."

"I'm not a Yank, but yes we are sitting this one out. As long as the United States isn't in this war I won't worry too much about him, except perhaps that he's in Paris with all those French women while all the French men are off fighting the Germans. I would think they would be mighty tired of doing that after so many wars. Europe is truly a mad place, you know, going to war again while no one can quite explain why. Tell me, what prompted England to rush across the Channel? Surely not because some mad Serb shot the Archduke of Austria, for God's sake. I can tell you America is not likely to get into the mess. We don't understand it, have had enough of war, can't afford it, and unless the Germans do something foolish enough to rile the American people, Ansel will have to be content taking notes as a neutral."

"You are beautiful, Beverly Bethany Quinn."

"How do you know my full name?"

"Rank does have some advantages, you know, especially for an old officer who is madly attracted to a mysterious lady somewhere in the middle of the Atlantic Ocean."

"Rank? But this is not a naval ship . . ." She stopped and suddenly looked at him very peculiarly. "Or is it? Yes! That would explain some things. You see, I know more than you may think. I know about her military cargo. That's why we're running blacked out isn't it? Your people are afraid the Germans know about the cargo." It was his turn to look surprised.

"Never mind," she said, "It would be a shame to waste what's left of the night talking about cargo. Are you going to fill my glass again, or are you planning to kiss me?"

He put down his glass and removed Bethany's from her hand. She looked into his gray-blue eye. "It's that damn patch!" she said, just before he kissed her.

"You will have to leave before sunrise," she said after the second kiss. "In the first place I'm a real grouch in the morning before I've had my coffee. In the second place, I'd hate to be responsible for tarnishing an officer's reputation. Jonathan always said the English Navy was very stuffy." He kissed her again. "Do I shock you, Peter? I shocked a young midshipman in your navy once, a long time ago."

"Yes, of course you do," he said, and kissed the nape of her neck, "I've never known a woman like you, doubt there is another." He pulled the pins holding her hair and watched it cascade down her smooth naked shoulders.

"For someone who is as clumsy with buttons as you are, Sailor, you talk too much."

I'm not sure I've really shocked Peter Hampton, but I'm certainly shocked by my own behavior. It's been a long time. What a strange and wonderful night.

"Damn," Hampton said afterwards as Bethany lay close to him.

"What?"

"Our last night at sea."

"Oh all right. You don't have to leave before sunrise, and I won't be grouchy before coffee. We will be wicked and have breakfast in bed," she paused and added with a mischievous smile, "eventually."

And eventually they did get around to a late breakfast. "The French are right about at least one thing," he said.

"And what is that?" she asked.

"They say they find a woman of a certain age much more fascinating than one in the unripeness of youth."

"Well of course we are! Now pass the jelly. And look at you. You're getting crumbs in my bed."

"Let's order more strawberries and cream and another muffin," he grinned. "I can't keep up the pace on an empty stomach."

"You are a wicked man, Peter Hampton, but such a nice wicked man."

Captain William Thomas "Bowler Bill" Turner (he insisted on wearing a bowler hat aboard ship except when he was on the bridge) was thought by some to lack polish. Turner was notoriously taciturn and didn't care a whit for the social duties normally assumed by the master of a passenger liner. If he didn't measure up to Cunard's social standards for their liner captains, none doubted his exceptional skill and steadfastness as a seaman. Under present circumstances that was the measure Cunard wanted in the man responsible for one of its finest and fastest ships afloat, even if he did consider most passengers "a bunch of bloody monkeys," and preferred to dine alone in his cabin. It was therefore somewhat of a surprise when Captain Turner not only personally saw to it that several invitations were issued to "that lovely Miss Quinn" during the cruise, but showed up at his table on the occasions when she was present.

Early on the cruise, Bethany had asked for and been given a tour of the bridge. It was there that she was introduced to Captain Turner. He had all but ignored her, as he did all visitors to the bridge. It was only after the first officer informed him that she was a former partner in a shipping company and knew a thing or two about ships that he took interest in the visitor he would later describe as "A fine figure of a sailor." It was evidence enough that Bethany Quinn still held the ability, learned as a child, to turn difficult men into pussycats.

On the morning of the last day at sea, the head dining salon steward delivered a personal invitation from Captain Turner asking Bethany to lunch at the captain's table. She informed the steward that she had already accepted an invitation to lunch with Commander Hampton and must regretfully decline the captain's invitation. The steward found her a short while later to say that room had been made at the table for Commander Hampton at the captain's request.

The first class dining salon was elegantly fitted out under a large dome decorated in frescos of the Louis XVI style. White gilt-crowned Corinthian columns supported a dining balcony and the whole salon was set off by white gilt-edged panels. The large captain's table sat in the center under the dome.

Bethany was seated at the right hand of Captain Turner. She had to sit forward on her chair to reach the table due to the fact that her chair, the table and all the grand furniture in the salon were bolted to the floor, a peculiarity not uncommon aboard ships. Commander Hampton was directed to a chair next to an elderly widow.

Turner gave his full attention to Bethany. He was fascinated by tales of "Uncle Jonathan" during his blockade running days. At one point, the captain leaned over to Bethany and remarked in a low whisper, "I fear we have been accused of doing a little of that ourselves, Miss Quinn."

She whispered back, "I am not surprised Captain, considering your cargo." It was Captain Turner who was surprised.

(Before departing, the customs house submitted to Captain Turner a single page list of the ship's cargo manifest. Captain Turner swore it was a true list all cargo aboard. A supplementary manifest presented after the ship sailed was twenty-four pages long and listed last minute additions to the cargo on board.)

The chef presented a marvelous menu. Miss Quinn chose Tortue Verte followed by Salade de Saison, Sirloin of Beef, Cauliflower a la Crème, Chateau Potatoes, and finally, Bavarois au Chocolat. Commander Hampton ordered Créme Chatrillon, Supreme de Sole-Palace, Green Peas, Rice and for dessert, Roll Currant Pudding with Sweet Sauce.

A string quartet played softly, the conversation was witty, and the mood, relaxed. Then, shortly after coffee was served, a stout, diamond-draped woman sitting next to Bethany, a Mrs. Tildingham, somehow knocked over a sizeable silver bowl filled with sugar cubes. The little blocks tumbled across the table, some onto the floor.

"Oh! Don't waste them!" Bethany said, and to the surprise of those present, began to gather up the little blocks with her spoon and put them back into the sugar bowl before the waiters standing nearby could react.

"Don't bother my dear, it's only sugar." The lady responsible for the spill laughed. She leaned to the lady next to her and said, "Such a fuss over a few silly little sugar cubes."

Bethany placed a single, sparkling cube of sugar in the palm of her open hand and stood up. Commander Hampton immediately stood. The other men at the table followed his courtesy. Bethany didn't notice. She was looking directly at the smirking faces of the two women.

"Just a silly little sugar cube?" she repeated. Her eyes blazed, her nostrils flared. She managed to keep her voice steady, but the words came loud enough to be heard at the surrounding tables. The area grew silent.

"Do you have any idea what this sparkling little block of sweetness represents?" Everyone stared at Bethany. "It represents the extinction of the Caribbean Indians, worked to death clearing the plains of Cuba to build a sugar empire for Spain. It represents the introduction of African slaves in the new world, shipped in to labor in the place of the decimated Indians. Just in your lifetime alone, sugar has cost the bones of three quarters of a million people who died to free Cuba from the heavy, greedy hand of Spain. Some of them were soldiers, Spanish, Cuban and American, but most were women and children and old people who died of disease and starvation in concentration camps. Think about that the next time you sit around at high tea and ask ever so charmingly, one lump or two?"

Bethany's eyes were points of green fire. She reached over and dropped the cube into the lady's coffee. "Ignorance is such a broad shield for society. Perhaps the next time y'all see sugar carelessly wasted you won't find it so funny. It has cost enough blood to float this ship."

She is formidable, Peter Hampton said to himself. *And quite regal when angry.*

Bethany turned toward the head of the table. "Captain Turner, sir, I apologize. I have ruined your lovely luncheon. Occasionally we Quinns have been known to let our tempers get the best of us. I'm sorry."

"Why not a'tall, Miss Quinn," the captain replied with a smile, "I'd say you gave us a well-deserved what for. You are always welcome at my table, Ma'am."

"I must have embarrassed you terribly back there," Bethany said as she and Peter stepped onto the promenade deck.

"I rather enjoyed it, though I don't think I would want to be the object of a Quinn's wrath."

"You're making fun of my childish tantrum."

"I'd say only a fool would do that after watching you chew up a whole table of two-lumpers. What would you like to do now?"

"Get lots of fresh air. The fog has lifted. Let's go sit at the bow with the wind in our face. It will chill my wicked temper while you tell me about this ship. I'll bet I already know more than you would imagine. Your British navy is being naughty. And I bet that little Winnie has something to do with it."

"You have me at a disadvantage," Peter protested. "I can't discuss the subject. Mum's the word; secrets and all that. Besides, you might be spying for the Kaiser. Beautiful women make the best spies, they say."

"Do they?" she said, and led the way up the stairs to the boat deck. "Would you look? All the lifeboats have been swung out on their davits. Does Captain Turner know something we don't?"

"I think it is standard procedure in these waters."

"Ah yes, we mustn't forget . . . you British are at war."

CHAPTER 25

It was the practice of the Admiralty to have one or more warships pick up passengers liners entering the declared war zone and escort then to port to discourage U-boat attacks. Captain Turner had orders to rendezvous with the cruiser *HMS Juno* ten miles south of Fastnet Rock near mid-day on the seventh of May, 1915. The cruiser was to provide safe escort for his ship north up St. George's Channel into the Irish Sea and to safe harbor at Liverpool. The morning had brought heavy fog and Captain Turner, being a cautious seaman, reduced speed to fifteen knots. Earlier, the ship's radio duty officer had delivered to him a decoded message warning of submarines in St. George's Channel and ordered him to sail with the lifeboats swung out on their davits as a precaution.

By the time the fog lifted, Fastnet was behind him. Turner expected to find *Juno* patrolling on station waiting for him, but there was no sign of her. Sailing orders called for radio silence forbidding use of the ship's transmitter. Turner could receive messages, but could send no inquiry to the Admiralty as to the position of his cruiser escort. He could have received a message concerning *HMS Juno* but none was sent. Now, free of fog, Captain Turner had no choice but to order up standard cruise speed of twenty knots and continue on course without an armed escort. He doubled the ship's lookouts. (*Juno* was steaming north more than 100 miles away. To this day, the Admiralty has refused to give an explanation.)

Bethany and Peter walked along the boat deck and sat on a bench beneath and just aft of the bridge on the starboard side.

"Well, you are certainly getting the fresh air you requested," Peter said. He turned up the collar of his coat.

"Too windy for you, Commander?" Bethany said, wrapping her lamb's wool shawl around her shoulders.

"Too mysterious," he replied. "Why don't you simply tell me what and how you obviously know about certain cargo this ship is carrying."

"Nothing mysterious about it," Bethany replied.

"Well?" Peter waited.

"It's a military secret. I'm not sure I should tell a sailor. He might arrest me for giving away such information."

"Oh for Heaven's sake! I'll grant you immunity provided I can take you to dinner in London."

* * *

Kapitän-leutnant Walther Schwieger, commanding officer of *U-20*, had run on the surface all night charging batteries and making maximum speed southward down the Irish Sea and into St. George's Channel. He planned to round Land's End, swing northward into the English Channel and run for home. He was delighted to find the morning of the seventh foggy and the sea calm. It allowed him to continue running at speed on the surface. Like Captain Turner, Kapitän Schwieger was a cautious seaman. He plotted a southward course 20 miles off the coast to avoid destroyer patrols in the narrows of St. George's Channel between Ireland and Wales. He submerged *U-20* when the fog lifted.

Bethany looked at Commander Hampton. "Well why not? Once we dock in Liverpool all this naughty British business will be over. I suppose you know most of it. You are probably the officer in charge or something." Peter said nothing. Bethany paused, then began. "First I received a mysterious telephone call from a fellow claiming to be a major in your army. He followed up with a letter in which he said he understood that Jonathan had some 10,000 modern rifles stored in a warehouse in Santiago de Cuba and that his government, that is, your government, Commander, would be most interested in purchasing them. I thought he was crazy. I knew of no rifles. The letter went on to explain that the arms weren't for England directly, mentioned something about giving them to a bunch of Arabs and setting them on the Turks. What sort of war is this y'all are fightin', anyway?"

Hampton ignored the question. "Were there 10,000 rifles there?"

"I wanted to disregard the whole ridiculous mess. Then the English major called me on the telephone again and insisted the information was correct. I checked with my accountants and was furious to discover that since late 1905 they had carried on the warehouse inventory books a large lot of crated machinery parts. It took four days of searching dusty J & Q ledgers to find any hint of the property. Then I found, entered in Captain Quinn's handwriting in 1905, a confirmation of crates of machinery parts received from the new government of Cuba as payment of a debt. It seems the new Cuban government owed J & Q a tidy sum for certain services performed during their War of Independence and didn't have much cash. In lieu of money, Jonathan accepted a cache of Mauser rifles, part of the arms surrendered by the Spanish army in '98. There was no record of what had become of them. I had the lot of 'machinery parts' quietly examined by a trusted employee in Cuba. It turned out that your British agent was correct. There were 200 dusty crates stacked to the roof in the very back of the warehouse. My man opened several at random. Each contained 50 rifles."

Peter did the math in his head. "You mean he simply forgot about 10,000 Mauser rifles? There's a hell of a demand for them today."

"I don't think he forgot about them, Peter. I think he was weary of the whole business. He carried a lot of guilt about it, about something that went wrong.

Besides, we were making plenty of money in the sugar trade. How your government found out about them I don't know. Jonathan never said anything about them to me, but he must have said something to someone, or maybe your man, going all over looking for rifles, traced them from Spanish or Cuban records."

"You must have made a fortune on them."

"I would have paid your government to be rid of them. Of course, an old J & Q friend, a shipping agent in New York, could have handled everything for me. In fact he did, but I decided it was the excuse I needed to travel to New York and take this lovely ship over to see Ansel. He's the one joy I have left, the last Quinn. I want to see if he's telling me the truth about not being allowed at the front. What I really want is for him to put away his uniform and run Shamrock and the Cuban holdings, but I'll settle just to know he's safe."

"One more question and then I'll change the subject. It's no joke having a lady casually allude to what should be a military secret. What else do you know about, well, what else?"

"If I tell you, I hope your government will not detain me for what I confess to know by accident."

"Don't be silly. It's just that I am concerned about such things being made public. It is a serious matter that could embarrass Britain and anger your government."

"It certainly is. There's enough ammunition and explosives aboard to frighten a saint, not to mention arms and gun parts. You can rest assured that because of my little part, the secret is safe with me."

"Yes, but how did you find out about the rest of, well what you obviously know?"

"My special cargo and I were supposed to go on another ship, Thomas & Dunlop's liner, *Queen Margaret II*, but at the last minute its cargo and passengers were ordered transferred to this ship. Before we sailed, my shipping representative tried to talk me out of going. He had stumbled upon what can only be called contraband military cargo as he was verifying the transfer of my small lot from *Queen Margaret* to this ship. Signing my cargo onboard it seems he saw other not so small consignments. He told me there were four million rounds of ammunition from the Remington Small Arms Company. Actually that *was* small compared to what he claimed was waiting on pier fifty-four. He said along with our and Remington's shipments there was at least a thousand tons of explosives waiting to be loaded aboard this ship. Rather extraordinary cargo for a passenger ship, wouldn't you say, Commander? By the way, our instructions were to consign the rifles as brass rods and label the cases accordingly. My agent said Remington falsely labeled theirs and that from what he was told there were explosives consigned in casks marked 'cheese'. Not quite cricket according to Queensberry rules, as you British say. It was all being loaded into the forward cargo hold when he left."

"How did you get your man to tell you all that? He must have known the rules, would have had to sign a secrecy agreement. He could go to prison for disclosing what you just told me."

"Men have always told me what I wanted to know." She smiled. "My God! So much for British secrecy. But if you knew all that, why on earth did you sail? Surely you heard about the warning the Germans placed in the *New York Times.*"

"Why not ask the other two thousand passengers and crew on board? They certainly didn't take the warning very seriously. Besides, standing on the dock looking up at this great ship, it's hard to conceive of anything happening so terrible as to sink her."

Bethany paused. "But then, it must have been the same for all those people milling around the deck that terrible night aboard *Titanic.*"

After a moment of reflection she continued, "Anyway, I heard several gentlemen discussing the warnings just yesterday. They said no single torpedo could sink her. Some said it would take half a dozen to do the job in the first place, and that in the second place, she was much too fast for a submarine to ever catch."

"Without explosives on board, that is if there are explosives on board," Hampton corrected himself, "they might be right, but . . ."

"I know what explosives on board can do to a ship," Bethany said darkly. "Oh, yes, I certainly know about that." She became very quiet and seemed to drift away in her own thoughts.

"Well now that we've discussed such a cheerful subject I think I should tell you that it will soon all be academic. Look over there on the horizon. That's Old Head Light House at Kinsale, Ireland."

Bethany could just make out the lighthouse on a high bluff. "Yes," she said absently. "Almost home free."

U-20 came up to periscope depth. The packing gland of the scope leaked cold water down Kapitän Schwieger's sleeves as he swept the sea around them. He confirmed his position as being still north of Fastnet and was about to lower the glass when he saw a smudge come up on the horizon. It quickly grew until he could see the origin of the smoke. He called for his channel pilot. The pilot's secondary duty was to aid in the identification of ships, especially those of neutrals. Schwieger called out, "Four funnels, upwards of 25,000 tons, speed twenty knots or better."

The pilot, a 1914 copy of *Jane's Fighting Ships* in hand, replied without hesitation. "It's either *Lusitania* or her sister ship *Mauretania*, both classified as armed cruisers used for trooping." Again taking the periscope, Schwieger said, "She's miles away. Looks like she's headed for Liverpool. We'll never touch her." As he spoke, he observed the great ship change course. Kapitän Schwieger guessed *Lusitania* had turned for Queenstown, Ireland. He couldn't believe his luck. *Lusitania's* new course would put her within his reach. He ordered a new heading to intercept the great ship. What Schwieger couldn't have known was that Captain Turner had received a new coded message warning him of the danger of submarines in St. George's Channel and ordering him to change course for Queenstown.

Schwieger had only three torpedoes left. He preferred to have at least two torpedoes in reserve for defense of his boat during the trip home. He would fire one of his three. If he hit, he would chance the other two and run for home naked.

* * *

"Looks like we're changing course," Peter remarked. "I'd say we're now heading for Queenstown." (Queenstown reverted to its old Irish name, Cobh of County Cork in 1922)

"Never mind where we're headed. I want to hear your story. It's your turn, Peter." Bethany sat back on the bench with the wind in her hair. "I want to know how you lost that eye and how you got that scar on your side."

"You were peeking if you noticed that scar," he said.

"Yes, I was," she smiled. "Do you know you have a cute little fanny just like a baby's?"

"Damn if you don't make me blush."

"Yes. Now go on, it's your turn to confess."

Glad for the change of subject, Peter began. "It certainly wasn't under such gallant circumstance as when your Jonathan lost his eye," Peter responded. "It happened on dry land in China when I was assigned to our consulate there."

"China! When was there a war with China?"

"It wasn't a war really. It was a rebellion by a bunch of fanatics back in 1900. They were members of a secret society that hated all foreigners; called themselves Yihequan. It means righteousness, harmony, and fists."

"Fists?"

"Yes. And since their symbol was a fist, we called them *Boxers*. The first we heard of them they were chasing down *foreign devils*, mostly Christian missionaries, out in the hinterland and chopping them up with short swords." He looked at Bethany for a reaction, but there was none. He continued, "They made quick work of that and turned against the international legation community in Peking. Got pretty sticky. All the legations wound up together for mutual defense: Frenchmen, Russians, British, Japanese, Germans, Americans, their wives and children, all crowded into a compound of buildings protected by walls and by barricades made from wagons, bedding, trunks, furniture and anything else we could find. For defense we had a hodge-podge of weapons and men: various embassy guards, military liaison people like myself, diplomats with hunting rifles, businessmen with pistols, and, thank God, a contingent of your American Marines."

"Back to Commander Hampton's story," Bethany teased.

"Right. Anyway, we got down to only one supply point for water, a well in an exposed position out in a courtyard. We couldn't get near it in daylight; lost a couple of chaps who tried. Could only fetch water at night. Being Navy, I was no expert in street fighting. Acting as water boy sounded like something a sailor could do. I wasn't very good at that either, I'm afraid. On the third trip, all after dark of course, I banged a water bucket on the well. The noise immediately drew fire. I think they must have sighted rifles in on the well in daylight and sandbagged them in place. Anyway, one shot hit the stone works in front of my face and a shard ricocheted into my eye. They kept up their fire and got me in the side, that scar you mentioned. They would have finished me right there except for a fellow who dashed out and pulled me back to safety. Damn fool thing for him to do, but I'll forever be in his debt. To my surprise, the fellow turned out to be a field grade officer, French. I remember he was calm as ice. Turns out he was an old hand in the orient. Colonel Bourget was his name. Hell of a soldier."

Bethany's heart jumped. She sat up almost gasping for breath. "Did you say Bourget, Henri Bourget?"

"My God! Don't tell me you know him, too!" Hampton said amazed. "Surely, you're pulling my leg."

"With me, Fate has always seemed to enjoy her little tricks," she answered, fighting to calm her own astonishment. Images flashed across her mind like flickers of lightening: his handsome, sad face, sunlight and laughter on a picnic green, the tiny apartment in Paris, a Legionnaire's insignia so alone on a pillow.

"Are you all right?" Hampton asked.

"What?" she looked up at Peter. "Oh, yes. It's just that you surprised me so. I knew Henri as a young officer in Paris a long time ago. Lord, it must have been thirty years. I was just nineteen. Did he get through that Boxer business?"

"Oh, I think so. That was fifteen years ago. I've not heard of him since. I'd guess him to be retired. Must be well into his sixties by now." Peter looked into Bethany's eyes. "By the look on your face just now, I suspect you knew him quite well. I think I'm jealous."

"Why, Peter," she smiled, "what a nice thing to say." She leaned over and kissed his cheek.

The boat deck stood 60 feet above the water. From that height they now could clearly see Old Head Light House some 12 miles away. Bethany took Hampton by the hand and they walked to the starboard rail where they could look out across the open sea, not another ship in sight. Bethany turned to face Peter and looked up to see a familiar figure standing on the bridge high above them. Captain Turner looked down at her and saluted. She blew a kiss to the rugged old sailor.

"That reminds me, Commander," she said looking back a Hampton. "Here I sit only a short distance from port and you haven't even asked me about my plans ashore. All you sailors are alike. Kiss the girls and leave them behind."

"I have been thinking about that," he said.

"Promises, Promises," she answered laughing.

"I'm serious," he protested. "I'm due several days leave after tomorrow. If you could be persuaded to come to London for a few days before going on to Paris to see Ansel, I promise to wine and dine you like a duchess."

"Will you take me to the London Zoo?" she asked.

"I'll take you to see the King if you'll just say yes."

"Range: 700 meters. Torpedo depth: Three meters. Angle of intersection: 90N. Target speed: twenty knots." Kapitän Schwieger called the numbers. They were repeated by the wachoffizier.

After a moment the wachoffizier informed the Kapitän, "We have a firing solution. All set and ready."

Schwieger shouted, "Feuer!"

High above the deck, a lookout in the crow's nest saw the sudden appearance of a small white wake off the starboard bow coming straight at his ship. Ironically, the seaman's name was Thomas Quinn. The starboard bow lookout, Leslie Morton, also saw the telltale track of the waterborne missile.

"TORPEDO! TORPEDO OFF THE STARBOARD BOW!"

"Dear God!" Commander Hampton said. He gripped the rail and fought hard to stave off panic as his eyes picked up the oncoming path of white frothy foam marking the torpedo's course as it blistered toward them at forty-five knots. Turning to Bethany, he was disconcerted by her apparent calm and confused by her statement.

"It's been a long time coming," she said quietly, her eyes fixed on the white line drawing toward them across the sea. "Hold me Peter," she turned to him, "Hold me as if you really love me."

It was a German G-type torpedo, a model with a reputation of poor reliability, often failing to go off unless it hit a target at a near 90° angle. When and if they did go off, they often would not sink even a small freighter. A U-boat frequently had to surface and finish the job with its deck gun.

The torpedo U-20 fired ran straight and true, its course terminating just forward of the ship's bridge. Schwieger witnessed the initial plum of water as his torpedo struck and exploded. A fraction of a second later he was amazed to see the plum enlarge in size, greater than anything he had ever seen. (A crewman from *Lusitania* who survived testified there were two explosions.) The sound of a tremendous explosion traveled swiftly through the water to reverberate through the U-boat's hull. The crew cheered. A hit! Kapitän Schwieger was stunned by a metal-rending explosion far greater than that of any previous torpedo he had fired. The Kapitän stepped from the periscope and motioned the pilot to take a look as if he needed confirmation of what he saw.

"Mein Gott! Es ist *Lusitania!*" The pilot could see the name painted on the ship's rapidly plunging bow.

Lusitania was making twenty knots when an explosion far greater than that of the torpedo's warhead blew open her bottom and bow ten feet below her waterline. Forced by her great speed, hundreds of tons of seawater per second drove into her hull, fracturing bulkheads and driving down the length of her longitudinal coal bunkers, blowing open the scuttle doors to quickly flood her boiler and engine room. As the flooded bow, driven by the ship's enormous momentum, plunged ever deeper into the sea, an additional four tons of water a minute poured through each of the hundreds of port holes that had been opened to the fresh spring breeze.

The torpedo struck at 2:10 on the afternoon of May 7, 1915. By 2:28, only eighteen minutes later, *Lusitania* was gone. Of her forty-four lifeboats, all of which were hanging out on their davits, only six could be seen bobbing on a lonely sea strewn with floating debris. One thousand two hundred and one souls were lost.

Hold me as if you really love me. Those words echoed to the finite end of his being. In the split second before he died, Peter Hampton knew . . . he really did love Beverly Bethany Quinn . . . as had every man who ever knew her.

EPILOGUE

Within hours, news of *Lusitania*'s sinking reached the intelligence section of French Army Headquarters but the message was immediately classified. As a result, Ansel did not know of the ship's loss until he read of it in the newspaper the next day. There was, at the time, no word on survivors. Three weeks before, Ansel had received a wire from Bethany telling him that she would be sailing aboard *Lusitania* for England on business and planned to visit him in Paris.

The French major to whom Ansel was assigned at French Army Headquarters, and the military attaché at the American Embassy, Ansel's direct commander, were very sympathetic. He was granted immediate emergency leave. The French major even arranged cross-channel transport via a courier flight aboard a Voisin aeroplane. It was the first time Ansel had flown, but he was too concerned about his aunt to be either frightened or exhilarated by the experience.

After landing at the Royal Flying Corps London Southend Airfield, Ansel crossed England and Wales by train to the port at Milford Haven. From there he traveled by boat to Wexford, Ireland and then by train to Queenstown. Bethany's name was not on the posted list of survivors. For several days Ansel visited the temporary morgue set up to handle recovered bodies. He insisted upon viewing the face of every female brought to the morgue. He checked the news from the ports of Queenstown, Liverpool and London for notices of survivors or dead brought in by the many vessels engaged in the rescue and recovery effort. There was no word of his aunt Bethany. Of the 1,200 souls that had perished, only a relative few bodies were gathered from the cold sea or found washed ashore. Lieutenant Quinn finally had to accept the fact that his aunt was gone and that her body, like the majority of those listed as missing, would never be found.

On the day of the mass burial of *Lusitania*'s victims, Ansel fell in amongst the hundreds of grieving mourners, military and public officials, curious onlookers, and an army of reporters. Together they formed a funeral procession that stretched for more than a mile. The cortege wound its way along a serpentine road to a cemetery on the outskirts of Queenstown. The mourners were greeted by a great oblong excavation in which one-hundred coffins lay in twenty rows, five abreast. To Ansel, the scene had the appearance of a log jam in a long, dry canal to nowhere. Each black coffin was marked with a white painted number. In addition, those coffins which contained the bodies of victims that had been identified had their names painted on the lids.

Isolated by his own thoughts during the long ceremony, Ansel did not hear the somber words spoken by half a dozen clergy in turn. His mind was painfully focused upon the realization that his beautiful Aunt Bethany, who had always been like a second mother to him, had died crossing the Atlantic for the sole purpose of seeing him. An agonizing sense of guilt increased the burden of grief that closed around him like a shroud.

As Ansel turned to leave, he thought of another mourner who must shoulder the most unbearable burden of all. Ansel had been brought up in the household of a sea captain and knew the responsibility Jonathan always felt for ship and crew. He asked a Cunard representative at grave-side to point out a survivor who probably wished he had not been washed from the bridge to be found clinging to floating wreckage . . . *Lusitania*'s captain.

Wearing a dark suit and holding a bowler hat in his hands, Captain Turner stood apart from the crowd, his eyes moist, his once proud shoulders bent. Ansel introduced himself. "My father was a sea captain, sir. I know how you must feel."

"Quinn? There was a lovely lady named Quinn in First Class. Was she your mother?" he asked timidly.

"She was my aunt," Ansel replied.

"I saw your lovely aunt just before . . . before we were struck," Turner said almost in a whisper. "She was forward on the boat deck below the bridge." The tough, weathered captain spoke with trembling lips, "She waved and blew me a kiss."

Ansel watched him walk away, a lonely man carrying a heavy sorrow no board of inquiry could ever lift from his heart.

Ansel went alone up to Old Head of Kinsale, a high rocky point of land thrusting into the Atlantic from the south coast of Ireland. Standing beside the lighthouse there, he stared out at the rolling sea. *Lusitania* was out there, he knew, down in the eternal darkness hundreds of feet below the waves.

She is not there, he told himself. *No watery grave for Bethany. She is in some other place, still bright and beautiful with laughter on her lips and a sparkle in her eyes.* He turned and walked away feeling more alone than ever in his life.

Nearly six months later, packets of documents began to arrive from attorneys representing Bethany's estate. The cover letter of each packet began,

Dear Lieutenant Quinn,

We understand your grief at this time, but the duties of representing such a large estate require us to ensure all proper formalities and legalities are carried out in the settlement of your aunt's estate.

One morning a package of a different sort arrived from the attorneys. Ansel sat at his desk in his cramped, dingy office with its one small and grimy dormer window on the top floor of the French War Ministry in the Rue St. Dominique and opened the well-wrapped package. Inside he found another parcel carefully enclosed in wrapping paper yellowed with age and tied with string. On the paper wrapping, handwritten in pencil, were the words, *For Ansel Quinn: To be delivered upon my death*. It was signed, *B. B. Quinn*. The contents consisted of two diaries and a most unusual pendant. *I'll be damned, it's a spent bullet!* Embossed in gold on the worn leather binding of the first diary was the single name, *Annielise*. The second diary had a soft, cloth cover bearing the hand-inked name, *Bethany Quinn*. Pinned inside its front cover was a French Legionnaire's insignia. At one point, as he read far into the night, he came across a folded loose note that had been stuck between the pages.

It was daybreak the next morning when Ansel finished reading the last page of the last diary. He got up from his desk and walked to the little window to stare out at a gray dawn accompanied by a light drizzle descending morosely upon the soot-stained rooftops of Paris.

Ansel had been astonished by the revelations contained in Bethany's diary. *My God! I'm not at all who I thought I was. No one was.* Of all the disclosures presented in the diary, one was so stunning as to burden Ansel with a dilemma Bethany could never have envisioned.

For days Ansel agonized over the most difficult moral and personal conflict he had ever faced.

What would you have me do? he asked her. And of himself, *If the roles were reversed would I want to know?*

Ansel had never suffered such emotional stress. *It was her secret . . . but now it is my secret too. I could let it die, do nothing . . .*

Ansel knew that to walk away would haunt him the rest of his life.

But what would facing the revelation, the burden of it mean? What would the consequences be? How the hell does one approach a situation like this?

In the end, he reasoned what his mother, his real mother, would have wanted given the inconceivable circumstances.

Lieutenant Ansel Quinn left his tiny, closet-like office on the upper floor of the French War Ministry, walked down the several sets of stairs leading to the first floor and down a long hall to a crowded outer office where several French clerks were working. He stepped in and spoke to the nearest clerk who directed him to the sergeant in charge.

"Sergeant, I have a pressing need to speak to your commander in private. I won't take but a moment of his time."

"Is it important, Lieutenant? A military matter?"

"It is an important personal matter, Sergeant. My mother was aboard *Lusitania*."

The soldier looked at the haggard, drawn face of the young American officer, paused a moment, then nodded toward the open door of a spacious inter-office. Ansel knocked on the door casing.

A distinguished looking, gray-bearded officer sitting behind a large polished desk stacked high with reports looked up at the intruder, "Well, what is it?" he said impatiently.

Unable to find the words with which to answer, Ansel walked forward, placed a cloth covered notebook on the desk, saluted and stood at attention.

"What is this?" The officer, agitated by the interruption, glanced at the book, picked it up, stared at the cover in silence for a long moment, and then gazed up at the young American standing silently before him.

Almost reverently, like a man that had recovered a lost piece of his soul, he spoke the name written on its cover.

"Bethany?" And looking up at the American Lieutenant, he repeated the question like a whispered prayer, "Bethany Quinn?" Ansel nodded and lowered his eyes to the engraving on a brass plate affixed to a polished wooden block sitting on the officer's desk. It read:

Général Henri Bourget
Armée de France

ACKNOWLEDGMENTS

Scores of factual details of places and events intertwined in this story were derived from careful research of historical books, papers, unpublished diaries and letters, as listed herein as the Appendix. It is unusual to include a bibliography with a novel but I would be ungrateful not to acknowledge that body of historical work for its contribution to this book. No published work stands on an author's work alone. The idea, words and style may originate with the author, but the finished book, tidy, free of awkward structure, grammatical errors and lapses in syntax, all the things that make a book acceptable to the reader, must be credited to the publisher's staff (editors, proof readers, fact checkers, layout artist, printers and book cover designers) whose work often goes unrecognized and unsung. I hereby sing the praises of the following persons at TouchPoint Press: Sheri Williams, Publisher; Tamara Trudeau, Senior Editor; Colbie Myles, Cover Artist and Media Liaison; Ashley Carlson, Associate Editor; and Media Coordinator; and Qihm Overstreet, Media Intern. Finally this work of mine may well have languished unpublished and unread without the faith and hard work of my tireless agent, Jeanie Loiacono of Loiacono Literary Agency, LLC. I also owe praise to my wife, Kay, for her love, support and especially patience exhibited in putting up with cantankerous me and two no-account dogs.

BIBLIOGRAPHY

Aimes, Hubert H. S., *A History of Slavery in Cuba, 1511–1868*, Octagon Books, 1967.

Beals, Carleton, *The Crime of Cuba*, Lippincott, 1933.

Blay, John S., *The Civil War, A Pictorial Profile*, Bonanza Books, 1958.

Buchanan, Lamont, *A Pictorial History of The Confederacy*, Bonanza Books, 1951.

Capers, L. G., MD, Vicksburg, Mississippi, "Attention Gynecologists! Notes From The Diary of a Field and Hospital Surgeon, C.S.A.," *The American Medical Weekly*, Vol. I. No. 19, Louisville, Kentucky, November 7, 1874.

Chestnut, Mary Boykin, *A Diary from Dixie* (Edited by Ben Ames Williams), Boston, 1949.

Coggins, Jack, *Arms and Equipment of the Civil War*, Double Day & Company, Inc., 1962.

Drescher, Bennie Howell, Daughter of Maj. William Howell, CSA, Niece of Varina Howell Davis, *Autobiography* (unpublished), Hannibal, Mo. 1933. Courtesy of Ed and Mildred Bounds.

Dufour, Charles L., *Nine Men In Gray*, Double Day & Company, Inc., 1963.

Eksteins, Modris, *Rites of Spring*, Houghton Mifflin, 1989. FLEMING, Thomas, "False Call to War," *Military History Magazine*.

Freidel, Frank, *The Splendid Little War*, Little Brown & Co., 1958.

Gebler, Carlo, *Driving Through Cuba, Rare Encounters in the Land of Sugar Cane and Revolution*, Simon& Schuster, 1988.

Ingraham, Mrs. Alfred, *The Vicksburg Dairy of Mrs.Alfred Ingraham, May 2–June 13, 1863*, (Unpublished) Edited by W. Maury Darst, Courtesy of Mr. Tom L. Wallace, Biloxi, Mississippi.

Jones, Wiley Cato and Miss Amanda Bailey, *Unpublished Letters, 1861–1865*, Courtesy of P. Robertson.

Judge, Joseph, Photos by Stanfield, James L., "The Many Faces of Old Havana," *National Geographic*, Vol. 176, No. 2, Aug. 1989.

Kemp, Daniel F., (Edited by John D. Milligan), "Gunboat War At Vicksburg," *American Heritage*, Aug./Sept. 1978, Volume 29, Number 5.

Lord, Walter, "Mississippi, The Past That Has Not Died," *American Heritage*, June, 1965, Volume XVI, Number 4.

Loughborough, Mary Ann Webster, *My Cave Life in Vicksburg, With Letters of Trial and Travel*, Kellogg Print Company, Little Rock, 1882.

Markham, Edwin, *The Real American in Romance, Brothers for Eagle's Wings, The Age of Expansion 1868–1910, Volume XIII*, William H. Wise & Co., Copyright, 1911 Funk & Wagnalls.

Morgan, Wayne H., *America's Road to Empire, The War with Spain and Overseas Expansion*, John Wiley & Sons.

Patridge, Bellamy and Vettmann, Otto, *As We Were, Family Life in America, 1850–1900*, Whittlesey House, A Division of McGraw-Hill Book Co. 1946.

Piehler, H. A., Editor, *Paris for Everyman*, J.M. Dent & Sons, Ltd. 1924.

Rickover, H. G., *How the Battleship Maine Was Destroyed*, Naval History Division, Department of the Navy, Washington, D. C. 1976.

Roberts, William Ransom, "Under Fire in Cuba, A Volunteer's Eye Witness Account of the War with Spain," *American Heritage*, Dec. 1977, Vol. 29, No. 1.

Rudolph, James D., *Cuba, A Country Study*, Foreign Area Studies, The American University, Copyright 1985 by the United States Government as Represented by the Secretary of the Army.

Semmes, Raphael, Admiral, CSA, *The Confederate Raider Alabama; Selections from Memoirs of Service Afloat During the War Between the States*. Edited by Philip Van Doren Stern. Gloucester, Mass., Peter Smith 1969.

Simpson, Colin, *The Lusitania*, Little Brown & Co., 1972.

Stern, Philip Van Doren, *The Confederate Navy: A Pictorial History*, Double Day & Co., Inc.,1962.

"The Daily Citizen," J. M. Swords, Proprietor, Vicksburg, Mississippi, July 2, 1863.

Thomas, Hough, *Cuba, The Pursuit of Freedom*, London, Eyre and Spottiswoode, 1971.

Wallace, Tom L., *History of the Wallace and Ingraham Families* (unpublished), Courtesy of Tom Wallace.

Webber, Thomas L., *Deep Like the Rivers, Education in the Slave Quarter Community, 1831–1865*, W. W. Norton, 1978.

Weisberger, Benard A., "The Carpetbagger, A Tale of Reconstruction," *American Heritage*, Dec. 1973, Volume XXV, Number 1.

Wheeler, Richard, *Siege of Vicksburg*, New York, Thomas Y. Crowell, 1978.

ABOUT THE AUTHOR

Thomas E. Simmons grew up in Gulfport, Mississippi, and attended Marion Military Institute, the US Naval Academy, the University of Southern Mississippi, and the University of Alabama. He has been a pilot since the age of sixteen and has participated in air shows, flying aerobatics in open-cockpit biplanes. In the late 1950s, Simmons served as an artillery officer in Korea. He is the author of *The Man Called Brown Condor*, *Forgotten Heroes of World War II*, *Escape from Archangel*, and the Quinn Saga. Simmons has also written numerous magazine articles and has been published in *The Oxford American*.

THE QUINN SAGA

FROM OPEN ROAD MEDIA

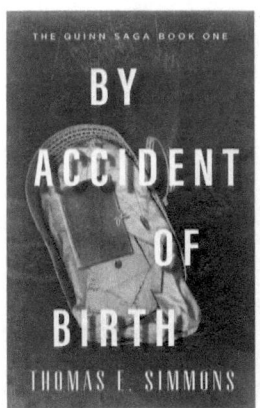

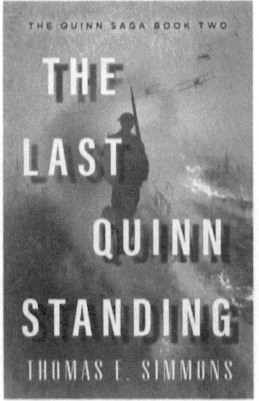

INTEGRATED MEDIA

Find a full list of our authors and
titles at www.openroadmedia.com

FOLLOW US
@OpenRoadMedia

www.ingramcontent.com/pod-product-compliance
Lightning Source LLC
Chambersburg PA
CBHW020839020726
47497CB00005B/1166